PLAYING THE FIELD

a novel by J.L. MEJIAS

Thank you for reading!

www. JLMejias.com

To my daughter, Valentina.

My mom, Blanca.

My fiancé, Vanessa.

Love you.

And to my dad.

CHAPTER 1

Sweetheart and Heartbreaker

Sitting in the booth of a diner, across from his best friend since the 7th grade, Casanova can't help feeling that pinch of envy that sometimes crops up around Jake.

"Are you OK?" Jake sounds annoyed; "You've been staring at me for a while, man. What's up with you?"

"Huh?" Cas snaps out of his cloud of thoughts and shrugs. "Nothing, man; I just zoned out for a sec. I wasn't staring at you, don't flatter yourself."

"Listen," Jake says sincerely, "I know it's been a while since you got laid, and you got no girls because you're ugly and nobody wants you."

"Thanks," mutters Cas.

Jake tilts his head to the side to take a better look at him, "And you're getting fat too."

"I'm not fat," he objects.

"Well, you're definitely out of shape."

"Barely." Cas looks down at his ever-growing belly, the pounds he's put on over the past couple of months stare back at him. "I just have to start hitting the gym again," he sighs.

"OK, I get that." Jake nods. "I feel you. If that's all it is, you just need to go to the gym more. Cool, man. Do it." He sits up in the booth. "But all I'm saying is, if you're gay, I'm cool with it. If you've decided to be done with women and be who you really are, just let me know now, man. It won't change anything between us. I'll support your decision. You're my brother, Cas, you'll always be my brother. Unless you want to become my sister. And even then, I'd still love you like a brother-sister. Or a sister-brother, whichever you prefer. I don't want to offend anybody."

Cas stares at him without blinking, his deadpan eyes looking straight through Jake, trying somehow to channel his own feelings of discontent.

The look doesn't faze Jake the slightest bit as he leans back in the booth. "Just do me a favor? If you change your name, go with 'Cassandra'. That way I can still call you Cas. You know what I mean?"

Cas stares at him for just a moment longer before blinking, and that slight pinch of envy fades into the background. "You're a clown, man."

"I know." Jake smiles smugly. "But seriously, dude, what's up with you? You been off in a funk for months now. I was hoping it'd pass already. I'm worried about you."

"What do you care?" Cas says, knowing he sounds far too drab.

"What do I care?" Jake looks genuinely confused as he leans forward in his booth, as if to say something very important, "See, that's exactly what I'm talking about! This, 'Woe is me, what do you care,' bullshit attitude you been rocking." He leans back in the booth and gets

2

more animated as he continues, "And what do I care? I care that you're my fucking roommate and you smell like ass."

A few diners from the surrounding booths look over at them.

Cas tries to act like he hasn't noticed the disgusted stares and looks directly at Jake. "Yo, lower your voice, man. The fuck's wrong with you?"

He lowers his voice so that only Cas can hear. "You're right, my bad. But seriously, man, you're only taking a shower like twice a week."

"I'm going green," Cas replies dryly.

"Green?" Jake asks in disbelief.

"Yup."

He stares at Cas, trying to figure if he's telling the truth.

"You mean going *green* as in saving water? Like you're going to take less showers to conserve water and save the environment?"

"Yes," Cas nods. "I'm woke."

Jake looks at him with genuine concern. "Don't start getting all weird on me, man."

"What's so weird about wanting to save water?"

"There's nothing weird about saving water. What's weird is not taking a shower every day. That's basic hygiene, man."

"For you, maybe."

Jake laughs, "For the whole free world."

Cas shrugs. "Whatever."

"Nova, there's a stench coming out of your room. You're not bathing daily. And lately, you seem to think deodorant is fucking optional."

"Deodorant causes cancer, man." Cas looks down at the menu.

"Then get some all-natural shit. You know there's that rock thing, right? The smooth rock you rub under your armpits? Get one of those – it's organic D.O. But you gotta do something, bro. You can't just show up at my events stinking like ass."

Cas discretely pinches the top left shoulder of his shirt and brings the fabric to his nose for a quick whiff.

"I don't stink," he says in a matter-of-fact way.

"Yeah, you don't stink right now because today you had the courtesy of actually showering and putting on some clean clothes like a normal functioning adult." Jake comments, "But your room? Your room smells like full court basketball."

Cas cracks a small grin. "It's not that bad."

"No, it's worse." Jake shakes his head. "It smells like a locker room dumpster, with rotting fish."

"I just have to do laundry. It's been a while is all."

"You *think*?" Jake laughs. "Your room *is* dirty laundry."

Cas ignores him and looks back down at the menu. "Do you know what you're ordering yet?"

Jake sighs. "Yeah, I think so." He looks up to signal to a waitress – none are available.

"I'm just saying," he continues. "You have to snap out of it already. It's been going on for way too long, and you're too old to be emo."

"Come on, man," Cas protests, still looking at the menu. "I'm fine. It's not like the last time. I'm just chilling."

Jake sounds frustrated. "No, you're not chilling – that's the problem. Shit, I wish you were chilling! Bro, you haven't gone out in months. We hardly hang anymore. You're spending all weekends in your dark-ass room playing video games and watching porn. What kind of a life is that? You're never gonna meet someone new like this. You need to get out there. You need to meet new women. You haven't even mentioned a girl, *any* girl, in like a year."

"A year?" Cas sucks his teeth. "Stop exaggerating – it hasn't been that long. Plus, Call of Duty is an awesome game."

"I know. I love Halo too, bro." Jake leans back in his booth. "But you know what I love more? Women! You know why? Because you can't fuck them video games."

Cas smiles. "With virtual reality expanding, I'm sure virtual porn is on its way."

Jake stares at him. "I'm talking about real woman, you pervert. I'm not talking about having sex with a virtual *Lara Croft*."

"Imagine that!" Cas looks at him and smiles wider. "I think it'd be pretty cool."

"That *would* actually be pretty cool," Jake acknowledges, "but that's not the point."

Just then, the waitress approaches their table.

"Hey, guys. I'm Megan. I'll be your server," she greets them in an accent that's definitely not from New York. "Are y'all ready to order? Can I get y'all something to drink?"

Jake gives Cas a look that says *Check out the waitress*. He looks back up and focuses on her name tag.

"That's a pretty accent you got there, Megan. I'm assuming you're from the South?"

She puts her hands on her hips in mock offense. "So, you just know I'm from the South, huh?"

"No," he smiles charmingly. "That's why I said I *assume* you're from the South."

She smirks. "Well, you know what they say about assuming, right?"

Jake raises his eyebrows. "So, I guess I made an ass out of myself? Great – not the first time," he says, and they both start laughing.

Cas smiles slightly and tries to be a part of the conversation.

"You should have used 'presume' instead of 'assume'."

The laughter comes to an abrupt stop.

"What's the difference?" Jake asks.

"Yeah, I didn't know there was a difference," adds Megan.

"Yeah, uh, 'assume'," he begins, "Means to almost know for certain – like you're almost positive about it. 'Presume' is more like you kind of know, but you're not quite sure about it. You're like 50-50 about it."

Jake seems skeptical. "Is that a fact?"

"That is very close to a fact, yes," Cas answers, quite seriously.

"Well, I should *presume* that you don't know what the hell you're talking about. Because I'm about 50% sure you're just making shit up."

Cas is annoyed. "I'm not making shit up – what are you talking about? I graduated college with…"

Megan cuts him off and tries to diffuse the situation. "Well, you know what?" she says, looking at Cas, "I *assume* that you're right because that was a very credible definition."

"Thanks," he responds.

She continues, "But I was just messing with y'all. Of course, I'm from the South."

Cas feels compelled to ask, "Really? Which part?"

"Florida."

"Florida?" Jake says excitedly, "I love Miami. I was down there this summer – had a blast."

"Nice. I lived a few hours north of Miami, but I been there plenty of times. I love it too." She looks over at Cas. "How about you? Did you go too?"

Cas smiles. "Oh, I've been there before. But I didn't go this summer."

"He was busy being a punk," Jake cuts in.

"Aww, that's not nice," Megan says playfully.

"I'm just messing with him," says Jake. "He's my best friend. We're like brothers."

"Now that's better," she smiles.

"And it's true," he replies. "But let me ask you something, Megan."

"Sure," she answers.

"You see my friend here," Jake begins. "He's a pretty OK-looking guy, right?"

Megan shifts her attention to Cas. He's of a medium build, not noticeably overweight but a little plump in the middle. He has olive

7

skin with sleepy brown eyes, and his hair is an overgrown fade in need of a trim.

"Don't get me wrong, I know he needs to hit the gym a little more. I always ask him to come work out with me." Jake looks like an athlete. His arms are lean and ripped with muscles and his fitted polo shirt perfectly hugs his well-defined chest. He has smooth, flawless dark skin and his haircut is a short and neat dark Caesar. "But I think he's okay."

Cas looks concerned – he's not sure where Jake is going with this.

Megan can tell he's uncomfortable. "I think he's very handsome," she smiles.

"Very handsome indeed," Jake says with a wink of reassurance to his friend, "And I'm glad you feel that way because we've been here a couple of times, and all he does is talk about how beautiful you are."

Megan is genuinely surprised. "Really?" she asks, directing the question at Cas.

He's tongue-tied, scrambling for words to say. He's never seen her before.

"Well... err... umm..."

Jake urges him on, "Just tell the truth, man. I've already blown your spot. Just admit it."

Cas nervously looks at the waitress. She has fair skin and nice lips, with her dark blonde hair up in a ponytail – the kind that looks effortlessly cute.

"Yes." Cas decides to follow his friend's lead. "It's true. I mean... yes – you're very pretty... of course."

"Aww," the waitress begins as she puts her hand on Cas's shoulder, "That's so sweet."

Jake is delighted his friend is playing along.

"Good, now let me introduce you two. Megan, this is Casanova Juan Carlos. Cas, this is Megan."

"Wow, that's some name!" She sounds impressed.

"It's actually Juan Carlos Casanova. Casanova is my last name, but everybody calls me Cas."

"Or Nova," Jake chimes in.

"Or that," he seconds.

"So, Mr. Casanova," Megan begins with her right eyebrow raised, "Doesn't *Casanova* mean like a *playboy* or something?"

"Playboy?" Jake cuts in before Cas can respond, "I can tell you right now – he's the furthest thing from a playboy. He's the kinda guy you take home to your parents. A real sweetheart."

"Is that right?" she asks, amused. "And what about you? What kind of a guy are *you*?"

"Me?" Jake says boastfully, "Oh, I'm the guy your parents warned you about. The one they told you to stay far, far away from."

She nods and smiles. "Okay, so you're the sweetheart and you're the heartbreaker."

"Yeah, something like that," Jake agrees.

Megan takes her order pad out, pen in her left hand, "Well, what can I get you, heartbreaker?"

Jake answers, "I'll have an egg white omelet with turkey bacon, boiled veggies on the side," he pauses briefly, "And wheat toast."

"Sure thing. And how about you, sweetheart?"

Cas smiles. "I'll take two eggs – sunny side up – corn beef hash, sausage, and buttered toast."

"Okay," Megan replies with a smile as she quickly jots down his order. "And do you guys want anything to drink with that?"

Jake answers first, "I'll just have water."

"Same here," Cas says, before adding, "Actually, I think I feel like a vodka and orange juice."

"Anything for you, sweetheart," she replies warmly.

He smiles at her. Megan smiles back.

"I'll be right back with y'all order," she quickly turns around and walks away from the table.

Jake turns to his friend. "A tad early in the day for a damn Screwdriver, don't you think?"

Cas loosens up a bit and shrugs. "I'm a G. I, been gangbangin' since pre-k."

Jake laughs. "Oh, word? You put that on your mama?"

"I put that on my mama's mama. That's my nana, fool!"

"Hey, leave grandma outta this." Jake laughs. "*BUT* real talk," he leans over the table as if to tell Cas a secret, "I think the waitress is digging you."

"Yeah, you think so?" Cas asks expectantly. "How do you know she's not digging *you*?"

"Well duh, she probably is. But I'm trying to throw some your way, bro."

"You're far too kind," he mutters sarcastically.

"Yo, cut the crap. I'm serious. You're interested or not?" Jake asks. "Because if you are, I can totally hook you up."

10

"Nah, I'm good, man." Cas doesn't really mean it. He's intrigued by the pretty, Southern waitress.

"What do you mean 'Nah man, I'm good'?" Jake asks in disbelief. "You better make a move on her and stop bullshitting."

Cas shrugs, in pretend disinterest.

Jake shakes his head. "You know what, man? Ever since you broke up with that fucking bitch Tiffany—"

He cuts him off, "Hey don't call her that!"

Jake is dumbfounded. "Don't call her what? *Bitch*? Are you serious? You gotta be kidding me now! You're only getting mad at me because..."

Jake's voice fades into the background murmur for Cas as his mind begins to drift towards thoughts of his ex-girlfriend.

Tiffany was a beautiful brunette with a body that eyes couldn't help but follow when she entered a room. She was big breasted with that perfect hourglass figure that magazines keep flashing. Her legs were long and shapely, complete with toned calves and slender ankles. She was the easy-going type; Cas and Tiffany rarely argued, and when they did, it was always about her busy and erratic work hours. She was a private nurse and was always on call.

Work schedule apart, Cas loved everything about Tiffany – her intellect and her beauty, but mostly her body. He thought she was the woman of his dreams: The *One,* as the happy-ending romances would tell it.

He was so sure of her that even before they had reached their first anniversary, he decided that he was going to propose to her. He knew a year of dating wasn't that long a time, but in his mind, she was too

11

good to be true, and he wanted to make his intentions official. He planned on spending the rest of his life with her.

On the Saturday morning that Cas was supposed to go looking for the perfect engagement ring to seal his love with, he woke up alone in his apartment. Tiffany had spent the night but had left before he got up. He saw a note on her side of the bed – it read, '*Had to run, babe, job called, I didn't want to wake you up. Dinner maybe? Call you later, XOXO*'. He smiled at the '*XOXO*'.

He got out of bed, excited to get the day started. He left his building and walked three blocks to his favorite deli.

"Hey, what's up, boss?" Cas greeted the deli worker. "Can I get a large coffee, regular, two sugars, and a small banana oatmeal, not too hot, please. Yeah, I gotta have my oatmeal, man, I'm trying to lose some weight," he said patting his small stomach.

"You're in good shape, my friend," replied the cashier.

He placed his money on the counter, took his coffee, and grabbed a copy of the *Daily News* on his way out. He also casually grabbed a copy of the free weekly newspaper, *The Village Voice*. He hardly ever read that paper and had only picked it up because the cover story that day was about one of his favorite baseball players.

In front of the deli, there were a few small tables and white chairs huddled in one corner, as if in wait for the weather to be nice to be brought out.

Cas sat down on the one furthest from the entrance.

Taking a sip of his coffee, he placed the two newspapers in front of him, with *The Voice* on top. He looked around to see if anyone nearby was looking at him, and then quickly turned the paper over and went straight for the seedy *back pages.*

The back pages of *The Village Voice* are where you can find advertisements for escorts, prostitutes, and other adult services. These ads are usually explicit, with pictures of sexy women wearing close to nothing. There's always a thinly veiled caption such as 'DISCRETE FULL BODY MASSAGE' or meet with someone for 'A NIGHT OF INTIMATE COMPANIONSHIP'.

Although he didn't read that paper often, whenever he did, he always made his way to the back pages. Cas never responded to any of the ads, nor did he intend to. He just enjoyed looking at the pictures, which basically worked as free soft porn.

His roving eyes casually looked through the pretty women of the back pages – little mental grins of approval registering in his brain. His eyes stopped abruptly and fixed on a face that seemed oddly familiar.

In the picture, there was a woman wearing fishnet stockings and black stilettos – her breasts – big, round, and fleshy – were bursting out of the top of her skin-tight nurse's outfit. She looked strikingly similar to Tiffany. The only difference was that Tiffany had short brown hair and the woman in the ad had long blonde hair and wore glasses. Her face flashed a sinister smile, and above her head, there was a caption:

'LET NURSE TIFFANY TAKE AWAY ALL YOUR PAIN'

His stomach flipped, and he felt like his heart would pop out of his throat.

This can't be her. Can't be, he thought. *But that looks just like her face. And her name is Nurse Tiffany!*

He scrambled to take his phone out of his pocket, pressed 'B' for 'Bae' in his contacts, and hit the 'Talk' button.

With the phone pressed against his ear, he anxiously listened to four long rings before getting directed to the voicemail.

"Hey, bae," Cas' voice cracked. "Uh, I just saw something crazy. Um, I'm not sure what I just saw. I think I'm just bugging. But, uh, call me back right now, please."

He put the phone down and grabbed the paper again. His forehead contorted in painful wrinkles as he intensely examined the picture. He slammed the paper back down, picked up his phone, and called her again – no answer.

He called her six more times – a few rings, then voicemail, every time.

His mind was dizzy with the sudden overflow of disturbing thoughts – *Why the hell she's not picking up?*

Cas was just about to call her for the seventh time when he looked at the ad again – there was a phone number.

Overcome with nausea and his mouth gone dry, he slowly dialed the number given in the newspaper ad. He looked at the screen of his phone – all the numbers were entered correctly. Cas took a deep breath and pressed the 'Talk' button.

His stomach started doing back flips.

It rang once, and someone answered. It was a female voice. "Tiffany here, how can I take your pain away?"

Cas was stuck – he couldn't speak.

"Helloooo? Is someone there?" the female voice asked.

His spirit perked up a little – that didn't sound like Tiffany's voice. A weary smile broke across his face as he began to feel relieved. *It's not her.*

The woman sounded annoyed, "Hello, this is Nurse Tiffany's phone. Who is this?"

"It's not you," Cas replied.

"I'm sorry, what?" the woman asked.

"Nothing. I'm sorry I bothered you. I called this ad for Nurse Tiffany, and obviously you're Nurse Tiffany, but you're not my Tiffany, or the one I thought you were," he said, laughing. "You know what? Never mind. Have a good one."

Cas was about to press 'End' on his phone, but he heard the voice respond.

"Wait. You want Nurse Tiffany, right?"

"Huh?" he asked, starting to feel nauseous again. "You're not her?"

"No, I'm Dominatrix Biffany, but this is her phone. Hold on. Hey, Tiff!" she yelled out, "Your phone!"

A second passed, and another female got on the line. "Hello?"

Cas recognized her voice immediately – it was his girlfriend.

"Tiffany!" he yelled.

"Bae?" she answered, "Oh my God, bae! What the hell?"

"You tell me what the hell!" He felt his knees go weak. "Are you… are you a prostitute, bae? Please tell me you're not a prostitute? Please tell me *MY* girlfriend, whom I was about to propose to, is not a fucking prostitute?"

15

"You're going to propose? Really, bae? Have you bought me a ring already?" she asked, sounding inappropriately excited, given the circumstances in which the conversation was taking place.

"Fuck the ring, Tiff! Answer the question!"

"Okay, okay. I'm not a prostitute," she said in a matter-of-fact tone. "I'm an escort."

"What does that mean, Tiff? That's pretty much the same thing, no?"

"No, bae," she answered quickly. "Well, I guess in a way it's kind of the same thing."

His face went completely pale as his phone dropped from his limp grip. It fell into the coffee, causing the cup to tip over and spill on the thigh of his jeans. The scalding hot liquid instantly made his leg jerk upward, and his knee crashed into the bottom of the table.

"FUCK!"

He punched the table in frustration and accidentally hit the spoon handle sticking out of the bowl of oatmeal. The spoon flipped in the air and hit him in the right eye, the oatmeal splattered all over his face and neck. Tumbling down his shirt, the spoon left a trail of little oatmeal globs.

Cas looked down at the floor and saw his phone lying there with a shattered screen and the battery popped out. He picked it up and put the battery back in, tried to turn it on but the power button seemed to have stopped working —it wouldn't turn on.

He just sat there in his coffee-and-oatmeal-stained clothes, trying to come to terms with what had just happened.

He was in pain, physical and emotional. And although he had a burning thigh, a throbbing knee, and a stinging eye, by far, what hurt the most, was his heart.

They broke up that day via email since his phone had gotten ruined after that fall.

The memory of that day was enough to make Cas sick for the first few weeks after the break up. Even now, four months later, he becomes a little queasy thinking about it.

His mind moves to the present, the sounds of the background murmur begin to dissolve as Jake's rant slowly comes into Cas's focus.

"...She didn't even have the decency to use a stage name, like Sparkle or Pebbles or some shit. She used her real name! Nurse Tiffany! Really, Cas? That's who you're defending? Nurse Tiffany? She lied to your face, telling you she's going to work – meanwhile she's out there turning all types of tricks. And ever since you broke up with that hooker, you've been walking around like a zombie. You're all sad and depressed and moping around the apartment. I'm so sick of it! Get over this bitch already, man. Life goes on," Jake concluded, almost out of breath.

Cas wasn't listening to most of what Jake had just said, but he knew his friend had a point.

"You're absolutely right, man," he says, embarrassed. "I don't know why I'm defending her."

"Because you're a pussy-whipped little bitch," Jake answers. "It's pathetic!"

"Yeah?" He chuckles. "It's that simple?"

Jake shrugs. "I knew she was bad news. Once she had you calling her *bae*, I knew at that point it was over. It was just a matter of time."

"What's wrong with *bae*?"

"It's stupid. *Babe* is already a one-syllable word. How much shorter does it need to be? You should have heard how dumb you sounded. 'I'm going to dinner with bae. Me and bae at the movies.' If a girl calls me *bae*, that's the first sign that it's not going to last."

"Yeah right, I've heard girls call you *bae* before."

"Once maybe. You don't see them anymore, do you? I'm serious man – a girl calls me bae, I might not even want to smash after that. I might just end it there."

"I don't think it's that bad. But, whatever, she's not bae anymore." Cas briefly looks at his phone, he doesn't have any missed calls or texts. "I'll be alright. I just need to get my mojo back."

"You're talking about mojo, and you got this pretty waitress right here digging you." Jake shakes his head in disapproval. "You're a fool if you don't try to talk to her."

Cas is annoyed. "Can you stop with the waitress? She's not into me."

"Alright, your loss." Jake gives up. "Anyway, what are you doing Sunday?"

"This Sunday? I don't know. Probably just chill in the crib, smoke out, watch games…"

"Fuck that," Jake cuts in. "Roll with me on Sunday."

"Nah, I'm good. I'm not in the mood to be in a club. And I didn't even know you had an event this weekend."

"It's not one of my events. I have a baby shower to go to."

"Baby shower?" Cas is curious. "Whose baby shower?"

"Veronica, Manolo's sister."

"Veronica? That's the younger one, right?"

"Yeah, the pretty one."

Just as Jake finishes his sentence, Megan comes over to their table. She's carrying two glasses.

"Here y'all go, water for you and a Screwdriver for you," she says, placing a glass in front of each. "I'll be right back with you guys' food."

"Thank you," Cas and Jake answer simultaneously as she walks off.

Cas continues, "Wow, Veronica is pregnant? How old is she now?"

"Like 23 or 24, I'm not exactly sure," Jake takes a sip of his water.

"That's cool, I guess. But I wasn't invited; so, I'm not going with you."

Jake puts his glass down. "What do you mean? I just invited you, she asked me to."

"She told you to invite me? Highly unlikely." Cas takes a drink from his glass – he gags a little. "Damn, this shit is strong as hell."

Jake puts his hand out. "Really? Let me try."

"No, no." Cas shakes head. "Get your own."

Jake pauses for a moment. He puts down his empty hand. "Whatever. Anyway, you gonna come?"

Cas goes back to talking about the drink. "You know I was just playing with you. If you wanna try it, help yourself," he says, offering the drink to his friend.

"I'm cool, I don't want any."

"Don't be like that, have some, man. I was just messing with you." He pushes the drink towards him.

"No, seriously, I'm good. I really don't want none," Jake says, and then adds, "You stingy fuck."

"Ha. Ha. Real funny."

"So, you're going to come to this baby shower or not?" Jake asks again.

Cas complains, "Such short notice, though."

"Short notice? What difference does it make? You're not doing anything anyway, so you might as well come."

"I don't even have a gift." Cas takes another gulp from his drink.

"So what? Neither do I."

"You can't go to a baby shower without a gift, you low life."

Jake sucks his teeth. "I'm not going empty handed, jackass. I'm going to get a gift – I just haven't gotten it *yet*."

Cas takes a sip through the straw, then puts the glass in front of Jake. "What you thinkin' about getting?"

"Whatever you're willing to go half with me on, bitch." Jake moves the straw to the side and takes a sip directly from the glass. He raises his eyebrows and says, "That's a man's drink right there. I wonder why she gave it to you?"

"Give me back my *drank*," Cas grabs his glass. "And did I hear you say you want me to go half with you on a gift? Is that the real reason you want me to go to the baby shower? So I can pay for half your gift, you deadbeat?" He uses the straw to stir the ice and takes a long sip. "Yo, where the fuck is our food? I'm starving."

Jake smiles, embarrassed, "Lower your voice, bro. Are you drunk already? Why the hell are you drinking so early in the day, anyway?"

Cas scuffs at the comment, "I'm not drunk. What, are you kidding me? This drink ain't shit – I need at least two more of these just to get a buzz."

"Oh please, you swear you can hold your liquor, but three drinks is your max limit before you start acting a fool. You're such a lightweight." Just as Jake finishes his sentence, the waitress returns with two plates of food.

"Okay boys, here you go," shes says cheerily as she places the plates on the table. "Is there anything else I can get y'all?"

Jake answers first, "No, I'm good, beautiful. Thank you."

"And what about you? Are you sure there isn't anything I can get you?" she asks Cas.

"No, I'm totally fine, thank you so much," he answers, his mouth stuffed with food.

"You sure?" she asks one more time.

"Yeah, I'm good. Thank you."

"Alright then, enjoy. Let me know if you want anything."

"Sounds good," Jake says politely.

Cas just nods.

The waitress smiles and walks away.

Once she is out of earshot, Jake begins talking in a feminine, Southern voice to mock Cas.

"Are you sure there isn't anything I can get you – anything at all? I mean absolutely anything you can think of? You New York City stud muffin, you."

21

"What are you talking about?" he asks with food still in his mouth.

"This waitress is so into you, and you're just too shook to see it."

Cas disregards his comment. "Yeah, whatever. Anyway, you serious about going to this baby shower?"

"Yes, and I'm serious about you going with me. So, stop bullshitting, and just say yes."

Cas continues to eat but doesn't say anything.

Jake looks up at him – he's beginning to worry that Cas is silent because he's thinking of an excuse to not go.

"Come on, Nova. What the fuck, man?" Jake pleads his case, "You don't want to do anything anymore. I've stopped inviting you to go to clubs because you never wanna go. I tell you about after-work spots, and you always say, 'I'm tired, I'm just going to stay home,' like a little bitch. I'm tired of it already, man. You can't live your life like this. Not going out, not socializing – it's not normal. I mean, what the hell! You're just going to wallow in this depression? You're my wingman. I miss my mother fuckin' wingman, man. Please, just come with me."

Cas continues eating his food, not saying anything.

After a few more bites, he nonchalantly looks up at Jake and nods, "You're *my* mother fuckin' wingman. Don't forget that."

Jake smiles – he can tell his friend is coming around to the idea of going.

"Alright, fine, I'm your wingman. Whatever you want, just come to the damn baby shower. I guarantee you, there's going to be a lotta chicks there, and free food and liquor too."

Cas feels good knowing his friend really wants him to go out. "Fuck it. I'll go," Cas says with a broad smile. "I'm down."

"Yes!" Jake says triumphantly. "After you basically make me beg you, you asshole. You're such a fucking diva, I swear." They both laugh.

Cas turns his focus back on his breakfast. He takes a bite of his corn beef hash. "You know we can't go empty handed."

Jake too begins to focus on his food. "I told you already – we'll go half on a gift."

"Alright, what we gonna get?"

"I don't know yet. They emailed me the registry; so, we'll just get something off there."

Cas has some more of his spiked orange juice. "Eh, I hate those gift registries. What the hell is that, anyway? A gift should be original, creative, not something chosen off a list. I never check those things. I just get whatever the hell I want, fuck it. I mean really, who are you to tell me what to buy you – you know what I mean?"

"Really?" Jake sounds unimpressed. "Who do you know that had a gift registry?"

"Nobody. That's my point, I wouldn't get them something off it anyway. I'd get them whatever I want, not what they tell me to."

"I feel you, bro. But for this gift, we're getting it off the registry."

Before Cas can respond, Megan comes back.

"Are you guys okay? Need anything else?"

"No, I'm good, thank you," Jake says with a smile.

"Likewise," adds Cas. "Everything is great."

"Alright, then. I'll just give you guys the check, and y'all can pay when y'all ready," she places two checks face down on the table.

"Take care, sweetheart," she looks at Cas and walks off.

He's caught off guard. "Okay, I will," he mumbles awkwardly.

"I wonder why she gave us two separate checks," Jake says out loud, without flipping the bill over.

"Probably because she overheard you try to hustle me for a baby shower gift and didn't want you to mooch off me any further," Cas says, only half kidding. "You cheap bastard."

Jake laughs and almost chokes on his food. "What! I'm not *cheap*. Ask your mom how many times I've helped her out."

"Oh yeah?" Cas asks mockingly.

"Yeah. When your daddy was ducking those child support payments, who do you think was paying for your *Cocoa Pebbles*?"

Cas grins. "Well, at least I know who my daddy is. Your mother is still waiting to go on the Maury Show. 'You are *not* the father!'"

Jake laughs. "You're stupid, man. Hurry the hell up with your food so we can get outta here. I have things to do." He turns the check over and looks at it for a minute. "What the hell is this? She charged me for your food too."

Cas finishes his last bite. "Seriously?" he asks. "Lemme see."

He takes the check from Jake's hand and immediately notices it's more than it should be.

"That's weird. I wonder why she did that."

"She's probably trying to pull a fast one and get paid twice. Can't trust those Southern girls, man. How much do you have on your check?" Jake looks around to see if he can spot Megan.

"Let me see." Cas flips the check over. He looks confused for a moment; then, his face breaks into the sunniest of smiles, the one that reaches the eyes, as he looks up at Jake.

Jake is curious to see what's on the check. "What are you smiling like a doofus for?" he says and puts his hand out.

Cas gives him the paper. He looks at it briefly before his eyes widen.

Instead of the bill amount, there's a phone number on the check, with a little hand-written message that simply says, *'Call me.'*

"See, man. I told you she was into you! You gotta trust me when it comes to things like this."

Cas can't think of anything bad to say. "I guess you were right," he replies, feeling a rush of excitement – something he hadn't felt in a long time.

Jake is just as excited and can't help but tease his best friend since the 7th grade.

"You sure she meant to give that to you? Maybe she got it mixed up and meant to place that paper in front of me and give you the check."

Jake's verbal jabs do nothing to douse Cas's mood even a little bit. "Don't hate the player, hate the game," he replies, still smiling wildly.

"Oh, now you're a *playa*, huh?" Jake smiles at him, "Unbelievable. I practically gift-wrapped her for you. All you had to do was sit there and look desperate."

"It's called playing hard to get. It's a subtle art form. I wish I could teach you, but I can't. You're not ready yet. You're too thirsty – eager to jump the gun."

Jake laughs out loud. "Wow, you get one number in a year, and now you're suddenly Mr. Cocky."

Cas folds the little paper with Meagan's number on it and places it in the fifth pocket of his jeans. He takes out his wallet. "Don't worry about the check, I got this," he says, pulling out some cash.

"Thanks, man."

"Eh," Cas grins, "It's the least I can do."

Jake smiles back, "I hear you. But I think the least you can do is pay for the baby shower gift," he says in a matter-of-fact way. "To me, that's the least you can do."

"Don't get greedy – you just got free breakfast, bro." Cas places two $20 bills on the table.

"Leave her a good tip," Jake says. "Not too good, though. You don't want her to think you're paying for her number, like she's a prostitute or something."

The smile on Cas face vanishes. "You're a dick," he says as his stomach starts to feel a little queasy.

"Why?" Jake asks in confusion, and then he realizes why Cas had said that.

"Ah, man. I wasn't talking about your ex. I mean, listen, every time I mention prostitute, or dirty whore, woman of the night, or even sexy nurse, you can't just assume I'm taking a jab at your ex-girl," Jake pauses. "Although, it's more than likely if I say any of those terms, I'm definitely talking about that bitch."

Cas doesn't want to laugh, but he can't help himself and chuckles – it eases his stomach.

"So, what are you doing now?"

Jake looks at his phone, "From here, I'm going to go work out, then get a haircut, and probably buy a new shirt. I've got a date tonight."

"With who? The new girl?"

"Nah, I don't think I've told you about this one. I met her last Wednesday night at a happy hour. I got her number, and whatever, and then I ran into her again yesterday at the same spot. We were chilling all night, vibing, laughing – it was cool. I asked her if she wanted to hang again tonight, and she said she's down." Jake brushes off a few crumbs that had fallen on his shirt while he was eating. "She's banging too. Mad beautiful."

"Cool, man. Sounds good." They both slide out of the booth and start walking towards the door.

Cas looks around for Megan – he sees her standing in front of a table, taking an order. He wants to say *bye,* but she's too far away to hear him without him having to yell.

Jake is walking in front of him; he looks back and lowers his voice so that only Cas can hear what he's got to say.

"If you want to hang tonight, let me know. I'm sure she could bring a friend. I'm talking low, I don't want the waitress to hear."

"Yeah, you helped me out a lot with that, I'm not even gonna lie," Cas says and looks back one more time for Megan, –she's still at the table. *I should go say bye,* he thinks.

Before he can make up his mind, she looks up at him. Their eyes meet.

She smiles and mouths, 'bye'.

27

Cas instantly feels that little twinge of excitement again. He waves back with a broad smile plastered across his face.

He isn't looking where he's going and bumps into a woman sitting at a table by the door.

"Ouch!" The woman looks up at Cas, her eyes wide in pain and anger.

"Watch where the hell you're going, asshole! You made me poke my mouth with the fork!"

Cas is immediately apologetic. "Oh, I'm so sorry. I wasn't looking where I was going. Damn, sorry about that."

Jake turns around to see what's going on. He sees Cas apologizing and doesn't hesitate to step in.

"What the hell did you do?" he asks sternly, purposely trying to embarrass him. "I turn around for one second, and you're stabbing people in the face with forks? What's wrong with you?"

The woman is holding her mouth. "Jim, am I bleeding?" she asks the man sitting across from her.

Jim is a big mass of a man – even when sitting down, he's huge, and he looks pissed.

"You better not be," he says looking at Cas. "Let me check."

Jake is enjoying the commotion. "Yeah, check it out, Jim." He looks at Cas. "I tell you what, she better not be bleeding, or me and Jim are going to kick your ass."

Jim examines her mouth – there doesn't seem to be anything wrong.

Cas is still apologizing, "Miss, I'm so sorry about that. I didn't mean to bump into you."

"Yeah, well…" the woman starts talking, but Jake cuts her off.

"I swear, I can't take you anywhere. What's the matter with you?" he says while grabbing Cas by the back of the neck. "Come on, man. Let's go. Get the hell out of here. Sorry, folks, jackass coming through."

Cas violently shrugs Jake off of him and apologizes one more time before heading for the exit.

"I'm really sorry, folks, again. Hope you enjoy the rest of your food."

There's no damage done to the woman's lip, but that doesn't stop her and Jim from scowling at Cas and Jake as they leave.

Just as he's about to walk out of the door, Cas looks back and sees Megan standing at the end of a row of tables. She looks embarrassed and avoids eye contact. Cas gives a quick nod and walks out. That twinge of excitement has evaporated.

Once outside, Jake laughs at his friend. "Watch where you're walking, you klutz."

"I feel bad, dude. But did I really bump into her *that* hard?" Cas says as they begin to walk up the block.

"You didn't bump her hard – she was a drama queen." Jake then adds, "But Jim was about to fuck you up, though. You ain't want that sauce. You wanted no part of Jim's sauce."

Cas shakes his head, "Man, please. We could've taken him on. The both of us together."

Jake snickers, "Both? Who? You and Megan, the waitress?"

"Oh, word?" Cas is amused. "It's like that, huh? You don't got my back? Alright, I see how it is now."

"Nah. Of course, I got your back. I always got your back, man." Jake smiles, "Someone's got to watch over your punk ass."

Cas laughs. "*Punk ass*? My man, I am straight thug life."

"Alright, Cheef Keef." They reach the corner of the block, "Hey, I meant to ask – did you look at the email I sent you about an event that's coming up next month?"

"Yes, I got it. Somebody's birthday, all-white affair, blah, blah, blah."

"It's not an all-white affair – it's a black-tie event."

"Same shit."

"No, it's not nearly the same shit. Stop fucking around. This is a big deal – there will be plenty of those industry types there, and I want the invite to really stand out. If this goes well, it might lead to some major contracts down the road."

"Yeah? Like what?"

"I don't want to talk about it – might jinx it."

"Well, when do you need this done by?"

"The sooner the better, but no later than Friday."

"Alright, I'll check it out when I get to the apartment." Cas looks down at this phone and continues talking, "But, you know, if this is such a big deal, why don't you pay a professional to do it?"

"Because you're better than most of the professionals. And don't worry, if this goes right, the next one, I'll definitely be able to pay you for it."

"I'll believe that when I see it. You've said that for the last three events."

"You know if you actually came to some of these things, you'd have a good time. I can get you free drinks all night – you'd sit in the VIP lounge. You'd probably get laid."

"Yeah yeah, I know," says Cas sarcastically.

"I'm serious, man. But anyway, I'm about to bounce the other way. I'll hit you up later, or maybe I'll see you at home. But either way, we're definitely on for Sunday."

"Sounds good." He reaches out to give Jake a fist bump – they touch their shoulders in a half hug.

"Be easy, man. Later."

"Later," Cas responds.

They walk their separate ways.

CHAPTER 2

Sunday

Cas finds himself lying in bed – Tiffany is standing at the edge of it. He has no idea how she's gotten into his room.

"Hey, bae. You miss me?" she says, naked but for a black mesh bra and panties.

He wants to say 'no', but when he opens his mouth, he ends up admitting the truth.

"Oh, bae, I miss you so much."

Tiffany begins to slowly lower down the strap of her bra off her left shoulder.

"I miss you too, bae, so much." Her voice is sultry and sexy. She lowers the other strap of her bra, exposing her beautiful breasts. They look much bigger than how Cas remembers them. "I'm going to show you just how much I've missed you."

She climbs onto the bed. As she slowly crawls on all fours, her back is arched, pronouncing the curve of her ass and hips. She smiles, sexy and mischievous – ready to indulge her old lover.

She reaches his legs, softly kissing his shins and working her way up to his knee. Tiffany slowly licks and kisses his lower thigh as her hands massage their way towards his cock. Her touch immediately reminds Cas of all that he's missed most about Tiffany. Her sensual, sexual ways that drove him crazy with blind lust. She grabs hold of his rock-hard assurance that he's loving every bit of what is being done to him and starts stroking it.

Cas is lost in the moment, anxiously anticipating Tiffany's skilled mouth wrapping around him. In the midst of this surreal moment of bottled ecstasy, there's a soft ringing sound in the distance. It's faint at first, but then begins to get louder.

"Is that your phone?" he asks her.

Tiffany's head is positioned between his legs – he can feel the warmth of her mouth cupping his balls.

Cas doesn't want her to stop, but the ringing is distracting him.

"Can you get the phone?" he says, but Tiffany doesn't look up. She keeps stroking and massaging with her hand and titillating him with her tongue that is trained to please.

It feels so good to be with her, but the phone is making Cas uneasy – he can't concentrate. He starts to remember why they broke up.

"Pick up your phone," he says.

She doesn't respond.

"I said pick up your phone."

She still ignores him.

"PICK UP YOUR FUCKING PHONE!" he yells, but to no avail. It's like she can't even hear him.

He's getting nauseous, thinking of all the times her phone rang in the past and she had to run out because *work* was calling. He can't take her ignoring him anymore.

"TIFFANY! PICK UP YOUR FUCKING PHONE! PICK UP YOUR FUCKING PHONE! PICK. UP. YOUR..."

Cas realizes that he's dreaming and opens his eyes. His cell phone is ringing.

"Aw shit," he mumbles to himself.

Reaching for the night stand, he grabs his phone and brings it very close to his barely open eyes. The caller ID reads 'Jake'.

"Come on, man," Cas grunts and hits the red cancel button, forcing the call to voicemail. Instantly, his phone shows two missed calls, both from Jake. Cas looks at the time – it's 9:00 AM.

Why the fuck are you calling me so early?

Cas had stayed up till almost 5 in the morning – drinking beer, smoking weed, and playing video games. He'd gone to bed late, knowing that he could sleep in as long as he wanted.

Sunday has become his favorite day of the week – it's the only day when he can stay home all day, do nothing, and still not feel like a total boring loser. The current story of his life.

He's so tired that as soon as his eyes close, he immediately begins to drift back to sleep.

His phone rings again – it's Jake. Cas hits the green answer button so he can take the call; he knows that if he doesn't, Jake will just keep calling.

"Hello?" he whispers, his voice low and raspy with sleepiness.

"Yo, what the fuck, man? I could be dying here, and you wouldn't even know because you won't pick up your fucking phone," Jake says quickly – he's also whispering.

"It's early, man. What do you want?" Cas is getting crankier by the moment. "And why are you whispering?"

Jake speaks low and fast, "Don't worry about that. I need you to do me a favor."

His eyes are shut – Cas is barely listening. His mind begins to drift.

"Nova!" Jake whispers louder.

"What?" he responds, wishing he hadn't answered the call in the first place.

"I need you to do me a favor. Call me back in ten minutes. As a matter of fact, make it fifteen. Call me back in fifteen minutes STAT."

Cas is annoyed and half asleep – he feels like Jake is talking utter nonsense. "What are you talking about, man? Why I gotta call you back? Just tell me what you want now?"

Jake sounds frustrated. "What I want is for you to wake your punk ass up long enough to call me back in fifteen minutes. Please, man, that's all I'm asking. So, don't forget."

Cas is too tired to question anymore. "Fine, I'll call you back."

"Thanks, man," Jake says, still whispering. "Don't forget, fifteen minutes."

"Alright," Cas grunts and hangs up the phone. Still lying down with his eyes closed, he thinks, *Fifteen minutes. Fifteen minutes. Fifteen minutes...*

***

When he opens his eyes again, in what feels like fifteen minutes later, he reaches for his phone and brings it close to his face to see the time.

It's 11:22 AM.

"Oh shit," he mutters to himself. He has a text message from Jake.

'Thnx for calling me back.'

Feeling bad that he let his friend down, Cas calls him. It rings a few times and goes to voicemail. He hangs up and sends a text.

'Sorry dude... fell back asleep, I'm dead tired... my bad, man... Where are you?'

Cas puts the phone down and lies in bed, contemplating whether he's ready to be officially awake. He decides his body needs more sleep. Just as he closes his eyes and begins to drift, he's startled by a loud banging knock at the front door.

He begrudgingly gets out of bed to answer it.

As he approaches the door, the banging gets louder.

He looks through the peephole – it's Jake. Cas opens the door.

"Don't you have your keys?"

"Don't you have a heart?" Jake shoots a bitter look at him as he enters the apartment.

Cas lowers his head and closes the front door. "Sorry about this morning, man. I was knocked out."

"I kind of figured that when an hour passed and my roommate, my supposed, reported, best friend, didn't call me back like I'd asked him to. But hey, what are friends for, if not to let you down when you need them the most?" Jake flops down on the sofa.

"Sorry, man. I mean that," he replies sincerely. "Why were you whispering anyway?"

"Man, I had a crazy night." Jake shakes his head. "I told you about the new girl, right?"

"Yeah, you mentioned her the other day. The *new* new girl. What's her name?"

"Cynthia. She kind of looks like Pocahontas. She has this beautiful tan skin and long straight black hair. And her body is crazy – she's super fit," Jake answers as he sits up. "Anyway, I take her out to eat – we go to that *B.B. King's* spot on forty-deuce. We get dinner – I have a steak and shrimp, she has a Mediterranean salad that's pretty good. The food was lit."

"Okay," Cas can tell his friend is enjoying laying out all the details, but all he wants to do is go back to bed. "Get to the crazy part."

"I'm getting there. So, after leaving the restaurant, we go to a bar around the corner, and this girl can freakin' drink. We're throwing back shots of Patron like it's water. I mean seriously, like eight shots and a coupl'a martinis too. Just pretty much getting toasted. And with each drink, she's getting more and more comfortable, telling me that, you know, even though we just met, she really likes me and she can see I'm a good person, and all this other shit."

Cas chuckles.

"But for real, she starts getting into how she doesn't want to be single when she's 30 – mind you, she's only like 27. She goes on about how she's tired of being lonely, and men are dogs, and all that single-woman-with-a-cat kinda stuff. And at this point, I'm wrecked, and I start getting caught up in my feelings and talking all types of emotional shit. I'm like, 'Yeah, I know what you mean, I'm still looking for the right woman to have that special bond with' – all this other drunken nonsense. Then, she's telling me how sexually frustrated she is, saying she hasn't had any in months because she doesn't want to have sex with just anybody – she's not into casual stuff. And the conversation is *deep*, we were both drunk like shit, but we were getting deep with our feelings. Talking about how sex is such an intimate and personal experience…"

"Sex is such an intimate experience?" Cas snarks, "Of course, sex is an intimate experience – it's called being intimate, for crying out loud."

"Yeah but check this out," Jake continues, "In the midst of all this deep conversation, she tells me the next guy she sleeps with, she's going to fuck his brains out."

Cas chokes. "Hold up, hold up. She didn't *really* say that in those exact words, did she?"

"I swear, dude – just like that. She said, 'The next guy I take home, I'm going to fuck his brains out'. Those same words. Very casual, very 'ho hum' about it."

Jake leans back, grinning in appreciation of his life.

"So, I'm like, man, the way this night is going, if I play my cards right, I'm going to be *that* guy."

Cas laughs aloud. He's wide awake at this point.

"Damn, that's some crazy shit for her to say."

"I know. But I play it cool," Jake leans back in his seat. "I'm like 'Yes, I know what you mean, I'm tired of being lonely, too' and all that. I don't say anything about the sex, nothing about the *fucking the brains out*. I just played it cool. I didn't want to seem like a thirst ball."

"Good move," Cas responds.

"Of course," Jake nods. "So, we're there for a while, ordering drinks, everything's lit. And now she's really digging me. Sitting extra close to me, she's a little more touchy-feely now, everything is going great.

"Before you know it, it's almost 4:00 AM, and the place is about to close."

"Okay." Cas leans back in the sofa, putting his feet up on the coffee table to make himself more comfortable. "So... what happened then?"

Jake continues, "We go outside to wait for the Uber. I give her a hug and a kiss on the cheek, but I can tell by the way she's holding onto me she doesn't really want to let go. So, I'm like, screw it, I'm drunk, she's drunk, I'm going for it. I start kissing her on the neck, real soft though. A little light bite here, a little lick there. Real classy."

"Keep it classy," echoes Cas.

Jake smirks. "I actually took your advice and played a little hard to get."

Cas feels that slight pinch of envy creep in again. "Oh yeah?"

"Yup. I look at her and say, 'Hey, girl. I hate for the night to end, but I have to go.'"

"*That's* what you hit her with? The old, 'Hey girl I gotta go?'"

"Hell yeah. But I had my R&B voice going." Jake deepens his voice. "I'm like, 'Hey girl, I know you been lonely for a mighty long time, but I'm here to tell you, I'm here now, girl. And although I really, really hate for this night to end, I have to go now.'"

Cas smiles and sings a background tune, "*Sha-na-na-na. Girl, I gotta gooo!*"

They both laugh.

"That's the name of the single, *Girl I Gotta Go.* It's the wave." Cas nods. "So, what happened next?"

"She grabs my face and starts tonguing me down."

39

"Get out!" Cas is grinning, but he's a little pissed off too, courtesy of that same old pinch of jealousy.

"Dead ass," Jake looks at him. "She was wild sexy – sucking on my tongue, biting my lips, grinding against me. Keep in mind, the Uber's already gotten there. I peek at the driver, and he's just staring through the window, a big ol' pervert smile on his face."

Cas laughs. "That's funny."

"I know, right? I even told him 'Sorry about that, man. You can go, I don't want to keep you here'. He was like, 'No rush. Take your time, my friend.' So, we're still kissing and stuff, and I'm all into it, but at the same time, I'm thinking, *Am I getting some or not?* Because I'm hard as shit, and if I'm not getting any, I need to get my ass home and beat off or something. So, I hit the R&B again. I'm like, 'Hey girl, am I coming home with you? Or am I going home alone tonight?'"

"Smooth," Cas nods in approval.

"It must have been. Because she grabs my dick, and is like, 'You're not going anywhere tonight!'"

"No way!" he smiles in disbelief, that grasp of envy getting stronger.

"I'm dead serious. Right there on the sidewalk, she just grabs it."

"Wow, how sick is that!" Cas is grinning ear to ear – he may be jealous of his friend, but he's also very happy for him. "So, what happened?"

"We finally jump into the car. We're going back to her place, she lives on the Upper East Side – so, from Times Square that's a bit of a ride. Especially with the Saturday night traffic. But nothing's stopping us, man – we're going at it hard in the Uber." Jake sits up and pretends like he's gripping an invisible ass. "She's sitting on top of me – grinding, going crazy. I'm kissing her, sucking her titties. I move my hand down to her panties, and she's dripping. I feel her through her panties, soaking wet. I slip my finger in, and she jumps back, letting out a sexy-ass moan. It was beautiful. I give the cooch a couple of good ol' flicks of the wrist—"

"Look at the flick of the wrist," Cas chirps in and quickly moves his fingers side to side. He smiles broadly as Jake laughs.

"I'm telling you, Nova, a couple of good ol' flick of the wrist, and the next thing I know," Jake pauses for a half a beat, "Water works."

"Water works?" Cas asks skeptically, but still grinning ear to ear. "What do you mean *water works*?"

"A fucking squirtter, bro!" Jake replies excitedly.

"Hell no!" Cas jumps up. "I don't believe it. That shit's not real. That's strictly fake porno bullshit!"

"I'm telling you – it was water works, dude. She was squirting everywhere."

"Ah, Jacob?" Cas pauses and looks at him.

Jake shakes his head. "You know every time you call me *Jacob*, I know you're going to say something stupid."

"Jacob, how do you know she wasn't pissing on you? How do you know it wasn't urine?"

"Uh, Juan, why would it be urine?" Jake smiles and looks dumbfounded. "I mean don't get me wrong – I have thought about it for a brief moment, but then I realized it couldn't be."

"Oh yeah? And why the hell not?" Cas reasons, "You barely know this girl, she let you finger her in the backseat of a random car and

41

squirted all over you. Would it be so crazy to think she could've pissed on you? Some people are down with the whole, you know, piss scene. *Golden tunnels* and all that shit."

"It's not called *Golden tunnels*, it's Golden Showers."

"Yeah, wouldn't you know."

Jake sucks his teeth. "No, she's not into the whole *piss scene*," he says using air quotes. "And even if she was into it, she wouldn't be pissing on me in the back seat of a fucking Uber, bro."

"Right. You're absolutely right," Cas nods in mock agreement. "She's not that kinda girl. She's a squirtter, not a pisser – put some respect on her name."

Jake stares at him blankly.

Cas gestures at him to continue. "I'm sorry I cut you off. I actually want to know what happened."

"You sure? I don't *have* to tell you the rest."

"No, my bad, for real. I didn't mean to cut you off, man." Cas starts chuckling. "Hey, what about the driver? What was he doing when all this was happening?"

Jake shrugs and chuckles a little too. "Man, I wouldn't be surprised if that dude was beating off. A couple times that I just happened to look up, I could see him looking through the rear view. Basically, we gave him a free show. That was his tip, watching us go at it like animals."

Cas leans back in his seat. "I swear I hate you sometimes, man. *All* the cool shit happens to you."

"Don't hate me yet, man. There's more still." Jake continues, "So, now we get to her apartment, and as soon as we get in there, she drops

42

to her knees and starts sucking me off. Just topping me, deep throat action."

"Deep throat?" Cas interrupts again. "You know, I never really like it when women deep throat my shit. I don't know why, but having a woman gag on my penis has never really been sexually gratifying for me. It just doesn't do it for me."

Jake shrugs. "Well, it did it for this chick because she was wild. She was gaggin', spitting on it, smacking herself in the face with it. I was actually a little afraid at one point; it was more than what I was used to.

"But I got into it real quick, though, and before you know it, I had her in the foyer, turned around and pressed against the wall, panties to the side, and I'm banging her from the back." Jake humps the air, his hands holding an invisible waist.

Cas cuts him off, "You had a condom?"

"Oh, hell yeah," he reassures him, "100 percent."

"Cool. So, you smashed? That's what's up."

"Nah, man, it was epic, though! We screwed in every room in the apartment on the way to her bedroom." Jake laughs. "Once we finally stumbled onto her bed, she got on top and rode me till the fucking cows came home, bro. She was in total control; she literally fucked my brains out."

Cas chuckles. "Sounds like good times."

Jake shakes his head. "You don't understand how crazy the sex was. For like, a one-night stand, for it to be that crazy, that passionate – what are the odds."

Cas laughs. "She put it on you, huh?"

"Hell yeah. Something special."

"No doubt – that's what's up, man. Definitely sounds like a great night," Cas replies. "But what was up with the phone call and the whispering this morning?"

"Oh yeah, that. Well, once we were done, we were just lying there, all sweaty and exhausted, pretty much dehydrated from all the wild, porno sex we'd just had. And you know, she's like, laying on top of me with her head on my chest, which was a little annoying because I was already really hot and tired. But it's cool, whatever. I wasn't going to be a dick about it."

"Such a gentleman," Cas chirps.

"I know. So, I start nodding off to sleep, but I could feel her looking at me. When I open my eyes to check, she's like wide awake, staring at me with crazy eyes and a *smile* on her face."

"Creepy," Cas agrees.

"Right. And I can see this look in her eyes. At first, I thought it was a look of drunken wonderment, like *Wow, I can't believe how good that was*. So, I just gave her a little kiss on the forehead, like *Yeah baby, we did that*. But I can still feel her staring at me. When I look again, I realize that she's not really staring at me in wonderment – it's more like *love lust*."

"Love lust?"

"That's the only way I can describe it. It's like when you lust for something so much, you think you love it. We just had this crazy sex episode, and she's caught up in *love lust*."

"So? What's wrong with that?" Cas asks, that little pinch of envy now grown to the point of making him want to choke. "Didn't you just say it was the best sex ever?"

"Yeah, it's up there. But still, I'm definitely not trying to have her fall in love with me. She even asked me what I was doing today. And I'm thinking like *You're not my girlfriend, you shouldn't be asking me what I'm doing.*

"But before I can even answer, she tells me, 'I really like you, and I don't do this with just anyone.' She said she's going to stop talking to other guys so she can just focus on us because she wants to see where this can go." Jake shrugs and looks at Cas in disbelief. "Isn't that little on the psycho side?"

"Eh, maybe a little." Cas shrugs.

"Apparently, somewhere in my drunk gibberish, I'd managed to convince her I'm ready to settle down and all this other crap."

Cas laughs. "Why the hell did you say that? You know you're not looking for a girlfriend."

"I don't know, man," Jake sighs. "Shit, to be honest, I don't really remember saying it. I know I was drunk and caught up in the moment," he pauses, "But I don't remember."

Cas starts to feel a little bad for the woman, Cynthia.

"I think I'm ready to settle down," he says out loud.

Jake looks at him. "Yeah, you think so? You're ready to call it a career?"

Cas takes a moment. "I'm pretty sure I am. We've been running around, chasing women for a long time. I'm 26 already, man…"

Jake interrupts him with a laugh, "You ol' bastard."

"What you mean? You're two months older than me."

"Exactly," he agrees. "And you don't see me pressing to settle down. You just need to live more. Sow your wild oats."

Cas looks at him in confusion. "What the hell does that even mean?"

"I don't know," Jake says with a smile. "It means to have fun and bang a lot of hot women before calling it quits. That's what it means."

"Seriously," Cas replies, "I know you probably think I'm just saying it, but I really mean it. I'm kinda ready to settle down."

Jake cuts him off, "Man, look, you think you're ready, but you're really not. That's just the loneliness talking."

"No, it's not. I know how I feel. And this is how I feel."

Jake doesn't believe him. "Please. You say that now, but when you've had good women in the past – and I'm *not* talking about Nurse Feel-Good-Tiffany, I'm talking about *real* good women – women who got their shit together, you've always fucked it up.

"Think about Joanne or Felicity. They were both smart, career driven, pretty, had a lot going for them, and you weren't pressed then to be with either. You cheated on them whenever you could and dumped them on whim. One day, you woke up and didn't want to be in a relationship anymore, and you broke their hearts. Why'd you do that? I can tell you right now – it's because you're not ready to settle down. You still got some wild oats left to sow – know what I mean?"

"You're right. I wasn't ready *then*, but I am now," Cas continues. "Plus, sometimes I wonder, like *How many good women are you allowed in life before you use up your quota?*

46

"Both of those girls were wife material, not to mention Rebekah, and I let them go because of some dumb shit. Spending too much time hoeing around with the likes of you."

"Hey!" Jake interrupts, "Who you calling a hoe?"

Cas laughs. "For real though. Sometimes I think, *how many good girls are left*? Maybe I already used up my quota, and that's why that whole Tiffany situation happened. Karma caught up with me. Think about it. I broke a lot of hearts, good hearts, just to be on some player shit. Yeah, it was fun, but what do I have to show for it now?"

"What do you mean?" Jake asks him. "You have priceless memories to show for it. We've had some crazy good times, bro. You remember that time we met those NYU chicks at Webster Hall? We had a fucking orgy, dude! That was insane. I mean, it sucks I had to see your hairy-ass balls in the process – but hey, no risk, no reward, right? I hope you've shaved that shit, by the way. I was embarrassed for you. You had a ball fro."

Cas smiles. "Yeah, shaved now. And that was a *pretty* crazy night."

"It was awesome," Jake nods. "And that's what life's about, man. When it's all said and done, and we're two old farts, we're going to be grateful for all those memories, you know?"

"Of course, and I wouldn't change those times for anything. But at the same time, I feel like I'm past that now. I mean, Jake, you do realize that was three or four years ago. We're closer now to 30 than we are to 20."

"Big deal," Jake interjects. "30 is the new 20, you know that. And if anything, settle down when you're 30."

"I'm pretty sure I want to be married before 30. Maybe have a kid by then too."

Jake stares at Cas for a moment, completely disgusted. "Have you been to the doctor lately? Because, seriously, I think you've shaved your hairy nuts too close, and you've cut your balls off. You just got a big fat pussy now where your balls should be."

Cas sucks his teeth. "Shut up. I'm trying to be serious, but as usual, everything is a joke to you."

"Nova, just listen to what you're telling me? You're killing me, bro. I feel like I'm losing my boy. You're changing on me."

"Changing?" Cas laughs. "That's what happens when you get older – you change. You evolve. Things that were important to me before, such as bagging as many women as possible, are just not that important to me anymore. It's called growing up, Jake. Try it sometime."

"It's called acting like a pussy, and I don't want to try it," he answers back sarcastically. "I'm gonna live while I'm young. We have our whole lives to settle down, when we're old and washed up. But right now, I'm just hitting my stride, man, and I don't plan on slowing down anytime soon."

"You know what? Let's just forget about it," Cas gives up trying to explain himself and is ready to change the topic. "So, what's the plan for the baby shower? And you never really told me what happened after you called me this morning?"

"Well, I was whispering because she was sleeping and I didn't want to wake her up. I was going to pretend your call was something important and I had to leave immediately."

"Yeah, I figured that." He feels guilty about not calling him back. "So, how'd you get out?"

"I texted Manny to call me. After he hit me back, I told her that I had to run to help him put together a crib for the baby shower."

Cas feels better after hearing that their friend, Manolo, was able to help him. "What did she say when you told her you had to leave?"

"Nothing really. She was probably a little disappointed, but she understood. She just asked me to call her later."

"What you gonna do now? You're still going to see her?"

"Oh, hell yeah, for sure. But I'm definitely going to fall back a little bit. I don't want her to fall too hard for the kid."

"Oh, please," Cas scoffs. "But anyway, what time you want to head to the baby shower?"

"It starts at 6." Jake looks at his watch. "I figure we get there at like 8 or so."

"You work tomorrow?" Cas asks.

"Yup, definitely. You?"

"Yeah, I actually have a meeting tomorrow at 10. So, I don't want to get home too late. I have to be up in the morning."

"Man, you be playing video games till like 2:00 AM, and you still manage to get up for work. Don't give me that bullshit," Jake says, before adding, "We'll go for a couple of hours, see how it is. If it's lit, we stick around – if it's not, we bounce early. Simple."

Cas feels anxious over finally breaking his reticent video game-playing lifestyle, but he is looking forward to doing something other than just going to work and coming home, pretty much his routine since Tiffany broke his heart.

49

"Alright, cool. Who else is going?"

"Me, you, and Chen. And Manolo will be there, obviously."

"Chen? Chicken Wing? He's around?" Cas asks.

"Yeah, he's around. But don't call him Chicken Wing – he doesn't like it. No one calls him that anymore," Jake answers.

"Shit, I'm a call him Chicken Wing as soon as I see him. I can't believe he moved back to the city. I remember you telling me he was coming back, but I thought he loved it over on the West Coast? How long was he in Cali for?"

"A few years already. Time flies, man. But seriously, don't call him 'Chicken Wing' – he'll fuck you up."

"Whatever," Cas ignores the comment. "Anybody else going that I would know?"

"As far as people you know? That's probably it. But I tell you what, Veronica has a lot of hot friends. I've met a few of her sorority sisters before, and they were all smoke shows. And of course, her cousins are going to be there too. So, I'm sure it's gonna be packed with women."

Cas likes what he's hearing. "Sounds good, man."

Jake gets up from the sofa and walks over to the small desk in the corner. "Is your laptop on? I want to check out the registry."

"Are you serious? You want to get something off the registry?"

"I already told you that's what we're going to do." He opens the laptop and begins typing.

"What's the registry looking like right now?"

"Damn, there are only two things left. A diaper genie and a car seat-stroller combo. It's a stroller that you can detach and use as a car seat."

"Cool, cool. What about the diaper genie? That's that special trash can for diapers, right?"

"Yessir. But damn, dude, the diaper genie is like 100 bucks and the stroller is 300."

"That's an obvious choice. We're getting the diaper genie."

Jake looks at Cas. "And you say I'm cheap?"

"What do you mean? Let's not get crazy, man. I'm not spending 300 dollars on someone I hardly ever see."

"It would only be 150 each. We're going half on it."

"Even 150, that's a lotta money. The most I'm willing to spend is 50 bucks, and I really don't even want to spend that much."

"If we show up there with a diaper genie between the two us, we're going to look like some broke-ass bitches, Cas."

"Why would we look broke? We're not family. Think about it. That stroller is still on her registry because no one else has bought it yet. If anything, her family and close friends are messed up because they didn't buy it for her already. They're the broke bitches, not us." Cas pauses for a moment, "And on top of that, we can always say that we bought something off the registry. We can be like 'Hey, you asked for this, I got it off your registry, here it is.' You know?"

"Oh, so now the registry is cool?" Jake looks at him with a raised eyebrow.

"Man, I'm not spending 150 bucks. Shit, if you want, I'll give you 50 and you can put the rest in."

"You can't spend 150? This is a Spanish baby shower. There's going to be free food, liquor, beautiful women, and you don't want to spend 150? And you know, the thing is I know you have it. You can afford it. You're just being cheap."

"Why're you all in my pockets? Don't worry about what I got, worry about what you got."

"I know what I got – I got 150 on it. I'm not being cheap."

"Call me cheap, then. I got 50. And you know what, I don't even really want to go. So, if that's not enough, just let me know and I'll stay home like I wanted to anyway."

"Alright, relax. No need to get butt hurt," Jake replies. "I guess someone has to get the diaper genie – might as well be us."

"Exactly," Cas says as he heads to his bedroom. He picks up a pair of jeans lying on the floor and takes his wallet out of the back pocket. Taking three $20 bills from it, he walks back to the living room and hands it to Jake.

"Here you go," he says to his friend.

"What do you mean?" Jake asks as he takes the cash. "You're not coming with me to get it?"

Cas yawns loudly. "No, I'm going back to sleep. Holler at me later so I can start getting ready."

"Aw, you suck. I thought you were going to roll with me."

Cas shakes his head and starts heading back to his bedroom. "Bro, I'm dead tired, I need to sleep."

Jake looks at him walking away. "You think I'm not tired? I was up fucking all night – I'm exhausted."

52

"I feel *so* sorry for all your pain," Cas answers. "And don't forget to return my change – I'm only giving you 50 out of that."

"Not only are you a hater and cheap, you're lazy too," Jake replies. "And you wonder why you're not blessed, Casanova."

"Sorry, bruh, I'm going back to sleep." Cas lies down on his bed and pulls the covers over himself.

"Fine, I'll go by myself," Jake says as he gets up from the desk and starts heading towards the kitchen. "What we got to eat?"

Cas yells out from his room, "There's some left over White Castle from yesterday, and a box of Yodels."

"Yuck," Jake interrupts, "Why do you eat that stuff?"

"Because it tastes good. And if you don't want any, take your ass to the store and buy your own food."

Jake finds nothing that he can eat in the fridge and stands in front of the kitchen cabinet, seeing if there's anything he can work with. After a few minutes, he gives up.

He walks over to Cas's room and stands in the doorway. "You cleaned your room?" He's pleasantly surprised. "It looks good, man. Still not perfect, but it's looking tidy. At least, it doesn't stink anymore."

"Febreze," Cas mumbles.

"It's a start." Jake nods in approval. "But you have to cut back on the junk food. Your blood is probably 90% corn fructose syrup, you know that? It's ironic that you're talking about growing up and maturing, and meanwhile you eat like an obese 13-year-old. It's all that weed you smoke. That's why you eat all these damn munchies."

"Stop talking shit and just order something," Cas calls out from his bed. "And while you're at it, get me a bacon, egg, and cheese on a roll. I'll eat it when I wake up."

"I'm not ordering shit," Jake says as he walks out the room. "I'm a go get the gift and probably get something to eat from outside. I'll call you when I'm on my way back."

Cas's eyes are already closed. "Alright, man," he says in as loud a volume as his tired voice would allow. "Make sure to lock the door on your way out."

He can hear the locks on his front door turning. Jake calls out, "Later."

Cas doesn't respond – he's already drifting to sleep.

He hears the door close and zones out.

CHAPTER 3

Chicken Wing

Cas sits on the sofa, thinking of a good reason to give Jake for sneaking out of the baby shower. Jake had called earlier saying he was on his way. That was over two hours ago.

Fully dressed and ready to leave, a wave of intense anxiety hits him – his stomach is in knots. It has nothing to do with Jake being late, he's used to that. Cas isn't exactly sure why he's so nervous, but that extreme feeling of uneasiness is making him want to stay home.

Before Cas had met Tiffany, he would go out all the time. Jake had gotten into club promotion and would organize stand-up comedy events, open mics, and small concerts at clubs across the city. Cas began designing the fliers for these events as a favor for his best friend.

Through Jake's ever-growing connections in the nightlife scene, they gained access to the VIP section in virtually every hot club. It was normal for them to be out partying four or five nights a week.

He always felt the prime objective for going out was to meet women. Sure, it's fun to hang with your boys and get a few drinks, but, ultimately, what determines whether you've had a good time is if you get a pretty girl's number, or at least, an email address. For Cas and his friends, the best-case scenario would be sleeping with a hot chick they've met at the club that very night. They lived for one-night stands, and if one of them ended their night with a new notch in their belt, they couldn't wait to tell their friends.

Once Cas started getting serious with Tiffany, he wanted to spend all his free time with her. The funny thing is, he had never been a *one-woman* kind of guy – he'd cheated on every girlfriend he'd ever had. Until Tiffany – with her, it was different, he *wanted* to be faithful to her. Cas took pride in telling the women who'd approach him that he had a girlfriend, letting them know he was taken, his chest puffed out with equal parts pride and happiness. He believed he'd found the woman he would be with for the rest of his life. So, he stopped feeling the need to go out anymore.

That was then.

He's single now, and he knows that he has to get back on the wagon. This baby shower is probably the easiest way to get back into the swing of things. There should be plenty of women there, and if he sees someone he's interested in, the awkwardness of approaching her and the difficulty of starting a conversation would be taken care of, since all he'll have to do is smile and say, 'So, how do you know Veronica?'

On a typical Sunday, Cas would be baked within an hour of waking up. He actively hasn't smoked any weed today because he knows if he does, he'll probably get lazy or paranoid and then end up not going. But as time passes and he feels more and more anxious, the idea of a toke becomes more and more appealing.

Maybe I should smoke a little? Just enough to calm my nerves, he thinks, inching towards his stash.

Before the thought has enough time to take seed in his mental ether, the intercom buzzes loudly. He doesn't move at first, he looks over at the time; it's 8:20 PM.

Should I hit the bong real quick?

The intercom buzzes again. He goes over to it and presses the 'TALK' button. "Yo."

"Yoooo," replies Jake. "Come downstairs. I have a ride."

"Okay," he answers as his stomach starts to sink.

Cas ignores the sinking feeling, grabs his keys, and heads for the door.

Slowly jogging down the four flights of stairs, he gets to the building lobby and walks out of the front.

There's a shiny black SUV, the windows are rolled up and tinted. The front passenger side window rolls down slowly – there's Jake grinning at him with his sunglasses on.

"What's up, brother? I'm glad you came. I was worried that you might flake out at the last minute."

"I'm here, man." Cas cracks a smile as he looks over at the driver – it's his old high school friend, Chen Wang. Cas is happy to see him. "Yooooo! Chicken *Wiiing*! What's good? Damn, it's been a minute, dude."

"*Chicken Wing*?" Chen looks at him with a half-smile. "Yeah, it definitely has been a while. I can't remember the last time someone called me that. But I'm good, man. Working at the MTA now, Junior Engineer. It's pretty sweet. Feels a little weird to be back in New York, though. I miss Cali sometimes."

"A Junior Engineer? Shit, I'm impressed, man." He gets into the back seat of the car. "Nice whip too. Let me find out Chicken Wing, doing his thing-thing."

Chen quickly turns towards Jake and shoots him a heated look as he pulls off.

"Hey, Cas," Jake clears his throat. "I don't know if I told you before but, uh, nobody calls him that anymore."

Cas looks confused. "What? Chicken Wing? Are you kidding? That's like the coolest nickname ever. I love that name, man. Chicken Wing, *Chicken Wang!*"

The car suddenly swerves towards the side of the road and stops. Chen now turns his head fully to face Cas.

"Yo, Nova. Remember when we were in high school, and you guys would always fuck with me?" he says as he widens his mouth to make himself look buck tooth. He starts talking in a stereotypical Chinese accent, "Ah chicken wing and por'fri' rice'. Ah french fri' an' chicken win', and we would all laugh. You remember that shit?"

Cas is hesitant to respond – he smiles meekly. "Yeah, I remember. That was…"

Chen cuts him off, "The shit wasn't funny to me, man! I only laughed because I was scrawny and weak, and I wanted you guys to be my friends. Well, I ain't weak anymore." He lifts his right arm up to flex his bicep – it's a massive, well-defined, chiseled chunk of muscle. "I don't play that *'french fri' chicken win'* bullshit no more, bitch! I will fuck you guys up, bro!"

"Hey," Jake jumps in. "What do you mean *you guys*? I didn't call you that. I specifically told him *not* to call you that. He don't wanna listen, he's a troublemaker." He looks back at Cas. "You see, I told you, don't call him 'Chicken Wing'. He'll fuck you up, bro."

Cas is dumbstruck. "Uh, I'm sorry, man. I didn't know it was that serious."

"Yeah, well it is that serious." Chen is tremendously agitated. "That shit used to bother me a lot. It's racist and disrespectful, and I don't tolerate that kinda shit anymore. I will not be disrespected."

"Damn, I didn't know you took it that way. I thought it was just a joke?"

"A joke? You think that's a joke? If I called you 'meeda meeda' or 'hey, rice and beans', would you think of that as a joke?"

Cas thinks for a brief second and says, "Actually, I think 'hey rice and beans' is pretty funny. You can call me that if you want; I don't mind."

Chen is about to say something but pauses instead. He stares at Cas for a moment, deadpan. "You think this shit is a game, Cas?" he asks in a matter-of-fact tone. "Get the fuck out of the car. I'm going to show you how much of a game this is!"

Chen gets out of the car, and it's obviously visible that he pretty much lives in the gym. His thick neck expands into wide traps and shoulders. He's barrel chested with a flat stomach, and his huge muscular arms are bulging out of the sleeves of his fitted polo. He dashes to open the back door, where Cas is sitting.

Cas quickly locks it. He watches Chen's Popeye-like forearms flexing as he goes crazy on the handle, channeling all his force into opening the door – the only barrier separating him from Cas.

His eyes widen in rage. "Yo, what are you doing! Open the door, and get the fuck outta my car!" Chen lets go of the handle and takes off his polo – he has a white tank top underneath. He starts flexing his muscles in different body builder poses to show Cas who's the man and who's the 'Chicken Wing'.

59

"I WILL FUCK YOU UP, BRO! THIS IS NOT A GAME!" He does the *Hulk Hogan* pose, with both his arms curled downward, causing his chest and biceps to look massive, thick veins protrude from his muscles everywhere.

Cas's eyes widen in panic – he looks at Jake in the front seat. "Yo, what the fuck is wrong with him! He's fucking psycho!" He looks back out of the car window – Chen has turned around to show off his wide lats and shoulders, his bulging back muscles resembling a mountain terrain.

Jake sighs and gets out of the car to reason with him. "Chen, come on, man, calm down. He didn't know you were sensitive about the name. You guys haven't seen each other for a few years. It's just a misunderstanding. He's sorry."

"Yes, I'm sorry, man!" Cas exclaims. "I promise I will never call you that again. I honestly had no idea you thought it was racist or anything like that."

Chen looks at him with a cocked eyebrow. After staring at him for a few seconds, he shakes his head and exhales. "Fine. I'm gonna let it slide this one time since you didn't know any better."

He grabs his shirt from the top of the car, puts it on, and gets back into the driver's seat. "Alright. Let's go."

They pull off in silence. Chen looks ahead, eyes on the road, focusing on driving.

Cas is in the back seat, speechless, wondering how and why that had escalated so quickly. He almost got his ass kicked by his old high school buddy.

Jake seems oblivious to them both. He's looking down at his phone, scrolling through his social media.

The ride is eerily quiet.

"What's up with the awkward silence?" Chen says lightheartedly, a diametrically opposite of the threatening tone from a couple of minutes earlier. "I hope you guys are not gonna let that little tiff ruin the whole night?"

"Nah, I'm good," Jake answers, nonchalantly. "I can't wait to get there already so we can get some of that Spanish food. I'm *starving*."

"How 'bout you, Nova? You okay?" Chen smiles at him.

"Yeah, uh, I'm good, man. Just happy you didn't kick my ass," he says with a nervous chuckle.

"I guess I did overreact a little bit, sorry about that. No hard feelings?" He reaches out behind him and extends his hand towards Cas in the back seat.

"Of course not, man." He shakes his hand and smiles. "Let's just forget about it."

"Cool, man, cool" Chen says, sounding happy and energetic. "So, what you been up to? Still writing?"

Cas is still quite tense after what has just happened but tries to play it off as if everything is fine. "Oh yeah, I still…"

The car suddenly jerks to the left – Chen pulls up in front of a store. "Hold that thought, I need to get something to drink," he says as he gets out the car. "You ladies want anything?"

"Nah, I'm good" Cas replies, still smiling.

Jake just shakes his head 'no'.

"Alright, be right back." He walks towards the store.

As soon as he is out of earshot, Cas's smile quickly drops from his face as he turns to Jake.

"What the fuck! This mother fucker is crazy! What the hell is his problem!"

Jake laughs. "I told you not to call him Chicken Wing. I specifically said, 'He'll fuck you up.'"

"Yeah, but I didn't know you meant that literally. How the hell did he get so big? He's fucking huge, man."

Jake takes off his sunglasses, breathes on the lenses, and starts rubbing them clean on his undershirt. "Think he's on gear."

"Steroids? Are you serious? He's a juicer? Why didn't you tell me that before?"

"Why would I just decide to give you info like that for no reason?"

"Oh, there was a very good reason – the reason is he's a fucking maniac, and I need to know that he goes through severe bouts of 'roid rage. Had you told me that, I would've definitely not said anything about his nickname."

"Well, now you know. Dry your panties and chill out."

Cas laughs sarcastically. "I knew I shouldn't have come out tonight. I knew it…"

Jake cuts him off, "Aw, man. Don't start with that shit again. It's going to be a good night – just relax. You almost got fucked up, but everything is cool now. You saw how calm and happy he was when he got out of the car?"

"That don't matter, he can snap any minute. What's he on, anyway? HGH? The guy is fucking huge."

"I'm not exactly sure what he's on, maybe Test and HG. Nothing too crazy."

"You say that like it's no big deal."

"Dude, I work in a gym. I know a lot of people who take steroids. Whatever he's on is not a big deal."

"It should be."

"Why? Because it's a *drug*?" he says, using his fingers for air quotes. "Last time I checked, marijuana is a drug too. That don't stop you from smoking plenty of the stuff, homeboy."

"That's different."

"It *is* different. Your drug makes you lazy and hungry. His drug makes him bigger, stronger, and more energetic."

"Yeah, but I don't smoke out and then have mood swings and try to kill my friends." Cas shakes his head with concern. Looking out of the window, he sees Chen returning to the car with a black plastic bag.

"I come bearing gifts," he says as he reaches into the bag. He gives both of them a bottled water, then reaches back into the bag and takes out a pack of cigarettes and extends them to Cas. "You still smoke?"

"Not really, but I'll take one. Thanks, man." Cas has been trying to quit for years. He's cut back drastically, down to just a few cigarettes here and there a week. Under normal circumstances, he would have turned them down, but tonight feels different. In one quick motion, he removes the plastic shrink wrap, opens the box, and takes out a cigarette. He holds it tight between his lips and begins patting his pockets for a light.

"Hey, uh, Chen, do you have a light?"

"A light? Who the fuck said you can smoke in my car?" Chen responds, sounding angry again.

Cas is dumbfounded, "Uh... err... I thought since you gave them to me, it would be okay if I..."

Chen bursts into laughter. "I'm just fucking with you. You can smoke in here – just try not to get ashes all over the place."

Cas lets out a nervous laugh. "Yeah, definitely, I'll be careful."

Chen fishes out a lighter from his glove box and hands it to Cas.

"Thanks," he says as he lights the stogie and draws in a deep drag.

"Hey, man. Roll down your window. Nobody wants to breathe that crap," Jake complains.

"Gotcha," Cas says, slightly apologetic.

He takes a couple more drags and gets disgusted by it. *Why do I even smoke this shit?*

Taking one more deep drag, he tosses the cigarette, still burning, out of the window. The car is moving fast, and as soon as he flicks it out of the window, the force of the wind blowing in causes the lit cigarette to shoot back into the car and hit him in the face before falling between his legs.

He immediately jumps out of the seat and starts whacking at his crotch to douse the cigarette. *Oh shit! Oh shit! Oh shit!* He instinctively knocks it to the car floor in blind panic and dashes towards it with urgent swiftness to pick it up. He finally grabs it and carefully tosses it out of the window.

"You okay back there?" Chen looks at the rear-view mirror. "You're not burning my shit, right?"

Cas glances down at the floor – he doesn't see any burn marks. "Yeah, right," he says with a forced chuckle, "Everything is good."

Chen nods and looks up at the road.

Jake glances back at his best friend. He can see that Cas is distraught. "Everything good, man?"

"Yeah, everything is great." Just as he says that, he sees a thin, faint cloud of smoke coming up from his crotch. Suddenly, he feels an intense pang of heat around his balls. Cas jumps up quickly and sees a small piece of cigarette ember, still glowing red, stuck in his pants.

"Oh shit!" He slaps away at the space between his legs and tries to smother the tiny fire.

Jake's eyes widen for a moment as he sees Cas burning the backseat. He quickly calms down as to not alert Chen and starts coughing to distract him from the commotion in the back.

Chen looks over at Jake. "You alright, man? Drink some water."

"Yeah, water is a good idea," Jake says, glancing back at Cas.

Water! Cas quickly unfastens the cap and pours some of the bottled water between his legs – the seat is leather; the water beads settle on top and stream down the side. He briefly shivers from the cold water seeping into his jeans. He extinguishes the small ember but is now left with water all over his crotch and pant legs.

His frantic movements draw the attention of Chen sitting in the front. "What the hell is going on back there?"

"Ah, my bad, man. I spilled some water." Cas tries hard to sound calm.

Chen shrugs it off and passes him some napkins. "It's only water, it'll dry."

65

Jake cuts in to change the subject, "I don't know why you took the local streets. We would've been there already if you'd taken the West Side."

"Where is this place, anyway?" Cas asks as he uses the napkins to dry himself off.

"Up in the Heights. 181st street and Audubon. It's a little lounge, a real low-key spot. We've been there once or twice," Jake answers.

"Oh really? I didn't know it was there." Cas smiles. "I love the Heights; all the hottest Dominican girls go up there. I remember when we used to cut class and go there to cop haze."

"Hell yeah." Chen smiles at the memory. "I would get my mom's car, and we would ride around, smoking out, blasting music. We thought we were the shit. Nobody had a whip but me." He starts to laugh. "Yo, we used to get twisted. Remember that time we were drinking E&J in Riverside Park? I got mad drunk and passed out on the train. I straight up fainted on the train, man."

They all burst out in laughter.

"Ah, man. I'll never forget that," Jake replies. "You were leaning on the door, sweating bullets, looking all pale and shit. You looked at me and you were like, 'I need air. I'm losing altitude.'"

Cas cuts in between laughs, "'I'm losing altitude,' oh, I remember that. One moment you were standing there, and then *WHAM*! you just dropped to the floor. Passed out cold."

"Hey, that was the best sleep I ever had."

"Was Manolo there?"

"Yup, he was there," Chen answers, "And those freshman chicks that used to follow us."

"Yes!" Jake says, clapping his hands as the memory comes back to him, "The freshmen crew. We were all freaking out. I thought you OD'ed or something. I really thought it was over for you."

Cas starts laughing even harder. "You remember the old lady who came to Chen's rescue?"

Jake puts on an old frail voice, "'Young man, are you okay! Someone call an ambulance! He needs CPR!' Oh man, that shit was so crazy."

"It definitely was," Chen says, still chuckling. "I didn't know what the fuck had happened. One second, I was talking to you guys, the next second, I'm waking up on the floor, looking up at an old lady about to give me mouth-to-mouth."

Jake laughs. "Yup, she wanted to tongue you down, man. But she did help us, though. She helped get you up and got you a seat. And for some reason, I don't know why, but you were just sitting there, with this stupid-ass grin on your face."

"That's because that girl, Melanie, was all over me, asking if I was okay. I was thinking like, *Wow, this girl really seems concerned for me. Maybe I can make this work to my advantage and finally get laid.* Shit, I was still a virgin at that time."

"Melanie with the huge tits? Can't forget her, she was the only chick in school with double D's."

"I know, she let me rest my head on her chest – they were like big, soft pillows. It was great," Chen smiles as he allows himself some fond flashbacks. He turns his head to Jake and points at him. "Wait! You totally blew up my spot that day."

"Oh yeah," Jake smiles broadly, "I was like, 'Look at him smiling – he faked the whole thing.'. But then you started laughing, that's where you fucked up. No one told you to start laughing. You made it seem like it was a joke."

"I couldn't help it, man – I was high and drunk. I just fainted on the train, and now I'm sitting there, laying my head on Melanie's big-ass titties. Why'd you have to hate on me like that? I probably had a concussion."

Cas chimes in, "That old lady was so pissed when you started laughing."

"I know, it was so wack. I got no love after that. Melanie got up and moved to another seat. She could have been my first."

"Jake, didn't you end up fucking Melanie?" Cas asks, already knowing the answer, just to raise the topic for fun.

"Yes, I did. And her rack was legendary," he answers with a big grin. "Those were some good times, man, good times."

Chen scoffs, "Good times for you, you cock-blocking bitch."

"Not me. I don't block anybody," Jake brushes off the comment. "It'd be cool if some of those girls are there tonight. Veronica was friends with some of them – I'm not sure if she still is, though."

"I'm telling you right now – if Melanie is there, you guys better fall back. That's all me," Chen says, sounding sure of himself.

"Hey, you don't have to worry about me. That's CB King over there," Cas says, motioning towards Jake.

"Cock Block King," Chen nods in agreement, "So true."

Jake shrugs and looks back down at his phone. "They hate me cause they ain't me."

Cas feels his stomach growl and changes the subject. "I'm officially hungry. Do you think it's bad form to go in and head straight for the food?"

"That's exactly what I'm going to do. Especially considering how nice a gift we got her. Oh yeah, that reminds me. Cas, you owe me 70 bucks."

"What? Why?" he asks angrily.

"When I got to *Baby's R Us*, I checked the registry from inside the store, and someone had already bought the Diaper Genie. The only thing left was the stroller-car seat combo. I got it on sale though, 260."

"Damn, man. What if I don't got that kind of dough?"

"Man, please. You got money. Cut it out, cheap-ass."

"And who's the asshole who bought the Diaper Genie?"

"Thirty-nine, ninety-nine," Chen says proudly. "Got it on sale."

"It was you?" Cas looks at him for a moment. "You cheap bastard."

Chen laughs aloud. "Why I gotta be all that?"

"You're an Engineer for the fucking MTA. You make more money than the both of us combined."

"No, I don't. I'm a *Junior* Engineer," Chen tries to defend himself. "I don't make the big bucks yet."

Jake isn't buying any of it. "Man, an Engineer is an *Engineer*. I don't care if it's Junior, Senior, Sophomore, whatever. If you got *Engineer* in your title, you're doing alright."

"You guys are just salty because I got the Diaper Genie before you. You slow, you blow," Chen boasts and goes on, "And both of you fuckers make money too. Don't cry broke."

69

"Hey, I'm not a personal trainer for the money," Jake says, sounding serious. "I do it for the satisfaction of transforming people's bodies and lives." He pauses for moment, "That, and the pussy."

They all break up in laughter.

"Exactly. Look at that – you get paid and laid. That's a job with benefits. And I been to some of your events, they've been pretty packed, man. So, I know you're making good money there too."

"I'm not complaining, man. It's this guy." Jake points at Cas.

"Hey, I freelance – so there's times when I have no clue when or from where my next check is coming. And sometimes, things are just slow, and I really have to be frugal."

"Cas, I know you – you're just cheap."

Chen looks over at Jake and nods in agreement, "I think you're right. He's just cheap."

Cas is offended. "Well, you know what? Fuck you guys. I'm not cheap. I'm frugal."

"Sure, that's what all cheap people say," Jake smiles and nods. "Look at the bright side, though – we're definitely going to stand out because we have the best gift."

Cas sucks his teeth. "Doubt it. Nobody is even going to notice. Just watch."

Jake looks back at him, his eyes squinted in annoyance. "Why are you so fucking negative? Damn." He faces forward and sighs, "Be a Debbie Downer if you want. All I know is you owe me 70 dollars."

"Can I see the receipt?"

"Receipt?" Jake sounds offended. "What, now you don't trust me?"

"Why can't I see the receipt?" Cas replies quickly.

"Wow. You're on a roll today, brother." Jake reaches for his wallet, takes out the receipt, crumples it into a paper ball, and tosses it at Cas's face. "There goes your receipt."

The paper bounces harmlessly off Cas's face and falls to his side.

"Not cool," he says as picks up the small piece of paper and unfolds it.

"I actually paid 264, but I was being nice and rounding it down to 260."

The receipt shows the $264.59 was paid via debit card. Cas jokingly holds it up to the light in the car.

"Looks fake."

"Good," Jake answers back. "Now, give me my 72.29 dollars. I want the exact amount."

"You're right," Cas concedes. He reaches for his wallet in his back pocket and takes out four $20 bills. He passes the money to Jake.

"I don't have any change," Jake replies as he takes the bills.

"Don't worry about it. Pay me back later." Cas pats him on the shoulder. "I know you're good for it, *papa*."

"You're stupid." Jake chuckles. "I'll pay you back later when…"

'Whap!' The paper ball receipt hits him on his ear.

Cas has a wide grin on his face. "Hey, truce. Truce! You started it, I finished it. Truce."

Jake looks at him impatiently. "You done?"

"As long as you are."

71

Chen cuts in, "All this money you guys throwing around, how much you got on my tank?"

"Yeah, Nova," Jake answers. "All this money you're throwing around, how much you got on gas?"

"What about you?" Cas asks defensively.

Jake looks at Chen. "See how cheap he is?"

Chen agrees, "Yes he is. But I'm talking to you too. Both of you."

Jake shrugs. "I don't know, man, but I think the fact that you only had to spend 40 dollars on the Diaper Genie, and we spent 265 on our gift, I think that should even out the gas money."

"What?" Chen looks over at Jake, confused. "What kind of dumb-ass logic is that?"

"That's good, sound logic to me," Cas pipes in. "It's like the law of averages. You saved earlier; so, now you gotta spend."

"Really?" Chen asks. "How you guys getting home?"

The car falls silent.

Cas digs back into his wallet. "I got 10 bucks on gas."

Jake reaches for his own wallet. "Give me that 10, I'll give Chen a 20."

He passes the $20 bill to Chen and takes $10 from Cas.

"Lit," Chen slips the bill into his pocket and adds, "You know what? You guys are alright in my book, man. Alright, indeed."

Cas smiles as he leans back in his seat and looks out the window, watching the blur of people and tall buildings go by.

***

Chen pulls up in front of a nice-looking building. The ground floor is an upscale steakhouse called *Bistec*. Over the big 2nd floor window is a black and purple sign that reads *Milky Lounge*; that's where they're headed.

They are lucky enough to find parking space right down the block from the entrance. Parking this good is a rarity in New York City.

"Great spot," Cas says to Chen as he backs into the space.

"Couldn't ask for anything better," he agrees.

The atmosphere has relaxed since Chen's earlier bout of 'roid rage. There's the sense of security one feels when hanging out with old friends. Everyone is comfortable.

Jake hops out of the car, puts his shades back on, and starts walking towards the Bachata music blaring from up the block. After a few steps, he turns around and yells to Cas who is still getting out of the car, "Yo, grab the gift, man. It's in the trunk."

"Cool," he replies and motions to Chen, "Can you pop the trunk, bro?"

"Got you." Chen presses a button and the trunk of the SUV begins to rise slowly. "I gotta grab my gift too. The good ol' Diaper Genie."

Cas chuckles. "Lucky guy."

"Thanks," Chen smiles gleefully. He grabs the Diaper Genie and lifts it out the trunk with very little effort. The box isn't too big, and it doesn't weigh much, no challenge for his bulging biceps.

The box with the stroller, on the other hand, is big and bulky, with twine tied around it and a little plastic handle. Cas reaches into the trunk, grabs the handle, and is surprised at how heavy it is. He tries to lift it with one hand, and it barely moves.

"Damn, this shit is heavy." He tries bending at the knees and wrapping his arm around the side of the box, trying to lift it up with proper form. He can't seem to wrap his arms around it far enough to get a good grip. It's cumbersome and uncomfortable, and he immediately starts to sweat.

Noticing that Cas is visibly straining, Chen decides to help him out. "Here, dude – hold my gift, and I'll grab that for you."

Cas's pride won't let him accept Chen's help. "Nah, man, I got it. It's just an awkward grab." He braces himself to make another attempt.

"Why don't you just grab it by the handle?" Chen says, wondering why is he bear-hugging the box.

"You can't grab it by handle – this thing is *way* too heavy," Cas answers, again trying to contain the box within his arms. He's just about to make his third attempt to lift it when Chen stops him.

"Wait, lemme check something."

Cas let's go of it and backs up. "What's up, man?"

Chen looks at the box for a moment, as if sizing it up.

"Hmmm…" He uses one hand to grab the handle and easily lifts the box out of the trunk.

"Yeah, it's definitely a little heavy." Chen raises his eyebrows sarcastically. "But, you need to start hitting the gym, bro."

And you need to stop hitting all those steroids, you muscle-head freak, Cas thinks, but only replies, "Thanks, tough guy."

They both turn their heads towards Jake who's yelling something out to them.

"What the hell are you guys doing over there? Grab the gifts, and let's go already."

74

"Yeah, you lazy bastard. Why don't you come help?" Cas is slightly annoyed with the both of them. He reaches for the handle to take the box from Chen's hand.

"You sure you got it, man?" Chen asks before letting it go. "I can hold it – it's not that big a deal. Just grab my gift."

"Dude, I'm not weak…"

"Yes, you are," Jake taunts him from up the block.

Cas doesn't find it funny. "Whatever, man. I don't see you volunteering to help."

"What! Help!" Jake answers, shocked. "Bro, I went to the store, bought the gift, carried it on the train. Took it all the way up to Chen's apartment, then I had to carry it back down and load it into the trunk when we were leaving to get you. And I did all that all by myself. What have you done?"

Cas can't think of a good comeback. "Well, whoop-dee-freakin' do." He grabs the box and begins walking towards the entrance of the lounge.

Jake is standing there with dark shades on.

"You look mad stupid wearing your sunglasses at night. It's fuckin' dumb."

"Why you mad, Cas?" Jake asks mockingly. "Because I look cool and you forgot your shades?"

He is secretly mad he didn't bring his own shades, but he's much more annoyed with the heavy box he's tugging along. He's trying to make it look like he's not struggling, but the weight is causing him to walk unevenly, wobbling as he goes up the block.

Chen and Jake wait for him in front of the entrance. Cas finally reaches there.

"You OK, Hercules?" Jake teases.

"Shut up." Cas gives him an annoyed glare.

Chen shakes his head. "You guys are like an old married couple."

"Yeah?" Jake grabs the door and holds it open to let them in first. "Guess who's the nagging wife?"

"You," Cas replies quickly.

They get through the door, and there is a long, narrow staircase that goes up to the entrance of the hall. Cas drops the box.

"Oh, hell no," he says out loud.

"What? The stairs?"

"Yeah, man, the stairs."

Jake sighs. "You want me to carry it?"

"Be my guest!"

"Are you serious?"

"Yeah, dude. I'm already starting to sweat," Cas answers defiantly. "If I carry it up the stairs, I'll be sweating balls by the time we go in there."

Jake shakes his head; "Wow, what a punk. Gimme the damn box."

He grabs the handle, gives Cas a disgusted look, and starts heading up the stairs with the big package.

Chen has already walked up and is impatiently waiting at the top of the landing. "You guys done acting like little pussies?"

"That's Nova whining, not me."

"It's both of you guys. You act like the shit weighs 300 pounds. Let's just go in already."

The heavy and cumbersome box makes Jake walk sideways up the narrow staircase. While he struggles with it, Cas takes the sunglasses off of his face.

"I'll take those." He grins and carefully places it over his own eyes. "Ah, these are sweet."

Jake is not amused. "Dude, give me back my shades. You're not worthy to rock them."

"Are you kidding me? They look better on me than you," Cas replies.

"I'm not kidding, man – give me back my shades."

He tries to reason with Jake, "Let me rock them for a little while – just a little while – then you can have them back."

Jake reaches the top step and places the box down. They're standing in front of the entrance to the lounge, loud music and laughter spilling from inside.

"Listen, man," Jake begins. "There are two types of people in this world, OK? There are the people who *think* they're cool, like you. People who might wear shades at night because they *think* it's cool. Then, there are those types of people who actually *are* that cool. Like me. Shades don't make me cool, I make the shades cool. You feel where I'm coming from?"

"Not really," Cas answers, unimpressed. "All I'm asking for is to wear your shades for a little while – I'm not asking for your philosophy on mankind."

Chen chirps in, "And all I'm asking is, can we go in now? I'm fucking hungry."

"Alright," Jake gives in. "You can rock them for a little bit. You need all the help you can get, anyway."

"Thanks, homie," Cas replies as he carefully places the shades on his face and pushes them against his eyes. He uses the tips of his index fingers to smooth out his eye brows.

"Feeling good?" Jake asks with a smile.

Cas shrugs his shoulders. "Feeling damn good."

"Let's do it." Chen opens the door to step into the loud Spanish music.

CHAPTER 4

The Baby Shower

Inside, there's pink, white, and blue streamers hanging from the ceiling, and balloons everywhere. Several large round tables, each adorned with a bright white table cloth and a colorful floral centerpiece, are lined up by the wall. There's plenty of space in the middle of the room for people to mingle and dance.

Cas scans the room to check out the crowd. The first couple of tables are all older people – grandparents and the elderly looking.

Oh great. It looks like a damn retirement home in here.

He continues scanning the room from under his confidence-boosting dark sunglasses. He looks at a few more tables – everyone he can set eyes on are mainly middle aged, all uncle and aunts with some older kids and teenagers loitering about the table, probably Veronica's cousins.

So far, no good.

But as he looks further, Cas's mood changes for the better. He notices there are a bevy of beauties scattered about a few tables in the back. Some are dancing, others sitting and chatting among themselves, everyone seems to be having a good time.

He sees his friend Manolo, dancing in the middle of a group of four or five beautiful women.

Chen nudges Jake. "Yo, there's Manny," he says, motioning towards the back.

As the three men enter, everyone looks up at them, except Manolo – he's too busy dancing. They begin walking towards the back to meet him.

Before they can take a few steps, a short and plump, middle-aged, auburn-haired, Dominican lady approaches Jake and talks to him in Spanish.

"*Oy, mi Negro, Yake! Como estas cariño?*"

A huge smile sweeps across his face – he leans over to give the woman a kiss on the cheek.

"Hi, mami. I'm good. *Todo bien, todo bien,*" he answers in the broken Spanish he's learned over the years.

The little lady smiles. "Good, I'm happy for you."

"Thank you, mama. You remember Juan and Chen?"

She looks at them for a moment. "*Oh si, Juan y el Chino.* Wow, long time no see you guys. How you all been?"

"I've been good, Mrs. Torres. Can't complain," answers Chen with a smile. "*Todo es mucho bueno.*"

"Good. *Gracia a Dios,*" she says, smiling brightly. "*Y tu, Juan Carlos?*"

"*Ayi ayi, más o menos.*" Cas can barely speak Spanish but the little he knows sounds legit because he can say it with an authentic Spanish accent.

"Well, *tú te ves bien,* you look good. Both of you," she replies. Her English is heavy with a thick accent. "Especially you, Chino. Wow, you berry berry big muscles. *Tú trabaja* in the gym *con Yake?*"

Chen likes the compliment and briefly flexes his chest muscles, causing the buttons on his shirt to pop.

80

"Thank you. I go to the gym a lot but I don't work there. I work for the MTA – I'm an Engineer."

"Oh, how nice! Good for you. *Eso un trarbajo muy bueno. Y tú Juan, que tu hace?*"

"*Yo escribo*," Cas says, feeling good about himself, "I write articles for different magazines and websites."

"OK, *eso es bueno*," Mrs. Torres responds, sounding impressed.

Cas smiles widely, his ego is quickly boosted. "*Gracias.*"

"Good, *de nada*," she replies smiling back at him, "*Pero*, where's the sun?"

"Huh?" he answers.

"*Por que tú ta* wearing sunglasses inside? What you think? *Eres un* big shot celebrity writer?" she says giving him a crooked look, "Or are you hiding your eyes because you're still crying over that bitch?"

Just as quickly as it had come, Cas's smile drops; his ego deflates.

How the fuck does she know? he thinks and quickly shoots Jake a skeptical look. Cas looks back at Mrs. Torres and smiles, "Uh, no, I don't know about any bitch. I just like the glasses, and, um, they're actually not even mine. They belong to..."

Jake cuts him off, "I told him, mama, not to wear the glasses inside. But he thinks he's cool like that," he says, looking at her and shaking his head. "He is *el stupido*."

Mrs. Torres frowns as she looks at Cas, thoroughly disappointed. "*No es* cool. That is stupid. *Por favor*, take off those glasses. It makes you look up to no good. OK, big shot?"

Cas quickly removes the shades. "Yes, of course."

Mrs. Torres reaches out and gently grabs him by the cheek. "There you go, very handsome eyes. And don't worry about that *prostituta*. You're a good guy, and you will find a very good woman. Maybe even here tonight, eh?"

Cas feels the old sense of queasiness return. He can barely speak, but he tries to shake the feeling and says, "OK, then. Well, uh, I'm going to say hi to Veronica and Manny." He smiles timidly.

"We'll come with you, Mr. Big Shot," Jake taunts. "Hey, you said you only wanted to wear the shades for a little while anyway, right?"

Cas eyes dart towards Jake. He moves closer to him, hands him his sunglasses, and mutters a cold, "Fuck you."

Jake is surprised by his tone. "Damn, what's all that for?"

"You know what that's for," Cas says, trying to contain his anger in public. "How the fuck does she know about Tiffany?"

"What are you talking about? She doesn't know about Tiffany. She doesn't even know Tiffany."

"She just mentioned something about a *prostituta*," Cas speaks louder then he intends to. He realizes people might overhear and lowers his voice and whispers to Jake, "She just said 'prostitute'. Why the fuck would she even mention that to me if she didn't know anything about Tiffany?"

"Nova," Jake begins, "People talk about prostitutes all the time. We're all adults here. She was just having an adult conversation."

"What!" Cas is pissed off. "What the fuck are you talking about?"

"Whoa. Chill out, man. It's cool. Let's talk later."

Cas looks around, some people have started noticing them. He tries to calm himself down – he closes his eyes and exhales deeply.

"Yeah. You're right. We'll talk later."

Chen interrupts, "I don't know what you guys are talking about, but where the hell is Manolo?"

They look up – Manny is no longer there.

"Where'd he go?"

Before anyone can respond, someone yells out from behind them, "Hey, who the hell let you low lives in, eh!"

The three of them turn around and see Manolo standing there with a wide smile on his face. The giddiness in his voice is a clear indication that he's been drinking. He reaches out to give a fist-bump to Jake. "What up, man? What the hell took you guys so long?"

Jake is about to answer, but Manolo cuts him off.

"Yoooooo! Juan Carlos, what up, bruh? I thought for sure you weren't going to come."

Cas smiles and answers back, "Nah, man. I had to come. Wish Veronica well and all that. What's going on with you, though?"

"I'm good, man. Work's going good, fam's good, I'm blessed. I'm glad you came, Cas."

"Thanks, man. Me too. I'm glad I came out. How's your son?"

"Manolito? He's bad as ever. He's in the kids' party, probably chasing around the little girls," Manolo answers, briefly looking around to see if his son is close by.

"Like father, like son," Cas says jokingly.

"Oh, hell yeah – he's a little player. He's only six, and he already knows he likes women. So, imagine when he gets older – I'm going to have to pack condoms in his lunch box," says Manolo, glowing in drunken pride.

"You're crazy, man. But, ah, what you mean kids' party? There's a separate party for the kids?"

"Yeah, we set up a separate room for the kids so they can wild out in there and we can party in here. Plus, you know, people are drinking and shit – we try not to have the kids sneaking away with beers, you know? Like the kind of shit we used to do."

"Hell yeah." They all laugh.

"So, we set up their own little area. They have their own party over there. A couple of my *tias* are in there, watching them."

Cas nods. "That's a good idea."

"Yeah, man. That was my idea. Hard to chill if you got rugrats running around, you know?"

Chen cuts in to greet Manolo, "What's up, biatch?"

Manny looks at him. "Oh, they let you outta the gym? Taking a break from the cardio?"

Chen leans in and lowers his voice, "Sheesh, I'm hoping to get some cardio tonight, you know what I'm talking about?"

"Oh, I hear you, brother!" Manolo smiles as he puts out his hand for a fist-bump and a hug. He lowers his voice as well. "Shit, I didn't even know my sister had so many hot friends. She's been hiding them from me. She knows – if I meet them, it's over."

"Get your son!" Their conversation is interrupted by an older Hispanic woman. "Get him right now!" she says to Manolo.

"Hey, Tia, what happen?" he replies.

"He won't leave the girls alone. He keeps on, Manny. It's not right."

"Where is he?" Manolo sighs.

Cas whispers to Jake, "His son is pretty aggressive, huh?"

Jake gives a half shrug and whispers back, "Eh. I guess you can say that."

Before Cas can reply, he's interrupted by Manolo's son, Manolito, approaching his father.

He looks about five years old.

"Daddy, they're bothering me. I want to wear the tiara," he says, holding a cheap pink plastic tiara in his little hand – the type that you can buy at a dollar store. He tries to put it on his head, but it falls. He quickly picks it up and stares at it fondly.

Manny shakes his head. "Son, you can't wear the tiara. Boys don't wear tiaras, boys wear crowns. Take off the damn tiara, Manolito."

The boy looks at him, confused and defiant. "No, daddy. Why can't I wear the tiara? Everybody is different."

"Why the hell you want to wear the tiara for?"

The boy smiles and puts the tiara back on his head. Using both his hands to hold it straight, he beings to sing a melody from the old musical, *West Side Story*.

"*I feel pretty,*

Oh so pretty.

I feel pretty and witty

and gaayyyyy!"

Manolo sighs and looks up at his group of friends. "I'll be back."

He gently picks up his son and starts walking back toward the kids' party. "You have to share, Manolito. You been wearing it awhile, and it's time to let the girls wear it now. OK, papa? You have to share."

"OK, daddy. I'll share."

85

The tia stops Manny. "Give him to me – I'll take him over there. As longs as he shares and doesn't be a brat, I can handle him."

The little boy cracks up. "Hey! I'm not a brat!"

She takes him from Manolo and puts him on the floor.

"When he's with me, he walks. I'm far too old for all that carrying shit." She looks at Manolito. "Right, *mijo*? When you with *titi*, you walk?"

"You know that's right, honey child." Manolito snaps his fingers.

The aunt laughs and looks at Manny, "Your son is something else, boy. Lord help you with this one."

"Hey, daddy", the little boy calls out to his father.

"What's up, son?"

"Cookie don't take no shit."

"Hey!" the aunt yanks his arm toward her – she speaks sternly with a finger pointing at his face, "Who you think you are, talking to your father like that? *Tú ta loco, chico?* Apologize to your father right now."

The little boy is frightened. "Sorry, daddy!" he says, holding back the tears welling in his little eyes.

The aunt immediately calms down.

"You have to show respect to older people. And you always have to respect you mother and father. You understand?"

Manolito nods in agreement. "Yes."

"Good," she looks up at Manolo. "He's been watching *Empire* with me. Anyway, get back to your friends."

Manolo nods. "Thanks, tia. You're the best," he says sincerely.

She nods back and walks with little Manny towards the kids' room.

As big Manny walks over to his friends, everybody has their phone out and pretends to be preoccupied – no one is making eye contact. After a minute or so, Cas puts away his phone and breaks the silence.

"Little Manny looks just like you, man – it's crazy."

"Yeah, that's my little guy, man," Manolo answers. He looks at Chen to change the subject, "But, hey, did you call that girl yet?"

"Who? The drunken Rebekah?" Chen replies casually, "I forgot her name, but nah, I haven't called yet. I'm not stressing it."

Jake butts in, "Who are you talking about?"

"We went out Friday night to that spot, *Velour*. Mad females everywhere. I mean like four to one ratio. There was this one group of girls celebrating a birthday, and they were wilding the fuck out, son. I mean WILDIN'! You guys definitely missed it," he says to Jake and Cas.

Jake looks offended. "Where the hell was I? Why didn't you fuckers call me?"

"I did call you – you were out with a girl," says Chen.

"Yeah, but you could've texted me and told me that shit was live," Jake complains, sounding totally disappointed. "Shit, if I was there, we would all have gotten laid. You know how I do it, baby."

"What difference does it make? You got some from your date anyway."

"That is true," Jake says in a matter-of-fact tone.

"Oh, so you've smashed that new chick already?" Chen asks.

Jake smiles at the thought of the recent encounter. "Yes, sir. I'll tell you about it later – it was amazing."

Chen asks Manolo, "Where's the mother-to-be?"

The smile on Manny's face quickly disappears. "She was on the phone with the baby's father. I don't like the guy for shit. In all honesty, if it wasn't that he's the father of the kid, I'd beat the shit out of him."

"Damn, it's like that?" Cas asks, surprised by the quick change in his friend's demeanor. "Who is he? Is he here?"

"Nah, he's not here. He was supposed to be, but he's not. He's some fake-ass hustler from the Bronx. A real thug, ghetto, mother fucker."

"Wow, I didn't think Veronica would be with that type of guy."

"That's because she's fucking stupid. The first time I met the guy, I knew he was full of shit. He had that look in his face – I could tell from day one he's no good. But you know how that goes, the worst person for you is the one you fall for."

"Yeah, I know how that goes." Cas feels sorry for Veronica. "Are they planning to get married?"

"Hell no! I would kill myself if she married that asshole. They're not even together anymore. He tried to play her when she first told him she was pregnant – he acted like it wasn't his."

"Damn, that's fucked up."

"I'm happy he did that because that's when everything people had been saying about the guy, that he's a loser and an asshole, really hit her. That's when she realized he's a horrible fucking person, and she dumped him. But you know, she's trying to do the right thing and allow him to be a part of the kid's life – so, she invited him to come today. When I overheard her speaking to him on the phone, it seemed like he's not coming. I'm not surprised." Manolo shakes his head. "But enough talking about that loser, fuck him. We're here to celebrate my sis and her first kid."

"I'll drink to that."

Manolo laughs. "Then, let's fucking drink. I know I need one. What you guys want?"

"I don't know. What you got?" Chen asks.

"We got everything, it's an open bar. You name it, we got it."

Jake thinks for a brief moment. "Alright, let me get..."

Manolo quickly cuts him off, "Hold up, I ain't taking orders. So, all tree of ya can get your punk asses to the bar and order your own drinks."

"All tree?"

"That's right," Manolo says, pointing at them, "One, two, tree. Let's go."

Cas smirk at the obvious mispronunciation. "No doubt. Lead the way."

They make their way to the bar. Manolo orders first.

"Hey, bartender. Bar-TEN-der! Let me get four shots of Hennessy."

"You got it," the bartender responds as he turns his back to reach for the bottle and four shot glasses. He places the glasses in a row, side-by-side, and pours the brown liquor right till the top of each shot glass. "Here ya go."

"Thanks!" Manolo slams his hand on the counter of the bar. "Let's toast to the old times."

They each grab a shot from the bar top.

"This is to old times," Cas says as he lifts his drink.

Jake, Chen, and Manolo all lift their glasses.

"To old times," they say in unison. All four quickly drink the shot and slam their glasses down on the counter top.

"Ugh," Cas grimaces, the taste of the strong liquor contorting his face. His chest burns as he feels the heat of the drink making its way down to his stomach.

"Bartender, another round, my man," Jake says, still wincing from the first shot. "Come on guys, another one."

Chen is amped up. "Let's do it!"

The bartender lines up the glasses again and pours another round of shots. The guys each grab one.

"This one's to new times," Jake says, lifting the glass. "Cheers."

"Cheers," Chen replies.

"Salud," Manolo and Cas slur in.

They throw back the second shot; the strong taste causes all of them to grimace even more than the first time around.

"Alright, I'm good with the shots for now," says Cas as the heat of the liquor settles in.

"Nah, one more, one more!" Manolo says, growing increasingly animated as the alcohol takes effect.

"What you mean, dude? You were drinking before we even got here. You're going to get wrecked," Chen says, laughing for no reason.

"No, I'm not. I was drinking champagne. That shit is light," he says, before adding, "And even if I do get fucked up, so what? I'm with my family and my people. If ever there is a good time to get twisted, that would be now, bro. My baby sister is about to have a baby! I'm about to be a *tio* for the first time."

Jake is smiling. "I'll drink to that."

"My man," says Manolo. "*Y tú Cas?* You up for another one?"

Cas knows that three back-to-back shots of Henny means it's going to be a really good night or a really bad one. Either way, there's no turning back after that next shot.

"Not really. But fuck it. Let's do it."

The bartender hadn't gone far, and he begins pouring out the next round.

Manolo lifts his glass. "To my sister, to a great night, and to me becoming a tio for the first time. I'm happy you guys came, man – it means a lot to me."

"Salud," they all say at the same time and down the shot. This time, they barely grimace.

"Wooooo!" Chen yells out, slamming his glass on the table.

The bartender walks over to them with a friendly smile. "You guys good?"

"Not yet." Manny looks over at Chen, "Red bull and vodka?"

Chen nods. He looks towards Cas.

"Red Bull and vodka?"

"Nope," Cas responds, "Long Island Iced Tea."

"Gangster," Manny nods, impressed.

"I'll take a Henny and cranberry," Jake answers.

Manolo looks over at the waiter. "Can I get two Red Bulls and vodka, a Long Island, and a Henny and cranberry?"

"You got it." The barkeep gets to work.

"Damn, dude – more Hennessy?" Cas asks Jake after he orders his drink, "Didn't you have enough of those shots?"

"It's better than mixing. You guys drinking all that rum and vodka after three shots of Cognac? No good, man."

"Tree shots," Cas says.

Jake chuckles, "Yeah, that's right, tree shots. But not for nothing," he leans in to whisper to Cas, "There's some bad bitches in here tonight. Play it cool – you'll probably get a few numbers."

"Eh, we'll see." Cas sounds unsure of himself.

"Nah, don't give me that. You better get at least one number, Nova. No excuses."

"Do emails count?" he asks.

Jake smiles. "Emails count, baby. Emails always count."

Chen cuts in, "Do emails count? You sound like a rookie out here. Of course, they count."

"What about Twitter handles?" Cas asks jokingly, "Do they count?"

"Hell no!" Jake and Chen say at the same time.

"Ah, no doubt. So, you guys are some playboys out here, huh?" Cas grins widely. "That's funny because back when I used to hang heavy, I don't remember you guys getting any action at all."

Jake gives a concerned smile. He leans in to talk to Cas.

"Could you say that any louder?"

"What?" Cas takes a big gulp of his Long Island Iced Tea. "Damn! This shit is strong." He looks at Jake, "Am I talking too loud?"

"Yes." Jake looks at him seriously. "Mad loud."

He's embarrassed and immediately lowers his voice.

"Ah damn, sorry, man. I'm kind of buzzing a lil' bit."

"Yeah, well, calm down, and get your shit together," Jake answers in a stern whisper.

"Got it," Cas replies.

After a moment, he begins to chuckle. "Calm the fuck down?" he says to himself. He looks at Jake and leans in to talk in a lower voice than before, "Yo, you calm the fuck down, and you get your shit together. I don't have to calm down, you have to calm down."

Jake leans back to see how serious he is. "What?"

Cas bursts out laughing.

"I'm just fucking with you, man!" he says, laughing so hard his eyes tear up a bit. "I love you, man – you're my brother." He bear-hugs Jake, "My brother!"

Jake stands perfectly still, locked in his friend's tight grasp. "Cas, can you let me go now?"

Cas releases him.

Jake tries to make direct eye contact with him.

"Look at me." Cas turns his eyes to Jake. Jake speaks very calmly. "Get your shit together. There are some fine-ass women in here, and you acting like a fucking frat boy."

"You gotta take it easy, Nova," Chen adds subtly, "Just relax, man."

Cas nods and tries to relax.

"You guys are right. I need to mellow down. I wish I could smoke right now," he says with a small smile. "But I'm chilling. Do your thing, guys – show me how it's done."

"Just be cool, dude. I mean, have you looked around? There's like a ton of women, and we're like the flyest mother fuckers here."

Cas scans the crowd to gauge the competition.

"You're right. All the other guys here are either young as hell or old as hell, or look like they're here with a girl."

Jake nods. "I know, it's great. I mean I expected there'll be a few hotties, but this is awesome. We're like lions with a bunch of gazelles prancing around us."

Just as he says that, three beautiful women come up to the bar.

The one closest to Cas speaks first. "Excuse me," she says, her voice is sultry and sexy with that hint of Spanish accent that Cas loves.

"Yes," he replies in his smoothest sounding voice.

The girl raises her right eyebrow, the look is absolutely sexy. Cas is hooked right in, itching to explore further.

"Excuse me," she says again.

"*Si, mi amor?*" he replies using the little Spanish he knows – the three shots of Henny have him smiling confidently. Cas doesn't notice the impatient look that is creeping up on the faces of the two girls standing behind the one he's talking to.

"Can you move out of the way so we can order a drink? Damn," snaps one of the impatient girls.

His smooth grin immediately vanishes, and he can feel his face turning hot with embarrassment. He quickly moves out of the way and looks back towards his friends for support. Chen is nowhere to be found, Manny is lost in the crowd of his family, and Jake has already moved to the end of the bar, engaged in conversation with an attractive brunette.

"Thank you," the same impatient one replies as she brushes past Cas to get to the bar.

The first woman he was talking to is still looking at him – this time, she has a sly grin on her face.

Cas lets out a nervous chuckle. "Sorry about that, I thought..."

"I know what you thought," she cuts him off, "You thought because you're a cutie I came over here to talk to you, right?"

"What? Ah, no, not really. I really don't know what I thought. I definitely didn't think you came over to speak to me just because I'm cute. I'm not even that good-looking."

"You're not," she answers with a serious face, before breaking into a smile, "But you're alright, cutie."

Cas gets tense with her first remark but relaxes with the latter.

"Thank you," he says, feeling good. "You're not too bad yourself."

"Not too bad myself?" she laughs. "Boy, you really know how to compliment a lady," she says playfully.

Her smile is stunning, beautiful white teeth under pink, full lips. Her complexion is olive, slightly lighter than Cas's tanned skin. Her hair is jet black and falls down in thick waves.

"You know I'm only kidding, right? I mean, you're absolutely gorgeous," he says as he stares into her light brown eyes.

"Wow, gorgeous? Please don't gas me," she says, laughing again. "I'm OK."

He looks at her more closely and notices that she's definitely older than him, at least in her late 30's, maybe early 40's. But she's sexy and confident. Cas finds himself very intrigued.

"No, I'm so serious. You're beautiful. What's your name?"

95

"Elizabeth. And yours?"

"Cas."

"Well, thank you for the compliment, Cas."

"It's not a compliment – it's a fact. You *are* beautiful."

She gives Cas a wide smile that makes her look prettier to him. "Thank you."

"You're welcome," he answers and smiles back. "So, how do you know Veronica?"

"I'm really close with her older sister Gloria, but they're both my girls. How do you know her?"

"I went to high school with her brother, Manny. She was a freshman when we were Seniors."

"Oh, so you're a dog, then?" she asks, casually.

"Ah, what?" Cas is confused.

"If you're friends with Manolo, then you gotta be a dog. Just like the other one, what his name, Jake? You're just like them. *Un mujeriego!*"

"Yo no soy *un mujeriego*, mami," Cas says defensively, but he's also impressed by how fluid his Spanish sounded. "Don't get me wrong. I know my friends have a reputation, but personality-wise, we're worlds apart. And even still, they're really good people. Jake is like my brother."

"Oh yeah, I'm not saying they're not cool. I've hung out with both of them a couple of times..."

Cas cuts her off, "Hung out with them?"

"I mean hung out as in a group of us at a club or something like that, and they're always trying to holler at anything with a skirt on. They have very little respect for women."

Cas is about to defend them as an instinctive reaction, but decides against it because, for the most part, she is right.

"Well, I can't totally disagree with you – but they *definitely* respect women. They just like to have fun."

"Fun? As in let me meet a girl, convince her I'm this great, fun guy, fuck her, and then, leave her. Is that your idea of fun?"

"Good times," Cas says sarcastically.

"Really?" she laughs at his candor.

"No, I'm only joking. Just messing with you because you're pretty, and I like how you look when you smile."

"Nice line, player."

"No, I'm really not like that at all. I'm so serious."

"Uh huh. Let me find out Cas is short for Casanova."

He lets out a laugh. "Wow, you're really gonna think poorly of me now, but it *is*, in fact, short for Casanova. Sadly, that is really the name I'm stuck with."

Elizabeth bursts out in laughter. "Are you serious? Oh, I'm definitely staying away from you. It was nice talking to you. You have a goodnight," she says and is about to turn her back at him to walk away when Cas gently grabs her arm – she is wearing a sleeveless shirt; her skin feels smooth and soft against his touch.

"No, wait – don't go. I can't help my name, trust me, I would have liked to have a choice. But I can assure you that the only thing Casanova about me is my name."

She turns around with a sly smile on her face. "I'm just messing with you, Mr. Casanova."

"Oh, so you got jokes, huh?" he says, feeling relieved.

"I try. So, Casanova, is that your first name?"

"No, it's my last name."

She laughs. "Really? Who does that? Who goes by their last name? Unless you're in the Army or something."

"I don't know. Ever since junior high, people have always called me by my last name. My first name isn't much better. It's *Juan Carlos*."

"Wow, that is a *puro* Latino name. Your parents weren't playing when they had you. *Juan Carlos Casanova* – it sounds like something out of a *novella*."

He shrugs with a smile. "I know. That's why everyone tends to call me Cas."

"Cas is cool, though. I like it." She smiles again. Cas, at this point, is quite smitten by Elizabeth's beauty.

"So..." He's about to say something when one of the impatient girls cuts him off.

"You done harassing my friend?" She looks annoyed. "Let's go, Liz," she says, passing her a drink.

"It was nice talking to you," Elizabeth says to Cas as she is being pulled away.

"Same here," he replies.

As she walks away, he admires her body. She's wearing a tight black shirt that is tucked into dark denims. Her jeans are tight, hugging the outward curve of her hips and making her ass pop out like a bubble

– it looks inviting and juicy, something he wants to squeeze. Her thighs are thick, and the tightness of her jeans accentuate her strong and sexy legs. Her walk is seductive, her plump ass sways side to side with each step.

Look at that, he thinks, briefly biting his lower lip, *Delicious*. He begins to imagine all the different sexual positions he would want to have her in.

Jake taps him on his shoulder.

"What's cookin', homeboy? How'd that go?"

"I think it went well," he says, taking a sip from his Long Island, still visualizing all the freaky things he would do to her.

"Which one you after? The shorty with the red or the one in the purple?"

"Neither. I was talking to the one in the black shirt."

"HA!" Jake mocks him, "Impossible. Go for one of the other ones – you'll have a better chance."

Cas looks at Jake sideways. "What do you mean *impossible*? How is that impossible?"

"Two reasons," Jake says matter-of-factly and takes another gulp of his drink, "One, she is way too hot for you, you're not ready for any of that MILF action. And two, I'm about to make a move on her."

Cas gets extremely tense but hides it with a laugh. "You trying to cock block me? Is that what you're doing?"

"Hell no," Jake says, sounding offended. "She's been digging me already. We have history."

"Really?" Cas is jealous, but he continues to smile and act unimpressed. "You have history?"

99

Jake shrugs. "I ran into her a couple of times here and there, and she's always given me the eye like she's digging me. I get all types of cougar vibes from her – I just haven't jumped in on it yet."

His feelings of jealousy quickly evaporate. He is truly unimpressed by Jake's history with Elizabeth.

"No doubt, playboy. Do you even know her name?"

"I think it's Jane or Carla. I don't know. Names are overrated."

"Yeah, OK," Cas answers quickly and scoffs. "You might at least want to know her name before you talk all this shit. It kind of matters if you're claiming *history*."

Jake finishes off his drink and turns to the bartender. "Can I get another cranberry and Henny?"

The bartender nods and quickly begins shaking the drink.

"Thanks, man." Jake takes a healthy swig of the light red liquid and turns to Cas. "Look, that doesn't matter. All that matters are the eyes. The eyes never lie, chico. And by way she looks at me, I can tell – she wants the Snake." He takes another gulp of his drink and places it on the bar. He taps Cas on the chest. "Watch."

Jake walks over to the table where Elizabeth and the two other women are sitting. Cas can't hear him but sees him leaning in to talk to her. They talk for a few moments before Jake casually reaches for her hand. His move infuriates Cas –intense jealousy burns within him as he watches his friend talk to her and then touch her.

Jake whispers something into her ear. She gives a half smile and shakes her head, signifying a 'no'. Jake leans back as if surprised by her answer. He leans back in to say something else – this time a big smile breaks across her face and she begins to laugh, but she still shakes her head in a 'no'.

Jake shrugs and lets go of her hand rather casually. He slowly stands up straight, looks around for a moment, and then starts walking back towards Cas, who is waiting with a curious grin on his face.

"What happen, Romeo?" he asks with noticeable delight, "Doesn't Carla like you?"

Jake tries to brush it off, "You know damn well her name ain't Carla. But yeah, it was cool. I think she's gay or something."

"Oh, so now she's a lesbian? Funny, because you made it seem like she was *so* into you. I thought you had *history* together?"

"Man, whatever. I'm not stressing it. Plus, that bitch is old. I really ain't into the whole cougar thing."

As he's talking, Cas's eyes are fixed on Elizabeth. She looks up and their gazes lock with each other's. She smiles and waves at him to go over and sit next to her. Cas's eyes light up at her gesture, but he tries to play it cool.

"It's funny you should say that because she just asked me to come over." He talks to Jake but his eyes stay on Elizabeth across the room. "I'll be back."

"What?" Jake's confused. "You're wasting your time, man."

Cas ignores his friend and grabs his drink from the bar as he makes his way over to Elizabeth.

I'm not drunk, he thinks, but the effort he's having to put into walking straight indicates otherwise.

He reaches her table where she's sitting by herself – her friends are dancing somewhere in the crowd.

"Hey, want some company?" he asks.

"Company? Oh no, I just called you over to get me a drink from the bar. I don't feel like getting up," she says with a devilish grin.

Cas is caught off guard by her request. "Ummm, OK. What do you want?"

She laughs out loud. "Are you serious? You really think I called you all the way to my table to get me a drink? Gosh, I would be a serious bitch if I did something like that. *Bendito*, imagine?"

He laughs, feeling relieved and foolish at the same time. "Damn, you got me good. But, I mean, I'll get it for you if you want – it's not a problem."

"No, silly. I'm fine. I have a drink already, but thanks. I called you over because we were having a nice little conversation over there."

Cas is ecstatic and shows it. "You know what, I feel the same way. I'll be honest, I was a little disappointed that we got cut off like that"

"So, tell me some more about yourself, Juan Carlos? Where are you from?"

"My family is from Puerto Rico, but I was born here, in New York. What about you?"

"I'm half Puerto Rican, half Dominican. My mom *es Dominicana, mi pai es Boricua, pero* – I was born here. I grew up in the Heights, not too far from this place." She takes a quick sip from the thin straw poking out of her drink. "Are you from around here?"

"No, I'm from the East side, Spanish Harlem."

"Don't tell me you're a hustler?"

"Oh, no, no. I have a job. I work."

"OK, because I swear every guy I've met from Harlem hustles something. Whether it's drugs or DVDs, t-shirts – Harlem guys are always hustling something."

Cas laughs, "Nah, not at all. I grind like a hustler, but I'm totally legal," he tries to jest.

"What do you do for a living?"

"I'm a writer."

Elizabeth is intrigued. "A writer? Interesting. What do you write about?"

"Everything," he says and takes a sip of his drink. "Sports, politics, music. Literally everything. It just depends on who I'm writing for. I work for several sites and magazines."

"Where all have you been published? Anywhere I might have read your name?"

"Maybe. I've been published on *Huffington Post*, *Bleacher Report*, been in *Playboy* a few times, too."

"Playboy? Wow, exciting. Have you been to the mansion?"

"Oh, I'm not nearly that cool or popular," he laughs. "But I've been published in their magazine."

Elizabeth raises her eyebrows, impressed. "Sounds like you have a good career."

"Yeah, it's not too bad," he humbly brags. "I also dabble in graphic art and web designing. It's definitely more of a hobby, but, like, I've worked on most of Jake's fliers for his events, and occasionally, when someone asks for something specific, I do it for them, you know, if I have the time. It's like a side gig on my down time. But writing is my main thing."

"That's pretty cool." She takes a sip of her martini. "Have you written a book?"

Cas shrugs. "I have an idea that I've been kicking around in my head for a while. I actually started writing it, but I only finished the first chapter. But that's a whole other story. What about you? What do you do for a living?"

"Paralegal. I work at a law firm in mid-town."

"Wow, that must be pretty interesting."

"What about that seems interesting?"

Cas is caught off guard. "I don't know. Paralegal stuff?"

Elizabeth looks at him intently.

Cas looks down and shakes his head. "I don't know."

"Did you just say it *should be interesting* because I said that to you about your work?"

"No," he says, looking up. "What I meant is, I don't really know what a paralegal does. So, for me it's interesting that you work as one because you can tell me all about it."

"I didn't plan on becoming a paralegal, but it's a very good job. I can't complain."

"Nice." Cas nods. "So, what does a paralegal do?"

"I don't want to talk about it," Elizabeth replies.

"Me neither," he quickly adds.

She laughs, "That's funny. I like your sense of humor." She takes a sip of her drink – the glass indicates it's a martini.

"What about kids?" she asks, "Do you have any?"

"No kids. I would like to have some, one day, eventually. What about you, you have kids?" he asks hoping that her answer is also no.

"Yes, *una*."

Cas is immediately disappointed with the answer but doesn't show it. His rule when it comes to dating women with kids is, 'Don't do it'.

"*Una*? You have a girl?"

She smiles as she begins to talk about her daughter.

"Yes, beautiful girl, my Alicia. She's 21 already."

"You sound like a proud mother," Cas pauses, "Wait. Did you just say your daughter is 21?"

Elizabeth laughs. "Yes, why? I look too young to have a 21-year-old?"

"Wow. I can't believe it!" Cas smiles and shakes his head. "I know it's rude to ask a woman her age…"

"So, don't," Elizabeth says with a wink as she uses the little straw to taste her Martini. She gets up. "Do you want to dance?"

Cas is instantly nervous. He isn't a good dancer, almost solely relying on the ol' *drink and a two-step* move. Unfortunately for him, the DJ is playing *Salsa* music, which is hard to dance to and even harder to fake.

"Ah, sure, I'll dance with you." He feels his face getting flushed. "But just to let you know, I'm not much of a dancer. And I'm even worse at Salsa – so, you're gonna have to lead."

Elizabeth gives him a seductive smile and grabs his hand. "Don't worry, *papi*, I'll lead you."

Her comment starts another problem for Cas – he's turned on and can feel his dick starting to get excited.

She leads him to the dance floor. The music is unreasonably loud, and there are several other couples dancing around them. Cas gently places his right hand on her waist as she places her left hand on his shoulder. Her free hand rests lightly in his.

Her hips and feet begin to move fluidly to the rhythm of the music. Cas, on the other hand, is stiff and rigid. Subconsciously, he keeps looking down at his feet to make sure he doesn't step on hers.

After a minute, Elizabeth begins to laugh.

"You weren't kidding when you said you don't know how to dance, huh?"

Cas laughs in embarrassment. "Yeah, well, at least I'm trying," he says as his hands move down her waist and settle closer to her hips.

She playfully grabs his hand. "OK, first, this hand belongs up here." She places it back on her waist.

He's genuinely apologetic. "Sorry, I really didn't notice it was there, my bad."

Elizabeth pretends to be angry. "Yeah OK, *fresco*. Now keep your hand on my waist – you feel how my body is moving? You need to relax and loosen up. Move them hips, boy, it's all in the hips."

The movement of her hips is driving Cas to want her more. He starts to move his body to the rhythm of hers. After a while, he's no longer looking at his feet, just moving naturally with her.

Their eyes meet and lock on each other.

"OK, I see you do have some rhythm," she says, "Now, turn me."

"Huh?" Cas asks, even though he knows exactly what she means. Dancing Salsa involves several turns and spins – he was, however, hoping to finish the song without having to do any of those.

"I want you to spin me..." Before she can finish her sentence, he turns her to the left, she does a 360 and is now facing him with a surprised smile on her face. He quickly spins her to the right, another 360, followed by a half turn to the left and then to the right. This leaves him holding her from behind, their bodies moving from side to side in unison.

He can feel her soft, round ass gently pushed against him and moving with the song. His manhood's growing, getting harder with each sway of her body. Cas is afraid that she'll notice and think he's a pervert. He moves his hip away to make some space between his crotch and her body. He doesn't get much distance, however, when she moves herself a little closer to him, seemingly liking the feeling of his hardening cock against her soft ass.

They rock back and forth for a few moments, the warmth of the alcohol settling in. His hands rest on her hips again, squeezing them gently, ever so softly. Cas closes his eyes and leans in to smell her hair. The fragrance is delicious, like a sweet fruit. He runs his fingers through it – her loose tresses feel nice in his hands.

He opens his eyes and softly kisses her neck – Elizabeth remains in his embrace for a moment. Then, she suddenly turns around and faces him

"Sorry," he mumbles, embarrassed that he kissed her.

"For what?" she asks.

The music switches to Reggaetón.

Elizabeth smiles and bites her bottom lip – she begins moving to the up-tempo rhythm. Her moves are seductive, her body fluid, her hips swerving from side to side. Cas is mesmerized by everything that he sees.

He's about to open his mouth to tell her how well she dances, when the impatient woman, with the red top on, cuts in.

"OK, you've been hogging my friend long enough," she says, getting between the two of them to dance with Elizabeth.

Cas is about to say something but decides against it and turns to fetch another drink.

The woman in red notices he's walking away and grabs his arm, "Where you going, *chulo*?"

He looks at her. She's attractive, about Cas's age, probably a little younger than him, but a lot younger than Elizabeth.

"I'm sorry, sweetie. I'm just going to grab a drink real quick. I'll be back," he says with a smooth smile.

"OK, you better come back. There's not a lot of cute guys here; so, you owe me a dance," she says with a mischievous look in her eyes.

"Don't worry, I got you. Let me just grab a drink." Cas is feeling good about himself – he likes the sudden flurry of attention.

He looks up at Elizabeth. She gives him a half smile; he returns it with one of his own, then turns to go to the bar.

He motions for the bartender. "Hey, can I get another Long Island?"

Someone yells from behind him.

"And four shots of Henny!"

Jake is standing behind him with Chen, and he can see Manolo making his way over. "You ready for the next round?"

"Not really," Cas says just as the bartender returns with the drinks.

"I'm not having anymore. I have to drive," Chen shakes head.

"One more, man, and that's it. You still have time to sober up." Jake hands him a shot. "And if worst comes to worst, I'll drive."

"Yeah, OK," Chen responds sarcastically. "You've been drinking more than me."

"Exactly. So, you're fine," Jake answers. He looks up at Manolo and hands him a shot.

They raise their glasses.

"To my best friends." Manolo is drunk and getting emotional, – his voice begins to crack, "I love you guys, man. You guys are my mutha fuckin' boys for life. And I won't say I'd die for anyone of ya, but I would kill for all of ya – so that's almost as good."

They all laugh. Chen adds, "Love you too, man. Salud."

"Salud," they repeat in unison and down the shots.

"WOOOOOOO!" Jake yells as each of their faces contort in ugly grimaces, caused by the bitter fire of the liquor

"Yuck!" The taste makes Cas squint his eyes. He reaches for the Long Island to chase down the shot. "Damn, that was nasty."

He goes for another sip of his drink when suddenly the hand he's holding the glass in is jerked downward, causing him to spill a little bit of the drink on himself.

"Oops, sorry about that." It's the woman in the red shirt.

She takes the drink from his hand, places it on the bar, and pulls him to the dance floor.

"You got your drink, now you owe me my dance."

Cas is about to get angry about the drink spilling, but his mood immediately changes when he looks at her. She's prettier than he

109

remembers from just a few minutes earlier, and with the buzz from the alcohol, she's getting more attractive by the minute.

Cas gives her a smooth smile. "No problem, *chula*."

She leads him to the dance floor. For the first time, Cas really looks at her body. Her red shirt is low cut and reveals the soft flesh of her round breasts. She's wearing black leggings that outline her toned thighs and shapely hips. Her body is tight – she looks like she works out regularly.

They find a little free space on the full dance floor. With her back facing him, she begins to move her hips from side to side.

When Cas tries to move with the music, he quickly realizes that he is more drunk than he thought. The heat from the crowd and the alcohol swimming in his system, along with the obscenely loud music, has him feeling hot and light headed; he's getting woozy. He closes his eyes to compose himself.

Alright, Cassy boy, get your shit together. You definitely cannot get sick in the middle of the dance floor.

When he opens his eyes, he's looking downward and staring directly at her deep cleavage. A big smile breaks across his face, and he regains some of his composure.

He puts his hands on her waist and begins to sway, letting her seductive moves guide him. His hands slide down to her thighs – they feel firm and soft at the same time. His dick responds to her proximity and begins to awaken again. Putting his arm around her lower back, he pulls her in closer; one of her thighs rubs against his cock. Not sure how she is going to react, he moves his hands to give her space – she backs off slightly.

They look at each other. Cas's eyes are drooping from the alcohol. She smiles and moves close to him, dancing. She turns around and thrusts her ass deep between his legs, pressing against Cas's crotch.

His eyes widen – he knows for certain that she is feeling his erection. Still dancing, he casually backs off of her, leaving some air between them.

She pushes her ass against him even harder and begins to grind. His cock is rock stiff. She bends over and begins to twerk against him as he holds her tightly by the waist.

Cas looks down at her grinding ass. He can see the outline of her thong. She is pushed up so close to him that any closer, and he'd be between her butt cheeks.

They sure are friendly around here, he thinks with a drunken smile. He decides to be bold and stupid and grabs a big handful of her ass and gives it a gentle squeeze.

She stands up straight, grabs his hand, and moves it off her butt – not aggressively, but in a way that implies she's setting boundaries.

Cas places his hands higher up on her waist. With her back still facing him, she reaches behind and puts her hand on the back of his neck.

With the way they're dancing, Cas's mouth is by her ear. So, he decides this would be a good time to find out who she is.

"What's your name?"

"Samantha," she answers, "And yours?"

"Casanova."

She looks back at him over her shoulder, their mouths not far apart. "Casanova, huh?" she says, grinding her ass harder against him. "Yeah, you gonna have to prove that to me."

Surprised by her aggressiveness, he is completely turned on. He's too drunk to come up with a smooth or clever response; so, "Oh yeah?" is what comes out of his mouth, followed by, "Everybody calls me Cas."

She ignores his words and keeps her body moving to the sexy beat, grinding against him so closely that his dick is pinned against her ass. He's about to say something but quickly forgets – his eyes are transfixed on her.

He glances over briefly at Elizabeth sitting alone at a table in the corner. She looks up at him, and their eyes meet.

He leans over to Samantha. "Hey, I need to take a little break."

"OK," she says, sounding a bit surprised.

He begins to walk through the crowded dance floor, towards Elizabeth's table. Before he can get close, the music stops and the DJ starts talking.

"What's up everyone! Hope everyone is having a good time at Veronica's baby shower. Are you all having a good time?"

"Yeahhhhh!" Several people yell out and start clapping.

The DJ continues, "That's what I'm talking about! Now, can everyone go to the big table in the back? Veronica will begin opening her gifts."

Jake comes up behind Cas and puts his hand on his shoulder. When he turns around, he hands him a bottled water.

"For you."

Cas takes the drink. "Thanks, man."

"No doubt, my brother. Let's go check out the gifts."

"Cool." Cas looks over at the table where Elizabeth had just been sitting; she's no longer there.

Jake talks in a low voice as they walk towards the back, "I see you doing your thing on the dance floor. The one in the red is really feeling you."

Cas feels the old bravado from his player days kicking in. "Yeah, she's definitely feeling me. But, to be honest, I'm digging the other one."

"Who, the MILF in black?" Jake scoffs, "Man, forget her. This one's giving you mad play."

"Yeah, maybe. But so was the other one."

They join the crowd surrounding the big table. Veronica is sitting in a big wicker chair, decorated with white, pink, and yellow streamers. Her mother and brother are standing beside her. Manolo is talking into the mic and has a big smile plastered on his face. They've already started announcing the gifts.

"The next one we have here is from tia Julia," he says as he hands his sister Veronica the gift box. She opens it and lifts up the contents for everyone to see. It has three packs of onesies and a pack of bibs with giraffes on it.

Everybody *"Ooohs"* and *"Awwwws."*

"Thank you, tia. Love you," Veronica calls out.

"Alright, let's open a big one now." Manolo grabs the biggest box of the lot. It's the gift from Jake and Cas. "Damn, this shit is heavy!"

"*Mira!*" interrupts the little red-headed Spanish lady, their mom. "Watch your mouth, *fresco. No habla asì con los niños aquì,*" she snaps, disapproving of the foul language.

"Sorry, mama; you're right. This *thing* is heavy," he says with an embarrassed smile. He pushes the box in front of his sister.

"This one is from Jake and Juan Carlos. My boys!" He points at them standing in the back.

As Veronica starts to rip the gift wrapping off the box, her face lights up with excitement.

"Wow, I can't believe you guys bought me this. Thank you so much!"

"What is it?" someone yells out.

Manolo looks over at the box. "They bought a stroller."

"And a car seat," Veronica chimes in; "It's a stroller-car seat combo. It's the one from my registry. Thanks, you guys; it's awesome."

"Niiice. And just in case ya' didn't know, those are my boys – they're standing in the back right there. Raise your hands, guys."

Jake and Cas are trying to play it cool, but they both smile widely. Manolo starts to slow clap, which causes other people to clap too. Soon, it turns into an applause.

"Give it up everybody – that's a great gift! And for all you ladies out there, they're both single, both employed, and obviously they're not cheap. They got that car seat-stroller money. They 'bout that life.'"

Several women laugh and look back at them; a female voice lets out a "Woot, woot!"

"Thanks again, guys. I love it," Veronica says gleefully.

Still smiling widely; they both nod in acknowledgment.

114

Manolo continues, "Moving on to the next gift..."

Jake leans over and whispers to Cas, "See, didn't I tell you it was a good gift? Didn't I tell you it'll make us stand out?"

Cas whispers back to him, "You ain't tell me shit."

They both laugh.

A few moments pass and then a beautiful voice whispers into Cas's ear, "Nice gift."

He turns around and is happy to see her there – it's Elizabeth.

"Hey. I thought I lost you in the crowd."

"Well, you found me."

"Really, *you* found me."

"That is true," she adds, "I think my friend Samantha likes you."

"Yeah, she might," he says before adding, "But I have a problem with that."

"Why?" Elizabeth asks, "She's a beautiful girl, you're a good-looking guy; what's the problem?"

"The problem is *I* might like you."

Elizabeth looks at Cas. "Might?" She says, her whimsical smile playing about her lips, "Really? You *might* like me?"

"Might. You know. maybe, possibly, there is some inclination of *like* brewing here," he continues, "I mean, you did say I was good looking; so, there is that."

"You're OK," she answers with a playful shrug.

"Hey, I can live with 'OK'. I'll take it."

They stare intently at each other for a moment, as if they're both daydreaming at the same time.

115

Cas finally breaks the silence. "Ah, listen, Elizabeth. I know we just met, and I'm not one of those smooth guys who always know the right thing to say and when to say it; so, I'm just going to come right out with it..." he breathes deeply, "I love you."

"What!" She chokes on her drink and laughs at the same time. "Did you just say you *love me*? Wow, what a psycho!".

Cas feels embarrassed and laughs as well. "Hey, it's just a joke! I don't really *love* you– we just met. I'm just missing you, eh, messing with you. That's not what I wanted to say. Totally joking."

Elizabeth raises her right eyebrow. "Damn, how much did you have to drink? I hope you were only joking because that would be kind of scary."

"Oh, hell yeah. Imagine?" he clears his throat. "No, but seriously, I would love a chance to get to know you better."

Elizabeth smiles and nods. "OK. And what does that mean to you? *Get to know you better?*"

"Well, for starters, can I get your number?"

She looks at him for a moment, contemplating. "You know what? I was just about to say 'no', because I never give out my number, but I'm going to do it differently this time. I'm going to give it to you."

"Great," Cas says while reaching for his phone. "What is it?"

"987-654-3210," she answers as Cas diligently types the numbers into his phone.

He repeats it to her, "987-654-3210..." He pauses for a moment, "Wait a minute, 9-8-7-6-5-4-3-2, huh?"

She bursts out in laughter. "Ha! Almost got you! You'd be surprised at how many guys I've given that number to and they don't even realize how obviously fake it is. You're pretty sharp; I like that."

Cas doesn't know how to feel. "I mean, honestly, if you don't want to give me your number, it's OK. You don't have to lie about it; you could've just said no. I won't bother you anymore. Have a good night." He turns back to walk away.

She quickly grabs his arm. "Wait. Where you going? I was just messing with you."

He's pleased with her response. "You better be joking."

Elizabeth rolls her eyes. "Oh my God, look who's Mr. Cocky now. Forget it, I'm not giving you my number. You blew your chance."

Cas laughs. "No, I'm really not cocky at all. I'm just being stupid. But seriously, I don't want to blow it. I'd just like a chance to take you out some time."

She squints and looks at him suspiciously. "OK, since you're acting so desperate, I guess I'll give you my number. It's 347-555-4391."

He enters it into his phone and presses the 'Talk' button. Elizabeth's phone begins to vibrate in her purse.

"That's me, save my number," he tells her.

"I can't believe I just gave you my number," she says, shaking her head. "You should feel lucky. I never give out my number. Never."

"I feel special," he says gleefully, making Elizabeth break into a big smile. She looks stunning.

"I know I told you this already, but I *have* to tell you again; your smile is gorgeous. I mean like really, really beautiful. I could look at it all day."

"Yeah? I bet you say that to all the girls."

"Only one," he replies quickly.

Before Elizabeth has a chance to respond, they notice everyone is looking towards the back of the room where all the gifts are. Somebody's arguing, and people are starting to crowd around.

"Yo, what the hell is going on?" Cas starts to walk towards the crowd.

"Hey!" Elizabeth grabs him. "Where are you going? You shouldn't go over there. It looks like someone is fighting." There's genuine concern in her voice – it turns Cas on.

He looks at her. "Stay here. I don't want you getting hurt. But I have to see what's going on, my friends are over there. I'll be right back."

Cas can feel Elizabeth's eyes following him as he puffs out his chest and bravely walks towards the commotion.

He gets close to the crowd and can hear Manolo's voice – he sounds angry.

"Listen, everybody's having a good time here, and my sister said you're not welcome. So, just do yourself a favor and get the fuck outta here."

Cas makes his way to the front of the crowd. He sees Chen standing next to Manolo and Jake right behind them. They're facing some people he doesn't recognize: three guys and a woman. He approaches Jake and talks in a low voice, "What going on?"

Jake looks intense. He talks to Cas but doesn't take his eyes off the group of strangers. "That's Veronica's ex, the baby's father. He came here talking shit. Get ready, cause it might go down."

Cas looks over at the opposition. They look like they walked out of a gangsta' rap video – skinny jeans sagging, with boxers showing, yellow bandanna hanging out of the back pockets, tattoos on the neck and face. The one woman in the group looks the most menacing. She's a gangsta' butch with the word *'SAVAGE'* tattooed across her neck. She's stout, about 5'5" and a solid 200 lbs. Her low-cut t-shirt reveals a detailed tattoo of two long barrel revolvers, one over each breast, pointing downward with the barrels almost touching and making a 'V' shape.

Nervous butterflies flutter in Cas's stomach. He's down to fight for his friends, but he'd much rather talk it out and keep the peace. By the look of this group, talking it out doesn't appear to be an option.

The one who appears to be the leader, a skinny, light-skinned Spanish dude with a long scar across his face, is standing at the front. He opens his mouth to talk. "Yo, that's my mutha fuckin' baby too, and I ain't going nowhere, nigga. If you want me to leave, then make me leave. You and your punk-ass manz and 'em."

Manolo is about to say something, but Chen cuts him off. "Look, Tony, that's your name, right?" he asks very calmly.

Tony answers, "Don't worry what the fuck my name is, nigga."

Chen shrugs and continues to speak in a very calm tone, "Alright, listen, whatever your name is, you've already been asked to leave. There's really no point in staying here and causing a scene. There's kids here, there's old people here, and not to mention, Veronica doesn't need this stress while she's pregnant. So, please, just make it easy for yourself and everybody, and just leave. I'm asking you nicely, man, please leave now. Please."

Tony looks disgusted and confused. "Yo, who the fuck is this fake-ass Bruce Lee on steroids mother fucker over here? Why don't you *please* mind your fuckin' business before I slap the shit out of you? *Please.*"

Chen remains calm. "Oh, word?"

Tony nods and claps his hands aggressively, "Yo! That's my word, my nigga. I'm telling you right now. If you want to get it poppin', we can get it pop—"

Before he can get another word out, Chen grabs him by the collar, lifts him a good three feet off the ground, and throws him through an empty table causing it to shatter into pieces. The force of his body crashing through the table and slamming against the floor knocks the wind out of him. He can't speak as he writhes on the ground in pain.

Tony's people stand there with their mouths open in shock. One of his boys looks at Chen.

"Oh, you wanna throw people?" he says as he reaches for something in his pocket. He pulls out a box cutter and quickly slides the blade open, but Manolo is even quicker in grabbing him by the wrist.

"What the fuck you think you doing! You gonna cut my boy?" Manny yells in his face as they struggle.

Just then, Jake rushes from behind and throws a heavy punch that lands hard on the guy's face – he drops the blade. The guy is dazed but still manages to take a wild swing; the punch misses Jake and Manolo and instead hits a little, gray-haired old man; the whole crowd gasps.

The punch jolts the little old man, but he remains on his feet. Staring in disbelief, he raises his old trembling hand to the side of his face he'd been struck on.

"Mira, cabron," he says in an old raspy voice – his eyes now filled with anger.

The stunned crowd erupts; a woman yells out, "HE HIT ABUELO! GET THAT MUTHA FUCKER!"

Several men from the party, old and young alike, relatives of Veronica and Manolo, rush to get him. An uncle dives at the assailant, tackles him, slamming his back violently against the wall, pinning him upright to hold him firm for an upcoming punch from one of the nephews; it lands solidly and knocks him to his side. Realizing that he's in danger of getting a serious ass-kicking, the assailant jumps up quickly and makes a run for the exit. He crashes through the doors, making it down the first couple of steps before losing his footing and stumbling down the rest of the flight. He meets the ground floor landing with a painful *'THUD'*. Despite being in agony, he wastes no time, getting up immediately and kicking open the exit door. The mob of relatives is already halfway down the stairs and hot on his ass. From inside, Cas can hear him running up the block with dozens of footsteps chasing him.

The third guy in the group looks like he's about to pick the box cutter from the floor when Cas kicks it out of reach. He stands in front of the guy and raises his hands up in a fighting stance. At this point, the butterflies are gone and replaced with adrenaline – even more so because he knows Elizabeth is watching. Cas's voice is topped with energy and anger, "What's good! You wanna go? Let's go, bitch!"

The guy quickly backs down, "Nah, nah, man; no beef, please. I'm just here to party. I ain't know he wasn't invited and all that, I promise you."

Cas believes him and puts his hands down. "Alright, man. So, just get your people and bounce."

The whole time this mayhem was taking place, Veronica has been sitting calmly in the big wicker chair made fancy with white and pink ribbons and lace.

She speaks nonchalantly, "You see? I told you, Tony, don't come here popping shit; my family ain't punks. Now, look what happen. Your ass got body slammed through a table. And your boy Willie is getting chased up the block, about to get his ass beat. Good work, tough guy."

The guy that Cas was going to fight is helping Tony get up from the floor; he's obviously scared. "Come on, Tone, hurry up, man; let's go, let's go."

Tony gets up slowly, a painful scowl on his face. He walks gingerly, holding his ribs and leaning forward. All the gangsta' bravado is knocked out of him, and he avoids eye contact as he limps his way towards the exit.

Cas looks around and sees the thugged-out lesbian with the gun tattoos over her tits. Looking at her face, he picks up on the fear in her eyes and begins to feel sorry for her. He walks over to her and speaks politely – she is a woman after all.

"I'm sorry, mama, but you have to go," he says, touching her shoulder and giving her a half smile as if to say 'sorry'. He looks at her face and realizes how young she is – she looks barely 18, a hint of innocence behind the heavy eye shadow and the gangsta' tattoos.

"You're a young girl; you shouldn't hang out with these assholes. You should really find new friends because guys like these will always get you into trouble," he says with more concern than he can explain. He looks at her for another moment, gives her shoulder another gentle touch, then calmly turns around and walks away.

Cas feels proud of himself. He just helped ward off some fake-ass gangsta's, he thinks he offered some words of wisdom to a troubled youth, and he met a sexy, mature woman who, he hopes, is eating all of this up.

His eyes quickly latch on to Elizabeth's lovely face. *Damn she's sexy,* he thinks, *I wonder how old she is? 40? She can't be 50, can she? I mean she did say she has a 21-year-old daughter, so there's that.*

Their gazes meet – Elizabeth looks worried. Cas gives her a wink of reassurance that makes her smile. Once again, totally awestruck by how gorgeous she is, Cas thinks, *Shit, who cares how old she is? She's fucking hot.*

He confidently walks towards her, admiring her beauty; *I'm so happy I came out tonight; this is awesome,* he thinks.

Suddenly, Elizabeth's eyes widen in horror – she sees something behind him.

"Look out!" someone yells.

Cas turns around in time to see the blur of something being swung at him; it crashes into the side of his head and shatters into pieces. His eyes shut tight from the impact; bright lights explode in his head like cameras flashing, a pain jolts through his body.

Then… everything goes dark.

CHAPTER 5

The Ride Home

Cas opens his eyes to find himself lying on a sofa, but he isn't sure whose apartment it is – the sofa looks unfamiliar. He can hear someone bustling about the room, he looks up; it's Tiffany.

She comes up to him and kisses him on his forehead. "Hey baby, just got home and saw you were sleeping. I didn't want to wake you up."

For a moment, Cas is relieved to see her, but the moment passes quickly as nausea takes over.

He opens his mouth to talk, his voice is weak, and he can barely manage to whisper, "What am I doing here?"

Tiffany looks at him, smiling, as if she's pleasantly confused, "Whatever do you mean? You came over last night. You always come over to my place."

Cas is confused. "Why did I come here? Who brought me here?"

"I did." It's Elizabeth; Cas cannot figure where she's come from. "You asked me if I could take you home and gave me this address," she says.

He begins to sweat. "Uhh, I did?"

"Yes, you did," Elizabeth says with her beautiful smile, "But why didn't you tell me you have a girlfriend?"

"I don't have a girlfriend. She's my ex," he answers, unsure of what's going on.

"Oh really?" Tiffany sounds surprised. "So, I'm your ex now? And why did you tell this girl you love her? Please tell her that's not true, and that you really love me."

Elizabeth interrupts, "Tell her, *papi*, that you really love me, not her."

Cas is caught off guard but actually feels rather happy to have these two women arguing over whom he loves.

"I don't love you," he says, referring to Tiffany. "At one time, I did, but after what you did to me, my feelings have changed, and especially now that I've met Elizabeth."

Elizabeth has a big smile on her face. "See? I told you he loves me."

Tiffany is getting agitated. She walks over to Elizabeth and points a finger at her face. "Listen, bitch, he didn't say he loves you. And I know, no matter what he says, he does love me. Right, Cas?"

Elizabeth pushes her hand out of her face. "No, bitch. He loves *me*."

Tiffany grabs Elizabeth by the back of her hair; she speaks very close to her face. "No bitch..." she says and pushes her head back, licking the side of her exposed neck, "He loves me."

Elizabeth grabs her by her waist, lifts her up, and they both go crashing to the floor, attacking each other. Hair is flying all over the place, asses are being spanked, titties are being grabbed, and Cas is loving every minute of it. The girls definitely seem to be more concerned with groping and aggressively feeling each other up then actually hurting each other.

They manage to separate and get to their feet, but Elizabeth throws Tiffany back to the ground and sits on top of her. Straddling her, she aggressively pins Tiffany's hands together.

"What now, bitch? I got you."

There is something very sexual about how Elizabeth mounts her. Cas is growing hard watching them go at it.

Tiffany frees one of her hands and slaps Elizabeth's tits. "Take that!"

"Owww! You little bitch!" Elizabeth says, "You like slapping titties? Well, take this!" She leans over, forcing her full breasts into Tiffany's face as if she is trying to suffocate her. "You like that, you little bitch, don't you?"

"Noooo!" Tiffany says and moves her head from side to side, trying to get out of the way of Elizabeth's big, smothering breasts. She looks up from the ground to where Cas is standing and watching the scene before him in awe. "Baby, get her off me," she pleads in a desperate voice that sounds terribly sexy to Cas.

Cas is frozen; he wants to get in the middle to break it up, but he can't move.

Tiffany says it again, "Help me, Cas."

Before he can answer, Elizabeth calls out, "No, Cas, help me," sounding just as seductive.

"No, Cas, me," says Tiffany again.

"Cas!"

"Cas!"

The women begin calling his name simultaneously, "Cas... Cas... Cas"

The sexy and desperate voices of the women suddenly turn into that of a desperate sounding man.

"Cas! Yo, Cas!"

The image of the two beautiful women fighting over him begins to fade as Cas opens his eyes. He looks around and realizes that he's laying down on the back seat of Chen's SUV. He looks to his left and sees Jake leaning over, looking back at him from the front seat.

Jake flashes him a tired smile. "There he is. Good morning, fella. Had a nice nap?"

Cas looks out of the window of the moving car – it's still night. He slowly sits up in the backseat. He briefly looks around for another moment to make sure he's not still dreaming. Convinced that he's awake, he begins to talk. "What the hell happen?"

"You got knocked the fuck out, my man."

"What? Are you serious?" As Cas speaks, he feels a throbbing pain on the side of his head. He puts his hand there to feel a large painful bump.

"Yeah, man," answers Chen. "That big ghetto bitch cracked you over the head with a bottle of Hennessy. You know the big half gallon bottle? She clocked you right on the side of your head, man. You went down like a ton of bricks."

"Tell me that's not what really happen?" Cas says, hoping his friends are just messing with him. "Please tell me you're lying."

Jake looks back at him and shrugs his shoulders. "I wish we were just messing with you, but that really is what happen. You said something to her and started walking away, and then suddenly the gangsta' bitch ran up behind you with a big ass empty bottle of Henny.

I actually yelled out, 'Yo watch your back,' but as soon as you turned around, *WHAM*, right across your noggin. You just dropped, straight to *la-la* land. It's a miracle you didn't get cut by the glass because that shit shattered over your head."

Cas can't believe what they're saying. "What? That's fucking horrible. I got hit over the head with a bottle of Hennessy? That dike bitch knocked me out?"

Jake laughs a little. "Yeah, I guess she didn't like what you had to say to her. What did you tell her anyway?"

He thinks for a moment. "I didn't tell her anything. All I said was that she has to leave; I was really fucking nice about it too." Cas touches the bump on his head again; it's sore and tender, "But what the fuck, man? How you guys let her run up on me like that? I thought you had my back?"

"Hey, man. I told you to watch out, but she was quick. She did it with no hesitation, straight thug life."

Chen cuts in, "Hey, Cas, don't worry about it. She definitely got her payback."

"What you mean? She got hit? One of you hit her?" he asks excitedly.

"No, not us." Jake looks back at him with a smile on his face. "That MILF you were talking to. I think her name is Elizabeth."

"What!" Cas raises his voice, which causes his head to hurt. "Ahhowwuch." He lowers his tone. "What do you mean? What happen?"

128

Jake explains, "She was right there when you got hit. She saw you drop and maaan, she let out a scream like you've gotten shot or something."

Chen starts to crack up, "Word. She was fucking livid, dude. She went off on the one who hit you. You would think that was your woman or something; that's how hard she went."

Cas is more shocked at this than with the fact that he was actually knocked out by a young woman, "They fought! No way!"

"Yeah, man," adds Jake. "And it wasn't even a close fight. Elizabeth threw her to the ground and just thrashed her. She left the girl with a busted lip and all that."

"Nah, you guys are just fucking with me." Cas doesn't believe it. "She couldn't have really fought that girl. That chick must have outweighed her by at least 100 lbs. How could she throw her to the ground? That's bullshit."

"No, man, dead-ass serious," Chen assures him. "Trust me, I thought the gangsta' bitch was gonna wreck her too. But I didn't know the MILF, what's her name? Elizabeth? I didn't know she could kick ass. She was on some OG shit. Right, Jake?"

"She was." Jake smirks in agreement. "She pulled the girl's shirt over her head like a hockey player."

"No!" Cas is shocked. "No way!"

"I was shocked too, but I guess you can't let a pretty face fool you, because man that woman could fight. And it's not like she was just scratching and slapping – she was throwing fists."

Cas is still in disbelief. "But how exactly did they start fighting? Like, I got hit, *BAM*, knocked out, then what happen?"

Jake explains, "As soon as you got hit, you just dropped, *boom*. Elizabeth starts screaming, 'Oh my God,' we're all standing there in shock. Even the girl who hit you is looking at you on the floor like, '*Oh shit*'. Next thing you know, Elizabeth is like, 'You fucking bitch!' and she grabs her by the hair with one hand and with the other hand, she lands like five or six quick punches to her grill – *bam, bam, bam*. Thug girl tries to duck, but when she leans forward, your girl pulls her shirt over her head, like a fucking hockey player, and starts hitting her with uppercuts." Jake uses his hands to demonstrate. "Then Elizabeth throws her to the ground, gets on top of her, and lands a couple more shots before we could grab her and pull her up. Shit, even when we were breaking it up, she was still trying to hit the girl." Jake shakes his head and leans back in his seat. "It was some surreal shit, man. A real wild scene."

Cas is coming to terms with everything he's being told. "The weird thing is I just had a dream she was fighting over me. That's crazy."

Chen asks, "Dream? You mean right now when you were knocked out?"

"Yeah. I was just dreaming about her fighting a girl."

"Was it the thug from the party?" Chen asks curiously.

"Nah, it wasn't the thug girl, it was..." He's about to tell them it was Tiffany but decides against it; he doesn't want to set Jake off on one of his 'Fuck Tiffany' rants. "Uh, I don't know who it was. Just some random chick. She was really hot, though. Both of them. They were wrestling all sexy like; it was actually one of the best dreams I've had in a long time. Too bad you woke me up."

"You were out like a light, man."

130

Cas laughs. "This is so nuts. I can't believe this happened to me."

"Yeah, it's pretty crazy, alright," Jake says, looking down at this phone. "We're actually legitimately worried about you; we're on our way to the hospital right now." He looks up from his phone and gives Chen directions. "Take a right at the next light."

"Hospital?" Cas sits up. "Oh, hell no. For what?"

"Man, you just got knocked out cold; you might have a concussion or something. You have to get it looked at."

"Well I'm up now, and I'm OK. So, no need to go to a hospital. Just take me home."

Chen looks back at Cas briefly. "Hey, Nova, I feel you on not wanting to go to the hospital and all, but you got absolutely rocked, man, and you definitely have a concussion. You should get it checked out."

"Yeah, Cas. She knocked you outta the game. If this was a football match and you got knocked out cold like that, they'd take you off the field, bro. I think getting knocked out is the definition of a concussion."

"I think you're right," Chen chuckles. "That's the concussion test. The question is, did you get knocked out? Answer: yes. Well, then your ass got a concussion."

"Take a left up here."

Cas sits in the middle of the back seat and leans forward to talk to the both of them. "Hey, I appreciate the concern, guys, I really do, but I'm fine. I'm not going to the hospital. I hate hospitals."

Jake looks back at him. "No one *likes* hospitals, but you really need to get yourself checked out."

"Not gonna happen. I'm fine, I just want to go home. I'm good."

131

Chen briefly looks back at him again. "You sure you don't want to go to the hospital? How many fingers am I holding up?" He holds up four.

"Eight," Cas replies with a smirk.

Chen puts his hand down. "Fuck it. I'm tired. I'll take you guys home. Nova, I hope you don't have a brain hemorrhage or something. Jake, GPS your house."

"You don't need GPS. The Henry Hudson is two blocks away. You can take it straight to my house."

"I see it. Cool."

There's a heavy silence in the car as everyone is sitting deep in their own thoughts. Cas feels a slight throbbing on the side of his head and briefly reconsiders going to the hospital but soon decides that the pain is not severe enough and ignores it.

His thoughts are interrupted when he feels his cell phone vibrate in his pocket. Slowly, he takes it out and looks at the screen. It's a text message from Elizabeth. '*Hey, I hope you're ok.*'

Seeing the message puts a smile on Cas's face. He texts her back, '*I'm fine. Just woke up from a nice nap :) but seriously I'm cool, more embarrassed than anything, but I heard you were kicking ass tonite, champ lol*'.

He presses 'Send'. While he waits for a response, he breaks the silence in the car.

"Hey, I don't remember much about being knocked out, but I do remember Chen body slamming one of those dudes. That was crazy, man. You power bombed that motherfucker."

Chen laughs. "The thing is I didn't even want to fight. I hate fighting. I really was trying to keep the peace, but that guy really thought he was tough. And he was so light, I mean, dude, like 150-ish. I lifted him with no problem. But I hate fighting in front of kids and old people. You know they get all worried and stuff, and that's not cool."

Jake adds, "Yeah, I didn't want to fight either, but when his boy pulled out the cutter, I had to snuff him. I hit him good too, nice and flush. Too bad I don't have knockout power like the bitch who laid Cas out."

The three of them break up in laughter.

"Shut up, man. She hit me with a bottle, that shit don't count. It ain't like she punched me. But what happened to that dude you hit? I saw him get chased out of there. Did he get caught?"

"Nah, I didn't chase him, but they said he was running for his life. Lucky for him he didn't get caught. He would have got beat down bad, you can't hit someone's grandpa. That's like blasphemous," adds Jake. "But, hey, did you get Elizabeth's number?"

Cas wrinkles his brow in confusion. "You mean the Elizabeth who you said was out of my league? The one you said I didn't have a chance with? Is that the one you're talking about?"

"No, the other Elizabeth," Jake answers sarcastically. "Did you get her number or what? I hope you did; shit, you were talking to her long enough."

"Yes, I got it," Cas says, sounding proud of himself. "In fact, she just texted me."

"That's what's up, man. I'm happy for you. I could tell she was into you."

"What? All you kept saying is I don't have a chance."

Chen cuts in, "Oh damn, Jake. Just because she shut you down before doesn't mean you have to mess it up for him," he says and briefly looks at Cas. "You know he tried to get with her a couple of times already, right?"

"Really? Wow, and you acted like you didn't even know her name. I'm not surprised." Cas shakes his head. "You're supposed to be my boy; how you trying to sabotage me? What a hater."

"Hater," Chen agrees.

"Hater?" Jake is defensive. "Man, fuck you guys. I'm not trying to sabotage you. I was trying to save you the embarrassment of getting dissed. Obviously, I was wrong, but you know I'm not a *hater*. I've hooked both of you up with women mad times. And you know that's true. A helluva lot more times than you guys ever hooked me up."

Chen looks over at him. "Now, you know I've put you on plenty of times too; so, what's your point?"

"My point is, I'm not a hater..."

As Jake continues talking, Cas's phone vibrates again. He looks at it; it's a text from Elizabeth. '*I hate fighting, but she had that coming... Are you going to the hospital?*'

He replies quickly, '*No, not going to the hospital, I'm fine, I have a hard head, lol... I want to give you a call, are you free to talk?*'

As he hits the 'Send' button, Chen turns up the block where they live. Jake is still talking, "...So, just because I told you not to talk to her doesn't mean..."

"Hey, just forget it, man." Cas is too ecstatic about talking to Elizabeth to let anything else bother him. "I know you were just trying

134

to look out for me, and you're right – you have hooked me up plenty of times. So, don't sweat it; I was just messing with you. Everything is cool."

Jake looks at him for a moment to see if he's being serious; he can tell that he is. He smiles and nods, "Thank you. That's what I'm talking about – real friendship. What a real friend, unlike some of these fair-weather ones, the names of which I won't mention, but they happen to be in the car right now. Possibly driving, even."

Chen starts laughing. "Oh, now I'm a fair-weather friend? Interesting." He pulls up in front of their building. "Well, gentlemen, it's been real. It's been fun. It's been real fun. Now, get the hell out of my truck. I want to go home."

"Take me to Cynthia's," Jake says, looking down at his phone.

"What? No, I don't want to make any more stops. I'm not a fucking cab."

"C'mon man, it's on your way home. It's not putting you out of your way at all."

"Why didn't you mention it earlier?"

"Because I just made the plans. I didn't get the green light until right now. Unless," he looks back at Cas, "You want me to chill at home tonight? You are under concussion protocol. I don't want you to pass out while I'm not around."

"Concussion protocol? That's funny," says Cas, opening the door. "I'm fine, man. You have plans already. I'm good."

"Don't worry about my plans – I just made them. I'll cancel if you're scared to be alone. I know you have that huge knot on your head."

135

"Hey!" Chen is tired and irritated. "You got two seconds to make up your fucking mind. I want to go home."

Cas quickly gets out the car and closes the door. He goes to the driver's window and reaches in to shake Chen's hand. "Good seeing you, my brother. We'll do it again soon. Thanks for the ride."

"No problem, Nova. Talk to you later, bro."

"Yo, Jake, have fun." He gives him a fist bump as he walks by the passenger's side.

"You sure, man?"

"Positive. Call me tomorrow." He nods, moving away from the car.

Jake and Chen watch him closely as he walks to the front of the apartment building, takes out his keys, and opens the lobby door. He feels like a little kid being watched by the adults. He feels good knowing that his friends care.

"Alright guys, later." He throws up a two-finger peace sign and walks through the lobby door.

CHAPTER 6

The Fifth Pocket

Cas is rudely awakened by the sound of his alarm clock. He reaches over to the night stand and hits the snooze button. *Too tired, must sleep.*

He had fallen asleep with his phone in his hand, waiting for Elizabeth to respond. Peeking through one eye, he brings the phone close to his face, hopeful that there's a new message.

It's blank. No new text messages, no missed calls. Instantly disappointed, he tosses the phone to the other side of the bed.

At this point, he feels the dull throb on the side of his head again. He touches the bump, it's painful. "Owww," he says angrily, "Fucking bitch."

The alarm goes off again.

"Fuuuuck," he grumbles and hits the snooze button for a second time.

Cas has a meeting with the assistant editor at the Mistro magazine. They're a contemporary arts and lifestyle mag, catering to the hipster millennial crowd. He's worked with them before, and they'd reach out to him occasionally whenever they'd have an idea for an article that complemented his writing style.

It's not like him to cancel meetings, but the throbbing pain in his head has him seriously considering it. Laying on his back, looking at the ceiling, he tries to decide what to do. His eyelids feel heavy. *I'll just close them for a minute.*

A moment passes before his alarm goes off again. The high-pitch ring of his alarm clock causes the pain in his head to pulsate.

"Fuck it," he says to himself and hits the 'Off' button. Picking up his cell phone, he looks through his contacts, finds 'Johnson', and presses 'Talk'. It rings four times, then goes to voicemail. Pinching his nose to make himself sound congested, Cas talks.

"How are you, Linda? This is Juan Carlos. I'm calling to cancel our appointment today. I'm so sorry for the short notice, but I'm really under the weather and I don't want to risk getting anyone in the office sick. If I don't hear from you, I'll give you a follow up call later this week, once I'm feeling better. I would definitely like to reschedule. Again, I apologize for the short notice. We'll speak soon, bye."

He hits the '#' key to end the message and presses '1' to replay it. His voice sounds nasal and congested, just the effect he was aiming for. *Good enough*, he thinks and hits the '#' key to send it.

As soon as the message is sent, he has second thoughts.

Damn, I should have just gone. Maybe I should call her back and tell her I changed my mind, and I still want to meet today? He thinks about it a little while longer. "Eh, fuck it. What's done is done," he says out loud.

He flips the pillow over to the cooler side and gingerly lays his head back down. Closing his eyes, Cas begins to drift. He's almost fully asleep when he hears the phone beep, indicating there's a new message. He assumes it's an email from Ms. Johnson. Reluctantly reaching for his phone, he turns his head to look at the message; it's from Elizabeth. A surge of energy rushes through his body as he quickly presses the button to view it. He is smiling even before reading.

'Good morning hard head, lol, sorry couldn't talk last night... how are you?'

"Ha!" Cas says aloud, happy to hear from her. He replies, *'I'm good. I canceled a meeting I was supposed to have today, so right now just lying in bed, very comfy n cozy, lol... how about you?'*

The excitement of hearing from Elizabeth has him wide awake. Getting out of bed, he walks over to the bathroom. Midway through brushing his teeth, he hears a notification from his phone in the room; it's a new message. He breaks into a big, soapy smile with toothpaste suds dripping down his chin. He hurries the brushing and anxiously goes to his room to grab the phone.

The excitement on his face quickly drops as he sees that it's not a text from Elizabeth; it's an email from Linda Johnson, the assistant editor for Mistro. He opens the message. *'Sorry to hear you're not feeling well, I was looking forward to meeting you today. Get better and call me to reschedule as soon as you're feeling well enough. Thank you.'*

He shrugs and writes back, *'Will do. Thanks for understanding, and I will be talking to you soon.'*

Cas sends the email and carries the phone with him to the kitchen as he looks for something to eat. Opening the fridge, he takes out a carton of eggs and puts it on the counter by the stove. He opens the freezer to see if there's bacon; there is, but it's frozen stiff. He leaves the frozen meat on the counter and heads back to the bathroom. *By the time I finish showering, it should be thawed enough to cook.*

Cas turns on the hot water, takes off his boxers, and steps in the shower. 20 minutes later, he steps out of the bath feeling fresh and clean. Hastily drying himself off, checks his phone – no new messages, touches the bacon – still frozen stiff. "Wack and wack."

Cas goes back to the bedroom to get dressed. He prefers to be stylishly understated; his favorite clothes are distressed jeans and vintage t-shirts. But he has plenty of options in his closet to cover any event, from business formals to night club wears.

He grabs a pair of faded denim pants and shakes them out, checking all the pockets to see if there's anything in them, hopefully money or weed. All are empty. He goes over to the drawer and grabs a black V-neck t-shirt and a pair of socks. After getting dressed, he looks into the full-length mirror hanging on the back of the bedroom door. He stands up straight to fix his posture and flexes his biceps. *They need a little work.* Cas drops to the floor and starts doing push-ups. It isn't long before he's winded and has to get up; his face is a little red; he can feel the heat from the blood pumping. He flexes his arms again.

"Alright, that's enough for now," he says, smiling at his ridiculously short work-out session.

Feeling good, he strolls back into the kitchen, grabs the bacon, tosses it into the freezer. *I'm not cooking shit.* As he takes his phone from the counter, he knows no one has called or sent a text, but he pushes the button to check anyway. Nothing. He goes over to the desk and turns on his laptop. *Might as well work.*

He opens an article he's working on – a satirical piece comparing political parties to professional sports teams.

After 15 minutes of reading the same three sentences over and over, he leans back in his chair and stares at the ceiling. He's thinking about Elizabeth.

As he is lost in thought, his cell phone suddenly vibrates; the huge smile makes a reappearance on his face. Reaching into his pocket, he quickly takes out the phone and presses the button to view the message. The smile quickly fades; it's a spam text, *'Come party tonight at The Point. Ladies free all nite, guys $25 after 12... $120 bottles all nite!'*

Deleting the text, he puts the phone back into his pocket, feeling annoyed with himself that he's so desperate for a response. *Slow down, man. You just met this woman. No need to get your feelings up.*

He leans back in his chair, thoughts swirling in his head, when he feels something in the small fifth pocket of his jeans. Sticking his index finger in there, he pulls out a small folded piece of paper. Opening it, he finds a phone number on it, with the words 'Call me.'

It takes a moment before he remembers. *The waitress from the dinner! Damn, I forgot all about her. Maybe I should call? No, it's been like a week, she probably won't even remember who I am. She was really pretty, though. What was her name again? Shit, I can't remember.*

Staring at the small piece of paper, he contemplates whether or not to call. He's interrupted by the vibration of his cell phone; it's another message. Almost knowing that the text is probably not from Elizabeth, he takes it out and looks at it; it's not her. It's from Jake, *'What up, homeboy? How's your noggin roggin feeling?'*

Cas gives a brief chuckle and texts back, *'The noggin is good, thnx.'*

141

He sends the message and places the phone next to his computer. His thoughts wander back to the waitress. Picking up his phone, he texts Jake again, *'Hey do you remember the name of the waitress who gave me her number?'*

Jake quickly responds, *'Megan.'*

"Megan!" Cas says out loud, "That's right, her name is Megan." He sends Jake another message, *'Good looking.'*

Leaning back in his chair, he plays with the small piece of paper in his hand, flicking it back and forth between his fingers. *Well, you know her name now; so, there's no excuse not to call.* He looks over at the time; it's 10:30 AM.

He tosses the small piece of paper on his desk, gets up from his chair, and drops to the floor to do push-ups. He knocks out 30 reps before he stops. Getting up and feeling a bit winded, he breathes in deep and exhales slowly. Looking at the piece of paper, he abruptly decides. *Screw it, I'm going to text her.*

He begins writing a message. *'Hey, Megan. This is Cas... I don't know if you remember me, we met at the dinner the other day... Anyway, just wanted to say hi...'*

After sending the text, he wonders if it sounded foolish. He doesn't have much time to mull over it before his cell begins to vibrate; it's a message from Megan. *'How can I forget a name like Casanova, lol. It's not every day I give my # out, so yes I definitely remember you :) What up, how you been?'*

Joy rushes through him; he begins to text her back, *'I'm just chilling, had a little accident over the weekend so I took the day off today, just going to hang around the house... how about you?'*

A few minutes pass and she writes back, '*Accident? Oh no, sorry to hear that :(I hope you're OK. I'm good though, I have the day off too, but no hanging around for me, lol, I have some errands to run.*'

Cas looks over the message and thinks what to write back. He would like to see her but isn't sure if it would be too soon to ask her on a date. After a little while, he begins to text, '*Do you want to meet up for lunch later?*'

Looking at what he wrote, he wonders if it sounds desperate and if she would think he's moving too fast. Closing his eyes, he presses 'Send' before he has more time to second guess himself.

He gets out of his seat and begins to pace around the room. *Damn, I hope I didn't just fuck myself up. I probably should have held off on asking to see her. She's gonna think I'm rushing her.* His thoughts are interrupted by his cell phone ringing. Looking at the screen, he's surprised to see it's Megan's number.

He answers, "Hello?"

"Hey! Is this Casanova?" asks the sweet, southern voice on the other end of the line.

"Yes, it is. This is Megan, right?" he asks, knowing it's her.

"It's me," she says, laughing, making Cas smile.

"I just texted you to see if you wanna meet up for lunch."

"Yeah, I got it, but I'm not too sure." She sounds skeptical. "I mean, I kind of want to, but at the same time, I don't really know you like that. How do I know you're not some psycho killer?"

"Me?" Cas says, playfully, "You're the one who gave me your number all secretive like. I should be worried, you could be a stalker."

143

Megan chuckles. "You got me on that one. That was a bit *stalkerish*."

He smiles. "No, that was actually really cool of you. But don't worry, I'm not a psycho killer. Besides, it's just lunch; it'll be in a well-lit public setting."

She laughs. "A well-lit public setting, you say?"

"I'm a gentleman," Cas answers.

There's silence for a few moments before Megan speaks again.

"So, what time are you thinking about having *just* lunch?"

"You tell me," he answers, excited at the prospect of going out on a date, even if it is *just* lunch. "I'm free all day; so, whenever you're ready, I'm good to go."

"Hmmm, OK, I have to go to my school to register, then I have to go to the bank, and after that I'm free. So, I say about 2, no make it 3. Is 3 cool for you?"

"3 is fine with me," he answers, trying not to sound overly excited.

"Great. So, I see you then. Where you wanna meet at?"

He thinks for a moment. "Ah, I'm not exactly sure yet, but we have some time, so I'll figure it out by 3."

"Sounds good."

"Definitely. I'll hit you up a little later. But we're definitely on, right?" he asks.

"Yeah, for sure. Why not? I wouldn't say yes if I didn't mean it."

Cas is relieved. "Cool, I'm looking forward to it."

"Me too," Megan's cheery voice assures him.

"Great. So, I'll see you soon."

"Alright, see you soon. Bye, Cas."

"Bye," he says and hangs up the phone.

Cas can't contain his smile. "Sweet!"

He looks at his bong and begins to talk to himself, "Should I smoke? Nah, don't do it, you don't want to be all slow and potted on your first date. But then again, you do have a few hours to kill. You can smoke now, play some games, and be sobered up by the time you have to meet with her." He likes to rationalize his stoning.

He walks over to the living room table, where there's a small wooden cigar box. From the inside of it, he pulls out a zip-lock bag that has several green leafy buds; he takes one out and begins to break it up.

Suddenly, he has a change of heart and puts the weed back in the bag and closes the cigar box. Cas gets down on the floor and starts doing push-ups. After several reps, he stands back up and admires his hard, swollen arms. "Nice."

He takes his phone back out and starts to write a new text, *'Hey, where's your school at? I'll meet you around there.'*
He sends it to Megan. Less than a minute passes before his phone goes off; it's a new message. He looks at the screen and his eyes widen in surprise. It's a text from Elizabeth. *'Hi you. Sorry took so long to get back... but what's up? What do you have planned for your day off?'*

Cas puts his hand on his head, annoyed by his mixed emotions. On one hand, he's really excited that Elizabeth has responded to him; on the other, he feels a little guilty because he's about to go meet Megan for lunch.

What the hell am I feeling guilty for? It's not like I'm doing something wrong. I just met these women, just getting to know them.

He grabs the phone and starts to text back. Not wanting to give too much information to Elizabeth, he decides that vague is the way to go. *'Hey,'* he begins to write, *'I was wondering what happened to you, I thought you forgot about me, lol... I'm actually going to meet up with a friend for lunch and that's about it... how about you?'*

Pressing the 'Send' button, Cas feels good about the text; he doesn't have to lie or tell her everything. He also likes that the message leaves room for mystery, thinking, *I'm sure she's probably wondering whether the friend I'm meeting up with is a woman or not, which is good. Lets her know her boy is a hot commodity. I'm a busy guy around these parts.* He nods, as if to agree with his thrilled ego.

The phone goes off with a new message; it's from Megan. *'I'm confused. I thought we were meeting up for lunch? Do you have other plans?'*

"Oh shit," he says out loud, realizing he sent his last message to the wrong girl. He quickly writes back, *'Lol, I'm sorry, that message was meant for one of my boys, they wanted to chill and I was writing back to let them know I'm going to lunch with a friend, which is you, lol, pretty lady.'*

He sends the text and begins to nervously pace around his apartment, slight panic swirling in his thoughts. *You gotta be careful, man; that could have been disastrous. Holy shit, that could have been disastrous. Thank God your explanation made sense, because technically, it is the truth. Except I told her it was one of my boys instead of another woman, which is cool because she doesn't need to know that anyway.*

146

He goes through his cell phone and forwards the correct message to Elizabeth. Then, flipping to his Contacts screen, he saves both numbers under their proper names.

A new message – it's Megan. *'Oh, that's cool, lol, it happens :) I go to Hunter on 68th street, you can meet me there at 3.'*

Before he can write back, another text comes in; this one is from Elizabeth. *'I'm actually getting out of work early today, so I'm looking forward to that.'*

Instantly, Cas thinks about asking Elizabeth to meet, even if it means canceling his plans with Megan. The thought rapidly vanishes. *No, I can't do that, that wouldn't be right. I'll keep my date.*

He replies to Elizabeth, *'Sweet! Getting out early is always a good thing.'*

He then writes to Megan, *'I'll be there at 3, right outside the train station... See you soon.'*

He sends the messages and leans back in his chair, holding the phone in his hand. He's looking forward to his date with Megan, but his thoughts continue to drift towards Elizabeth. He compares the two women in his mind. *They're both very pretty in their own way. Megan has a sweet, southern disposition, bubbly even; but there's something about Elizabeth, she's just so damn sexy. She's curvier; her legs, ass, hips, tits are all thicker, juicier. She's a full-grown woman, someone fleshed out as a MILF fantasy, a cougar goddess...*

As he continues pondering on the difference between the two, his phone goes off; it's a new message from Elizabeth. *'Yes it is. I'll probably just relax in the house by myself, cuddled up in bed with a book.'*

Cas sits up and types, '*Maybe I can keep you company,*' but doesn't send it; he's not sure if he should. He doesn't want to come across as aggressive, even though the thought of her cuddled up in bed makes his dick take immediate notice.

Pressing the delete button, he erases the message without sending it. *It would be foolish to try and see both girls on the same day. Just play it safe.*

'*Sounds like you have an exciting evening planned out, lol, don't hurt yourself.*' He sends the text, gets up, and goes to his room; he is not sure he wants to wear what he already has on to his lunch date. He goes to his drawer and begins to go through some of his vintage-looking tees. He finds a gray one that has an ace of spades card on the front. He hasn't worn that one in a while and decides to put it on. The shirt sleeves fit tightly around his arms, which he especially likes, since his arms look a little swollen from the sets of push-ups he'd just done.

Going back to the living room, he grabs his cell phone from the desk; it has a new message from Elizabeth. '*Yea, my exciting life, lol... well I know you have things to do so I'll speak to you some other time, call me later if you want.*'

Cas feels that she's waiting for him to ask to see her. It's driving him crazy because he wants to see her too, but he already has plans. He gives in and presses the 'Talk' button on his phone to call her. It rings thrice before she answers.

"Hello." Elizabeth's voice sounds sultry and sexy, just how he remembers it.

"Hey, what's up? It's Cas. What's going on?"

"*Nada.* Leaving work now; can't wait to get home," Elizabeth says.

Her voice is turning him on. "That's cool," says Cas, trying to sound smooth, his hand absentmindedly reaching down and grabbing his dick that is starting to stiffen. "You know, I wish I had known before that you were gonna be free so early today; I would have loved to see you."

"Even if you'd known," she begins, "How do you know I would have wanted to see you?"

Her smart remarks and breathy voice are getting him hard; he wants this woman bad.

"That's true. I don't know, but I guess, I would hope you would want to hang," he pauses for a moment, "Would you have wanted to see me?"

"Eh," Elizabeth says, sounding unimpressed. "It doesn't matter now since you already have plans."

"Yeah, I know I have plans, beautiful, but if I didn't have plans, would you have wanted to see me?"

"Beautiful?" she responds nonchalantly. "Maybe."

"Maybe? Damn, just maybe?"

She answers, "Just maybe."

Cas can tell she is playing hard to get, which turns him on more, he tightens the grip around his cock. "Oh yeah? Well, maybe I can just hang up the phone on you now, and then maybe I'll call you later. Alright Miss Maybe?"

She laughs at his comment. "Oh, so you gonna hang up on me?"

"Maybe," Cas answers playfully.

"That's not nice," she says, her voice getting sexier.

149

Cas lowers his voice, trying to match her sexiness, "Who said I was nice?"

"Oh, so you're a bad boy?"

"I'm as bad or as good as you want me to be."

"Really?" she answers, "Well, I don't want you to be bad, only good."

He's rock hard. "Oh, I'm *good*."

"Good at what?" she asks curiously.

Cas is thrown off by the question. "Eh, I'm, ah, good at..."

Before he can finish, she laughs and cuts him off, "No, let me stop, this is getting a little crazy. I'm just messing with you, *papi*. So, what time you going to lunch with your friend?"

Feeling lame he couldn't come up with a quicker response to what he's good at, Cas lets go of his cock and exhales deeply. "I'm meeting up with them at 3," he says.

Elizabeth asks, "Who's *them*? A hot girl?"

"Not as hot as you."

"Is that supposed to be a compliment?"

"No, just the truth," he replies, smirking at how cool he thought that sounded.

"Okay. So, who is this girl? Your girlfriend?"

"No, no, not at all. I don't have a girl. I'm very much single."

"Yeah, I should have known you're a player. You did say Jake is your best friend."

"He is. But I'm not Jake. We are very different people. Judge me for me, not by the company I keep."

150

"Said like a true writer. Give me another one of your lines," she says, sounding sarcastic but still very sexy.

"Wow, you're something else. You know that? But I mean it though, I'm not like him; I'm my own person."

"They say dogs run in packs."

Cas laughs. "Oh please, then what about you? Using your logic, I have to be careful with you, considering how your friend got down at the party. She was pretty crazy with it; so, you're just like her?"

"Samantha is a friend of a friend," Elizabeth says defensively. "We're cool, but we're not close at all. And you shouldn't be talking bad about her because you sure didn't mind grinding all up on her."

"I'm not talking bad about her. I'm just saying from the limited amount of time I had around her, she doesn't seem very shy, and you hang out with her; so, what does that say about you?"

"It doesn't say anything about me. She's a grown woman and can do whatever she likes; it's not a reflection on me."

"Exactly," Cas says, enjoying his conversation with her. "That's precisely my point. You can't be judged by the friends you have. I mean you can be, but it's unfair."

"Yeah, but it's different."

"How do you figure? Because you're a female, it's different?"

"No," Elizabeth begins, "It's different because Jake is your best friend and I barely know Samantha. Yes, we've hung out before because we know some of the same people and occasionally run in the same circle, but again, we're not close at all. We've never gone out, just me and her, and we've never talked on the phone."

"Fair enough. But still, like I said, I'm not Jake; we're two very different people."

"Okay, I got you. I will judge you based on you, just like you said."

"Thank you."

"Anyway, let me let you go. I've been standing in front of the train station for like five minutes talking to you, and I'm about to go downstairs."

"You been standing talking on the phone with me instead of going into the train station? I feel special."

"You should."

"I do."

"Good, I'm glad I can make you feel special," she says, laughing lightly. "Anyway, it was nice talking to you, Mr. Casanova."

"Same here, Ms. Elizabeth. Talk to you later."

"Bye."

The phone goes dead, but Elizabeth's voice lingers in his ear; Cas wishes she was still on the line. He puts the phone down and shakes his head. "Damn, she's sexy."

He drops on the floor to do push-ups, counting out loudly at first, "1, 2, 3, 4..." then continuing in his head. His intentions are to pull off 30, but he gets to 26 and his arms feel dead. He counts out loud again to motivate himself, struggling to finish the last few.

"Arrhh 28...," he says as he holds his body up with his arms extended from the ground; he goes back down for the next one, his chest an inch off the floor, he extends his arm up again.

"29." *One more!* Bending his arms, he goes back down to the floor and tries to lift himself up one more time, "ARRRHHH!" His triceps are on fire, his forearms are trembling, the weight of his body overcomes his will and he falls flat on his chest. "Ahhhhh," he moans, sprawled out on the ground, out of breath but pleased with himself, even though he couldn't finish the full 30.

Still breathing hard, he picks himself up off the ground and flexes his arms. *Not bad.* He is especially surprised because this was the first iota of exercise he'd done in a few months.

Picking up his phone from the desk, he checks for messages – there are none; so, he closes his laptop, steps into the living room, and flops himself down on the sofa. He takes the cable remote laying on the coffee table and turns on his TV. He starts watching the local news. A few minutes go by before his eyes start to feel heavy – he's sleepy. He looks at the time, it's 11:47 AM – plenty of time to squeeze in a power nap before he heads to lunch with Megan.

Using the remote, he lowers the volume on the TV, lays out on the sofa, and closes his eyes. A little faint smile shows on his face as he eases into sleep.

CHAPTER 7

Just Lunch

Cas steps out of the train station on East 68th street, Hunter College. Walking up the stairs leading out of the subway, he looks at his cell phone; it's 2:58 PM.

He never did make breakfast; by the time he'd woken up from his nap, he figured it would be better for him to hold his appetite for lunch. His stomach regrets making that decision, manifesting that regret through hunger pangs. He's not used to going that late into the day without eating.

There's a hot dog cart on the sidewalk just outside the school. It's a halal grill with chicken and rice; the smell has him salivating instantly.

Cas walks away from the aroma and tries get his mind off food. Looking at his phone again, he realizes it's 3:06 PM. *Damn, where is this girl? I'm starving.*

He sends her a text, '*Hey I'm in front of the train station outside your school.*' A couple of minutes pass, then his phone vibrates with a message.

'*Hi, I'm coming down now. See you in 2 mins.*'

Slipping the phone into his pocket, he sits down on the concrete bench in front of one of the entrances to the college. He takes out his phone again and begins catching up on some social media, just trying to kill time. After a few more minutes pass, he's bored with the phone and his hunger pangs make him feel nauseous. He checks the time; it's 3:21 PM.

Damn, what the hell is taking her so long! I just wanna eat!

While contemplating whether he should send her another text, he feels someone tap him on his shoulder. He turns around; Megan is standing there with a big smile on her face.

"Hiya! Sorry I'm so late," she says in her Southern drawl, "It took me much longer to register than I thought it would. I had to choose a bunch of different classes than the ones I wanted since they were all about full. I know you must'a been thinking 'Where the heck is this girl,'" she says with a laugh.

Her sweet Southern voice and easy-going smile erase any bad feelings Cas had developed during that 20-minute wait.

Smiling back, he replies, "Eh, don't worry about it; it was just a few minutes."

"No, it was longer than that, but thanks for waiting," she says, looking at her watch.

"It's cool; don't mention it." The noise in his stomach reminds him that it needs food, "So, ready to eat?" he asks.

"Oh gosh, I am so hungry."

"You're not the only one; I'm freaking starving. What's good around here?"

"There's this great diner over by 62nd and 1st avenue; we could go there if you like."

"That'll work. Let's do it."

He gets up, and they begin to walk. After half a block, he asks her, "So what's your major?"

"Child psychology."

155

"Child psychology? So, what's that like, being a psychiatrist for kids?"

"Yup, I could become a child psychiatrist if I like," Megan replies, looking at Cas. "I can do that or become like a social worker or even a high school guidance counselor. I can also become a coordinator at an adoption agency and find kids good homes. I mean, there are so many options in that field."

"So, I take it you like kids?"

"Oh, for sure! I love kids. I want to work in a field that helps 'em, you know? It kills me when I see stories about child abuse or neglect on the news; I just don't understand how anyone could really hurt a child! They're so innocent and precious."

Cas is thoroughly impressed with her passion to help children. "I think it's great how you want to do something that actually makes a difference. I respect that. Do you want to have any kids of your own?"

"Moving a little too fast there, partner," replies Megan with a smirk, "Slow down, cowboy."

"Ha! I didn't even think of that. But you're right. That does seem a bit forward."

"Just a bit," she teases, "But, shoot, I don't know. Maybe."

"Really? *Maybe*? That's surprising; you seem to be so into children, I would think, without a doubt, you would want to have kids."

"I mean, don't get me wrong – I love children, but being a parent is such huge responsibility. And at the present, my life is so hectic with work and school, and just adapting to the big city and all. I can't even think about having a child now. But I reckon one day, when all the dust settles and I'm happily married, that's when I'll really start to think about it."

"I hear ya," says Cas.

Megan looks at him. "What about you? Do you want to have kids?"

"I already have."

"Really?" She sounds surprised. "How many? One?"

"Four," he answers calmly.

"Four! You have four children? Are you serious?"

Cas bursts into laughter and shakes his head, "No. I don't have any kids."

"Oh man, you got me so good." Megan smiles. "That was a good one."

"Thanks. But yeah, maybe at some point I'll have a kid – just one, though." He looks at her. "Like you said, it's a lot of responsibility."

"Exactly," she agrees. "Have you finished school already?"

"High school? No, I dropped out. I'm still planning on getting my GED online at some point, but I've been really busy with this whole bike messenger thing for the last couple of years; so, there's that."

She looks at him, her face a mixture of shock, horror, and intrigue. "You didn't graduate high school?"

Cas looks back at her skeptically. "Why? Is that a problem?"

Megan's unsure of how to respond. "Um, I guess, uh, not..."

Before she could finish, Cas interrupts, "Ha! I'm totally fucking with you. Of course, I graduated high school." He chuckles. "You should've seen your face. You didn't know if you should judge me or feel sorry. I just got you twice in like five minutes. You're too easy."

157

Megan shrugs and smiles. "No, you didn't get me because I didn't believe you, and if you were telling the truth, I wouldn't have judged you anyway."

Cas winks at her. "Right."

She looks at him, a quizzical expression on her face. "But you all did graduate high school, right?"

"Yes. College too."

"Nice. What school?"

"I graduated from Stony Brook."

"Oh, I know Stony Brook. I hear it's a party school; is that true?"

"All schools are party schools," he says as they approach the entrance of the diner. "Is this the spot?"

"Yeppers. The food is so good here," she replies and opens the door. Cas walks in behind her; he briefly looks down to steal a sneak peek at her body.

Just beyond the entrance, there's a hostess waiting.

Megan smiles and lifts two fingers up. "Table for two."

The hostess smiles back. "Table for two, follow me please."

She grabs two menus and leads them towards a booth by the window. They take a seat and the hostess lays out a menu in front of them both. "Your server will be right with you."

Cas and Megan sit down across each other. Before they have a moment to speak, a waiter approaches the table. He greets them dryly.

"Hi, my name is Lee. I'll be your server today. Can I get you something to drink?"

Megan answers first, "I'll have water and..." she looks at Cas, "Are you ready to order?"

158

"Yeah, I think so." His hungry eyes intensely viewing the menu, he says, "You can order first."

"OK. I'm going to get the grilled chicken salad," she answers.

"Grilled chicken salad," the waiter confirms, "And what about you, sir?"

"Let me get…" Cas's eyes continue to scan the menu as he talks, "I'll take the triple decker sandwich, ham, roast beef, and instead of turkey, can I have it with bacon?"

"You want turkey bacon?"

"No, I want *bacon* bacon."

Megan laughs, causing Cas to chuckle too.

"You want bacon instead of turkey?" the waiter asks.

"Exactly."

"You got it. Would you like something to drink with that?"

"Yeah, I'll take a Pepsi, please."

"No problem. I'll be right back with your drinks." He takes the two menus off the table.

"Thank you," says Megan as the waiter walks away. She looks at Cas with a sly smile. "Hungry?"

"Oh yeah, I'm starving. I haven't eaten all day."

"Yeah, I can tell. What did you get? Ham, roast beef, and bacon? Sounds super heart-healthy."

"Oh, you got jokes? Well, sorry I'm not a vegan. I like to enjoy the food I eat. Unlike you, Miss Salad rabbit food."

"Hey, salad isn't rabbit food. And just because it's healthy doesn't mean it tastes bad. I like myself a good salad."

159

Cas grins. "Maybe that's my problem; I've never had a good salad."

"I'll make you one, one day."

He raises an eyebrow. "OK. I'm gonna hold you to that."

"Good," Megan answers.

They both sit silent for moment, seemingly searching for something to say. Megan speaks before the silence becomes awkward.

"So, Casanova, tell me something."

Cas reaches for his water. "Something," he replies quickly and takes a sip.

"Ha, ha. I'm serious."

"OK, serious. What do you want to know?"

"How old are you? If you don't mind me asking."

Cas sits up straight and clears his throat. "Actually, I do mind. I'm very sensitive about my age, and I would appreciate if you stay out of my personal affairs."

"What?" Megan looks at him skeptically. "No, you can't be serious."

"No, I can't be," he concedes with a smile. "I think it's funny to say *I do mind*, when someone asks, 'Do you mind?'"

"So, you like being a jerk? That brings you joy?"

"No, of course not. It's just a funny response. Next time someone comes up to you and is like, 'Excuse me, do you mind?' just answer, 'Yes. In fact, I do mind.' It's funny as hell."

Megan nods, "Yup, you sound like a total New York City a-hole."

"No, I'm really not." Cas laughs. "But seriously, to answer your question, I'm 26."

Her eyes widen. "Stop lying. You're at least 30."

"No." He's offended. "Why? Do I look that old to you?"

"Well, you certainly don't look 26-young."

"Ouch."

"And you have the cynicism of a person who's lived a longer life."

"Damn. Tell me how you really feel."

"Oops, sorry about that. But you know what I mean."

"No, I don't know what you mean. And I don't think you're really sorry. I think you hide behind that sweet Southern accent to make some very pointed comments."

"You're right, I'm not sorry," she says with a wicked smile. "I can be an asshole to an asshole."

Cas stares at her, trying to think of a witty comeback, when he's struck by just how pretty she is. Her eyes are light blue, her mouth is small but her lips are cute and full; she has a perfect pair of puckers.

"You're very pretty; do you know that? You have a great smile."

She half smiles and tilts her head. "You mean that? Or are you just playing with me again?"

"I'm serious; no fooling around this time. You're very, very pretty."

"Aww, that's sweet. Thank you."

"You're welcome," he says, still staring at her, appreciating how attractive she is.

"So, you never asked me how old I am?"

161

Cas smiles, "How old?"

"Guess."

"Hmmm, if I had to take a gander..."

Megan cuts him off, "Yes, please gander away."

"I would say, 24?"

"I'm 22."

"Wow, 22! You're a baby."

"Oh please. What are you, four years older than me? Yeah, you're a real old foogie. How old did you think I was anyway?"

"I knew you were young; I just didn't think you were *that* young."

"Really? Does my age bother you? Can't keep up with a young country gal?"

"Oh, I can keep up." He says with a grin, "I like 'em young and supple."

"Spoken like a true dirty old man," Megan remarks with a laugh as the waiter approaches the table with their food.

He places the chicken salad in front of her and the triple decker sandwich in front of Cas.

"Enjoy," he says and walks off.

Megan looks down at her food. "Yummy."

When she looks up, Cas has already taken a big bite from his sandwich and is chewing with his mouth full.

Nodding his head in agreement, he pushes the food in his mouth to the side so he can try to talk. "Delicious."

"I told ya, they make good food here."

"So, Megan, I have to know something." Cas swallows the bite and takes a drink of his soda to wash it down. "You seem really cool and sweet, and you're obviously very driven and very pretty; so, why are you single?"

Megan looks at him with a confused look. "Who told you I was single? I never said that."

"Ah, what do you mean? I just assumed." Cas is caught off guard. "Why would you be here with me if you have a boyfriend?"

"Who said anything about a boyfriend?" she answers with a smirk.

"What?" Cas laughs and half-jokingly adds, "What, do you have a girlfriend?"

Megan shrugs. "Maybe."

"Are you serious?"

She just shrugs again, which Cas translates as a 'yes'.

"Wow, wow, wow." He smiles widely and nods as he processes this revelation. "And here I am, thinking you're this sweet, innocent, Southern girl. Little did I know that you're a little bisexual freak!"

"Hey, I am sweet and Southern," she says while taking a bite from her salad, "I don't know too much about innocent though."

Cas is staring at her with his mouth open, dumbfounded. Megan laughs. "You gonna eat or what?"

Abruptly closing his mouth, he looks down at his food and smiles. "Oh yeah."

He's still hungry but has lost interest in his food; all his attention is on Megan and her dual sexual preference. Taking a modest bite from his sandwich, he asks her, "So, how long have you been into girls?"

"How long? Well, in high school, I noticed that I was attracted to girls."

"Aren't most girls attracted to other girls?" he asks.

"No. That's actually ridiculous. Why would you think that?"

"Because I always hear women talk about how hot other women are. Saying stuff like she has a gorgeous body or she has a beautiful face. Women stay on other women's shit, man. That why I think women, for the most part, are really attracted to other women."

Megan laughs out loud. "That's so funny. Just cause a female says another female is pretty doesn't mean she's attracted to her; it just means she's acknowledging her beauty. That has nothing to do with being gay or bisexual."

"It's just crazy to us because guys are not like that at all. You'll never really hear a straight guy say another guy is attractive."

"Yeah, you do – guys just do it differently. I've heard guys says stuff like, 'that guy is buff' or 'his arms are huge.' Subconsciously, all you're doing is commenting on things you think are attractive about a guy."

"Yeah, maybe. I never thought of it like that."

"Of course, you haven't," she says with a smile. "But when I said I started finding girls attractive in high school, I'm not talking about just thinking another girl is pretty; I'm talking, like, looking at another girl and getting aroused. Looking at her and having visions of being with her romantically."

As the conversation progresses, Cas can feel his dick starting to beef up in his pants.

"I see. So, when did you actually pursue your first girl?"

"Freshman year in college."

"Oh, so that's fairly recent – only a coupl'a years ago."

"Yeah, I guess. It was on a ski trip with a group of friends. During winter break, we rented this really cool cabin for like four days; it was awesome – a great trip. But the first morning there, everyone had left the cabin for breakfast, and I was in there alone, taking a shower," she pauses to take another bite from her salad.

Cas inhales deeply, trying to appear calm. "Okay, go on."

"Whoa, you seem a little too eager to hear this story. And you called me a freak?"

"Hey, you brought it up!" he says defensively; trying not to sound like a complete horn dog. "You don't have to tell me if you don't want to. We can talk about whatever you want. I'm just interested in getting to know you." He takes a drink of his water. "But if you want to continue with the story, that would be fantastic. No pressure whatsoever."

"Yeah OK, perv." She laughs, taking another bite. "Anyway, I heard someone come into the bathroom; I didn't know who it was, but I didn't really pay it any heed because these are all close friends. So, I just kept taking a shower. Then, out of nowhere, someone dumped a cup of freezing cold water over the shower curtain. I screamed because it was so freaking cold." She smiles and shakes her head at the memory. "I peek outta the curtain, and it's my friend Anu, cracking up like it's the funniest thing ever, which is making me start to laugh a bit, and I'm like 'Anu, you bitch, what are you doing?' And she's just staring, grinning ear to ear. So, I'm like, 'Alright, guess my shower is done.' But before I can grab my towel, she pulls the curtain back while I'm still naked. I'm like, 'Anu, close the freaking curtain!' and obviously

165

my first reaction when she pulled the curtain back was to cover my chest with my hands; so, she's like 'Why are you covering your tits?' and I'm like, 'I don't know'. So, she grabs my hand and pulls them away, leaving me standing there, my breasts fully exposed."

Cas and his cock are thoroughly immersed in her story, paying full attention.

"She's just staring at me, and I'm like, 'What's up? Why are you staring at me? And she's like, 'These' and she grabs my tits, gentle, you know, and I was going to stop her, but for some reason I didn't. I just stood there and let her feel my breasts, and she started sucking them." Megan pauses for a moment. "I can't believe I'm telling you this."

"Hey, I'm an open-minded dude; I don't judge," Cas says, hoping that she continues.

"I guess it's too late to stop now, seeing how I've told you this much already." She laughs again. "Before I knew it, she was finger banging me. And it felt different, and it felt a little weird, but I knew I was into it because I didn't feel grossed out about having a girl touching me like that. It actually felt good, like really good."

Cas is listening with his mouth open, crumbs falling off his lips; he's lost all interest in the sandwich.

"And that's pretty much how it all started. The rest of the trip, every chance we got, her and I would sneak away to make out and stuff." She ends the story nonchalantly and puts a fork with pierced salad leaves and chicken in her mouth.

Cas tries to play it cool, but he's hard and horny as hell and would love to passionately bang Megan right there on the table.

Trying to gather himself, he clears his throat and starts talking, "Ahh, OK, that is pretty, pretty intense. I'm thoroughly impressed. Next time you and Anu are going to see each other to catch up on old times, let me know – I'm treating."

Megan laughs. "Oh, shut up. Such a typical male. Why do guys love to see two women together? I know there's some women who like to see two guys together, but for the most part, women are not aroused seeing two guys go at it. What is so special about two women having sex?"

Cas is amazed at the question. "Where do I start? I mean, what's not to like about that? You gotta understand, women are beautiful, sensual, sexual, beings; and if you have two of them going at it, it's like magic. Like looking at a unicorn or something like that."

Megan almost spits out her food laughing. "What! Like looking at a unicorn? You're so extra right now."

He starts to laugh too. "Yeah, I guess that is a little extreme, but you know what I mean. To us, to men, there's just something exotic about two women being together. It's hot."

He takes a bite of his sandwich. After chewing for a moment, he asks, "Which do you prefer, men or women?"

Megan shrugs. "It depends." She chews her salad and ponders on it a little. "It depends on who I'm with and how I'm feeling at that point. The girly girl side of me prefers a man, someone who is strong and overpowering and makes me feel safe."

Cas raises an eyebrow. Megan feels the need to clarify her comment. "Of course, when I say overpower, I don't mean I want a guy to try and flex on me. I'm not into being pushed around or anything like that. I don't like guys who are overly aggressive. I just mean the feeling of knowing someone is stronger than me – it can be a turn on."

"I got you," Cas assures her. "So, when are you usually in the mood to be with a girl?"

"When I'm feeling really sexy and strong and just want to let go of all my inhibitions. I'm a lot freakier when I'm with a woman as opposed to when I'm with a guy. Even the way I dress is different."

"What you mean? Like you dress all masculine when you're with a girl?"

She gives Cas a crooked look. "C'mon, me? Dressing up masculine? Of course not. I always dress feminine to a certain extent. What I mean is when I go out with a woman, I tend to dress even sexier than I would for a guy," she says as she takes another forkful of salad. She chews for a moment, "I'm always going to try to look nice, and for night-out dancing, I want to look sexy, but I wouldn't dress as sexy for man as I would for a woman."

"Why?" Cas asks. "I would think it would be the opposite; I mean, doesn't it make more sense for you to look sexier for a dude than what you would for a chick?"

"Heck no. Women appreciate it more. Like a man would just think 'Damn, she looks hot, I wanna hit that'. A woman knows, she understands the effort a female puts in to look really nice. They appreciate everything more. When you go out with a woman, and she looks all hot and sexy, there is the understanding that it has taken a lot of thought and effort to put that look together. Women get that."

"That makes sense. It really does make sense," says Cas, envisioning Megan in sexy black lingerie, wearing stilettos, with a whip in her hand, spanking the ass of a hot chick.

"Just so you know," Megan begins talking, which brings Cas back from his mini daydream, "I'm not the type of girl who goes sleeping around. Yeah, I like guys and girls, but that doesn't mean I just go bed-hopping from one to the next. I'm not into casual sex at all. If I have sex with someone, man or woman, there is definitely more meaning behind it than just a screw."

"No doubt," Cas answers, a little surprised by her tone. "Just so you know, I didn't think of you like that anyway."

"Yeah, but I know how you guys are," she begins talking in a deep manly voice, "Yo, shorty is bi, bro! I'm gonna have a threesome, yo!"

Cas cracks up. "Oh, word; that's what men sound like?"

"New York men? Yeah, bro," she says in the same tone; they both start laughing.

"Well," Cas begins, "Don't worry because I don't look at you that way, anyway. I do think its insanely sexy that you're into women, but that in no way suggests I think you're easy or anything like that." He pauses to take a bite from the sandwich, before nonchalantly adding, "I just think you're a little freak, that's all."

Megan nods her head and speaks, her tone is condescending, "Is that all that you think? Really? I'm just some little freak to you? Interesting."

"It *is* interesting, isn't it?" he says jokingly.

"Oh, shut up," she says, laughing at him, "So what about you, Cas? Why are you single? You seem like a good enough catch – college grad, successful writer..."

He cuts her off, "Successful writer? That's up for debate. I don't know what you would qualify as successful."

"Success to me is very easily definable. Do you enjoy writing?"

"Yeah, I enjoy it. I'd like to think I'm good at it too."

"Do you make enough money to pay your bills and live comfortably?"

"Yup."

"So, you enjoy writing and you make enough money from it to support yourself?"

"Yeah. I mean I'm not well off or anything like that, but I definitely make enough to cover my bills and not live completely check to check."

"Alright then, in my book, that's true success. You're making a living doing something you enjoy doing; it doesn't get much better than that. There are a lot of people in this world who make a lot of money but are miserable because they don't like their job. Worse than that are the people who make a little bit of money and still hate their job. So, you should consider yourself a success."

"Hey, according to your criteria, I guess I am," he says, feeling good about himself.

"Okay, then; so, *why are you* single?"

Cas's momentary elation dissipates as his stomach starts to turn. *I'm single because my ex girl was an escort from the back pages of the Village Voice*, he thinks, but decides against actually saying it aloud.

He looks down at his sandwich before saying, "I guess I just haven't found the right one yet. I thought I did with my last serious relationship, but over time I realized we weren't compatible, and we had to end it."

"Oh, okay. How long did you date?" she asks, genuinely interested.

"Almost a year. We broke up right before we would have made a year."

"Dang, that's tough. Was there any particular reason why y'all broke up?" Megan asks, sounding sorry for him.

"Oh yeah, definitely."

"What? If you don't mind me asking."

"Actually, I do mind."

Megan laughs. "Ha! I get it now. It is pretty funny."

"Oh yeah, *I do mind*. See, told you it's funny. But to be totally, totally honest, I'd rather not talk about it. It's in the past, and I've moved on; so, there really is no point in talking about it."

Megan tilts her head to the side and looks at Cas, endearingly. "I can tell you're still hurt."

He replies, "Yeah," and then thinks about it for a moment, "Well, no, I'm not still hurt. I mean, it was hurtful, of course, like most break ups are, but I'm over it now. You just learn from it and move on."

"I completely understand."

"Yeah, so, what about you? Why are you single? Or are you seeing a woman?"

"Oh, I'm definitely single. I'm talking to a few people, but it's nothing serious – just hanging out here and there."

As she talks, Cas is imagining what 'hanging out' would mean for a bisexual girl. He envisions Megan and her girlfriend in lingerie, caressing each other's breasts while sitting on the sofa watching TV. He suddenly realizes how silly it is to think these girls would just be hanging around watching TV in sexy underwear, fondling each other. He chuckles at his foolishness.

171

"What?" Megan asks with a suspicious look.

Cas lets go of the thought. "Huh? Oh, nothing, just thought about something. It has nothing to do with what you were talking about."

"I wanna know," says Megan.

Cas clears his throat. "Ah, it's nothing. Just something dumb thing I remembered, but it's, ah, not worth repeating," he answers, and then quickly changes the subject. "So, when was your last male-driven relationship?"

"Male-driven?" Megan asks with a small frown on her forehead. "That's a funny way to put it, but I haven't been in a serious relationship, guy or girl, in almost two years. There's no one particular reason besides the fact that I'm very busy with work and school; so, I don't have much time to date."

"I feel you," Cas says and takes a bite from his sandwich. "But are you looking for anything?"

Megan shrugs. "Not really. I mean if someone whom I find interesting comes along, then I would see where it goes, but I can't say I'm actively looking."

"Same here," Cas says and looks at his sandwich, which is a little more than half eaten. "Big sandwich."

She shakes her head and mocks him. "You said you were hungry; now look at you – can't even finish one sandwich. Wimp."

"Hey, be quiet and eat your salad, alright? You know how many hungry bunnies are out there right now that would give their left rabbit foot for that salad?"

"Oh, whatever." She smiles. "Are you done?"

"Yeah," he looks down at his plate, contemplating if he wants to try and finish the rest of it. He decides against it. "I'm gonna take the rest of this with me. It *is* a really good sandwich though."

"I'm glad you liked it. My salad is really good too, but I'm not a wimp like you. I'm going to finish all of it now."

"I could finish it if I wanted. I'm just saving room for dessert."

"What do you want to have?" she asks.

Cas looks at her. *You.* He smiles at the thought of saying that and wonders what her response would be, but he decides not to. Instead, he says, "I'm not really sure. Maybe some ice cream, or maybe this bakery by my place that has great cheesecake. But I'm not sure, I just want something..." he locks his eyes with hers, "Sweet."

"Oh, I have something sweet for you," Megan answers.

Cas's dick instantly stands in attention. "I bet you do."

"You know I do," she says with a sinister smile.

"Well, when can I have it?"

"Right here, right now," she says and gets up from her seat.

Cas's lips curve into an embarrassed smile. "What, eh, what are you doing?"

Megan looks at him, the glint in her eyes suggests she enjoys making him feel uneasy. "I told you I'm going to give it to you right here, right now." She reaches into her pocket and pulls out a chocolate granola bar and hands it to him. "Something sweet."

He takes the bar and looks at her, disappointed and relieved at the same time. "Thanks, appreciate that."

"You're mighty welcome," she says, feeling pleased with herself.

173

"I see your little smile over there. I'm glad it makes you happy to get me riled up."

"Riled up?" she says with an exaggerated look of confusion. She puts her hand on her waist and leans to the side causing her hip to stick out; it looks rounded and feminine. "All I said is I have something sweet for you, and that I'll give it to you right now. How is that getting someone *riled up*?"

He smiles. "I don't know; maybe it's the way you said it."

"What? You don't want my candy? I'll take it back." Megan reaches out.

"Oh, I want your candy," he says, stealing a glance at her hips, "Believe you me."

Megan starts to laugh. "Okay, you really are a dirty old man." She turns around to reach for her bag. "Where's my money?" she says, as she rummages through it before sliding her hand into her tight back pocket; her butt is perky and toned. Cas's eyes are glued to her ass when she looks back at him and catches him staring.

He quickly looks away. "Uh, err, money? What do you need money for? I'm paying."

"No, no, I'll pay for half," she replies. "Or at least I'll pay for my own food."

"I can't let you do that," he answers flatly. "And, anyway, you can't find your cash; so, more reason for me to get it." Looking back for the waiter, he catches his eye and makes a motion with his hand, indicating he's ready for the check. The waiter nods, reaches into his apron, and pulls out a note pad; he comes up to the table with a smile. "Anything else?"

174

"No, we're good," Cas responds. "Just the check, please."

"No problem," he says and rips the bill out of the notepad, "Here you go. Thanks for coming." The waiter leaves the check on the table and walks away.

"Found it!" Megan exclaims as she pulls out a woman's wallet from her purse. "How much is it?"

Cas quickly grabs the check and looks at it, "Let's see. It comes out to free-ninety nine," he says with a big grin.

"Hey, that's not fair." Megan purses her lips in a frown. "Plus, you should be happy I want to pay for half the bill."

Cas lets out a half laugh. "Happy about what? You insulting my manhood?"

She rolls her eyes. "Oh please, insult your manhood? Is it really that serious?"

"No," he answers, smiling. "But I want to pay. Look, if you want, you can get the tip."

Megan squints her eyes at him. "Alright, alright, if you insist."

Cas nods. "I do insist."

He gets up and walks toward the cashier by the door. Handing over the check, he pulls out his debit card and gives it to the cashier. Turning around to look for Megan, he sees her leaving a few dollars on their table. When she looks up and sees him, he winks at her; a big smile breaks across her face.

"What's up?" she asks, walking towards him.

Cas smiles and answers, "Nothing, you ready?"

"Yep."

He leads the way through the entrance and holds the door open for her as she walks out. They begin walking side by side.

"Lunch was good," he says, looking over at her.

"Definitely," she agrees. "Where you headed now?"

He shrugs. "Not sure. Probably go back to my place and try to get some work done. What about you?"

"I have to go to Brooklyn to drop something off for my roommate, and then I'll probably just hang out with her for a while."

"Cool. So, when can I see you again?" he asks, immediately realizing how desperate that came out.

"I don't know. When are you free?"

"Tonight," he replies, half-joking.

"Tonight?" she asks, "You serious?"

Cas can tell she's considering it. "Yeah, why not? I'm down to hang tonight. We can go get a drink or whatever."

"You know what?" She seems to be contemplating the idea for a moment. "Why not? You seem like fun." She playfully looks him up and down. "I'll buy you a drink."

He laughs. "Sounds good. Where you wanna go?"

"I don't know; you tell me."

"Well, I know a couple of chill spots. It really just depends on where you would be coming from."

"I live in downtown Brooklyn; so, I'm near the city."

"Oh cool, I know a spot in the Vill, by West 4th street."

"What is it, like a club or a lounge?"

"It's a low-key little lounge."

"Okay, that sounds cool. What time?"

"Is 9 good?"

"That's fine."

"You sure?"

"Yep, 9 is fine."

"Cool," Cas says with a smile, "It's a date."

Megan looks over at him and gives him a little smile of her own. "It's a date."

After a short walk, they approach the train station.

"Are you taking the subway?" she asks.

"Nah, I'm gonna walk for a little bit. I would if we were going the same way, but I'm going uptown and you're heading to Brooklyn, right?"

"BK."

"No doubt," he says, looking into her eyes. "Then, I guess I'll leave you here."

Megan puts her hands out and Cas moves in for a hug. She holds him closer than he expects; it feels good. He notices for the first time just how petite and slender she is; her waist is small and he feels like he can wrap his arms around her twice.

"Thank you for lunch," she says, still locked in the embrace.

"Anytime," he pauses, "Shorty."

"Hey!" she says, playfully pushing him away, "I know I'm short; don't make fun."

"I like it. I'm not making fun at all; you're cute as hell."

177

Megan raises her eyebrows. "Cute? Don't be fooled by my size, honey; I'm a firecracker."

Cas laughs. "I bet you are. But calm down, firecracker, I like your size. A lot."

"You better," she says, biting her lip and coming in for another hug.

Their hold on each other is tighter this time. Her eyes look up at him, seemingly searching for a kiss. Cas sees it – he can feel that's what she wants. *Just do it*. He hesitates for a moment too long, and before he can react, Megan lets go of their embrace. The moment is gone.

"Ah, right, so umm..." Cas clears his throat. "Can I get a kiss?"

Megan bursts out laughing, "What! No, you weirdo! Are you serious? You can't just ask me for a kiss, I'm a southern belle. You have to court me."

Cas feels stupid but tries to play it off. "I was just joshing, ya. You know I didn't mean that."

"I don't know, Casanova, it sounded like a pretty sincere request." She's having fun teasing him. "But it's fine. We'll hang out later."

"Cool beans. So, we're definitely on tonight; Village, right?" he asks, feeling excited about the date.

"Yeppers. I'll meet you downtown, but call me later so we can map it out."

"For sure. I'll speak to you soon."

"Alright, byeee," Megan says as she walks down the stairs. She looks back once, right before going through the turnstile and disappearing into the subway.

CHAPTER 8

Local

After dropping Megan off at the train station, Cas decides to take advantage of the nice weather and walk back home. He crosses a couple of blocks before his cell phone starts to vibrate; it's Jake.

Cas answers the phone, "Yo."

"What's good, man?" Jake asks.

"Just chilling, baby. What's good with you?"

Jake can tell by the tone of his friend's voice that he's in a good mood. "Damn, you seem rather chipper today."

Cas's face breaks into a wide smile. "Do I?"

"Don't you?"

"Well, in fact, I am feeling rather chipper today, my good man. I've just come out of a lunch date with Megan."

Jake is happy for him. "Oh, word? That's what's up. How did it go?"

"Pretty damn good. We gonna hang out again tonight."

"Oh shit!" Jake can't contain his excitement. "He's back, ladies and gentlemen. Nova is back in the building!"

Cas chuckles. "Ah, man, you're stupid."

"So, come on, man, give me some deets."

"To be honest, there's not much to give. We had lunch, and it was cool; now, we're hooking up tonight."

"Come on, bro. You gotta give me more than that. I know you holding out on me."

"No, I'm really not. We just ate and talked, and it went well. That's about it... for now at least."

Jake presses on, "Did you get a good-bye kiss?"

"Nah, just a good tight hug."

"Did you cop a feel?"

"What? No. What, are we in junior high? I didn't try to *cop a feel*, bro."

Jake sounds disappointed. "Are you serious?"

"Are you?"

"So, no kiss, no feel, no nothing. You're giving me nothing, man. What good are you?"

"Sorry."

"Well, at least tell me who asked to see who?"

"She asked me when is the next time we can hang, and I said tonight."

"So, she asked *you* when she can see you again? That's a good sign, a very good sign."

"To be honest, it might have been me who asked her when we can hang again. I really don't remember. But regardless, we're hanging out tonight."

"Sweet. Where you gonna take her?"

"I'm thinking about taking her to *Madam's Lounge*, in the Village."

"The Vill? No, don't do it, too far. Take her somewhere local."

"What? Why?"

"Take her local, I'm telling you. I know a spot on Pleasant Ave, a little bar lounge spot. You should take her there, it's real cozy and intimate."

"Okay. The place I'm going to is cozy and intimate; so, what's the difference?"

"Think about it. Say you're out, everything is going great. You're into her, she's really into you. And now she might be ready to do the do."

Cas interrupts him, "Do the do?"

"Yeah, you heard me, do the do. Now, the vibe is good, and she wants some alone time with you, but you're like a 30-minute cab ride away from home. Unless..." Jake pauses for a moment, "Where does she live? In the Vill?"

Cas answers, "Nah, she lives in Brooklyn."

"Okay; so, that's what I am getting at – so you're both feeling good, there's a potential for it to go down, but it doesn't because you live too far and it gives her too much to think about."

"So, what's the difference if we go somewhere local? She doesn't have time to think? That's stupid."

"No, it's not about time to think, it's about how much stuff she has to think about. For example, if you say, 'Hey you wanna go back to my place?' She says, 'Where do you live?' You say, 'Harlem,' and she's like, 'Oh, hell no, that's too far,' and 'I have to get up in the morning,' and blah, blah, blah.

"The further you are from home the harder it will be to get her to come to your place. She's thinking, 'Do I want to take a cab with him all the way Uptown? If I go all the way home with him, he might automatically think he's getting some,' and so on and so forth. It's not just about sex either, like she might get tired and just want to come back to your crib just to relax; but you're so far that in her mind she's better off just ending the date and going home by herself."

"And if I'm close to home? You think that works out differently?"

"Absolutely. You say, 'Hey, it's a little loud in here, and I kind of want to just chill for a little bit; you wanna continue this at my place? It's right down the block.' Now, she's thinking, 'Well I'm already over here,' and 'Why not? It's close by, and he seems like a nice guy. It wouldn't hurt to go back to his place for a little bit.' And because it's so close to the spot, just a short walk away, she's gonna be more up for it. Next thing you know, you guys are strolling out of the bar, walking hand in hand back to your apartment. And if you're lucky, fast forward another hour and she riding your brains out."

Cas breaks out laughing. "Wow, you really got this down to a science, huh?"

"Hell yeah, man. Especially for a first or a second date, I always try to go somewhere local. Whether it's local for me or local for her."

"She might get offended if I ask her back to my place so soon."

"What, are you kidding me? She agreed to go on a second date on the same day as the first. This girl is into you, man; I could tell from that day at the diner."

Cas is unwilling to admit Jake's right. He says nonchalantly, "I don't know, man. Maybe."

"I'm telling you, bro, go local," Jake says, "Just imagine if the tables are turned, and you're out with a girl and things are going good and she says, 'Hey, you wanna go back to my place and hang for a while?' And you say, 'Where do you live?' And she's like, 'Brooklyn.' You're probably going to have to really think about whether you wanna go all the way out there or not. But say she's like, 'I live right around the corner.' Shit, you're not even gonna think twice about it, you're gonna be like, 'Hell yeah, let's go.'"

"That is true."

"I know it is. And that's why I'm telling you – local is the move, Cas."

"But I already told her to meet up in the Vill."

"So what? Plans can change."

"Maybe I'll do that."

Jake chuckles. "You and these maybes. You'd be foolish not to do it."

"Yeah, well, what about that new girl you took out this past weekend? You didn't take her to a local spot, and it still worked out."

"Yes, but that's me." Cas can feel Jake's cocky grin all the way through the phone. "My game is on 100, bro; yours is somewhere in the 60's. Maybe."

"Oh please."

"I'm serious. Women will tread through hail and high water for a piece of the Snake. I'm a beef cake, often referred to as a dream boat. You, on the other hand, are what I would refer to as lame-ass, also known as a cornball. You need everything intricately planned out to get laid. Me, I can get it on the fly. Improvise, if you will."

"It's amazing you can carry the weight of that inflated head of yours without tipping over."

183

Jake laughs. "Nah, you know I'm just messing you," he pauses for a moment, "I mean, I am quite the stud, but you're no cornball lame-o. You just need to get your swagger back."

Cas knows Jake is right, but won't give him the satisfaction by admitting it. "Yeah, yeah, whatever. Shouldn't you be working now? What the hell you doing calling me at this time?"

"I'm just killing a little time; my next client is running late."

Cas imagines Jake's tardy client being some hot young woman in gym tights with a perky ass and flat stomach. The twinge of jealousy stirs again.

"Yeah, who is she?"

"Not a she, a he. This old gay guy. I think he just likes looking at me because I've been working with him for like a month, and he still asks me to demonstrate the same exercise over and over. But whatever, he's a steady client."

"So, you're basically, like, a whore. A little chocolate eye candy for an old man, sugar daddy."

"Yo, watch your mouth," Jake says, sounding disgusted. "And no, I'm not a whore, your ex was a whore. I'm a trainer, asshole. I can't help it if people enjoy looking at me."

"Are you sure it's just looking? You sure there's no touchy-feely thing going on in there?" Cas asks with a laugh.

"First of all, fuck you. Second of all, I just called Tiffany a whore and you didn't throw an emotional fit like a heart-broken teenager. What's up with that?"

Jake is right, Cas didn't even care that he'd brought up Tiffany.

"I guess I didn't notice. But who cares."

"See, I knew once you started to go out a little bit and meet some new women, you'd forget all about her."

"Yeah, you're right." Cas likes that he didn't feel queasy at the mention of Tiffany, but he wants to move on to a safer topic before his old feelings resurface. "Anyway, let me ask you something. How much do you charge for your sessions?"

"It all depends. Different people, different price. For women, I usually charge like 150 dollars for three sessions. For men, I charge a minimum 200 dollars for three. But if I can tell they can afford to pay more, I charge more."

"How much do you charge the old man you're waiting for today?"

"He's got some money, so I charge him 100 dollars per session. Basically 300 for three sessions."

"Does the extra charge come with a happy ending?"

"Fuck you!" Jake sounds like he's got his middle finger up in the air.

"No doubt. What's the most you've ever charged?"

"500 for three sessions. I have this rich lady from Whitestone I train. She's my best client. Off her alone, I make about two grand a month."

"Damn, not too shabby, man."

"Yeah, works pretty sweet for me."

"Think you can give me a coupl'a free lessons?"

Jake laughs. "Ha! Free? Hell no. I only give free sessions to chicks I'm trying to bang. And even then, I charge like 25 bucks."

"C'mon man, you owe me for the damn fliers anyway."

"The fliers?"

"Yeah, the party fliers. You know what the hell I'm talking about."

"What do you want to do exactly? What are your fitness goals?"

"You know." Cas looks down and pats his pudgy stomach. "Just lose a coupl'a pounds. Lean out a little bit."

"Alright, Nova. I'll give you some free sessions. But on one condition."

"What's that?"

"No whining like a little bitch. If you train with me, we train. My time is expensive, and if you want me to give you free workouts, you better be putting in the effort."

Cas nods his head, determined. "I can tell you're a good trainer because that was pretty motivating. I'm motivated to work out right now. Let's do this!"

"Slow down, Casanova." Jake laughs. "Hey, my client just got here. We'll talk later."

"Alright, cool. Later, man."

"And don't forget," Jake adds right before he hangs up, "Local. Trust me, bro, *go local*."

Cas replies, "I hear you. Talk to you later, man," and hangs up the phone.

CHAPTER 9

Time to Kill

Cas walks into his apartment and tosses his keys on the desk. He decides that Jake is probably right, and that sticking with a local spot is his best bet. He texts Megan to let her know about the change of plans.

'Hey, it's Cas... I know we were supposed to hang in the Vill, but I was just put onto a better spot uptown... would you be cool coming up here?'

He sends the message and enters his room to decide what to wear. Of the several shirts he has in his closet, he narrows his choice down to a long-sleeved navy-blue shirt with vertical gray stripes and a solid color short-sleeved forest green shirt.

Putting on the navy-blue shirt, he looks at himself. "Alright, this looks nice but it'll probably look better with shoes; sneakers just won't look as good." Taking that off, he puts on the short-sleeved green one. "I could definitely pull this off with some nice jeans and all-white kicks. Not to mention," he says as he flexes his biceps, "I can show off the guns with this shirt and…" Before he can finish the sentence to himself, his phone beeps loudly; it's a new message.

He goes to check it, expecting it to be from Megan; instead, it's a new text from Elizabeth. His eyes light up as he reads it.

'Hey, chulo. I found myself thinking about you for some strange reason, lol… anyway just wanted to say hi… What u up to?'

Although he's happy that she's texted, he strangely finds himself feeling a little guilty. Cas thinks out loud, "What the hell am I feeling feel guilty about? I'm not doing anything wrong. I'm just a single guy, gauging my options. So, why the hell do I feel so damn obligated? And, obligated to who?"

Before he has a chance to answer his own question, his cell goes off again. He looks at it; this time it's a text from Megan.

'Hey hey. I can come uptown, not a problem. Where do you want to meet? Do you still want to meet at 9?'

Cas's feelings of guilt quickly dissipate and are replaced by the excitement he feels about tonight's date – his first real date in over six months. He texts back, *'Yes, we're still on for 9... what train do you take?'*

Less than a minute passes before he gets a response. *'I'm by the A train.'*

The A train runs from Brooklyn to West Harlem and Washington Heights. Cas lives in East Harlem, but he's familiar with the route. He writes back, *'Ok, that's cool... just take it to 125st and I'll meet you there.'*

She replies quickly, *'Sounds good. I'll call you when I'm leaving.'*

He writes back, *'Cool, I'm looking forward to seeing you :)'*

After he sends the text to Megan, his focus switches to Elizabeth. He opens her message to read it again.

'Hey, chulo. I found myself thinking about you for some strange reason, lol... anyway just wanted to say hi... what you up to?'

He smiles at the little phone screen, as he thinks of what to write back.

'Well, hello stranger, lol... I'm fine, just living my life and what not... so what do you mean for some strange reason you were thinking about me?' Hitting the 'Send' button, he waits for a response.

After a few moments, he has a new text message. *'I guess that sounded kinda bad, lol... what I really meant is I thought about you and wanted to reach out.'*

He writes back, *'Well for some strange reason I find myself thinking about you as well... when are you free so I can take you out?'*

He quickly gets a new message. *'You wanna take me out on a date?'*

He thinks for a moment and then sends, *'Not a date... a hot date! ;)'*

As he holds the phone, it lights up with a new text. *'A hot date? Lol, well, just so you know, I only do hot dates.'*

Cas smiles at her text. *'I was just making sure ;p'* He sends, and then quickly follows it up with *'When can I take you on a date mas caliente?'*.

The next text from her reaches promptly. *'I can maybe sneak in a drink with you after work... just maybe.'*

'Why maybe?' he asks.

'Because I don't know if I'm ready to see you... I don't know if you're worthy, lol.'

"Ha!" He laughs to himself. "Playing hard to get? I like that."

He decides to play along. *'How can I prove my worthiness?'*

'Beg me... say pretty please!

Cas raises his eyebrows. "What the? Oh, we got a live one here."

He writes back, *'Pretty please with sugar on top!'*

His cell quickly lights up. *'Are you free tomorrow?'*

'I can make myself free for you ;)' Cas sends, feeling good about his smart reply.

As he waits for her reply, he looks at the clock; it's 6:30 PM. He decides that since he has some time to kill, he's going to pack up his bong and take a couple of tokes. Going to his dresser, he grabs a small metal box. He takes it to the living room and pulls out his bong, stored behind the TV stand.

Sitting on the sofa, he opens the box and pulls out a small zip-lock bag with weed in it. He takes out a generous leafy bud, breaking it into a small mound of crushed green flower on the coffee table. Using his finger, he takes a healthy pinch of the greenery and places it snugly in the bowl of his bong. Placing the neck of the water pipe to his mouth, he flicks on a lighter, places the flame against the bowl to light the bud, and inhales deeply, filling his lungs with the thick smoke. He holds his breath, capturing the smoke in his chest; after a few seconds, he exhales deeply – a thick cloud of smoke funneling out of his mouth.

As he's breathing out, he begins to choke and cough; it's been a couple days since he'd last smoked and the monster rip he's just taken is hitting him especially hard.

"Oh shit," he says, finally catching his breath. Even though he's already feeling light-headed, partly from the smoke, partly from the hard coughing, that doesn't stop him from going in for another toke.

He puts the neck of the bong to his mouth again, lights the bowl and takes another big hit. This time, he calmly holds the smoke in his mouth without choking. As he slowly exhales, the weed aroma he finds so exotic engulfs him into a calm cocoon.

With his eyes half close, his mind starts to drift, random thoughts about all aspects of his life fill his mind. Eventually, as is usually the case when he has too much time to think, his thoughts wander onto Tiffany.

There's no doubt in his mind – he truly loved her. He begins to have a conversation with himself – something he often does when he's alone.

"What the fuck did you ever see in that girl? *What do you mean what did I see in her? She was beautiful and sexy and cool as hell.* Yeah, but she was a phony, dude; the whole time she was living a double life. You always thought she was such a good fuck, only to find out it's because she had been getting a lot of practice. That's just dirty. No wonder she always insisted on using a condom. Thank god you never hit that raw. *Damn, Tiff, how could you do that to me? I loved you, girl.*" He sits up slightly to grab his bong, he lights it up and finishes whatever's left in the bowl. He inhales deeply and exhales slowly. Placing the bong back on the table, he leans back in the sofa and continues the conversation. "I loved you, girl. I would have married you, had kids, grown old together. I really loved you." This is usually when he starts to feel sorry for himself. But today is different; he doesn't pity himself, he's angry instead. "Man, fuck that bitch. *Loved* is the keyword here, you *loved* her, you don't love her anymore. You don't need her. She played you, plain and simple. Plain and *fucking* simple."

His anger doesn't last long, and he starts to chuckle. "Damn, Cas, she got you good, man, she really pulled a fast one on you." His light chuckle turns into a loud laugh, and he starts cracking up. "Oh shit, she played you, son, she played you lovely. Ah, man, what a bitch!" He laughs so hard that he starts to cough and tears come out of his eyes.

The laughter slowly starts to taper off as he catches his breath. He continues his conversation.

"Fuck it, man, you had it coming. How many girls you cheated on, playboy? I mean, really, did you think you were going to live your whole life without all of that bad karma biting you back? It had to happen." His thoughts remind him of a love song by an underground hip-hop artist; he doesn't remember exactly how the song goes, but he remembers his favorite lines.

'I was feeling you so much, I was talking marriage

But you can't fight the laws of average.

What I mean is, I broke so many hearts, that eventually

Someone was gonna do the same to me...'

Sitting up, he reaches for the bong. Before he lights it, he peeks at the time on his cable box, it's just before 7:00 PM. Because Megan is meeting him uptown, he has more free time than he'd expected. He can leave his house at 8:30 PM and have plenty of time to meet her at the train station near him at 9:00 PM.

I'm good for now, he thinks as he puts the bong down. He decides to shut his eyes for a couple of minutes instead.

He lies down on the sofa and squints at the ceiling through half-closed eyes, lost in his thoughts.

You know what, man? There's really no reason for me to even continue thinking about her. She's the past, Tiffany is the past, and I need to forget about her.

His eyes blink slowly.

You're going to be fine. You just need to meet someone new. You've met women before and you'll do it again. I mean look what happened in just the past couple of days; you went out and good things happened, you met Elizabeth and Megan. You're all good, man.

His eyelids get a little heavier.

You gonna hang with Megan tonight, take her some place local, like Jake said, and who knows?

He cracks a small smile as his eyes close completely.

Although it doesn't feel like much time has passed since he'd closed his eyes, something tells him he should check the clock just to make sure he isn't cutting it too close.

He slightly opens his right eye to take a peek at the digital time on the cable box. It reads 7:47 PM.

Alright, cool. Just get a few more minutes, and I'm up and at 'em.

Shutting his eyes again, he turns over to his side to make himself a little more comfortable.

Life is good. It's gonna be a good night, is his last thought as his mind drifts into sleep.

CHAPTER 10

Rude Awakening

Cas's dream isn't very vivid, if he is dreaming at all. He just feels at peace in the blank tranquility of his mind.

When he wakes up, the first thing he notices is the grogginess in his eyes, suggesting that he's been sleeping longer than he might have liked.

"Alright, time to get up, let's go." He turns to check the time on the cable box, it reads 10:50 PM.

His eyes widen in terror, and he jumps off the sofa. "Oh no! Oh no, no, no, no." He looks around in disbelief. "How?" he angrily questions himself, "Hoooowww?"

His cell phone is on the table – the little message light is blinking red.

"Shiiit."

He has a sinking feeling in his stomach as his picks up the phone. Bracing himself for the worst, he looks at the screen – two missed calls and three texts messages. Checking the calls first, he finds that both are from Megan, one at 8:07 PM, the other at 8:52 PM.

"Damn it," he says out loud.

He opens the first text, 8:09 PM from Megan. *'Hey, I'm about to leave, call me back so we can map this out.'*

Her second message was at 8:23 PM. *'hello out there. I'm ready to leave, I'm just waiting on you... I know you said let's meet at 125th but*

I'm not comfortable going without speaking to you first. so holla at ya girl, lol.'

Her last message was at 8:54 PM, *'I just called you... I got kinda tired and lazy waiting to hear from you so I'm just gonna stay in... I hope you're ok... good nite.'*

Cas feels like a total jerk. He starts to type a text on his phone, even though he is not quite sure of what he wants to say. He presses two letters on the keypad before he decides that he is better off just calling her.

He highlights her name and presses 'Talk'. The phone rings three times before she answers, "Hello," Megan answers calmly.

"Hey, what's up? It's Cas. I'm so, so, so sorry about tonight. I feel like a real jerk right now."

She sounds unsympathetic. "You should, you stood me up."

"Damn, that sounds so bad. You know I would never do that on purpose."

"How am I supposed to know that? I hardly even know you." He can tell from her tone that she is not letting him off easily.

"Well, I'm not..."

Megan cuts him off, "So, what happen? Why didn't you answer your phone before?"

"I was just killing time in my place and wound up falling asleep but I just..."

"Wait," she cuts him off, "You fell asleep? Is that the best you could come up with? You fell asleep? How lame is that?"

Cas feels horrible. "I know it's lame, but it's the truth. I really did fall asleep, I just woke up right now."

195

"Hmm, I don't know whether to believe you or not. Either way, even if you are telling the truth, it's still very rude."

"I mean it's not that late now; we can still meet up."

Megan lets out a sarcastic laugh. "Yeah, OK, buddy. I'm already in bed, and there's no way I'm getting up and going out now. I'm staying right here."

"I can join you, if you like?" As soon as the words leave his mouth, he wishes he could take them back.

"What? Are you fucking dumb?" She doesn't find the suggestion amusing at all.

Cas quickly backtracks. "No, of course not. I'm just joking."

"Yeah, you might have the wrong impression of me. I don't play like that, especially with a guy I've just met. I'm a little more Southern belle than you're probably used to."

"No, I'm sorry. I was just joking." At this point, Cas can sense any attraction she felt towards him evaporate with each stupid word that comes out of his mouth. He tries to salvage the conversation.

"Listen, I was really looking forward to seeing you, believe me, and I'm so..."

Before he can finish, Megan cuts him off, "Look, guy, I'm not trying to be rude here, but I really don't want to hear it. You said you were looking forward to seeing me, yet you fell asleep? Unacceptable. I like a man who keeps his word. And let's not forget it was *you* who asked to see me today; so, why would you do that if you knew you were going to be tired? It just sounds kinda lame and, to be honest, a little shady."

"Damn. I know I've really fucked it up, but I guarantee you there's nothing shady about it at all. I really did fall asleep, and I can't apologize enough..."

"No, you can't."

"Well, how can I make it up to you?"

Megan lets out another light sarcastic laugh. "Make it up to me? Please, you don't have to make up anything for me. Just the next time you tell a woman you want to see her, mean it, and don't go home and sleep, like a lame-ass."

Cas is offended by the several 'lame' references, but he stomachs it, knowing he deserves it. "I promise I will make it up to you. Just tell me when you're free again, and I'll..."

"I'm not sure when I'll be free again. Anyway, I'm tired and I'm ready to go to sleep; so, I'm gonna let you go now. Bye."

"Wait!" Cas hates that he sounds so desperate. "Can, uh... Can I call you tomorrow?"

"I don't care."

"Okay." He's not sure what else to say. "Alright, I guess I'll let you go to sleep. Good night."

The line goes dead.

He looks at his phone to make sure she'd really hung up; she had.

"Fuck!" he yells out to the empty apartment, gripping the phone in his hand. He flops down on the couch. *Shit, you fucking suck, man! Why the...? How the...? How the hell did you sleep that long?*

Cas is sick with regret and disappointment and briefly contemplates calling her back to apologize again. After a second thought, he decides not to, figuring it would only make things worse.

197

My first date in months, and I overslept. He shakes his head. *What a lame-ass.*

Just then, his phone rings. It's Jake.

"Hello?"

"Yo, yo, what's up, man? I left my keys at home; where you at?"

"I'm home."

"Why? I thought you were going out? Did you stay local?"

"Yeah, real local," Cas answers sarcastically, "I didn't go anywhere."

He can hear the disappointment in Jake's voice. "Aww, man, why not? Did she cancel on you?"

"Nah, I fell asleep. By the time I woke up, it was already two hours past the time we were supposed to meet. We were going to meet up at 9, I woke up damn near 11."

Jake is hesitant. "Tell me you're lying right now?"

"I wish I was, man," Cas says, sounding defeated, "I really wish I was."

"How the hell did you fall sleep? Were you high?"

Cas laughs to himself, although he doesn't find it funny. "Yeah, I smoked a little bit because I had some time to kill. But that had nothing to do with it."

"Of course it did, you're fucking pot head..."

Cas cuts him off, "Man, it had nothing to do with smoking. I was just tired," he says, sounding annoyed.

"Dude, if you hadn't smoked, you probably would have never fallen asleep and would have made it to your date with shorty. You suck."

"Thanks, man, I appreciate that. I wasn't feeling fucked up enough. I needed you to kinda rub it in my face a little bit more."

"Hey, I'm not trying to be a dick, I'm just saying you really fucked up, man. You can't be standing people up, especially this early in the game. Now, she's gonna think you're just a flake."

"Well, you know, if I didn't take you stupid advice and stay *local*, then I would have never gone to sleep to being with. I wouldn't have had the time."

Jake sounds completely unconvinced and sucks his teeth. "Fuck outta here. You can't blame me for you being a pot head and making the stupid *stupid* mistake of smoking before your date. I thought you knew better than to get high before you met up with her."

"What the hell are you talking about?"

"I'm just saying, even when I used to really smoke..."

Cas interrupts him, "You still smoke."

"Yeah, but rarely. I'm talking about when I used to smoke every day, like you. I never smoked before going on a date because it just made me too slow, too mellow. I never had the same wit or energy."

"Wit? What wit? You don't have any wit. And anyway, you stopped smoking because you couldn't get it up when you were high. Have you forgotten you tell me everything?"

"Oh, hell yeah, that too." Jake starts to laugh. "I mean, shit, that was the main reason. But even besides that, I'm telling you, I just wasn't as sharp. It's like going to work high. It doesn't matter how productive you think you're being, you're not going to be as productive high compared to when you are sober."

199

"Yeah, maybe. But I'm a writer; sometimes, smoking helps get my creative juices going."

Jake mocks him in a whiny little kid's voice. "*I'm a writer, I'm an artist, I'm creative...* Blah, blah, blah. Man, please. I've read some of the stuff you've written when you're high; it's creative gibberish."

"OK, whatever." Cas is tired of this topic. "So, what's up? You forgot your keys?"

"Yes, I was actually going to meet up with you to get yours, but since you're home, I guess I don't need them anymore. I should be there in about an hour."

"Alright, I'll be here. See you then."

"Cool. Later."

They both hang up.

Cas looks over at the bong on the coffee table; he thinks about Jake calling him a pot head.

"I might as well; it's not like I'm going anywhere," he says out loud as he grabs the water pipe and looks for the lighter.

CHAPTER 11

Chance Encounter

A few weeks have passed since Cas stood up Megan under pot's influence. He did send her a text the very next day saying, *'Good morning... I know you're probably tired of me apologizing for last night, but I'm gonna say it one more time... SORRY! have a great day and hopefully I'll hear from you soon.'*

He still hasn't heard from her yet.

In the meantime, Cas has had his meeting with Ms. Johnson from Mistro magazine, and they've published two of his articles on their website. *Money in the bank*, he thought as he signed the disclaimer and release for his work.

It's a Thursday, and Cas is shopping in the East Village, looking for a new pair of sneakers at his favorite shoe store. He's always able to find exclusive kicks there that he can't find anywhere else.

As soon as he walks into the shop, he finds a pair of sneakers that catches his eye. As he goes to grab the shoes, his phone rings; it's Jake. Cas is about to answer but notices his battery is low; he sends the call to voicemail instead. He shoots Jake a quick text, *'Battery almost done, out shopping, hit you in few.'*

A minute later, he feels his phone vibrate with a new message; he assumes it's from Jake and doesn't bother looking at it. He continues with his shopping.

Twenty minutes pass before his phone buzzes again with another message. With two shoe boxes in his hand and as he's standing in line waiting to pay, he can't reach the phone in his pocket.

The cashier is slow and uninterested; it takes her 15 minutes to ring up the two people in front of him. When Cas gets to the front of the line and puts the shoe boxes on the counter, he gives her a half smile. "Busy day?"

"Yup," the cashier replies without looking up at him.

As she scans the boxes, Cas takes out his phone to check his messages.

He opens the first text, and to his surprise, it's not from Jake; it's from Elizabeth. He feels the heat of excitement rush to his head. "Oh shit."

They had texted each other the first few days after they'd met; it was more like Cas texting her. Elizabeth was always very slow to reply, often taking several hours to get back to him. Once Cas texted her, *'How's your day going?'* on Monday 10 AM, and she replied *'Pretty good, how about you?'* at 11 AM, on Tuesday.

He tried calling her a couple of times, but she wouldn't answer. He thought she might be trying to give him a hint that she's not interested; so, the last text he sent her read, *'I can tell you're not much for texting and phone calls, lol... But I want to take you out this weekend. Are you free?'*

That was at least two weeks ago, and she hadn't gotten back to him. Until now.

He anxiously opens the text. *'Hey you... been kinda busy lately, that's why I haven't returned your calls. I'm downtown right now, Alphabet city at a hookah lounge... are you busy?'*

The second message from her reads, *'Hello? Are you out there? Lol.'* And the last says, *'Alright, guess you're busy.'*

Cas quickly selects her name and presses 'Talk' on the phone as he walks away from the counter without his merchandise.

The cashier looks up. "Hey, you don't want this?"

"No, I'm good. You took too long," he says as he walks out the store with the phone pressed against his ear. It rings twice.

"Hello," comes in the same sultry feminine voice Cas had been longing to hear.

"Hey!" he says sounding more excited than he would have liked to; he quickly tones it down, "Sup, pretty lady?"

"Hey, *chulo*. I'm in the city right now, downtown at a hookah bar. What are you doing?"

"I'm actually shopping in the Vill; I'm probably not that far from you. Where you at? I'll come meet you."

"I'm on 7th St and avenue A. It's called Touch."

"Cool. I'm not too far, so I will see you in a little while, I'm getting into a cab now."

"Okay, see you soon."

"Bye," he replies and puts the phone into his pocket.

Hailing down a cab, he jumps in and gives the driver the address. He's not far from the place and gets there in less than 10 minutes. Cas's high spirits make him give the driver $10 for a $7 trip.

The hookah lounge has a red sign with *Touch* written in gold letters. He takes out his ID and passes it to the guy at the door. The abnormally large doorman looks at the card quickly and hands it back to him; he steps aside to let Cas in.

The place is dimly lit with a thin veil of flavored smoke. It's early afternoon, and it is pretty much empty; the after-work crowd won't be arriving for another couple of hours.

His eyes catch a glimpse of the silhouette of a female figure in the back; it's Elizabeth. He contains his excitement and walks coolly to the rear of the lounge where she is sitting.

He talks in his smoothest voice. "Hello, beautiful. Are you waiting for someone?"

Without missing a beat, she answers, "Actually, I am, but he's kind of lame, and you seem a lot more my type."

Cas smiles. "Lucky me."

He leans over to give a gentle kiss on her cheek, Elizabeth barely moves her face; his kiss lands not far from her mouth.

As he sits down next to her, she begins to talk, "So, Juan Carlos, how have you been?"

"I was OK, but then you called, and now I'm great."

"Great, huh?"

"Yup," he says with a boyish grin. "And I'm gonna be even greater once I have had a little of what you're sipping on," he says, referring to the champagne glass she's holding, filled with what looks like ice-cold orange juice. "What is that?"

"A mimosa, Champagne and orange juice," she answers, offering her glass, "You want some?"

"Sure," Cas says, grabbing the glass from her hand; he takes a small sip, and it is delicious. "Oh, hell yeah. I need one of these."

She gives a huge smile that soon turns into a hearty laugh, showing her perfect-looking teeth. "I told you, *papi*."

"You were right." Cas looks at her; their eyes connect. Her gaze is filled with glassy mischief, indicating she might be a little tipsy.

A waiter approaches the table and speaks with a foreign accent, "Hello, what can I get you, please?" He hands them a menu.

Cas briefly goes over it and looks at Elizabeth. "Did you already have hookah?"

She takes a sip from her glass while pointing at the tall, elegantly decorated hookah pipe on the table in front of her. "Yes, but there's only a little left."

"OK," Cas says as he looks up at the waiter, "Let me get two mimosas and a pineapple hookah."

"Right away," the waiter says and takes away the menus.

"Wait," Elizabeth says, "I'm not finished with my drink; you don't have to bring me another one."

Cas looks at her drink, which is more than half gone.

"Let me see?" he says, putting his hand out. She passes him the glass. He looks at it briefly, and then in two big gulps finishes what's left in it.

"Ahhh, refreshing," he says, as the sweet-tasting liquor goes down into his system. He passes the empty glass to the waiter.

"Hey!" Elizabeth says in disbelief as she fails to hold back the smile that creeps into her face. "That was mine!"

"It's OK, I have another one coming for you, so don't worry. Plus, I needed that more than you did, I'm trying to catch up," he says, giving her a wink.

"Oh, so, you think you can just wink at me and everything is all better?"

"I didn't even wink at you; I just had something in my eye."

Elizabeth replies, "Yeah, uh huh, sure. *Que mentiroso.*"

Cas loves it when women speak to him in Spanish; he can't speak it very well, but he does understand it.

"What? *Mentiroso*? I'm not a liar, babe."

"Oh wow, now, I'm your babe? Who told you I was your babe?"

Just as he about to say something, the waiter comes in with two champagne glasses filled with the orange liquor.

"Here you go," he says, placing the glasses on the small dark wood and stone table in front of them. "I'll be right back with the hookah."

"Thank you," Cas says as he reaches for the drinks; he passes one to Elizabeth, and then takes a sip from his own; the carbonated sweetness tickles his tongue. "It's good."

"Yes, it is," she says taking a sip of the drink as well. "You got here fast; you were in the area already, for what?"

"I was about to ask you the same thing," he says smiling. "I was just shopping, I was about to buy something when I called you."

"Really? What were you shopping for?"

"Just some sneakers and maybe a book. Nothing specific."

"Nice. So, I messed up your shopping plans?"

"No, I can shop whenever. You, on the other hand, you're a hard lady to get a hold of. I have to take whatever time you give me."

"Aww, that's sweet. Well, you have me for the next couple of hours, if you're free."

Cas likes the sound of that and his cock immediately starts to stiffen. "I actually did have a few things to do," he lies – he had nothing to do. "But I'd much rather hang out with you."

"Don't blame me if one of your girls get mad at you for standing them up," she says with her eyebrow slightly raised; she is making a statement and asking a question at the same time.

"Hey, I'm single as a dollar bill. I don't have to worry about any of that."

She lowers her eyebrow. "Only if you say so."

"I do," Cas says, and then adds, "You never told me what you were doing down here?"

"One of my friends from work is leaving for vacation today. She'll be gone for two weeks, and she wanted me to check in on her apartment every couple of days or so. I came here to pick up the keys, and we had a couple of drinks before she had to leave. She actually just left for the airport like 10 minutes before you came."

"Oh cool. Where is she going?"

"Egypt"

"Wow, cool."

"Yeah, she doesn't have any kids, so she's always going somewhere or the other. Anyway, I decided since I'm in the city, I'll ping you and see what you're up to."

He takes a healthy gulp of the sweet bubbly drink. "I'm really glad you did. I was hoping hang out with you."

"I know, and I feel bad, but it's just with my daughter and my family, it's just hard to have free time. But I'm free now." She laughs.

***

Two hours, and four glasses later, they're completely engaged in conversation, laughter constantly streaming from their booth.

Cas tries to talk as he catches his breath. "Aww man, but seriously though, thank you for having my back that night. That was a big bitch."

"Oh please, the bigger they are the harder they fall. And you? You should have gone to the doctor to get your head checked out."

"Nah, it wasn't that serious."

"Wasn't that serious?" Elizabeth starts to crack up again. "The girl cracked a liquor bottle over your head; you were out like a light! What do you mean *it wasn't that serious?*"

Cas tries to put on a serious face as he says, "Yeah, go head and laugh. It's just the funniest thing in the world to see someone assault people with a glass bottle. I'm surprised you didn't have your phone out to record it, yelling *World star!*" he remarks sarcastically.

"*Aww, bendito.* Don't worry, *chulo*, I got her for you."

"Oh, now I'm your *chulo*?"

Their eyes meet; Cas feels a connection that is stronger than mere lustful attraction. He wants this woman – he wants to be with her, he wants her to belong to him, and he wants to belong to her.

She looks at her glass – it's empty. Cas still has a little drink left in his; Elizabeth grabs it from his hand and drinks the rest. Handing the empty glass back to him, she says, "You are whatever I say you are."

The tone of her voice arouses Cas, and he feels his crotch start to bulge.

"Really? So, you think you got it like that?"

"You tell me if I got it like that."

Cas is totally intrigued. "Yeah, you got it, babe."

She gives him a sexy yet wicked smile. "I thought so."

He doesn't want to break the flow of their conversation, but he has to use the bathroom – the several glasses of orange juice and champagne have filled his bladder to the brim.

"I'll be right back, I'm just gonna go to the loo real quick. Do you know where it is?"

Elizabeth points to a dark narrow doorway towards the back of the lounge. "It's through there, down the steps."

"Thanks." As soon as he gets up and begins to walk, he leans a little to his right as if the floor is slanted. He smiles to himself. *Whoa, dude, I'm kinda tipsy right now.* He looks back to check if Elizabeth has noticed. He finds her looking right at him, covering her mouth to hide her smile.

"Hey," he says with a chuckle.

"Hey to you," she answers back, "Are you okay? You look a little thrown off."

"Oh yeah, I'm good," he says as he straightens out his posture and tries to walk cool and easy.

He makes his way to the narrow flight of steps leading down to the bathroom. Carefully taking the steep steps, he uses his hands on either side of him to hold onto the wall. He reaches the bottom and opens the door – there's a urinal and toilet bowl.

Standing in front of the urinal, he unzips his pants and takes a much-needed piss, leaning his head back in relief. "Ahhhh... Thank you, lord."

It's longer than a normal piss, which always happens when he drinks. He is almost done when someone knocks at the door.

"Someone's in here," he says as he is just about done. They knock harder, which startles Cas. "Someone's in here. Hold on."

He finishes and reaches over to the sink to wash his hands. The person begins knocking again – Cas is drunk and agitated.

"YO!" he yells at the door, "What the fuck is wrong with you? Wait a minute." He quickly washes his hands and dries them with a paper towel.

Angrily, he opens the door. "What the fuck is..." he stops mid-sentence. Standing in front of the door is Elizabeth.

"Oh, I'm sorry, I didn't know someone was in here," she says looking Cas in the eyes, a sexy smirk playing about her face.

Without thinking, Cas grabs her by her waist and pulls her close to him. The glasses of sweet champagne have him feeling supremely confident.

"So, it was you, huh?" he says.

Both of her hands are on his chest as she looks up at him. "Mmm-hmm."

He tilts his head sideways, closes his eyes, and goes in for a kiss; Elizabeth does the same. Their lips touch, fitting perfectly with each other's. With his eyes still closed, he blindly reaches for the door behind her and closes it, pressing the button on the knob to lock it.

Their kiss is sensual and intense. He moves his hands to her head and carefully holds her face. He sticks out the tip of his tongue and softly licks her lips. Elizabeth stands there with her eyes closed, mouth slightly open, seeming to feel each slight caress of his tongue.

Her hands still resting on his chest, she grabs his shirt to pull him in even closer, tilts her head further to the side, and places her whole mouth over his – their tongues vigorously swirl around each other.

Cas moves his hands down her back to cup and squeeze her ass. She starts to slowly grind her body against him. The bulge in his pants is pressed against her thigh. Elizabeth slips her hands down the front of his pants and rubs his hard cock. She allows his hand to go under her spacious skirt, and it grabs a handful of her fleshy ass; she starts to rub his cock harder.

He moves his mouth down to the crook of her neck and showers her with licks and kisses. Elizabeth stands there, eyes closed, head tilted to the side to expose her neck, biting her lip with pleasure. Her hands begin to undo his belt.

Cas's liquor-tainted brain begins to process what he's doing.

Holy shit, is this really happening? And am I really about to have sex with her in a bathroom right now?

As these thoughts cross his mind, Elizabeth has already unbuttoned his pants. Sliding his zipper down, she puts her hand inside his boxers and grabs his rock-hard dick. She maneuvers it through the hole in the front of his boxers and begins to stroke it.

Yup, this is really happening. He moves his hand down the front of her skirt, in between her thighs. He rubs his hand against her panties – its moist and inviting, he slips them to the side and slides his finger in.

211

Damn, she's so wet

Elizabeth moans and strokes his dick faster. She suddenly drops down on her knees and reaches for his cock; opening her mouth, she begins to suck it.

Cas is in awe of the beautiful face that is now wrapped around his man meat. Looking down to watch her, he gently holds her silky soft black hair away from her face. He can't take his eyes off her, her head bobbing back and forth, his cock glistening from her saliva. For Cas, watching her is almost more pleasurable than the act itself.

She looks up at him, their eyes meet. She closes her eyes and begins to suck harder and faster. Cas's hands tighten around her hair as he begins to thrust his hips in rhythm with her mouth.

Suddenly, he feels like he is about to cum.

Oh no! Cas closes his eyes tight. *Not yet, man, not yet!* He clenches his dick, trying to keep himself from exploding. *C'mon man, Think of something. Baseball, basketball, who's on first...* His thoughts race, trying to distract him from the pleasure he is receiving. Before he has more time to think, Elizabeth stands up straight. She begins kissing him, their tongues deep in each other's mouth. She grabs his shaft and places it between her thighs. She doesn't actually put it inside her; she just traps his cock between them, squeezing her legs together.

Cas can feel the wetness of her pussy rubbing against his meat; her clenched thighs around him feel amazing, and he feels his cum wanting to flow out. He has to tell her to stop or he'll risk creaming her legs.

"Chill, chill," he whispers in her ear.

"What's wrong, *papi*? It doesn't feel good?" she asks, already knowing the answer.

"It feels too good. You gonna make me cum."

"Don't cum yet, *papi*. Don't you feel how wet you got me? Don't you wanna feel that pussy?"

Cas pushes her away from him, puts his hands under her ass, and lifts her up onto the sink. She spreads her legs. He quickly reaches into his back pocket and pulls out a condom, rips the wrapper with his teeth, and rolls the condom down onto his pulsating cock. She grabs it, aligns it with her position, and pulls him forward so he can enter her.

With him all the way in her, she moans in his ear, "*Aye papi, que rico. Domelo, papi, domelo.*"

They kiss fervently as he crashes into her repeatedly. A few moments later, they are interrupted by a knock on the door. Cas freezes and looks up.

"Ah, someone's in here. One minute."

He hears murmurs on the other side of the door but can't make out what it is.

Elizabeth whispers in his ear, "Don't stop." She grinds her body hard against him, getting the momentum going again. Her movements drive him crazy, and he begins to fuck her aggressively.

"Yes! Give it to me!" she says as she wraps her legs around him, "Oh God, just like that! Keep fucking me just like that!" She tightens her legs around him as her pussy squeezes his cock. The pressure has him on the brink.

"Oh, fuck yes!" she yells as her body begins to gyrate; she's cumming. She squeezes herself so tight around him that holding back anymore is impossible, and they climax at the same time. Cas gives her a few last hard deep thrusts, squeezing every drop of milk out of him.

Their bodies collapse into each other as they embrace, breathing heavily. After another moment, someone knocks on the door again.

Elizabeth yells out now. "Coming out, one second." She looks at Cas with an exhausted grin. "We have to go," she whispers.

Cas slowly nods. "Okay" he says, still trying to catch his breath.

Elizabeth pulls down her skirt and tries to make her disheveled hair presentable by finger combing it. Cas pulls up his pants.

They look at each other and smile. "You ready?" Cas asks.

"Yes," she answers, "Let's go."

They open the door. There are two tipsy-looking women on the other side, wholly engaged in their own conversation. They barely notice a man and a woman walk out of the bathroom together.

Cas leads Elizabeth up the narrow staircase to the main floor where the bar is and go over to the small sofa where they were sitting.

"Oh shit," Elizabeth says.

"What happen?" Cas asks.

"I left my purse here like a freaking *loca*," she replies, busily looking through it to make sure her valuables are all in there. "Phew, everything is still here, thank goodness." She unzips her wallet and takes out some cash. "Here, for the drinks. I have to run."

"Are you kidding me? I got the drinks, please. But why do you have to leave?"

"I have some things to do and thanks to you," Elizabeth looks at him with a beautiful, sly grin, "I'm running late."

"Really? Well, that sucks. When can I see you again?" he says, immediately feeling a wave of disappointed that he doesn't have more time with her.

"I don't know. Soon, I hope. But call me, and we'll figure it out," she replies as she gets her things together and look at her phone, "My car is outside."

The rush she is in to leave makes Cas feel as if Elizabeth is running away from him. He tries to think of something to say, but before he can, she leans forward, grabs him buy his shirt, and gives him a soft and sensual kiss on the lips.

"Bye, *chulo*." Elizabeth gives him another soft kiss and walks out the door.

Cas follows her outside, truly confused by how hastily she's leaving.

There's a black sedan out front; Elizabeth quickly gets in the backseat and closes the door. Looking back at Cas, she makes the gesture of a phone call with two fingers by her ear and mouths the words, 'call me'. Then, the car pulls off.

"I will," he answers back, but she isn't around to hear it – she's already gone.

CHAPTER 12

Happy Hour

The next day, Cas wakes up shortly after 10 AM, feeling happy with the world. Almost as soon as he opens his eyes, he reaches for his phone to see if he has any messages from Elizabeth. He'd sent her a text after getting home last night, asking her if she would be free to go out that weekend. He feels slightly disappointed that there were no new messages from her, but he quickly shakes off the feeling; he had way too good a time the previous day to allow anything to dampen his mood.

Cas contemplates going to gym. He's had a membership for over three years now but rarely puts it to good use. He abruptly decides he's going; he wants to work up a sweat. On his way there, he takes out his phone and writes a text to Elizabeth, *'Good morning chula. I had an amazing time yesterday. Hopefully we can see what's good for this weekend. Can't wait to see you again.'* He sends the message, feeling good about how it sounds.

He wonders if he should send a text to Megan as well, but he isn't sure of what to say. After walking a couple of blocks, he figures that short and simple would be the best way to go. He writes, *'Hey just checking up on you, hope we're still cool.'* He reads it over before sending it out. *Eh, what else can I really say?* He hits the 'Send' button on his phone.

***

After his workout, he gets himself a sandwich, takes care of a few brief errands, and finally finds himself sitting on the sofa, watching news as he eats his lunch in his apartment.

Throughout this whole time, Cas has been thinking about Elizabeth. He tries to actively put her out of his mind by focusing on other things, but subconsciously, he's checking the phone every few minutes to see if she has called or texted.

By the time he's done eating and has had his fill of the news show, he decides it's a good time for him to start working on another article for Mistro.

As is usually the case with Cas, once he commits himself to writing, he gets so focused on the work that he loses all track of time.

A few hours pass as Cas types away on his keyboard. Just as he's about to take a break, his cell phone begins to ring; it's the first time his phone has lit up all day.

He looks at the screen hoping it's Elizabeth; instead, it's Jake. He looks at the time; it's 6:30 PM.

Cas answers the phone, "Yo."

"What's up, man, what you doing?"

"Nothing, just working on a piece. What's good with you?"

"Eh, I'm contemplating whether to go home or meet up with Chen and Manolo for happy hours at this bar," he pauses for a second, "Are you up for going out? It's not too far from our crib."

"Nah, not really. I'm a little tired. I think I'm just going to chill at home."

Jake knows how to spark his friend's interest. "You sure? You know Elizabeth might be there."

Cas's face glows with the mention of her name. "Well, speaking of Elizabeth. Guess who hung out with her last night?"

"You? Shut up!"

"Yessir. Took it down too." As soon as the sentence leave his mouth, he feels guilty about it. He doesn't want to make her sound cheap.

Jake is extremely excited. "Shut the fuck up! Why didn't you tell me?"

"I never got the chance. I've barely seen you the past coupl'a days."

"That's what's up! Was it good?"

"It was great, man," Cas replies as a smile automatically appears on his face thinking about the previous night.

"Well, give me some dirty deets, man."

Cas hesitates. "Nah. Not yet. Maybe later."

"Why?"

"Because I don't want to tarnish her name. I like her, like a lot, man. We got this crazy, *beautiful* chemistry. I don't know, it feels like we're already connected. Something about her..."

"Oh please, cut it out. Here we go again, Nova is in love."

"See, I knew you were going to say something stupid. Nobody is talking about love, I just..."

Jake cuts him off, "Well then, you should come out with me because she's almost definitely, probably, maybe going to be there."

"What makes you say that?"

"Manolo's older sister Gloria is going, and they all hang in the same group."

218

"Word?"

"Yeah, man." Jake can tell he has him now. "You sure you don't want to go?"

"Eh…" Cas has already made up his mind, he's going, but he acts as if he's not sure. "I don't know. Are you sure you're going?"

"If you go, I'm going too."

"Eh, I just don't know..."

Jake doesn't let him finish, "Whatever, man, we're going. Save the excuses for another time. I'll meet you downstairs in like 10 minutes."

Once he has heard that Elizabeth might be there, that is enough reason for him to go. "Alright. But I need like 20 minutes to get ready."

"Smooth. See you in a little bit."

Cas hangs up the phone and goes to his room to pick out some clothes. He decides on a vintage-looking gray t-shirt and some dark indigo denim jeans with a pair of black kicks.

15 minutes later, Cas walks out the entrance of his building in time to see Jake approaching.

"What's up, doggy," Jake says with a smile.

"What up," Cas says and gives him a fist pound and a half hug.

"Thanks for coming with me."

"Shit, I didn't come for you; I've come for my girl, Elizabeth."

"Oh yeah," Jake pauses for a moment, "I'm not exactly sure if she's there. I said she might be, *might*."

"Man, you said *definitely*."

"I said *definitely, probably, maybe.* That means I don't know," he answers with a sly grin.

219

Cas stares at him dead-pan.

Jake doesn't appreciate the stare. "Stop looking at me like that. What, she's your girlfriend already?"

Cas sucks his teeth. "She's not my girlfriend."

"Alright, then. So, stop acting like a little biznatch and let's get some drinks."

"Cool." Cas drops his cold gaze and gives a reluctant smile. "Let's get drinks."

They head to a bar that is about a 15-minute walk from their apartment.

For the most part, they walk in silence. Cas's mind drifts with thoughts of Elizabeth, while Jake is texting on his phone. It's not until they're about a block away that Cas speaks.

"I hope she's there."

Jake answers, "Hopefully, for your sake anyway. But even if she's not, there's always a really good ratio here and *definitely* some hotties."

They get to the entrance where a huge bouncer is waiting at the door. "What's up Jake," he says in a baritone voice.

"What's up, Big John. He's with me, does he need to show his ID?"

The bouncer looks over at Cas. After a moment, he nods. "He's cool. Have a good time, guys." He moves out of the way to let them both in.

As they enter the spot, Jake puts his hand on Cas's shoulder and points to the back. "There they are," he says as they start walking towards the rear of the bar.

Chen notices them approaching first and gets up. He has a big smile on his face and gives Jake a fist bump. "What up, brother." He looks over at Cas, surprised to see him. "Can this be? Is it a full moon? We have a rare Nova sighting." He teases his friend and shakes his hand.

"Yeah, man" Jake adds, "I had to drag him out."

"Oh shit," Manolo jumps in and pound hugs both guys. "Nova making another guest appearance. Niiice."

Cas laughs at their cracks. "Thanks."

"Hey, what are you guys drinking?" Manolo adds, "Chen is treating this round."

"What? I ain't treating you to shit. Except for my boy Cas. What you want, man?"

Jake interrupts, "What about me? I can't get a drink?"

Chen shakes his head. "Nope. You two deadbeats get your own drink. Nova, what you drinking?"

"Ha," Cas laughs at Manolo and Jake. "Good looking out, Chick, uh, Chen." He was about to call him 'Chicken Wing' but recovered nicely; "I'll take a Long Island."

He nods and looks over at the bartender. "Hey, can I get a Long Island for my buddy here?"

"Sure thing," the pretty bartender responds.

After a minute, she passes him the light cola-colored drink. "Here you go. That would be 12 dollars."

"Put it on my tab," Chen tells her.

"You got it," she says, walking back to the register.

Cas takes his first sip; it's very strong and his face shows it. "Damn, that's good. Thanks, Chen."

"Of course, man, don't mention it."

"I can't drink anymore anyway," Manolo says, feigning offense, "I have to leave for work in a little while."

"That office building downtown you were telling me about?" Jake asks.

"Yup. We're redoing the carpet in six elevators. It should be a pretty easy job. Only thing is, we have to get there after 9:00 PM when the building is completely empty."

"Damn, so late? That sucks, no?"

"I don't mind at all. We get paid more for night jobs. Only bad thing is I kind of want to hang out," Manolo replies with a smile.

Cas takes a few more sips from his drink and begins to ease into the atmosphere. "This place is pretty packed for a Tuesday."

"Yeah, this spot is usually live during the week," Jake answers, "It's actually better during the week than on the weekends."

"No doubt." He takes another swig from his glass.

Before he knows it, he's done with his drink and orders another. It arrives quickly.

**

An hour and a half later, the guys are sitting in their booth, finishing off the latest of the several rounds of drinks they've been downing. Cas is helping himself to a Long Island and has nice buzz going.

Manolo has had to leave for work, leaving Jake and Chen in the midst of a lively conversation.

222

"It's cheating, man. At the end of the day, it is cheating."

"Technically, yes," Chen replies to Jake, "But what I'm saying is that it shouldn't be considered cheating. If you're willing to risk your own life to take steroids for becoming the best possible physical version of yourself, then I think to be called a cheater is wrong. You need to have the courage to go for it."

"If the rule is that you can't take steroids, and you take them anyway, then you're a cheater. That's it."

"Yeah, well, the rule is you're supposed to report all income to the IRS so you can be taxed for it. I know for a fact you don't report all the cash you make; so, by definition, you are a cheater. A criminal, even."

Jake shakes his head; he's about to respond when Chen cuts him off.

"Yo, Cas, I think that girl is waving at you," he nods towards the end of the bar.

Cas looks up to where Chen is motioning – he sees a very pretty girl giving him an inviting smile. He returns her smile, and gives her a little wave to say 'hi'.

"Damn, she looks familiar," Jake says. "I know that's one of Veronica's friends but I don't know her name. You know her?"

"I don't think so," says Cas, feeling the effect of the several Long Islands kicking in. "But she's hot."

"Yeah, she is. Go talk to her," Chen says, stirring the little red straw in his drink.

"You think I should?"

"Definitely. If she was looking at me like that, I would have already been over there by now."

Cas stares at her, hoping his face doesn't show the mix of liquor and nerves that is causing his stomach to flutter.

"Fuck it." He throws back what's left of his drink and gets up from the booth. He walks over to the woman with the inviting smile.

"Hey you," she says as he approaches.

"Heeeyyy," Cas responds, feeling loosened up from the drinks.

"How you been?" she asks.

"I'm great," he says with a smile; he still has no idea who she is. "How you doing?"

"I'm good too, hanging in there." Her easygoing tone makes it seem as if they know each other from somewhere.

"Cool, cool," Cas says, his mind racing, trying to put a name to the pretty face. "Can I buy you a drink?"

"Sure. I'll take a vodka spritzer."

"Got you," he says happily and motions to the bartender, "Can I get a vodka spritzer and a Long Island?" The bartender gives him a nod of acknowledgement and begins to make the drinks.

"Look, I'm not gonna lie." The liquor has Cas feeling bold and honest. "You are so beautiful, but I'm ashamed to say, I forgot your name."

"Wow," the pretty girl says as she grabs the drink the bartender just put beside her. "How'd you forget me? You don't remember that wild night we had?" She bites her bottom lip. "I rocked your world."

Cas chokes as he takes a sip from his drink. "Okay, now I know you're messing with me. I'd never forget a night with you, not in a million years."

"That's a long time." She smiles. "We met at the baby shower."

224

His mind quickly makes the connection – she was the girl in the red shirt, they'd danced together.

"Yes! Of course, I remember you. We danced."

"And you still don't remember my name?" She takes a sip from her glass, allowing him a moment to think.

Cas is drawing a blank. "Uh, yes, I do remember, um, it's right there..."

She shakes her, amused. "Samantha. My name is Samantha."

"Samantha!" Cas says out loud as if he has had an epiphany, "That's right, I remember."

"That's what I'm saying," she agrees, "How can you forget about me?"

"No, I didn't forget about you, I'm just bad with names. But you're absolutely right, you did rock my world, on the dance floor." His mind quickly flashes back to her soft ass grinding against him on the dance floor.

"Yeah, yeah, whatever," she says playfully, "You were too into my friend to remember me. I bet you didn't forget her name."

Cas turns pale. *Is she talking about Elizabeth?* He plays dumb. "Who are you talking about?"

"Oh, so now you don't remember anybody, huh?" she says, grinning, "Maybe that bottle over your head gave you amnesia."

"Ah damn, you saw that?" Cas says with a huge smile, "That shit ain't funny, girl. I got hit with a freaking big-ass bottle over my dome. That shit *hurt*."

Samantha gives him an embarrassed smile. "I know I shouldn't joke like that, sorry, sweetie. That was really messed up. I'm glad you seem OK."

"Yeah, I'm fine. I got a hard head."

"I bet," she says with a sly smile. "So, what you doing here?"

"I'm just chilling with my boys," he says and motions towards his friends. Jake and Chen are talking to the pretty bartender.

"Same here. I'm out with my girls. Just wanted to get a drink before I went home."

"Long day?" he says, contemplating asking about Elizabeth but decides against it.

"Oh, hell yeah. I was running around like a crazy lady all day."

"I feel you," he replies, "You look great, though."

"Oh please," she says with an appreciative smile and tosses her hair, "I look like a hot mess."

Cas looks her up and down. She has a charcoal gray pencil skirt on, with black-red bottom high heels, and a white blouse. The long, tight skirt hugs the pronounced curve of her hips. She looks professional and sexy, like a sexy secretary. Thoughts of what she'd look like under her clothes start flooding his mind.

"Seriously," he begins, the liquor in his system, working in full swing, makes him feel smooth and confident, "You're so hot. You're killing it with those shoes." He knows no woman can resist a shoe compliment.

She backs up a bit to lift her right leg straight out and show off the shoe.

"Thank you, thank you. They are pretty hot, if I may say so myself. You really like them?"

Cas quickly imagines those heels resting on his shoulders, as he's burying himself deep inside of her. "Oh, hell yeah, I'm telling you those are hot."

She pulls her leg back in. "You have good taste."

"Thank you; so do you, obviously." Cas finishes the rest of his Long Island.

"Excuse me," he calls out to the woman behind the bar. She looks up, and he points to his empty glass.

She turns around and walks to where Cas is positioned on the bar. "Another Long Island?"

"Yes, please," he nods happily, "And another for the pretty lady here."

Samantha cuts in, "No, I'm good sweetie; thank you, though."

"You sure?"

"Yes, if anything, can I just have some of your drink?"

"Of course," he replies with a big smile. Cas thinks it must mean something that she wants to share a drink with him.

The more he looks at Samantha, the more he wants her. He's trying to play it cool and behave because she's friends with Elizabeth, but he wonders if the lust in his eyes is apparent.

As if reading his mind, she says, "So, you really like Elizabeth, huh?"

"Huh?" Cas is caught off guard.

Samantha gently takes the drink from his hand and uses the straw to stir it slowly. "It's funny because you don't look like the kind of guy

227

who would be into married women." She delicately wraps her lips around the straw and takes a long sip.

Cas's stomach flutters. "What are you talking about?"

"You know, you just don't look like *that* type of guy." She takes another sip, and then passes the glass back to him; he's doing a bad job at hiding his confusion and pain at this new knowledge.

"Oh, I'm sorry," Sam says, doing a bad job at looking surprised, "You didn't know she was married? I thought you knew. I thought she tells everybody."

Cas takes another sip from his glass, his stomach flipping inside out as he slowly comprehends what she's just said.

His mind races with questions but he maintains his composure. "Honestly, it's not like I'm really talking to her or anything like that; we just had a good conversation at the baby shower," he pauses for a moment, "But no, she didn't tell me she was married." As the statement leaves his mouth, he feels his throat get constricted; he coughs to clear it out.

"Yep," Samantha says nonchalantly, "Married with a kid."

"She did mention she has a daughter. And to be honest, she might have mentioned she was married too." Cas says, knowing full well that Elizabeth hadn't. He tries to play it off like it's no big deal and forces a laugh. "I really don't remember a lot from that night."

"Got you," Samantha replies, sounding disinterested in the topic that she had brought up.

Cas's mind is spinning with questions. *She's married? What the fuck? Why didn't she tell me? Why every time I really like a woman, something like this happens?*

He wants to ask Samantha how long Elizabeth has been married, but he feels a little choked up and is worried about revealing his emotions.

He moves the straw aside on his glass and takes a huge gulp of his drink. The rush of alcohol in his mouth causes his eyes to water a bit. "Wooooo!" he yells out loud as if trying to scare away the hurt he's feeling.

Samantha starts to laugh. "You okay?" she asks, placing her hand on his chest; he's instantly thankful that he's been doing push-ups lately.

Cas opens his eyes wide and tries to refocus. He realizes he probably looks like a nut and starts to laugh. "Yeah, I'm good," he says, clearing his throat, "I feel great."

"You sure?" she says, her hand still resting on him.

He slightly flexes and makes his pec muscles hard.

"I'm sure."

"Okay, if you say so," she says as she slowly moves her hand off his upper body.

They stare at each other. *She seems to like touching me.* The thought makes him smile.

He looks over at Jake who is talking to a girl in the corner; he has his phone out, probably getting her number.

Suddenly, a thought enters Cas's head. *Local.*

Blocking thoughts of Elizabeth out of his head, he looks at Samantha and is suddenly completely attracted to her. Feelings of lust fill up his cock; he decides he wants her.

"Hey beautiful?" he says to her.

229

"What's up?" She places her hand on his forearm that is resting on the bar.

"I'm actually about to get out of here soon and..." he pauses for a moment, contemplating what he's about to ask her, "And well, I got a nice buzz going right now; so, I kind of just want to go back to the crib and chill."

"Yeah, I'm kinda feeling it too. I'm dreading my ride home," she says, taking the drink back out of his hand and taking another sip from it.

"Oh. Where do you live?"

"The Bronx, 187th and Jerome."

"OK," he hesitates, trying to find the right words; liquid courage takes charge in time, and he speaks freely, "Well, ah, I mean I don't want the night to end. Like, I'm going to be up for a while; so, if you want, you can come back to my place and chill for a bit."

She gives him a suspicious look. "Are you asking me to come home with you?"

"No. You know, when you say it like that, it sounds so... I don't even know what it sounds like. But I didn't mean any offense by it," he pauses and takes a deep breath. "Basically, I'm a little drunk, and I'm ready to get out of here, but I still want to hang out with you. That's all; it's completely gentlemanly. If you're not ready to go home, but you wanna get out of here, then we can chill at my place."

"Where do you live?"

Cas tries to contain the smile waiting to break across his face with her question. "Oh, I'm local, just a few blocks away. I walked over here."

"Don't think just cause I asked where you live, I'm going over. I was just curious."

Cas feels like she wants to come, but she's hesitant because it doesn't seem *classy* to go home with guy she had just met.

"Hey, listen, I didn't think anything."

"Yeah right," she says, "Let me find out you're trying to take advantage of me because I'm a little drunk."

"Take advantage? Shit, with those shoes you rocking right now, I think you trying to take advantage of me."

"No, *papi*, I don't take advantage," she says playfully as she checks him out, up and all the way down, "I just *take*."

Cas smiles broadly. "Well, you can take whatever you like."

"Really?" she asks seductively.

The back and forth flirtation has Cas's manhood at full attention.

"*Whatever* you like," he says again. He's definitely drunk and feels extremely loose.

"Check it out," he says taking the drink from her and finishing the rest of it in one gulp, "I'm about to leave. If you wanna stay here, I totally understand." He looks up and sees Chen and Jake engaged in a conversation with a group of Samantha's friends.

"Actually, I'm gonna have one more drink, chill with my boys for a little bit and then, I'm out. So, you have a little more time to think about it."

"Okay, I'll think about it," she says smiling; Cas feels as if he has her.

"Hey, bartender, let me get another Long Island and another Red Bull and vodka."

231

"No, I don't want anymore," Samantha quickly says.

"Well, I'm not sharing my drink this time; you drank more of it than me."

"Damn, greedy," she says jokingly.

"How am I greedy? I'm getting you your own."

The bartender returns with the two drinks; Cas hands his debit card to her and grabs the drinks, handing one of them to Samantha.

"Here you go," he says and lifts his glass, "*Salud.*"

"*Salud,*" she says back as they clink their glasses, take a sip, and start walking towards their group of friends.

"Yo, Nova!" Jake says, putting his arm around him. Cas looks at his face – it's obvious he's feeling really nice. "Hey ladies, let me introduce my best friend; basically, I love this guy like my brother. Cas, these are the ladies; ladies, this is Cas."

"Hey," the group replies in unison.

"Hey, ladies," he says with a deliberate shy wave, "So, are you all like in a girl band, and I should just call you *The Ladies*, or do you have individual names?"

"Funny," one of them responds dryly.

"I'll introduce," says Samantha; she points out each girl and states their names, "This is Kim, Terry, Lisa, and Myra."

"Nice to meet everybody," he says politely.

The pretty one named Myra asks, "Cas? That an interesting name. It short for anything?"

Jake enthusiastically answers for him, "It stands for Casanova! Isn't that fly? His real name is Casanova."

"That's my last name," he says with a lazy smile, "Juan Carlos is my first name."

"I like that name," Samantha adds, "It's a very true to the roots, straight from the island name. *Juan Carlos*."

"Does anyone call you J.C.?" the girl named Kim asks.

"Nah, either Cas or some people call me Nova. But no J.C."

"Nova. I like that," says Myra.

The conversation switches to sports, and all are talking about how improved the Knicks are. As everyone gets caught up in the talk, Jake tugs on Cas's arm, letting him know he has something he wants to tell him. Cas tilts his head towards him to hear it.

"What's up with you and shorty?" Jake asks.

"Who? Samantha?" he answers, barely above a whisper.

"Yeah. She's bad, dude, for real."

He smiles at his friend's comment, "Yeah, she is. I'm trying that whole 'Local' approach you swear by."

A huge smile comes over Jake's face as he puts his hand out to fist bump Cas. "My man."

Cas gives him dap. "You know how I does it." They laugh.

"Get the hell out of here," says Jake, "That's how *I* does it. That's how I been doing what I does when I does it." They both break out in laughter at their drunken foolishness. Jake continues talking low. "So, how's it looking?"

"I don't know for sure yet; she hasn't given me an answer, but I think she's into me."

"I can tell you right now she is."

"Yeah, that's what I figured, but I don't know."

Suddenly the guys are interrupted by a female voice; it's the same pretty girl, Myra, who asked about his name. "Hey, guys, what are you talking about over there? You wanna share with the whole class?"

"Sorry, teacher," Cas answers quickly and surreptitiously winks at the girl; she smiles.

"You know that's funny," she says looking at him in his eye.

"What?" he asks.

"I'm really a teacher."

"Wait, you serious?"

"Yeah. All of us are teachers in the same school. I teach 4th grade," she says with her eyes still focused on him.

"Yeah or yes?" Cas responds, kidding.

She laughs. "Yes, OK, yes. Damn, I didn't know I had to be on top of my pronunciation."

"Hey, I was an English major," he says proudly.

"Really? Interesting; did you ever think about teaching?"

"Yeah... ah, I mean yes." He smiles. "But I'm happy with what I do. I'm a writer."

"Wow," she says, sounding genuinely interested. "Published?"

Samantha cuts in, "I didn't know you were a writer?"

Cas looks at her; there's a hint of jealousy in her eyes; it catches him off guard for a moment, but then he realizes that he's kind of been ignoring her since they came over to where the friends are.

"Oh yeah, not any books or anything like that. But I have articles and pieces published all over the web. I'm in magazines and sports sites."

Samantha is about to say something, but Myra speaks first, "How exciting."

"Yeah, how exciting." Sam is annoyed and sits down on a nearby sofa.

"Not really. Just sometimes." Cas goes to Samantha sitting on the edge of a U-shaped sofa; there's very little room next to her, but he's been drinking and feeling good; so, he goes to sit down.

The space is really tight, and he can only partially sit on it. He looks at her; she smiles, the jealousy in her eyes is gone. She moves over to give him a little more room.

He puts his hand on her knee and leans into her as he whispers, "Thanks." It could be the drinks, but Cas is pulling off all the smooth moves.

"For what?" she leans away from him; they both look at her knee.

Cas quickly moves his hand, embarrassed at how comfortable he was acting. "I'm saying 'thank you' for making room for me to sit down."

"Oh!" She laughs and puts her hand on his knee. "Don't be silly. Of course, I'll make room for you."

Her touch makes him feel good.

Everyone in the group is engaged in different conversations among each other.

"Samantha." Cas leans in again. This time she leans forward as well; he whispers close to her ear, "I'm about to get out of here, and I want you to come with me." He knows he's being bolder than he normally would be; he feels confident tonight.

235

"To your house?" she asks, already knowing that's what he meant. "Where do you live again?"

Her question lets him know that she's at least considering leaving with him. He feels his dick harden with the possibilities of what can happen this night.

"I live just a coupl'a blocks away. We could walk there or jump in a cab, it's literally like five minutes away."

"How do I know I can trust you?"

"Trust me? I'm bringing you to my house, I should be asking *you* that question. For all I know, you could be a serial killer."

She laughs. "And you're willing to take that chance?"

"I am if you are," he replies.

"That's true. But we're not talking about me, we're talking about you. How do I know I can trust *you*?"

"You don't know. That's what makes it fun."

She's not impressed with his answer. "Listen, mister writer, don't think you're going to convince me to come with all your slick talk."

"I'm not trying to make you come with slick talk. I'm trying to make you cum with something else," is what he thinks about saying, but instead he replies, "Of course, you can trust me. I mean look at this face." He grins boyishly, which makes him look young and innocent.

Samantha leans away from Cas and stares at him with a raised eyebrow, as if trying to determine his trustworthiness.

"I can't believe I'm even considering this," she says, shaking her head, "When are you leaving? Now?"

"I'm ready to go now," he says as he tries his hardest to contain the excitement in his voice.

"Okay. I'm going to go to the ladies' room real quick. I'll meet you outside, I'll be right there."

"Cool." He quickly gulps down his drink, as she gets up to go to the rest room.

"Hey," he says before she walks away, "Are you going to finish your drink?" He's referring to the Red Bull and vodka.

"No, I'm definitely good."

"Alright, cool," he says, grabbing the glass and finishing the rest of it; he grimaces at the change of taste.

"I'm out of here." He gets up and puts his hand out to give Jake a fist bump.

"You out?" Jake returns his gesture.

"Yeah," Cas responds, as they move in closer for a half hug. He whispers, "She's coming back to the crib."

"Sweeeet!" Jake whispers back happily, "Do your thing, homeboy. I'm probably not coming home tonight, but if something changes, I'll text you."

"Bet."

Although he's not far from where the two are standing, Manolo yells out, "Yo, Nova, you bouncing?"

"I didn't even see you come back."

"I sent my cousin to do the job. He really needed the work. So, I took him over there, set him up, and just got back."

"Sweet. I'll catch up with you the next time, for sure."

"Definitely." Manolo puts his hand out for a pound and they slap hands.

Chen gets up from his spot on the sofa. "Well, ladies, I'm about to leave too."

"Bye, Chen," the girls say.

"Aww, you out too?" Manolo asks Chen.

"Yes, sir, I have to get up early."

Jake adds, "It's not even that late."

"It's late enough."

"Alright." Manolo gives him a pound hug.

"Be safe man," Jake says.

"Definitely. Cas, I would drive you home but I don't have my whip with me."

"It's all good, man. I feel like walking a little."

"No doubt," he says and starts heading for the exit.

Cas puts his hand up to wave at the group of girls. "It was nice meeting ya. You all get home safe."

"You too," Myra, the pretty teacher, says, "Too bad you have to be a party pooper and leave so early."

"Sorry, it's past my curfew."

"Oh, my bad, you got wifey at home clocking you?"

"Nah, not at all." Cas smiles broadly. "I'm just kind of tired and ready to go home."

"I hear you," she says, looking him in his eyes, "Well, good night. Get home safe."

"Thanks, you too." He smiles and proceeds to make his way to the exit.

Once he is outside, he sees Chen trying to hail a cab; one pulls up in front of him

"Later, bro."

Chen looks back. "Yo, you wanna share a cab?"

"Nah, I'm good. I'm actually waiting for somebody."

"Who, Myra?"

Cas is surprised that he took her name. "Samantha. The one I was sitting next to."

"Yeah, I know, but that other one, Myra the teacher, she was on it."

"I kinda got the vibe too."

The cab driver grows impatient. "Hey, buddy, you coming o'what?"

Chen ignores him. "Yeah, she definitely seemed interested. Anyway, let me get out of here before I have to body slam this cab driver."

Cas chuckles. "Alright, man. Get home safe."

"You too. Good luck, bro." Chen gets in the backseat of the cab and closes the door; the car drives off.

"Thanks." Cas waves.

Cas gets on his phone to look through his social media. After a few minutes of staring at the small lit screen, he closes his eyes.

He suddenly feels a little woozy. *Damn, how much did I friggin' drink?*

The liquor is turning sour on him; he concentrates on standing still.

Fuck, I feel so shitty.

After a long blink, 20 minutes have passed. He starts to have doubts about bringing Samantha home. With each passing moment, he's becoming increasingly tired and agitated. His thoughts give way to drunken ramblings.

I'm tired of women with all their bullshit. Always lying, always doing shit behind your back. You're fucking married? Are you kidding me? I've had it. I'll never let somebody get me like that again. Elizabeth thinks she can toy with my heart? Toy with my feelings? Well, here's some news for you, Tiffany, you bitch, I'm done. I'm outta here... Wait, what the fuck? Why did I say Tiffany? Why am I even thinking about her or Elizabeth? Fuck 'em both, I'm out. I'm going home, I'm not waiting another minute.'

Right as he turns to leave, he hears Samantha's voice. "Hey, sorry I took so long. My girls didn't want me to go home alone. I tried to tell them I'm OK, but you know that goes."

Her voice is soft and feminine; it quickly eases his tension and puts away his doubts.

"No worries." Cas stares into her eyes and smiles easily. "You didn't take too long."

"Yes, I did."

"Yeah, you did." He chuckles. "I was just about to leave."

"Well, hey, nobody is stopping you. Bye, Cas. I'll gladly see myself home."

"No, I wouldn't leave. Just teasing. I'd wait out here all night for you if I had to."

"Oh, cut it out. Is your place far?"

"No, just a few blocks away."

"To be honest, I'm not trying to walk anywhere; my feet are killing me right now."

"No problem. I'll get a cab then." As they walk off the sidewalk into the street, a green cab quickly pulls up.

He opens the door for her and watches as she bends down to get in; he follows her and closes the cab door behind him.

Just then the reality of what's happening dawns on him. *This woman is truly coming home with me. Wow.*

Their ride pulls away.

CHAPTER 13

The Drought, The Flood

As the cab pulls up to his building, Cas is filled with nervous energy. Before yesterday, it had been six months since he'd had sex. Now, he's possibly about to have sex with a second girl in two days.

Cas hands the cab driver a $10 bill. "Let me get two back." The driver nods and passes him his change. "Have a good night," he tells him as he opens the door. Samantha follows him out on to the side walk.

"So, this is your building?"

"Well, I don't own it," Cas shrugs.

Samantha laughs. "That's corny, come on. I'm drunk right now, and I still know that's corny."

He chuckles. "But you laughed, so, who's really corny?"

As they begin to walk towards the entrance of the building, Samantha comes close and leans against him, interlocking her arm with his. He looks at her and notices that she is a little shorter than Elizabeth.

Elizabeth.

Suddenly, he feels a wave of guilt rush over him – like he's cheating.

What the hell is wrong with me? I have no reason to feel guilty. The freaking woman is married! I'm not doing anything wrong.

Shaking off the feeling, he focuses on Samantha. He looks at her and smiles. *You have a beautiful woman right here in front of you, and you're wasting thinking about the one who's married. Just enjoy the moment.*

He pulls her in closer, caressing her arm gently. She looks up at him – a subtle smile on her lips.

They reach the front door; she let's go of him so he can grab his keys.

"I live on the third floor. It's a walk up."

"Oh great, more walking," she remarks sarcastically.

"I'll carry you up," he replies.

Samantha smirks. "Oh, whatever. I'm good."

"Let me know, I'll do it," he says, unlocking the front door of the building and leading the way through the lobby to the staircase.

As they walk up the steps, his stomach becomes a little uneasy with anticipation.

Dude, it's about to really go down; this is not a drill. Maybe she doesn't want to do anything. Don't get ahead of yourself; she could just want to chill. But then again, it's almost midnight on a Tuesday. I doubt she came over for tea and biscuits.

They get to his apartment. Using his keys, he opens the door and hits the light switch. "Welcome to mi casa."

As Samantha enters through the foyer, she sees a glass and silver computer desk straight ahead. To the right is a sunken living room with a burgundy micro fiber sofa and love seat. Beyond the desk, there are three doors; the bedroom on the right is his, the one on the left is Jake's, and the middle door leads to the bathroom.

He leads her into the living room. "Have a seat. Do you want anything to drink?"

"No, I've had enough for tonight. I have to work tomorrow."

"Oh yeah, me too. I meant 'drink' like water or juice."

"My bad," she laughs, "But, no, I'm good. Where's the bathroom, though?"

"The middle door past the desk."

"OK, thanks." Samantha leaves the living room.

Cas hears the bathroom door close; he heads to the kitchen to get some water.

As he holds the pitcher of water, his hand suddenly begins to tremble; cold sweat breaks across his forehead. He feels woozy.

"Just take it easy," he says to himself, "Everything is fine."

His stomach cramps violently. "Oh, what the fuck?"

The sudden pain causes his body to tense. He leans over the kitchen sink.

"Brrraaawwaaaaaawwwhhh!" Fluids, alcohol, and bacon flow out of his mouth like an open faucet.

It abruptly stops.

He catches his breath and gasps in pain. *Oh shit, oh shit.*

Another violent cramp.

"Brrraaaaahhhaahawwwahhhhhhhhhrrrrrrr!"

It stops again; he's panting heavily.

Quickly turning on the kitchen faucet, he washes the vomit down the drain.

He can hear Samantha coming back into the living room.

"Cas, you OK?" she calls out.

"Be right there," he answers.

There was no reason to drink that much. Just calm down and breathe. You hurled; so, you should be good now.

His cock has gone woefully soft; he gently pats his crotch. *Hang in there, buddy, night's not over yet.*

Grabbing two glasses of water, he heads to the living room.

Samantha is standing in front of the sofa, resting her hand on her curvy hip; Cas is struck by how sexy she looks. He walks up to her with the two glasses in his hands.

"I told you I didn't want anything to drink." Her voice sounds soft and seductive. "But thank you."

"You're welcome," he says, his voice slightly cracking.

"What's wrong?" she says to him with a sinister smile, "Nervous?"

"Nervous? Not at all. My throat was a little dry." He quickly takes a drink from his glass.

Samantha moves closer to him, looking deep in his eyes. "Don't be nervous."

She puts her hands on his. "Don't be nervous." Closing her eyes, she leans in, expecting a kiss.

Suddenly, her eyes shoot open and her head darts away from him.

"Oh God! Cas, your breath smells like shit."

He immediately turns red and puts his hand over his mouth.

"Sorry!" He moves his head away from her so she can't smell his breath. "I had a little too much to drink, and I just threw up in the kitchen real quick."

"For real? You got sick?" She's sounds concerned. "*Bendito.* How you feel now? You still feel sick?"

245

"No, I'm totally fine. I feel so much better. I'm going to go to the bathroom to wash my mouth."

"Good idea." Samantha sits down on the sofa. "Use some of that mouthwash under the sink."

Cas looks back at her, confused.

"Oh yeah, you know I peeked into your bathroom cabinet. I saw a prescription cream in there that looked a little suspicious, but you're good though."

"HA!" Cas's hand still covers his stinky mouth. "You are foul. How can you go through someone's bathroom cabinet? That's violation. Sheesh." He walks into the bathroom. "And as far as creams go, I don't know what you're talking about. But I do have a roommate, you know? So, whatever."

He reaches for the bottle of mouthwash under the sink.

A few minutes later, after brushing and rinsing, he comes out of the bathroom with his mouth feeling cool and clean.

Samantha is standing in the living room, looking at a painting.

Cas comes up to stand behind her. "You like it?"

"It's interesting." She turns to face him and gently taps his mouth with her finger. "How's this situation doing? You got that worked out?"

"Yes. It's good."

"Good." She smiles and closes her eyes.

Cas moves in slowly and very lightly kisses her on the lips. The kiss is brief but sensual.

Samantha moves back and looks up at him – her eyes are coy and inviting at the same time.

Cas's manhood is suddenly at rock-hard attention. *Oh, it's on now.*

Putting his arms around her waist, he pulls her into a tight embrace. He tilts his head to the left and goes in for a kiss. It starts off very soft, like the one just before, with their lips gently pressed against each other. He slips his tongue into her mouth, feeling her body tense for a moment, and then relax.

As their tongues lustfully play with each other, she grabs him by the sides of his shirt and pulls him in as close as possible. His hard cock is pressed against her thigh as she grinds her body against him.

Their kissing is passionate – she bites his lower lip and then pushes her tongue into his mouth again.

Cas falls onto the sofa; Samantha straddles herself on top of him, sitting directly on his crotch.

He leans forward, causing her head to tilt back; he begins kissing and softly licking her neck.

She moans into his ear, "Oh yes…"

As Cas continues to kiss her, his hands slide down and pull up her tight skirt, exposing her round ass, barely covered by a thin thong. He squeezes her soft ass cheeks lustfully, and she begins to grind against him harder; his cock feels trapped in his pants.

He lifts her up ever so slightly to adjust his meat under her. He slides his hands to her front and begins to grab her breasts. She moans and kisses him passionately, reaching for the belt on his pants, undoing it as quickly as she can.

Cas helps her with his belt; she slides a little back on his lap to give him space. He gets it open, slides his zipper down, and pulls his cock out of his boxers.

247

Samantha looks down at his thick meat, bites her lower lip, and grabs it. She holds it gently at first, stroking it as they kiss. Her hand tightens its grip and strokes faster.

Cas leans his head back and moans in pleasure. "That feels so good."

"You like that, baby?" she whispers into his ear.

Samantha lets go of his dick and positions herself on top of him. He can feel the heat and moisture of her pussy through her panties. She moans in his ear as she grinds against his cock

"You got a condom?" she whispers.

"Yeah, in my wallet," he whispers back.

Samantha lifts her body up slightly and moves her panties to the side. She rubs the head of his hard penis against her wet pussy lips, moaning and breathing deeply.

Cas wants to reach for his condom but he doesn't want her to stop what she's doing.

"Let me get the condom," he says softly.

"Okay," she whispers back but keeps rubbing his cock against her drenched pussy.

She stops rubbing it and positions herself directly on top of him.

He feels the head of his penis as it starts to slowly penetrate her. He wants to tell her to stop but he doesn't. He feels the tip of his dick getting engulfed between her lips. "Wait, wait," he says, realizing he is partially inside her.

"Okay," Samantha whispers again, and then completely slides her pussy down on his rock-hard meat. The warmth and wetness of her tight twat feels wonderful as it wraps itself around him. "Oooo baby," she moans as she slowly rides him.

Cas can't believe he's inside her raw, unprotected. He feels like he should be panicking but he's not – her tight, wet pussy feels so good. Leaning back and closing his eyes, his hands grip and squeezes her ass under her tight skirt. They both still have their clothes on.

As she slowly rides him, he can feel the friction from the lining of her panty rubbing against the shaft of his penis.

Cas, what are you doing? You shouldn't be fucking her raw; you just met her. But, damn, this feels good.

He opens his eyes. "Wait!"

He sits up straight and puts his hands on her waist to lift her off of him. "Hold on sec. I need to get a condom."

As he stands up to look in his back pocket, he grabs his wallet and his unbuttoned pants fall to his ankles; his hard cock is pointing straight outward.

Samantha comes close to him and grabs it; it's wet from her juices and her hands glide along the shaft smoothly. She lustfully kisses him, using her tongue to lick his lips and explore every corner of his mouth.

Her passion is driving Cas wild; he grabs her by the back of her long black hair and pulls her head back, exposing her neck. He starts to furiously kiss, lick, and bite her neck, while squeezing her breast through her blouse.

He speaks in a low and assertive tone. "Turn around."

Samantha quickly turns her back to him and bends over the arm of the sofa. He gets a full view of her firm bubble ass. He spanks and grabs it, loving the way her flesh feels in his hands. He pulls her panties down to her ankles; she lifts her legs up to move them out the way. Sliding his hand down to her soaked pussy, he starts to rub his middle finger over her clit, causing her to quiver with pleasure.

He uses his teeth to rip open the condom wrapper, using one hand to continue rubbing her clit, with the other, he rolls the condom down his cock.

With the hand that's in between her naked thighs, he sticks his finger inside her.

"You want me to fuck this tight little pussy?" he grunts, "That's what you want?"

Samantha is horny and pleads aloud, "Yes, fuck me, now, please!"

He positions himself behind her, grabs her ass cheek, and slides his cock into her. He feels her tightness around him as he penetrates deeper, until he is completely inside her.

Bending his knees slightly to give himself leverage, he positions his hands on both sides of her waist, holding her exactly where he wants, and starts banging her hard, slamming himself into her over and over again.

The sound of his balls slapping against her wet pussy echoes throughout the house.

"Yes, baby, yes!" Samantha screams out, "Fuck my *pussy!*"

He's pumping into her from behind, hard and fast. With each inward stroke, her ass jiggles as he rams into her. The sight of his cock sliding in and out, between her thick ass cheeks, makes him go completely wild; his adrenaline is shooting through the roof.

Cas is lost in the moment. He closes his eyes; the room feels like it's spinning.

Sweating profusely, he has to remind himself to calm down and breathe. He slows down, from fucking like a rabbit, to long, rhythmic strokes.

Each time he goes all the way into her, he stays there for a few moments, rotating his hips in a circular motion, and then he slowly slides himself outward, watching the meat of his cock come out of her pussy. He brings it out almost to the tip, and then slowly starts going back into her till his cock is buried deep inside her again.

With each slow stroke, Samantha moans softly as she moves her ass to the rhythm of his hips.

He slides out of her and smacks her ass. "Let's go to the bedroom."

Samantha reaches down to take off her shoes; it drops her height by several inches.

She stands up straight and Cas unzips the back of her skirt; slipping it off her, he tosses it on the sofa.

She is wearing a dark gray matching lingerie set.

Cas kicks off the jeans and boxer that were around his ankles.

Grabbing her by the hand, he leads her to the bedroom.

CHAPTER 14

The Morning After

Cas is groggy; his eyelids are heavy, and he can barely open them wider than two little slits. He's not sure how he got home, and he's sleeping in the nude, which he rarely does.

Lifting his head, he glances to his right; there's a woman sleeping on her side with her back to him. Her body is covered with the bed sheets but a little part of her bare shoulder is exposed.

For a second, he thinks he's dreaming again; but the thought quickly vanishes as it dawns on him it is all real.

His mind slowly tries to piece together what had transpired the previous night. Glancing at the alarm clock, he sees that it reads 4:47 AM.

A name starts to slowly appear in his mind. *Samantha.*

Damn, I don't remember shit. His body feels dehydrated and sore, dead weight. Slowly moving his hand, he reaches to lift the sheet up and look underneath.

His eyebrows raise as he admires her naked ass. He puts the cover down and lies back.

Not sure of what to do or how to feel, and being too tired to think straight, Cas slides over to where she's lying. As he gets closer to her, he can feel the heat radiating off her body – it feels good. He lays his arm across her shoulder.

Without saying anything, Samantha moves her arm so that his can slide under hers; she takes his hand and cradles it with hers.

He gets comfortable behind her, their bodies spooning. Holding her feels warm and cozy; he softly kisses her shoulder and closes his eyes.

He drifts back to sleep. *This is nice.*

***

When he opens his eyes again, he finds himself looking at Samantha's head – she's lying on his chest. He touches her dark brown hair – it's very soft; it makes him smile.

Cas glances at the alarm clock; it reads, 8:50 AM.

Wait? Doesn't she have to be at work?

His body is stiff and his mouth is very dry; that makes it hard to talk.

"Hey, uh…" he clears his throat, "Hey, Samantha," he nudges her softly.

Her body begins to move, and she slowly turns towards him. Her hair is messy, it covers half of her face.

"Good morning." Samantha's voice is low and raspy, her drowsy eyes peeking through strands of her hair.

He smiles at how cute she looks. "Aren't you supposed to be at school? You're a teacher, right?"

"I called in sick," she replies sleepily.

"Really? You can do that?"

She pauses, her tired face looks at him dead pan. "Of course. You remember substitute teachers?"

"Oh yeah, of course. Duh."

Samantha suddenly sits up in bed.

"Unless you want me to leave? If that's why you're asking, you can just say it and I'll step."

"Step?" Cas grins. "What are you, one of the fly girls from *In Living Color*?"

She laughs. "Shut up."

"That was a throwback word. 'Yo I'm about to step, son,'" he laughs. "But no, I don't want you to leave. I can chill if you can."

Samantha smiles. "I can hang for a bit."

"Sweet." He moves the hair away from her face.

She tilts her head and closes her eyes. Her body collapses gently on his chest.

"I hope you don't mind; your chest is comfortable right now."

"Not at all," he says, looking down at the top of her head, his fingers running through her soft dark brown hair.

"*Mmmm*," she whispers low, "That feels good."

Cas closes his eyes, thinks for the briefest of moments, and answers, "Yeah, it does."

***

After what feels like just a couple of minutes, Cas is awakened by a few gentle nudges to his side. Sam is standing over him smiling; she's fully dressed.

"There you are, sleepy head."

"Hey," he tries to get his bearings, "You're leaving?"

"Yeah, I have some stuff to do. I would have left you sleeping, you look so peaceful, but I didn't want to leave your door unlocked."

254

"Appreciate that," he says, his head throbbing.

"God forbid if somebody would have come in here and murdered your ass, it'd be my fault because I didn't wake you up to lock the door."

"So true. Thank you," Cas chuckles. "How are you so chipper? I'm so hungover."

"Don't let this smiling face fool ya, I'm wrecked." She laughs. "But I gotta do what I gotta do."

Cas just nods slowly.

"Alright, sleepy guy, get up. Come lock the door," Samantha says, standing in his bedroom doorway.

"I'm up." His head hurts, and he doesn't feel like getting out of bed; but he has to take a piss so badly, it's causing a pain in his stomach.

He slowly removes the cover and stands up – he's naked.

"Oh shit." He quickly covers himself.

"No need to be shy now, boy. I already seen it all," she says playfully.

"I guess you're right." Cas drops the covers and stands there naked.

"Oh damn." Samantha looks away with a huge smile on her face. "You gotta warn me when you going to be whipping your dick out like that."

Cas is embarrassed and quickly grabs a pillow to cover his cock. "Well, you're the one who asked me not to be shy."

"Yeah." Samantha is still looking away and smiling broadly. "I just wasn't expecting that."

Cas stands there, bare-assed, holding a pillow against his crotch. "Can you pass me those boxers on the floor, please?"

"Sure." She bends down to grab the underwear and hands it to him. She turns her head to make eye contact.

As Cas pulls up his underwear, Samantha peeks down at his cock.

"You know, that thing is good," she says, looking at his penis, "You were good."

"Thanks," he answers, grinning ear to ear. "You were too. Last night was amazing from what I remember."

"You don't remember everything?" She sounds a little disappointed.

"I remember mostly everything. Some of it is a blur. How about you?"

Samantha comes up to him and grabs his meat.

"I remember everything," she says, smiling, as she softly bites his bottom lip.

Cas is instantly hard.

Samantha gives him a sinister smile. "Oh, I see someone's awake now."

"Rise and shine," he replies playfully.

"Sorry, stud, but I have to go."

"Ahh, you suck!"

"No, not yet."

"Wow," Cas says with a smirk. *This girl is something else.*

"OK, seriously, I really do have to go." Samantha walks out the room and heads to the front door. Cas walks behind her, admiring the sway of her hips with each step.

She opens the door and turns around. "I had a lot of fun last night."

"Same here, definitely."

"Call me later?"

"For sure."

"Good." Samantha leans in and gives him a soft kiss on the lips. "Bye."

She turns around and walks out.

"Bye," Cas answers back, his dreamy eyes watching her disappear down the steps.

He heads to the bathroom to take a long piss. Standing in front of the toilet, he closes his eyes and flashes of the previous night start coming back to him.

"What a night." He shakes his head and smiles at thoughts of Samantha bending over the sofa. "What an awesome, *beautiful* night."

Finishing up in the bathroom, he shuffles into the living room and lies down on the sofa; the scene of the go down from a few hours earlier.

Still half drunk, his words come out slow and lazy. "Damn, dude, you put it down last night."

He writes Samantha a text. *'Hey sexy, I had a great time last night. I know you just left, but I'm looking forward to seeing you soon.'* He sends it with a smile on his face.

While waiting for a response, he goes to sit at his desk.

Only a moment or two later, his phone lights up with a message. He grabs it, grinning, expecting it to be from Samantha.

The grin drops a little. It's from Elizabeth.

"Oh shit," he mumbles; his stomach turns as he realizes that Samantha and Elizabeth know each other.

He looks at the message.

'Good morning handsome. Just wanted to say hi.'

Before he could write back, the phone rings.

"Hello," Cas answers, his voice raspy.

"Yoooooo! What's good, man? How was last night? Did it go down with the go down?"

"Yeah, man." He indulges his best friend, "It went down with the get down. I'm back in business, baby."

"Owwwww! That's what's up." Jake is excited for him. "See, aren't you happy you came out?"

"Hell yeah. Thanks, man."

"Of course, my brother. But damn, you sound like shit. How much did you drink?"

The thought of last night's liquor consumption makes him nauseous.

"Shiiit. I don't even know. Maybe like five Long Islands, a couple of Red Bull and vodkas. Shots of this, shots of that. It was too much. *Waayyyy* too much."

Jake laughs. "Aye, small price to pay. She was looking hot as hell."

"Yeah, she was," Cas agrees.

"What you doing right now?" asks Jake.

"Nothing, just chilling out in the crib. I should be working, but I'm not."

"Alright. I'll be there in like 20 minutes."

"No doubt."

"Yo, you got weed?"

"Not for you," Cas answers quickly.

"Stop playing. For real, man, do you have some?"

"Yeah, why? You feel like token smokin'?"

"I don't know. A little bit. A little smokey-dokey."

"I was just about to light up, but I'll wait for you. Hurry your ass up, though."

"Alright, be there in 20. Later."

"Later."

Cas ends the call and immediately looks for the text from Elizabeth.

'Good morning handsome. Just wanted to say hi.'

As he contemplates what to write back, it suddenly hits him like a ton of bricks. *This chick is married!*

His body gets hot with anger, and he talks to himself out loud.

"What the hell am I worried about? Who cares if she finds out? She's a married woman!"

Thinking for a little while longer, he decides to take a very simple approach to get to the bottom of the situation.

'Are you married?' He sends her the text and waits for her reply.

A few moments pass, nothing happens.

A few more moments pass, and he begins to feel anxious. Sitting on the sofa and staring blankly at the TV, he tries not to think about her.

"What the fuck is wrong with me?" He talks to himself some more, "I had great night with a great woman, and here I am, thinking about Elizabeth. Stupid."

Just as he finishes his sentence, the phone rings. It's Elizabeth.

"Hello."

"Hi, Juan Carlos." Elizabeth's voice is very feminine and alluring.

"Hey, what's up?" He sounds nonchalant, even though he really is excited to hear from her.

"Um, I just wanted to talk to you," Elizabeth breathes deeply before continuing. "Look, I am married, but right now, we're separated."

Cas feels queasy as she explains her relationship status. "Okay, and why wouldn't you tell me that from the beginning?"

"I'm sorry." She sounds sincere. "I guess I never had the chance to. But obviously someone beat me to it."

Cas talks quickly to distract attention away from the *someone* who told him. "It would have been nice for you to make that clear to me from the get go. Had I known you were married, I would have kept myself from pursuing you. Now, I like you a lot – more than I should, obviously – and that sucks."

"And I like you too." Elizabeth is about to say something else, but she doesn't. She stays silent.

Cas is not sure about what to feel. "So, are you getting divorced?"

"I don't know. I still love him but I'm not sure if it's going to work."

"Well, if you still love him, what's the problem?"

"He cheated on me."

"So, what am I supposed to be?" he asks sarcastically, "Payback?"

"No, nothing like that. To be honest, I never give out my number, ever. But something about you made me want to take that chance."

"I guess that's a compliment."

"It is. It absolutely is." She pauses for a moment. "But I am still married. And I don't know for certain if I'm getting a divorce."

"Really?" Cas is not thrilled by anything he's hearing. "So, what was the point of us meeting up the other day and all that happened?"

"I don't know what the point was." Elizabeth sighs. "I don't think there was a point. I'm just going through things in my life and I wanted to, I needed to, let go. I needed to feel good and have fun and not care. You did that for me, and that's all I needed you to do."

As he digests what he's being told, he says the only thing that comes to his mind. "You used me."

Just then, the intercom rings; he knows it's Jake.

"I'm sorry, I have to go."

"What? Why?" Elizabeth sounds a little desperate.

"I have company."

"A woman?"

Cas is thrown off and gets defensive. "You're nobody to ask. Don't worry about who it is."

"Don't be an ass."

Is she serious? He replies, "How am I being an ass? And no, it's not a woman."

"Can I call you later?" she asks.

Cas wants to say 'no', but when he opens his mouth, he says, "Sure."

"Okay," Elizabeth replies quietly, "Speak to you soon."

"Okay, bye."

He ends the call and looks at the phone, wondering why he feels so hurt.

"Damn," he sighs to himself, "Why does she have to be married?"

He gets off the sofa and walks to the intercom to let Jake in. He unlocks and opens the apartment door so he doesn't have to get up again.

A moment later, Jake comes in with all his energy.

"What up, brah!"

Cas gives him a half smile. "What's up, man."

"Don't '*what's up man*' me!" Jake says excitedly, "You better wake your lazy ass up and give me some damn details. SIT UP." He looks around quickly. "And where's that weed at?"

"Oh yeah, that's right, you're in one of your smoking moods." Cas points to the tin box under the coffee table. "It should be in there."

Jake reaches under the table, grabs the box, and opens it. There's a dark blue vape pen and a small zip-lock bag with several green buds in it. He takes out one of the smaller buds, crushes it between his fingers, and packs it into the bowl of the vape.

He presses his friend, "Tell me, man, did you hit it or what?"

Cas's mind quickly flashes back to last night, sitting on the sofa with Samantha on top of him.

"Yeah, it was good, man. Great night; we definitely connected."

"That's what I'm talking about." Jake puts the pen to his mouth and takes a deep pull.

While holding the vapor in his lungs, he begins talking – his voice sounds nasal.

"I'm proud of you. Two women in the past couple of days? You're on a roll."

Cas doesn't feel proud. "Yeah, it's alright."

"You're coming out of the abyss. You *needed* this." Jake exhales, letting out a long, thick cloud of vapor. "Did you get head?"

"No head."

"No head? Why not?" He takes another pull.

"I don't know, it just didn't pan out like that."

Jake exhales. "That's wack. But hey, you hit it; that's all that really matters."

"Is it?" Cas directs the question more at himself than at Jake.

"What?"

"Nothing."

Jake pauses, "Damn, dude, this is some good-ass smoke."

Cas looks up at him from the sofa; he sees his friend's eyes have already gotten small and a silly grin is plastered all over his face.

"Dude, you look lit already." He laughs and sits up. "Pass that already. You always have been a steamboat."

Jake puts his hand up. "Chill, let me get one more hit." He inhales deeply.

As he exhales and passes the pen, he starts to choke, gasping and coughing from the strong exotics.

263

"You OK? You want some water?"

Still coughing, Jake emphatically nods his head 'yes'.

Cas grins. "Cool. You know where the kitchen is; hook me up while you're at it."

Jake sticks up his middle finger as he continues to choke.

"Sheesh, you're a light weight." Cas gets up and goes to the kitchen to get some water.

Jake sits up on the sofa and leans forward, looking down at the floor.

Cas returns to the living room and hands him a tall glass of water.

Jake finishes more than half in three quick gulps. His coughing subsides, but his eyes are red and teary.

"Ahhhh," He shakes his head. "Thanks, man. That shit hit me hard."

"You think?"

Jake shrugs. "I'm high as hell. I need to sit down."

Cas pauses, "You're already sitting down. I hope you know that."

Jake shakes his head. "Then, I need to stand up."

"Yo, just chill out, man; you good." Cas laughs. "You just haven't smoked in a while."

"You're right. I'm good." Jake slouches in his seat next to Cas on the sofa.

"What kind of smoke is that? I never got this high over just a couple of tokes. I know it definitely isn't some Arizona bud."

"Arizona? Nobody smokes Arizona anymore; that's old school. This shit is called Super Punch Berry Holiday Kush."

Jake looks over at him and starts laughing. "Get out of here. There's no way that's the name of this thing. What did you say? Crunch Berry Hawaii Punch?"

Cas laughs. "It's Super Punch Berry Holiday Kush. That's the name of it, for real."

"Well, that Captain Crunch Berry is some serious shit, dog."

"It is," Cas says, feeling the effects of the smoke setting in.

Jake looks at him. "So, tell me, man, did you kill it last night?"

A smile slithers across Cas's face. "Yeah, I think so. I was kind of really, really drunk, though. I actually threw up. I think?"

"That sucks. Do you remember anything good?"

"Oh yeah, I remember her riding me right here..." he pauses a moment, "Right here in my bed room, which was fucking great."

Jake smiles. "You were going to say 'right here on the couch,' weren't you?"

"No, we didn't fuck around on the sofa."

"I think you're lying. I think you did, and that's really gross, man. No sofa-fucking, you know that. We both sit here, we both lay down here, it's so unhygienic. I hope I'm not sitting in your jizz."

"No, I'm telling you, we really didn't mess around on the sofa like that."

"Fine," Jake replies reluctantly, "Anyway; what else happened?"

Cas is about to give some more explicit details but stops himself. *Samantha is cool, let me not put her out there like that.*

"I just remember I had a really good night. She's pretty awesome, and I definitely did my thing."

"Good stuff, man; nice."

265

"Yeah, I just wish I could remember more. So much of it is fuzzy."

"Do you remember using a condom at least?"

The memory of her riding him raw comes crashing into his mind. "For the most part."

"No doubt..." Jake begins, mechanically, but then pauses as he realizes what Cas just said, "What you mean, *for the most part?*"

"We were making out on the sofa and she got on top of me and started grinding me and before I knew it..."

"You sofa-fucker!" Jake cut him off. "I knew you sofa-fucked! I saw it in your face."

"It was really quick. In and out."

"Raw?"

"Like less than two minutes, probably."

"But still, a little while is all it takes. All that shit you be talking to me and you hit it raw? Wow."

"Dude, I'm not worried about it. She looked fine and healthy and all that; I'm sure everything is cool."

"Shit, I hope so." Jake looks at him, shaking his head. "You know, she been with Manolo, and that fool got herpes."

Cas's stomach flips inside out. "What?"

"Just joking man." Jake shakes his head with a grin. "He doesn't have herpes. Not confirmed, anyway."

"Wait, wait; so, why would you say something like that? That shit ain't funny, man. You almost made me sick."

"Man up, it was a joke. Smoke some more and calm your ass down."

Cas starts to relax again and chuckles. "I really thought you meant that for a second."

"Think about it, man. If that shit was true, I would have told you before you left with that chick."

"Yeah, that's true."

"But I am pretty sure Manny hit it before."

"Yeah right," Cas says with a smile. "Sure, he did."

"No, I'm serious. I was joking about the whole herpes thing, but I'm pretty sure he slept with her. I think that's what he told me."

Cas's stomach tightens up again. "Dude, why the fuck didn't you tell me that last night?"

"First of all, I didn't know about it until after you left. Secondly, what difference does it make?"

"It makes a lot of fucking difference! Manolo is my dude, but he's fucked a lot of questionable chicks, dog, you know that. I would have definitely made sure to strap up the whole time. Ahh, I feel sick."

Jake looks at him deadpan. "I feel like you're slut-shaming him. You think you're too good to be with a girl he had before? He gets some hot-ass women. A lot better than those fuglies you be bringin' around."

"I don't care if he gets super models; I don't want to have something he's had already."

"Again, really, what difference does it make? You and I have had the same women before."

"Yeah, but that was a long, long time ago. I'm too old for shit like that now. This is so wack."

"Why are you so disappointed? It was a one-night stand, what's the big deal?" Jake is confused. "Unless, you really like the girl or something. Which you probably do because you're a sucker like that."

Cas pauses for a second. "I mean, I don't know how much I like her. But she's cool, and I'm attracted to her..."

"So what?" Jake cuts him off, "You gonna marry a girl that let you fuck on the first night? I can't believe you. You get whipped so easy."

Cas is frustrated. "Did I say that? I didn't say that. All I'm saying is that I don't want to fuck a girl who already fucked one of my friends. What's so crazy about that?"

"Alright. So, let's say Manny did hit it; you wouldn't see her anymore?"

"I don't know."

As Cas finishes his sentence, his phone lights up with a message. Looking at his phone, he tells Jake, "It's her."

"What'd she say?" Jake asks, reaching for the tin box to break up some more weed.

Cas quickly reads it to himself before reading it aloud, "It says, *'hey, same here, last night was great and I want to see you again soon :)* '" He smiles as he feels a boost to his ego.

"This is perfect timing. Now, you can just ask her yourself."

Cas sucks his teeth. "I'm not going to ask her if she slept with Manolo; come on, man."

Jake shrugs. "Why not? It's a fair question."

"Because if I ask her and she hasn't, then it's going to look like I think she's some sort of a fast-ass girl. Might just ruin everything."

"Cas, she let you hit it the first night. That's kind of the *fast-ass girl* calling card, bro. What's there to ruin? It's a one-night stand."

"I don't know," he replies, "I really don't think just because a woman sleeps with you the first night, that makes her fast. Well, maybe it makes her fast, but it doesn't automatically make her a hoe. I don't think she's a hoe; I think we were both drunk, and we were digging each other, and we just went with the moment. I can tell she wouldn't have done that with just anybody. I think there was something about me and something about her, and it just clicked. Regardless though, I'm not asking her if she slept with him. Not now anyway."

Jake takes a hit from the vape pen, holds it in for a moment, and then exhales a big cloud of vapor.

"So, let me get this right. You think you're special, and that's why she had sex with you the first night?"

Cas looks up from his phone. "That's right."

"Okay, playboy. Well, do you want to know if Manolo hit it? Cause I can call him right now and find out."

"Eh, I'm not sure I want to know." He ponders on it for a moment. "I mean there's a part of me that really wants to know, but then, there's another part that's thinking, maybe it's better I don't."

"Why?"

"Because she's really cool, and we had a good time last night. Do I really want to taint this because of something that happen a couple of years ago?" He pauses for a moment. "If it even happened at all."

"I can't believe you." Jake says, shaking his head, "One night with the girl and you're in love. You're so desperate. How pathetic."

"You're pathetic."

269

"I'm awesome." Jake takes another hit and continues in the nasal voice, "And you know what? Eventually the truth is going to come out. So, you better make a smart decision now about whether you really want to know or not. Ask yourself – how serious do you wanna be with this girl? And is it a deal breaker if she did sleep with him? Because if the answer is yes to both of those questions..."

Cas cuts him off, "How serious do I want to be with this girl is not a yes or no question."

Jake brushes him off, "You know what I mean. If you dig her, and she slept with Manny and you know you wouldn't mess with her because of that, you should probably find out now before you invest serious time into a situation in which the occurrence of past events has already doomed the possibility of a future. You feel me?"

Cas nods to his friend's logic. "You're high, bro."

"True that," Jake acknowledges, "But I'm making sense, am I not?"

"Am you are, my friend. Am you are, indeed."

He takes out his phone and texts Samantha.

'*For sure. Just let me know when you're free. I'll call you later.*' He hits 'Send'.

"But I just decided. I don't want to know. Plus, I'm almost sure he didn't. He was either messing with you or you misunderstood him. But either way, I'm good not knowing."

"Hey, whatever lets you sleep at night. But I'm pretty sure I didn't misunderstand; I'm pretty sure he hit it. I think he said it was like two years ago."

"I doubt it." Cas's phone vibrates with a message. He checks it; it's from Samantha.

'Great ;'*

Smiling at the message, he looks up. "I seriously doubt it."

"If you say so," Jake says as he slouches back in the sofa, "But I still think you should find out sooner rather than later."

Staring straight ahead at the TV, Cas answers, "And I think you should shut the hell up."

They both look at each other and start cracking up.

Jake shakes his head, grinning. "Sucker for love, man. You're a sucker for love."

CHAPTER 15

I've Been Hurt

When Cas wakes up the next morning, his first thought is of Samantha. He checks his phone and sees that doesn't have any new messages. He is about to text her but decides to call instead.

"Hello," Samantha answers the phone

"Hey pretty face. I would like to take you out to dinner. Are you free tonight?" Cas asks.

"Am I free? For you? Not at all," she answers playfully.

"Alright, then," Cas plays along, "On that note, I believe I have to go now. Thank you, and have a good day."

"You're so silly." Samantha laughs. "Yes, I'm free. For you, I'm always free."

"Just for me?" he teases.

"Just for you." She laughs seductively. "Where should I meet you?"

"Wherever's most convenient for you. Where would you be coming from?"

"My place, the Heights."

"Cool, I know a great Spanish restaurant in the Heights. How far up do you live?"

"Remember where Veronica had her baby shower? I live like five minutes from there."

"What time should I pick you up?"

"No, you don't have to do that," she answers quickly, "I'll meet you there directly."

Cas laughs. "Are you serious? I can come get you, it's not a problem."

"No, really, it's fine. I appreciate the offer, but I don't want you to have to come all the way up here just to get me. Just text me where it is, and I'll meet you there."

"Listen, little miss independent, I can..."

She cuts him off before he can finish, "Oh shut up. I'm trying to make this easy for you."

"Well, you don't have to," he replies dryly.

"Trust me, I know I don't," she answers coyly, "I just want to."

He gives in. "OK, you got it."

"OK is right; so, shut your mouth and text me the address."

"Wow!" Cas bursts into laughter. "Say what now?"

Samantha's voice is dripping with sensuality. "You heard me very clearly."

"I think I heard you, but I'm going to act like I didn't. Because I don't take orders." He clears his throat. "But what I am going to do is text you the address so you can meet me there. And that's not because you said so, but because that was *my* intention from the very beginning."

"Okay, tough guy," she answers with the hint of a smile in her voice, "I'll see you tonight."

***

Cas gets to the restaurant at 8:00 PM. He looks around outside; Samantha is not there yet.

Not wanting to go in without her, he waits outside and enjoys the light breeze on the mild autumn night.

A beautiful dark-skinned Spanish girl walks past him; they make brief eye contact as she passes by. He watches her as she walks down the block, his gaze locked on the sway of her hips. *Damn, that's nice.*

Cas is caught off guard by the sudden tap on his shoulder. He turns around.

"Hey? You sneaking up on me?" he jokes.

"Maybe," Samantha replies.

They both smile and go in for hug.

"Hi," he says into her ear.

"Hi," she answers, hugging him a little tighter.

The embrace lasts longer than expected, neither seemingly wanting to let go.

"And hi to you too," she says with a slight giggle in her voice.

"Huh?" he replies before realizing what she meant. Engrossed in the embrace, Cas had failed to notice his arousal, and that his erect penis is pressing against her thigh.

"Oh," he answers, embarrassed, "Hello there."

Samantha laughs as she lets him go, grabs his face, and gives a quick soft kiss on the lips.

"You ready to go inside?" she asks.

Cas is hesitant. "Uh, give me a minute."

Samantha moves in close. "Why, is he still up?" She discretely moves her hand down towards his crotch and grabs it through his pants. "Holy shit, you're so hard."

He whispers back, "Uh, yeah. And you're not making it any better."

"You sure I can't make it better?" she asks with a seductive smile, squeezing his manhood.

"Stop!" Cas says, looking around, "You gonna make me skip dinner and take you straight home for dessert."

"Oh no, I'll stop." She quickly lets go of his dick. "We need to eat. I'm hungry."

Samantha grabs his hand and starts leading him towards the entrance.

Cas chuckles and tries to casually adjust his crotch to make his hard-on less noticeable as they walk into the restaurant.

"*Buenas*," the pretty hostess says with a smile, "*Para dos?*"

"*Buenas noches. Si, para dos.*"

The hostess grabs two menus and motions for them to follow her. The place is fairly packed, and she leads them to a table towards the back.

They have a seat, and she places a menu in front of each of them.

"Enjoy," she says with a parting smile.

"The food here is really good, especially their *pernil*." Cas looks over the menu.

"Mmmm, *pernil* sounds delicious. I think that's what I'm going to order."

A male waiter appears. "Ahh, the *pernil*. Excellent choice."

Samantha and Cas look at each other for a moment and burst into laughter.

The waiter looks a little confused. "Oh, I'm sorry, did I interrupt something?"

"No, not at all." Cas smiles at him. "I'm actually ready to order a drink."

***

Two hours later, Cas and Samantha come out of the restaurant, arm in arm, laughing loudly.

"That is so freaking funny!" she says, stumbling and almost bringing them both down in the process.

Cas has just enough balance to keep them upright; she falls into his arms.

"Whoa, whoa, easy girl. I gotcha."

They hug each other close, gently rocking from side to side. Her body suddenly starts to tremble, almost as if she's crying. He can't see her face because it is buried in his chest.

"Are you OK?" he asks.

She starts to tremble harder.

"Hey." Cas is concerned. "What's wrong? Are you crying?"

She slowly moves her face away from his chest and looks up at him, her eyes closed and her face brightened up with a huge smile.

"I'm just thinking about that story you told me about the dog peeing on your foot!" Her body shakes with loud laughter.

He starts laughing too. "That's so not funny. I mean it is now, but at the time, shit, I was mortified. For the whole rest of the year, people would say I smelled like dog piss."

Samantha doubles over in laughter.

"Oh," she says between breaths, "That's rich, that's really rich."

He wraps his arms around her waist and pulls her in.

"Easy now, don't hold me too close," she says, "You don't want to wake up 'you know who.'"

"Oh, we can go to my place now. So, he can be as wide awake as you need him to be."

"Really?" she replies, "And what makes you think I'm going back to your place?"

"Shit, you know how much I just spent on dinner?" he says, grinning widely.

"Oh, helllll no, you didn't," she answers back, pushing him away, "I hope you didn't just say that."

Cas changes his voice to sound like Tony Montana from *Scarface*, "I was only kiddin'!"

"Yeah, I bet." Samantha moves back and looks him up and down. "Well, news flash, honey. It takes a lot more than dinner at a run-down restaurant to get these goods," she says while playfully running her hands down her breasts and waist.

"That's what I'm saying," Cas chimes in, "It takes a lot more than a pretty face, a sexy body, and a great personality to get me home. So, sorry, your loss."

"Oh yeah, what else does it take?"

"Well," he begins, "It takes a big hug and lots of kisses."

"Like this?" Samantha grabs his shirt and brings him in close.

They begin to make out, Cas gently holds her face in his hands as he kisses her slowly and passionately.

They're interrupted by the horn of a passing car. "Get a room!" the driver yells out of the window.

Cas gives an embarrassed smile as he looks at Samantha.

"Are you going home with me?"

She looks down and slowly shakes her head.

"No? Really?" he says as he begins to playfully pinch and poke the side of her stomach.

She smiles and squirms. "Stop!"

He stops and places his hands on her hips. "So, do you want me to walk you home or put you in a cab?"

She looks down again and shakes her head.

"Well, I'm not letting you go home by yourself," he says, slightly squeezing her hips and then sliding his arms around her waist, "Unless, of course, you are going to come home with me."

This time, she slowly nods her head.

"Yes? You are coming home with me?"

She shakes her head 'no'.

"What?" Cas laughs in confusion. "Talk. 'Yes', you're coming with me, or 'no', you're not?'"

As Samantha looks up, wide-eyed, Cas can see the desire in her eyes – she bites her lower lips and nods her head 'yes'.

Cas kisses her forehead. "Cool".

Grabbing her hand, he leads her to the street to hail a cab. A livery cab quickly stops in front of them; he opens the door for her, and she gives a curtsy bow as a thank you.

The cab ride is quiet. They both choose to watch the concrete city scenery swooshing past the car window – they barely speak or look at each other.

Cas looks over at her to say something, but doesn't. Instead, he reaches for her hand and gently caresses it. She opens her palm up and lets him entwine his fingers with hers. They hold hands for the rest of the ride.

***

Cas takes out the keys for his apartment.

"Here we are," he says as he opens the door.

He tosses his keys on the desk. "You want anything to drink? I have some wine."

Samantha replies, "Thanks, love, I'll just take water."

"You sure? Cause I'm gonna have me some wine."

She laughs. "You lush."

"I be that," he answers with a smile. "Make yourself comfortable."

Cas goes to the kitchen to prepare the glasses.

Returning with two glasses, he hands the one with water to Samantha.

"Here you go, beautiful."

"Thank you very much."

She slips her heels off and folds her feet under herself on the sofa.

"I had a good time tonight," she says, looking at him.

"Good." He takes a sip from his glass. "So did I."

They're silent for a moment, each quietly sipping from their glass.

"Hey." The silence is broken by Samantha. "Do you smell that?"

"Huh?" Cas answers, breathing in deeply through his nose, "I don't smell anything. Does it smell bad?"

"Cas?" she asks, fighting back a smile, "How can you not smell that?"

"Oh, damn," he says, sitting up. Pinching the chest of his shirt, he pulls it outward so he can stick his nose inside to see if the smell is coming from him. "Is it that bad? I honestly can't smell it. I hope it isn't me. What does it smell like?"

"It's hard to say, but I think." Samantha inhales deeply. "I'm pretty sure the smell is dog piss."

"What?" He looks at her with a half-smile. "You got jokes? Is that what's going on here?"

Samantha bursts into laughter.

Cas shakes his head slowly in pretend disapproval. "You know, that was a traumatizing experience for me. I'm glad to see my pain brings you so much joy."

She tries to catch her breath. "Aww, poor baby. It must have been pretty traumatizing to have a dog piss on you, huh?"

"Yes!" He responds, playing it up, "It really was."

Samantha sticks out her lower lip in a pout and puts her arms around him; she lays her hands gently on the back of his neck.

"I'm sorry for messing with you." She leans in to give him a kiss.

They begin to softly make out.

After a moment, she starts to chuckle. "Well, I see someone is up again."

"Uh huh," he says as he reaches behind her and grabs a chunk of her ass. He begins to squeeze it. "Mmmm, I want some of that."

She gently grabs his hand and moves it off her. "Not now," she says with a weak smile.

"OK." Cas is confused. "Is everything alright?"

"Yes. It's just..." She looks down and her voice trails off.

"You're on your period!" Cas says, sounding sure of himself.

"No, stupid," she answers, "I'm not on my period."

"What is it, then?" He's concerned. "What's wrong?"

She leans in slowly and gently hugs him around his waist, her head lay against his chest again.

"I don't want you to think that's what this is all about."

Her comment makes him nervous; he feels a wave of guilt rush over him.

Why do I feel guilty? I haven't done anything wrong.

"Hey," he says as he starts to put his arms around her. Once she is in his embrace, the feeling of guilt quickly dissipates. "It's not all about that at all." He pulls her in a little closer.

"I hope not," she says, not looking up.

Cas laughs to lighten the mood. "What you mean you hope not? I'm telling you it's not."

"OK," Samantha says, and then looks up at him. Their eyes lock, she leans forward and gives him a light tap kiss on his lips.

He smiles at the gesture. "You wanna watch a movie?"

She gives him a soft punch in his stomach. "Let's do it."

***

A few hours later, after the movie is over, they're lying on the sofa, fully clothed. The TV is still on but barely audible, just white noise in the background.

Her head is positioned in the crook of his arm, his fingers absentmindedly caressing her shoulder.

Just as Cas begins to doze off, he is pulled away from his nap by the sound of her voice. He looks up at her through sleepy eyes.

"Cas?" Samantha says.

"What's up, baby?" he replies, smiling at how naturally that 'baby' came out.

"Can I tell you something without sounding all weird?"

"It's too late for that," he says jokingly, "I already think you're weird."

"Shut up." She giggles. "I'm serious."

"Hi, serious, I'm Cas. Nice to meet you."

"Oh my God," Samantha says with a smile in her voice, "How corny can you be?"

"OK, OK." He laughs. "What's up, babe?"

She breathes in deeply. "Do you know I've had a crush on you for years?"

He opens his eyes all the way now. "What? Are you serious? We haven't even known each other for years."

"Oh yes, we have, you just never noticed me." Samantha sighs. "I've seen you plenty of times."

"Really? Where?" Cas says, interested in her answer.

"At Veronica's house. You would come over to hang out with Manny, and I would be there. You just never noticed me."

"Really? Are you serious?"

"Yup. You would hardly ever even look at me."

Cas grins and shakes his head. "I find that so hard to believe. How could I have not noticed you?"

"Easy," she says, sitting up and looking at him, "You were a jerk."

"Yeah, I was kind of jerk-like when I was younger. But I don't think I would have been a jerk to *you*."

"You weren't exactly a jerk to me per say, you just never paid me any mind."

"Wait." Cas sits up as well. "You're talking about when? High school?"

"Yeah, you were in high school."

"Of course I didn't notice you then; I'm like three years older than you. When I was 16, you were 13. That's a huge difference in teen years."

"But I was around you when we were older too. You used to come home from college to visit; I was older then, and still you completely looked through me."

"Wow, now you're making me feel bad. I can't see myself ignoring you."

"Well, in your modest defense, I was kind of shy around you."

"You see!" Cas says, "You should have been a little bolder."

"Oh please, I tried. I would laugh really loud, or like, just look at you, just hoping you would notice me. But you never did."

"I'm sorry, baby, but you were too young for me back then. I never was into younger girls. And anyway, you have *all* my attention now." He leans in for a kiss.

Samantha moves her face away.

"Cas, how do you see me?"

"I see you as a beautiful woman."

"Thanks," she says, "But I mean, how do you see us? Where do you see this going?"

He pauses for a moment.

"What do you mean?" he asks, although he knows exactly what she means.

Samantha answers quickly, "I mean do you see us being together? Or is this just some bit of fun for you? Am I just a piece of ass?"

Her frankness catches him off guard.

"Well, you're definitely not just a piece of ass," Cas says with a huge smile. "You've got a nice rack too."

"Ohhhhh!" Samantha begins to pinch his stomach. "You got jokes? Mister funny guy," she says with an extra hard pinch.

"Owwwww!" Cas is laughing in pain. "Stop, that hurts!"

"Keep on with the wisecracks when I'm trying to be serious and I'll pinch your balls the next time."

The thought makes him shudder. "No, no, that would not be cool at all. I will behave now. Promise."

Now she laughs. "Good, cause I'll really do it the next time."

Samantha moves back in to lie on top of him. She sighs. "Look, I know we just started dating, and to be honest, I regret sleeping with you on the very first night because it was way too soon. We should have waited longer."

"Hey," Cas begins to assure her, "I don't judge you, or me for that matter, for us getting down with the get down. It felt absolutely right, and by no means do I think you just go around doing that normally. I felt like we connected."

"I hope you mean that because I felt that too."

"Listen, I've been hurt before and..."

She cuts him off, stands up, and begins to pace, "And I've been hurt before too, lots of times, unfortunately. And I don't want to be hurt again. I like you a lot, but if you don't see this as having potential for something serious, then just tell me that now. No hard feelings. You go your way, I'll go mine. But I'm definitely not going to put up with bullshit. So, if this is bullshit, just be honest with me now, so I can remove myself."

The seriousness in her tone causes Cas to sit up. "I don't want you to remove yourself. And I don't think this is bullshit. I think I like you, and I'm looking forward to getting to know you better."

"Really?" she asks, trying to figure out from his face if he's being sincere.

"Dead ass," he responds as he gets up, grabs her, and tries to pull her in closer to him.

Samantha playfully resists. "You better mean it. Because, if not, I'm gonna hurt you, mister."

"Oh, baby," replies Cas without missing a beat. "You can hurt me anytime you want."

She laughs and gives in, allowing her body to fall into his embrace.

He hugs her tight and kisses her on her forehead.

Samantha looks up at him and leans in for a kiss.

It starts off subtle, only for a moment; then, she pushes her tongue deep into his mouth.

Cas is caught off guard – and instantly aroused.

CHAPTER 16

Sleep Well

Over the next month, Cas and Samantha go on several dates; he frequently stays over at her place.

Samantha has a one-bedroom apartment in Washington Heights, overlooking the Hudson River. Cas prefers going over to her place because she doesn't have a roommate, so it's more intimate.

When he's in his own apartment he wishes he was back in hers. He notices that when she's not around, he misses her. He doesn't want to, but he does. He knows it's way too early to even consider real, strong feelings for her, but he can't help himself. The thought of Samantha makes him smile.

This morning, Cas wakes up next to her – the sheets are off her back, revealing Samantha's soft skin as she lies on her side, facing away from him.

While he admires her, his mind begins to drift.

What makes people fall for each other?

This question has occurred to him many times over the years.

Throughout his life, Cas has been fortunate enough to have dated many women. Beautiful, intelligent, independent women who would have gladly given their hearts to him. Of course, not every girl he dated fell for him, not even close. But the ones who did fall, always fell hard.

He remembers an old fling named Lisa; they'd met on the internet, through a free dating site. She was from a small town in upstate New

York, and although she was only younger than him by less than four years, judging by her admiration of Cas, one would've thought he was decades older than her. She was fascinated by Cas; he was this good-looking young writer from the city, nothing like the guys in her small town.

They went on two actual dates – the first one being dinner and a movie. The second date was at a small dark lounge in the East Village where Cas has taken many dates. It's a place where the drinks are good, the lights are dim, and the small crowd and music are both diverse and chill. The kind of place anyone would feel comfortable in. They had a great time. He slept with her that night. After that, they didn't go out on dates anymore; she strictly came over for sex.

She lived almost two hours away, and they didn't see each other often, rarely more than twice a month. But when they did meet up, it was always the same thing. She would drive a long way over to his house; Cas would always have some take-out food ready for her and a bottle of whatever liquor they'd decided on for the night. They would eat, drink, talk, and laugh. Then, eventually, one of them would go in for a kiss, and it would be *on* from there.

It was always hard and aggressive; they fucked each other like each time could be the last. Cas always felt obligated to have his 'A' game on with her. *She drove two hours for me, better give her that good dick.*

Lisa adored Cas. She adored him before she ever met him in person, just based on the messages they exchanged on the dating site. When they did meet in person, by the end of the first date, she was completely and hopelessly in love with him.

Cas knew how Lisa felt about him, but he always acted as if he didn't. He pretended they had this mutual understanding, that they simply enjoyed hanging out every once in a while and having hot sex. Nothing more.

But inside, he knew better – she loved him. Lisa never said it– she just showed it by catering to everything he wanted, always eager to do anything to gain his approval. If he would have asked her to suck his toes, she would have done it enthusiastically and gratefully.

Of course, Cas played dumb to this, willfully denying the fact that she was in love with him. Because he knew that acknowledging Lisa's feelings for him, and still continuing to fuck her, knowing that it meant nothing to him, would make him a pretty heartless person. So, he would deny it in his mind to avoid feeling guilty for continuing to have sex with her. It didn't work, though. He felt guilty about fucking her, just not guilty enough to stop.

For reasons he couldn't figure, Cas never fell in love with Lisa. They generally had a good time with each other; she was attractive, smart, and always laughed at his jokes. That was a plus because he knew he could be corny at times. The sex, however, was his favorite part – kinky and passionate. They always went at it hard, as if it were a work out. They'd bang each other to dehydration – their bodies spent and sweaty, trying to catch their breath. Too exhausted to get up, they would usually fall asleep right afterwards, often in each other's arms.

Cas actually *tried* to fall in love with her – it just seemed like the logical thing to do. She treated him great, she was loyal, and they had awesome sex – what more could he possibly want? But it just wouldn't happen for him. His feelings never grew beyond like and lust, and he could never understand why.

There were times when Lisa would stay over at his place. On these occasions, Cas would wake up in the middle of the night and look over at her sleeping next to him, overwhelmed with guilt. He knew no matter what she did, he would never love her – she was just not the one for him, and that what they had going was only temporary. Eventually, it would be over and she would be hurt.

And just as he couldn't figure out why he didn't fall in love with Lisa, he can't figure why he's starting to fall for Samantha.

As these thoughts float through his head, Samantha turns over in her sleep and lays her arm across his stomach – the warmth of her skin feels good against his. Cas looks down at her sleeping face and smiles. She looks so pretty, so peaceful.

He lies on his side and gently wraps his arm around her. She instinctively moves in closer, their bodies cuddled together with a familiarity that makes him feel like he's known this woman a lot more than just a few weeks.

His thoughts slow down. He closes his eyes and absentmindedly rubs her back as he drifts back to sleep.

***

He wakes up to the inviting smell of bacon and lets out a loud yawn.

"Good morning, sleepy head," Samantha yells out from the kitchen.

"Morning, baby," Cas says from the bed, feeling too comfy to get up.

Samantha calls out, "Did you sleep well?"

He smiles at the question.

How sweet is this girl? You gotta really care about somebody to ask them if they slept well. He nods in agreement with his own thoughts.

Samantha peeks in through the door way.

"Hey, booger face," she says, "Did you hear me?"

"Booger face?" He looks at her from the bed. "You're the only booger face around these parts. It's well known," he says in a matter-of-fact tone. Samantha opens her mouth in shock, then scrunches her face as she begins to saunter into the bedroom.

"What did you say to me?" she says as she approaches him, looking especially short without her shoes on; she's barely 5'3".

Cas laughs and lies back in bed, his hands behind his head. "You heard me."

Samantha climbs into the bed and mounts him. She leans in and grabs his wrists to pin him down.

"What did you just say?" she asks and playfully bites him on the side of the face, lightly at first, then a little harder.

Cas lets out an exaggerated yell, "Owww! Don't bite my face!"

"I'll bite it again!" Samantha answers, chomping her teeth in front his nose.

Cas moves his head from side to side, trying to dodge her bites.

"No, you can't do this to me!" he says as he pretends to struggle to get his hands loose.

"You called me a booger face. A booger face!" she yells and quickly leans in for another bite.

"Wait!" Cas exclaims, "That's not what I said. I never said any of that!"

291

"Oh really?" Samantha says, still holding him pinned down by his wrists. "So, what did you say then?"

"What I said *was* that it's not nice to call me a booger face. And in this day and age, with the anti-bullying campaign and you being a teacher, you should really know better."

Samantha lets go of his wrist and sits on top of him, with the weight of her thighs and ass pressed against his crotch. He begins to get hard. She can feel it, and grinds against him ever so slowly.

She tilts her head, her mouth pulled into a sad pout.

"Aww, did I hurt the baby's feelings?" she says, grinding harder.

Cas gets dreamy-eyed; he slowly nods his head 'yes'.

Samantha leans forward, slightly lifting her ass off him. She reaches between his thighs and grabs his hard cock.

"I know what will make you feel better."

She pulls his dick out of his boxers and moves the fabric of her panties to the side, exposing her pussy. Samantha positions herself directly on top of the tip of his penis.

Cas is throbbing. His hands grip her thighs, squeezing them.

I need a condom.

She rubs the head of his dick between her lips – it's wet. She slowly sits on it, letting herself wrap around it, urging his rock-hard meat inside her. Samantha closes her eyes and lets out a slow moan; she moves her hips, each movement making her wetter. She opens her eyes and looks at him more intensely, gyrating harder. She leans in and bites his chest. Cas moans – it's a bit painful but he doesn't really mind.

Samantha kisses the spot she'd just bitten, then bites him even harder – sinking her teeth into his chest as she rides his cock. Cas tries to take it at first, but her bites get harder – it becomes too painful.

"Arrhh," he yells and pulls her by the back of her hair. She looks deep into his eyes, still moving her hips. Cas pulls her hair tighter, yanking her head closer to him, and begins to kiss her – her lips, neck, and breasts, his mouth touches her everywhere. He uses his other hand to grab her ass and begins thrusting upwards rapidly. Samantha moans loudly and slams down on him with each hard stroke, their skin slapping loudly.

The sex is hot, and Cas is getting ahead of himself. He's been inside her for less than five minutes, and he's about to cum already. He fights it.

Fuck, man, don't do it. You don't have a fucking condom, you idiot.

It's too intense – he's about to explode.

Pull out!

He goes to lift Samantha off of him, but she forces all her weight down, not letting him come out. "Wait," she says, biting her lip, riding him hard, "Almost there."

"Oh fuck!" Cas clenches his jaws and closes his eyes tightly – he's about to lose it.

Hold!

He uses every muscle in his body to prevent himself from ejaculating.

Hold!

This is it, he can't hold another moment.

Nooooo!

"Oh shit!" Samantha stops moving and looks at him, her eyes wide open.

"The food!" She jumps off of him and runs towards the kitchen.

Cas lies there, his eyes shut tight, his dick bobbing in the air like a flag pole. He held.

"Wow," he says to himself; breathing hard as his tense body begins to relax.

"That was close," Samantha calls out from the kitchen.

"Tell me about it." He shakes his head and chuckles to himself.

"It's cool though, nothing burned." She turns off the stove. "But I have to be more careful."

Cas exhales, "You and me both."

***

Samantha falls into his embrace, her cheek pressed against his chest; laying on top of him, breathing heavily. They both lie in silence for a moment, basking in the afterglow.

"You didn't answer my question," she says.

"What?"

She moves her head back and looks up at him. "Did you sleep well?"

Cas puts his arms around her, pulling her in closer. "I always sleep well when I'm here."

Samantha's eyes crinkle from the big smile on her face. "Oh yeah?"

He looks down at her and leans in for a kiss. "Yes."

"Yessssss," she says, still looking up, her eyes tightly closed and her lips puckered. Cas chuckles and gives her a soft kiss.

Samantha smiles and leans into him, her cheek pressed against his chest again. "I slept well too," she says.

They hold each other tight for a moment. Cas's hands begin moving down towards her ass; he's about to grab it when she pushes him away and gets up.

"Don't start. What are you, a machine? Can we just pause for a second to eat? Jesus, I'm hungry, and you trying to bang me again. Can I finish making breakfast already?"

Cas laughs and goes to slap her butt as she walks away, but misses it.

"Don't burn the house down," he yells out.

"Shut up!" She shoots back from the kitchen.

He smiles and shakes his head as he gets up from bed and begins to stretch. Looking over at the night stand, he sees that his phone is blinking red. He grabs it, there are four text messages.

The first is from Jake at 1:30 AM, *'You coming out?'*

Cas ignores it. *I'll hit him back later.*

Looking at the next message, his eyes widen, his heart begins to race, and his cock pulsates. All three are from Elizabeth.

The first was at 8:30 AM. *'Hi ;)'*

The next was at 9:04 AM. *'Hello???'*

And the last was at 9:24 AM. *'Guess you're sleeping... Anyway I been thinking about you and just wanted to say hi...'*

Cas hasn't spoken to Elizabeth in well over a month. He's excited to hear from her, but his excitement quickly turns into guilt as his conscience pulls him towards Sam.

Samantha's a good one, Cas. Don't be stupid.

His thoughts are brought to a halt as she peeks through the door.

Samantha looks at him and instantly senses something is off. "You alright?" She asks.

"Yeah," Cas replies casually, hitting the button to close his messages. He places it back on the night stand. "I'm good, babe. Just checking my phone."

Samantha motions to the night stand and says, "Let me see it."

Cas smiles as his stomach flips. "What?"

"Let me see your phone," she says almost casually.

"For real?" He smiles, trying not to seem nervous.

"Of course not." Samantha laughs. "I don't want to see your phone, player."

He laughs with her. "How am I a player?"

She smiles and shrugs. "I'm just messing with you, but look how nervous you got. Anyway, do you want toast?"

"I wasn't nervous." He acts normal. "But, yes, I'll take some toast if it's not too much trouble."

Samantha puts her hands on her hips. "You know, making toast is a whole lot of trouble. But I think you're worth it."

Cas smiles sincerely and relaxes. "Aww shucks." He moves in for a kiss.

"Aww shucks." Samantha smiles and kisses him back.

As she turns around and walks out of the room, the smile slowly drops from Cas's face. He looks at his phone sitting on the night stand.

Don't do it.

You're happy with Sam, you don't need to complicate things.

His reasoning begins to drift away as his cock begins to pulsate again.

What's the big deal? It's just a text. Plus, me and Samantha haven't made anything official, we never said we were exclusive. Technically, I'm still single; so, it's not like I'm doing anything wrong. And, damn, Elizabeth is fucking hot.

He grabs his phone and looks at it.

Before he could do anything else, Samantha calls out, "Breakfast is ready."

Cas is overcome with guilt.

You're a real douche, you know that? You have a good thing in the works here, and you would consider fucking it up just to get a piece of ass. A married piece of ass at that.

Standing there for a moment, he nods in agreement with his own thoughts.

Don't be stupid, man. Don't be a douche bag.

Without writing anything, he tosses it on the bed.

You're happy with Sam.

He walks out of the room with a pep in his step, feeling good about himself.

"Yo, Chef Boy'r dee. What are you doing over there?"

"Messing with your butt, I almost burned the eggs," Samantha answers.

297

"I'm sorry my manliness distracted you. I'll try to keep my swag to a minimum from now on."

"Oh please." She sucks her teeth. "What you really need to keep to a minimum is your stink-ass breath."

Cas starts to crack up. "Oh damn, babe, it's that bad?"

"Yes, seriously," she says from the kitchen, "It makes the Ozone layer cry."

"Oooooh…" Cas chuckles. "You got jokes now?"

"I'm serious," she replies, "I had second thoughts about kissing you this morning because that's not the way you wanna start your day."

Cas looks at her deadpan. Bringing his hands to his face, he breathes into his palms and tries to smell his own breath. He inhales deeply.

"Smells like roses," he replies.

"What!" Samantha exclaims. "Dead roses. You're king of the stinky-breath people. And I'm gonna keep making fun of you till you stop smoking for good."

He goes into the bathroom, turns on the sink, and grabs his toothbrush and toothpaste.

"What are you taking about? I hardly smoke cigarettes anymore, only when I drink. And I'm gonna quit eventually."

She yells back, "I'm not just talking about cigarettes. It's the weed too, weed breath."

He stops brushing for a moment and looks at himself in the mirror.

"This bitch crazy," he says through a suds-filled mouth.

"What'd you say?" she yells over.

"Nothing, babe," he replies and continues brushing.

"Well, hurry up, breakfast is ready."

"OK, be right there." The aroma of bacon starts his appetite's engine.

"That smells really good," he says, as he walks into the kitchen.

"It tastes even better." She takes a crispy piece of bacon and places it in his mouth. He eats it out of her hand and acts like he is going to bite her fingers off.

She quickly pulls her hand back. "Hey, my fingers are not on the menu."

Cas comes in close and playfully grabs her ass. "Are these buns on the menu?"

With his other hand, he cuffs her breast. "How about these cupcakes?" He bites his lower lip as he squeezes her breast.

"Chill out, horn dog." She laughs and pushes him away. "Cupcake? Buns? What the hell? You're comparing me to food?"

"Yes," Cas adds with a smile, "Your body is like a buffet, I just want to eat it all up."

The smile drops from her face. "My body is a buffet? You trying to say I'm fat?"

"What? Of course not. You're in great shape, you put me to shame. So much so that after I eat this big ol' plate, I'm gonna go to the gym." He grabs another crispy piece of bacon and shoves it in his mouth, grunting like a caveman.

"Pig!" Samantha exclaims, softly smacking his chest.

He smiles, takes a bite of toast, and then grabs both of their plates. "C'mon," he says, nodding for her to follow him into the living room.

299

They sit down next to each other on the sofa; he grabs the remote and turns on the TV.

"No sports!" she calls out before he has a chance to pick a channel.

He starts to laugh. "OK, no sports. You cooked, so you pick what we watch."

She looks at him with a big smile and goes in for a greasy-bacon lip kiss.

***

After breakfast, Cas gets dressed and lies on the couch, while Sam takes a shower and starts getting ready. As he waits, he closes his eyes and dozes off. Shortly afterwards, he's awakened by Samantha planting a kiss on his forehead.

"You ready?" She's standing over him, her eyes admiring his face.

"Let's do it." Cas gets up from the sofa and follows her as she walks towards the door. He puts his arms around her and gives her a kiss on the top of her head.

"Am I gonna see you later?"

Samantha gives an exaggerated frown and pouts. "Probably not. I have a lot of papers to grade, and if you come over, you'll just distract me."

"Me, a distraction?" He laughs. "You're probably right though; I wouldn't let you get anything done."

"Exactly, with all your manly manliness and what not." She gives him a quick kiss. "Plus, you have work to do too. You need to finish your article."

"That's true," he answers.

Just as she reaches out to undo the locks and pull the door open, Cas grabs her by the arm, turns her around, and kisses her; she gladly obliges. They make out softly for a moment. Samantha pulls away.

"Stop, you're making me not want to leave."

Cas smiles with sleepy eyes. "That's the plan."

She laughs. "I have to go, baby. I'm meeting up with my mom, and you're not lying around my apartment all day. So, you gotta get the heck out of here."

"Fine," Cas begrudgingly agrees. "I'll go home and get some work done."

"Good." Samantha leans in for a quick kiss, grabs his hand, and leads him out of the door.

CHAPTER 17

The Grande Maduro

A few hours later, Cas is sitting at his desk, with his fingers on the keyboard, staring at the screen. He's paid some bills online, looked at sports highlight videos, and read a few articles. But he's yet to get any of his work done. In fact, he hasn't punched a key in 20 minutes; his mind is elsewhere.

Elizabeth.

He stares at his phone for a long time, feeling compelled to call her, but he resists. Looking up at the blank document on the computer, he tries to think about what to write. His fingers are on the keyboard, but his thoughts are obstructed. He looks back at the phone.

"Should I?" he asks himself. "Let me just read her text again."

He grabs the phone and goes to his text messages. He looks at the last one.

'Guess you're sleeping... Anyway I been thinking about you and just wanted to say hi...'

He reads it over and over.

Should I write back? For what? The woman is married. You're happy with Samantha, things are going well. Just leave it alone, man. Just leave it alone.

His conscience is telling him all the right things to do, but his thumbs find themselves on his phone's touch keyboard. Suddenly, the phone rings and his heart jumps.

Elizabeth?

Looking at the screen, he realizes it's Jake; his heart relaxes.

Cas answers, "What's up, brother?"

"What up, bro? I noticed you haven't been answering my calls, and I just wanted to say fuck you."

Cas laughs out loud. "My bad! Sorry, dude. I just been chilling, man, nothing major. Hanging out with Samantha a lot."

"Sucker for love ass." Jake laughs. "So typical."

"What do you mean *typical?*" Cas is already annoyed. "Nothing's *typical.* She's mad cool, I like spending time with her, and I don't give a fuck how you feel about it."

"Wow, look how defensive you got. *I like spending time with her,*" he mocks him. "You're whipped so quick. You've known her for two hours. Slow down, cowboy."

The phone is silent for a moment.

Cas relaxes and chuckles, "I know, right? It's only been like over a month. But fuck it, dude, it feels good right now. I know it's early and things always seem great in the beginning, but whatever. We'll see how it goes."

"I hear ya." Jake messes with his boy. "So, I guess you got over the whole Manolo thing? That's cool."

"Dude." Cas tries to remain calm. "She didn't sleep with him. He lied to you."

"You asked her about it?" Jake is curious. "She told you this?"

"No." He's trying his hardest to sound nonchalant. "I'm not worried about it. I know she didn't."

303

"I'm almost certain he said she did," Jake pauses, "But you know what? That's none of my business. As long as you're happy, that's what's up. The past is in the past." He sounds sincere.

Cas is getting irritated and wants to change the subject. "So, what's up, man? What you up to?"

"Nothing. I've hardly been home the past couple of weeks, and you don't even call to check on me. I could be dead and you wouldn't even know."

"Jacob, we text almost every day. And you're right, I wouldn't know because I've hardly been home either. I thought we've just been missing each other."

"Two ships in the night, man. Are you home now? I'm on my way. I have some time to kill before my next session."

"Yup, I'm here. I'll see you when you get here."

"Bet. See you soon."

Cas hangs up the phone, feeling sour that Jake brought up Manolo and Samantha.

"Asshole," he says under his breath.

A few moments pass and his intercom rings.

Cas presses the 'Door' button and unlocks the front door. Sitting back at his desk, he keeps looking at his phone, wondering if he should text Elizabeth back. Another moment passes and Jake walks in.

"What's up, Novocain?"

Cas spins around in his desk chair and stands up to greet him. Although Jake can annoy the shit out of him, he's happy to see his best friend and roommate. They give each other a pound hug.

"What's up, man?" he says with a smile.

"Chilling, dude." Jake drops his gym bag to the floor. "Just running around, working. I want to thank you again for that flier you made for me. It came out great. The whole interactive component with the champagne bottles popping, it was really dope."

"It was pretty cool, huh?" Cas smiles.

"Definitely." Jake nudges him towards his phone. "I don't know if you saw, but I just sent you my half of the rent."

He looks at his phone. "I saw the quick pay. But you gave me too much, did you realize that?"

"I sent you an extra 300 bucks. That's for your work on the flier."

"Yeah?" Cas's smile widens.

"Yup. The event was a success. I made a nice profit, and you came through big time with the fliers. A lot of people complimented them. Actually, I gave out your contact info to a few people who want you to do some work for them. I'm sure you don't mind."

"Of course not. Thanks, man. I think I did get an email from someone but I wasn't sure if it was spam."

"Check it when you get a chance. It's probably potential work."

"Will do. Thanks, man. And thanks for the moolah."

"You earned it, man. But you definitely missed out on that night. Some crazy times; you should have come."

"Maybe next time."

"Yeah, if you're not too far up your new girl's ass." Jake grins. "So, what's this stuff with Samantha, bro? You really like her?"

Cas shrugs, trying to play it cool. "Yeah. She's pretty dope. But I know it's still early, so we'll see. She's definitely my main squeeze, though."

Jake laughs. "Your only squeeze."

"No," Cas replies, walking over to his desk and sitting down. "Not my only squeeze."

"Oh really? You have another one?" Jake asks in happy disbelief. "You're talking to someone else? Who's the other?"

"The *other*?" Cas looks away, eyes glancing at his phone. He looks up at Jake. "You. You're the other. You're my side chick."

"Ha," Jake replies, deadpan, "I knew you were lying."

Cas chuckles and spins around in his chair to face the computer screen; Jake has a seat on the sofa. He picks up the cable remote and turns on the TV.

"So, are you really talking to someone else or not?"

Cas clears his throat. "I might be. Remember Elizabeth? Veronica's friend?"

"Of course, I remember her," Jake answers, not looking away from the TV, "And I told you already, she's out of your league."

"What? Out of my league?" Cas scuffs. He closes his laptop and goes into the living room.

"What are you talking about? How is she out of my league when I hit it already?"

Jake quickly glances over at him. "Yeah, right. Sure, you did."

A smile slowly creeps across Cas's face, he shakes his head.

"Wow, Jake, really? You just proved that you don't listen to anything I say. What a friend. Lucky me." Cas snatches the remote from his hand and plants himself on the opposite side of the sofa.

Jake sucks his teeth. "Man, stop it." He gets up and heads for the desk chair. "I always listen to all your tall tales."

Sitting down in the very comfortable, mahogany leather computer chair, Jake slowly spins the seat around and reclines as far back in the chair as he can, smiling the whole time. He looks up at Cas. "When did you tell me you had sex with Elizabeth?"

Cas motions for him to get up. "Dude, why are you sitting in my chair? You know I don't like anybody sitting in my work chair."

"Are you serious?" Jake laughs. "This fucking chair is, like, two years old, bro. Get over yourself." He spins around again.

"Alright, sorry to ruin your fun, but get up. I'm working anyway. I need my chair."

"Whatever." Jake sighs and puts his hands on the armrest as if he's about to get up but freezes, almost in a sitting squat.

Tossing the remote back on the sofa, Cas stands up and walks over to his desk. "Get up, man."

"Hold on," Jake replies, "I have to fart." He smiles broadly as he gets up. "Ahhh, there we go."

"Yo, what the hell!" Cas is pissed. "What's wrong with you!"

Before he can say anything else, Jake cuts him off.

"Relax, man." He puts his hands on Cas's shoulders. "I was totally fucking with you. Geez, lighten up."

Cas feels foolish for getting so angry. He quickly shakes his shoulders to move Jake's hands.

"Get the hell off me," he says as they both start laughing.

Jake takes a seat on the sofa. "So, when did you tell me this lie about fucking Elizabeth?"

Cas reluctantly goes to his chair, sniffing hard to make sure Jake really didn't pass gas; not smelling anything, he sits down.

"I told you about it when it happened. It was a while ago. Over a month already, probably close to two."

"I can't believe it," Jake says, shaking his head, "I would remember something like that."

"You should." Cas turns his chair to face the computer. He looks at his phone – no new messages.

"How can you not remember? I told you we went for hookah, we got ripped, and we went at it in the bathroom. It was intense."

"Holy shit." Jake sits up on the sofa. "You did tell me that. But I thought you were talking about that waitress?"

"Who? Megan?" Her face flashes through Cas's mind. "No, not her. I told you, Elizabeth."

"Wow, dude, that's awesome! I can't believe I didn't realize you were talking about her. I keep forgetting her name is Elizabeth. Lovely. I remember you telling me you hit it in the bathroom, and it was crazy."

"Yeah." Cas smiles at the thought of her. "It was cool. I mean, we were in a tight-ass bathroom; so, I couldn't really do my thing the way I wanted to. It would have been better if we'd gotten it on somewhere else."

"So, you still seeing her?"

"Well, I haven't since that day." He reaches for his phone on the desk. "But..."

Jake cuts him off, "You didn't hit it right. You probably nutted too fast."

Cas ignores the comment and points at his phone. "But she just hit me up today and said she's been thinking about me. So, there is that, you *hater*."

"Sweet!" Jake sounds impressed. "Did you text her back?"

"No, not yet, I didn't see it until like two hours after she'd sent it, because I was at Samantha's place..." Cas pauses for a moment. "That's the other thing, Sam is really cool. And as steaming hot as Elizabeth is, she has plenty of issues. She's married, she's not sure if she's getting a divorce, she has a kid that's a few years younger than me; like, everything about it is off. There's really nothing there as far as future potential is concerned."

"There's potential." Jake laughs. "Potential to get more of that hot ass! Are you kidding me? If she's okay with it? If she's D.T.F? You have to do it. She's too beautiful to pass up. You said you hit it in a bathroom? That's no way to treat a woman like that. You have to lay her down on a bed, like a gentleman, at least one time. I don't care how hot and heavy you got in a bathroom. If you get another chance to take it down, take it. Otherwise, you're going to regret it for the rest of your life."

Cas looks at him. "Yolo and all that?"

"You only live once, bro."

"Alright, heartbreak Jake. I know what it means. But it's also an excuse to do dumb shit." Cas alters his voice to sound like a suburban teenager. "Dude, let's rob a bank. Why not? YOLO! Let's do some heroin, dude! Yeah! YOOOLOOO!"

Jake shakes his head. "C'mon man. That's not Yolo – that's yo' dumb. That's just being stupid."

"Yeah, well, messing things up with Samantha would be pretty stupid too." He begins flicking through channels on the TV.

"If you really don't wanna mess this up, just throw Elizabeth my way. If she gives me one night, oh lord, she would love me. I'd take her to heights she's never seen. She'd introduce me to her husband. I'll cuckold him." Jake laughs at his own joke.

"Ha! That's funny." Cas laughs too. "She's out of your league, man. You got no swag."

"Swag? You know damn well they call me Jake McSwagger a.k.a. Mr. Swaggly Waggly."

"When you say, 'They call you,' are you referring to the voices in your head or actual, real, live people?"

"Both." Jake gets up and heads to the kitchen. "What we got to eat? Ho-Ho's and Ding-Dongs, or is there some real food?"

"Ho-Ho's and Ding-Dongs?" Cas follows him into the kitchen. "Sounds like an 80's porno flick."

"Starring your mom, oh!" Jake answers as he opens the fridge and takes out a carton of eggs.

"Ha ha, funny guy. I actually been staying away from the junk food lately. Trying to be a little more health conscious."

"Good to hear that. You actually look like you lost a little weight."

Cas smiles and pats himself on the stomach. "Thanks, man, I've been trying to."

Jake nods and pokes him on the side. "Well, you need to try a little harder, tubby."

The smile drops off his face. "Just make sure you clean up whatever mess you make and do your own dishes. You have a habit of leaving your trash around. I'm not your freakin' maid."

Jake looks at him. "Relax, roomie. You sound like my mom."

"No," Cas replies, "If I said, 'Oh Juan, you do me so well,' then I would sound like your mom."

"Ha!" Jake laughs. "You got mom jokes now?"

"You started it." Cas grabs the orange juice and pours it out into a glass.

"Hey, can you pass me a bowl?" Jake asks. "And where's the cooking spray?"

"Cooking spray?" Cas looks at him in mock disgust. "Real men don't use cooking spray. We use butter. Be a fucking man, bro."

"I thought I bought cooking spray?"

"You did. That was like two months ago. It's finished."

"Damn." Jake goes back in the fridge to grab the butter. "So, what's good with the cougar? You got pics?"

"Elizabeth?" Cas shrugs dismissively. "No, I didn't ask for any."

"Real men get pics." Jake places a frying pan on the stove and turns it on. "She must not be feeling you that much."

"Why you gotta hate?" Cas sighs. "I'm not gonna ask her to send me pics like I'm some horny teenager."

"Why not? What's the big deal?"

"She's not some dumb young chick. You just said it yourself, she's a beautiful, grown-ass woman. Asking her for a pic seems so juvenile."

"Oh, I see." Jake nods, cracking open two eggs in the bowl. He grabs a fork and begins to beat them. "Sounds like you're chicken to me."

"Chicken? How can I be scared? I already took it down. If I never see her again, we still had that time at the hookah lounge."

311

"Yeah, but think about it." He pours out the eggs on to the hot pan. "This gorgeous woman, married for years, probably hasn't had another man but her husband in, like, forever – you get a shot at it, and you fuck her in a bathroom? That's wack. Don't let that be your one and only time. Look, with a woman like that, like I said, you gotta lay her down on a bed, take your time with it. Treat her right, you know?"

Cas's shoulders slump. "I've thought about that." He stares at the ground, shaking his head slowly. "A bathroom was definitely not ideal. Don't get me wrong, it was super hot, but still. We couldn't really get down the way we wanted to. I mean, shit, after a few minutes, there were people who had to use the bathroom, knocking on the door. That was a blower."

"Exactly. That's my point. If you're going to do it, then do it right, you know?"

Jake put a few slices of cheese on his eggs as they cook. Cas watches in silence as he thinks.

"I mean, the woman is gorgeous," Cas ponders out loud, "But I don't know. I just don't know if I want to."

Jake mocks him, "Aww, you just don't know if you want to? Is it because you're in love? You've been dating a girl for what? Two days? And now you think you're in love?"

"Shut up. Who said I'm in love?" He's annoyed. "That's just you speaking nonsense, I never said I'm in love."

"Yeah, but I know you. You start with the 'I think this is the one' crap. You cut off every other girl you're talking to and dive in head first. Then, after two or three months, you start with the 'I don't think she's the one' crap. You start to panic, the relationship goes sour, and you're alone again. And then you're like, 'Man, I should have fucked that cougar Elizabeth when I still had the chance.'"

Jake flips his omelet.

"True," Cas agrees. "But this time could be different."

Jake laughs. "Yeah, I forgot about the 'This time might be different' crap."

"It might be."

"Hmm." Jake pauses and flips over his eggs again. "Did you forget about the fact that there's a really good chance that Manolo hooked up with her?"

"Dude, please shut up. I never said I'm in love, and Sam did not sleep with Manny. Why you keep saying that stupid shit? What do you have against Samantha? Is it that you like her?"

"No. And I don't have anything against her. I'm just trying to make you see that you really don't know her that well. Maybe she is great and you all get married in the future, but the future's not promised; only the here and now."

He uses a spatula to slide the eggs on to a plate.

"And in the here and now, what I'm trying to say is, if there's ever a time to holler at Elizabeth, that time is now. She's not leaving her husband for you, she made that clear before; so, that kind of lets you off the hook as far as confusing things goes. She probably just wants to hook up every once in a while. You know, they say older women's libidos are crazy; she's in her sexual prime right now. She's probably tired of her husband – he doesn't appreciate her, takes her for granted, and she wants a young stud to bang her. Make her feel good. Make her feel sexy. I know, I've fucked plenty of MILFs. They don't always have the best bodies, but they've always got some good-ass pussy."

Cas laughs. "You're stupid."

"I'm serious, man. She wants to get worked. You have to hit it at least one more time, maybe more, make it worth her while. If things progress with you and Samantha, then you end your hook ups with Elizabeth; that's it. But this is your window to go get her, man. If you and your Sam make it official – and that's probably going to happen sooner rather than later – once that happens, the window is officially closed; it's shut tight. After that, if you reach out to Elizabeth, you'll be cheating. Right now, you're technically not in a relationship, so you're technically not doing anything wrong. *But* time's a-ticking."

Jake grabs his plate and a fork and goes to sit down in the living room to eat. Cas follows him and takes a seat on the opposite coach.

"Your logic is not totally flawed. I would definitely love another crack at Elizabeth, and it wouldn't be cheating on Samantha because we're not *technically* together."

"That's all I'm saying, brother, that's all I'm saying," Jake replies and turns his attention to his plate.

A few moments pass. Jake is eating his food and watching TV. Cas is lost in his thoughts, still contemplating if he should reach out to Elizabeth. His cell phone beeps with a notification; it's a new text.

"Is that her?" Jake asks, looking over at the phone.

Cas is excited. "Let me check." His excitement quickly turns into shame – the message is from Samantha. *'Thinking about you.'*

Looking at the text, his mouth forms a weak smile.

"It's from Samantha."

Jake can tell his friend feels bad. "Dude, if you really like her, then don't mess it up."

"Oh, now you say that, after you tell me if I don't fuck Elizabeth again I'm going to regret it for the rest of my life?"

Jake cuts him off, "Hey, that's just my suggestion. Do what you want."

"Yeah, thanks for the suggestion."

"You're welcome," Jake quickly replies. "And stop stressing out so much over it. You haven't texted Elizabeth back yet, right? And even if you did, you're not doing anything wrong."

"Yeah, but it don't feel right either."

Jake shrugs as he goes back to chowing down his food.

"Hey, just to be clear." Cas looks over at Jake. "You can't tell anybody about this Elizabeth thing. I need to keep this low. Not only is she married, but her and Samantha know the same people. So, I don't need any drama bullshit."

"I hear you. But I think you're stressing that Samantha thing too hard. I mean she's had her fair share of fun too."

"What the fuck are you talking about?" Cas is clearly agitated. "Why you always taking shots at her? You barely know her."

"No," Jake begins, "*You* barely know her. I know people who know her that way; I know she's fucked Manolo."

"Yeah, right."

Jake takes the last bite of his food and puts his fork down. "Bro, let's just settle this once and for all, right here, right now. I can hit Manny up and just ask him."

"You know what? Go ahead, call him now, in front of me. Put him on speaker. Fuck it."

"Bet." Jake takes out his phone to call Manolo; he puts it on speaker, it begins to ring.

"Do you want me to tell him you're here with me?"

"I don't care, go ahead." As the phone rings again, Cas says, "Actually, no, don't tell him I'm with you. I don't want him to change his answer one way or another."

As he finishes his sentence, the ring stops and Manolo picks up, "*Demlo*."

"*Demlo*," Jake answers back. "Yo, Nolo', I got a question. You know that chick Samantha, the one Cas is messing with? I was going to tell him you hit it, but I'm not sure if you actually told me you did or not. I was too drunk to remember."

Cas's heart races with anticipation.

Manolo laughs. "That's what you call me for? No, 'Hey, Manny, how are you, my friend? How's the family?' None of that, huh? Just go straight to some dumb shit."

Jake cracks up. "My bad, my bad. What's good, Lo? How's the fam?"

"Nah, too late, man. I know it's not heartfelt. But, yeah, I hit it before."

Cas's stomach drops, and he feels his heart jump to his throat. *Damn.*

"But that was years ago. Like five years, maybe even longer. Don't tell him about it, though. Why would you even want to?

"I don't know. I feel like he should know."

"I mean, I'm sure he wouldn't mind anyway, it was such a long time ago. But I still don't think you should tell him. He's just starting to get back into the swing of things, and she's actually a cool person. I don't want any awkwardness or anything like that. It was a long time ago, man. Just leave it alone."

Jake looks up at Cas. "You're sure you don't want me to tell him? I think it's only right that he knows."

"It's up to you, if you want to," Manolo answers, "But there's really no point in him knowing. It was a long time ago. I have no interest in her, she definitely has no interest in me. Plus, you know, not for nothing, I got a really big dick, man. After she had this, it's hard for any man to size up. I don't wanna put that kind of pressure on him."

Jake smirks. "Is that right?"

"I'm the original *Big Papi*. The *Grande Maduro*."

"What's that? The big sweet plantain?" Jake is cracking up.

"You know it." Manolo chuckles out loud.

Cas grows pale and nauseous as he listens to them laugh.

"Alright, cool, man." Jake relents. "If you don't want him to know, I won't say anything. Anyway, what's good with you? What are you getting into tonight?"

"Nothing. Get some sleep, I got work tomorrow. I'm just going to take it easy."

"Sounds boring as hell."

"Fuck you." Manny laughs.

"I'm out of here, man. Holler at me later if anything comes up."

"One."

Jake presses end on his phone and places it in his pocket.

317

"Well, there it is. I told you."

Cas is hurt but tries to play it off. "Oh well, fuck it. It's not like she's my girl."

"That's what I been trying to tell you." Jake gives him a sympathetic smile. "I know you're upset, but it's cool. It's better to find out now than investing more time with this chick and getting hurt like the last time."

Cas feels his anger rising. "What you mean, like the last time? Why you always gotta bring up Tiffany? What's wrong with you?"

"Nothing's wrong with me. I'm trying to look out for you." Jake gets up, takes his empty plate to the kitchen; he rinses it quickly and comes back to the living room. "But hey, it's none of my business. If you wanna to see the broad, or if you don't wanna see the broad, do whatever makes you happy. Do you, boo boo."

"You're right, it's none of *your* business. And I'm going to do me, boo boo. And Samantha and Elizabeth, too too. I'm taking all the bitches."

Jake shrugs with a smile. "I hear you, pimp, I hear ya. Just save a few for me, you know what I'm saying?"

They both laugh, but Cas is faking his.

Jake heads to the front door. "I'm outta here. I'm going to try to sneak in a little cardio, burn off some of this food before my client gets there. You want to come to the gym, get a little work out on?"

"Nah, I'm good." Cas smiles nonchalantly.

"You sure?"

"Fuck you."

"Whoa?" Jake is caught off guard. "What's that about?"

"I don't know." Cas looks at him, still smiling. "It's just funny how you insist on ruining my thing with Samantha. Like, it doesn't even make sense why you would want to? I feel like you're a hater sometimes."

"What? I told you about it because I feel like you have a right to know. I didn't think it was a big deal, but I also felt, as your friend, that, hey, this girl you're dating, or fucking, or whatever, she actually was with one of our very good friends at one point, you know, just as a heads up. That's all. How does that make me a hater?"

"Yeah, sure, I guess. But it feels like you're hating on me through the guise of doing something nice."

"Through the *guise*?" Jake sucks his teeth. "If I didn't tell you, and you'd have found out, of which there is a high probability that you would have, you would come at me like, 'Why didn't you tell me? You didn't think I would want to know that?' Come on, you know how you are. It's like damned if I do, damned if I don't."

Cas slowly nods. "You know what, Jake? You are absolutely right. Once you knew about her and Manny, there was no good way to play it. If you tell me, if you don't, damned if you do, damned if you don't. You're right."

"Thank you." Jake gives him a fist bump. "Damn, I wish I didn't have to go to work, but I'll catch up with you later. We good, man?"

"Yeah, for sure, it's all good, man," Cas replies and walks him to the door; he opens it for him. "Now get the hell out of my house, you're ruining my vibe."

"Hey, it's my house too," Jake says as he walks through the door. "I'm just trying to look out for you. Real talk."

"I know. Now, I'm going to look out for you. Hurry up and move so the door doesn't hit you in the ass on your way out. Real talk." Cas slams the door hard behind him and locks it.

Jake bangs on the other side of the door. "Yo, if that shit would have hit me, I would have fucked you up!" He starts walking towards the stairs. "I knew you were hurt," Jake calls back, his voice growing fainter as he walks down the staircase. "Fronting like you don't care. Ha! I still love you, Nova. You little bitch."

"Yeah, fuck you," Cas mutters under his breath. He turns around and starts walking back to the living room. "I don't need anybody to look out for me. I can look out for myself. Everybody is full of shit."

He flops down on the sofa, grabs his vape pen, and takes a long hit as he leans back in the couch.

What to do, what to do? He's lost in his thoughts. *Samantha is great, there's no doubt about it.*

But damn, why did you have to sleep with my friend, though?

And it is very early on, so who's to say what's to come out of this?

Not to mention, I already had sex with Elizabeth, so would it be that wrong to do it again?

It's not like I'm pursing a relationship with her, it would just be physical.

Jake is right, if I don't do it, I'm probably going to regret it forever.

Cas sighs out loud and takes another hit from his vape.

I don't know, man.

Are you going to pass up the opportunity to have a night of unbridled passion with one of the sexiest women you have ever seen in person?

And are you going to pass it up for a relationship that's not even official yet?

For a woman who has already slept with one of your friends?

Cas puts the vape pen to his mouth. "A wise man once said, 'You only Yolo once.'"

He takes a hit, grabs his phone, and goes to his contacts.

He texts Elizabeth, *'Are you free tonight?'* and hits the send button.

CHAPTER 18

The Past Is the Past

A few days have passed and Cas hasn't heard back from Elizabeth. He's disappointed and bad-tempered.

He's also been passively avoiding Samantha. His responses to her texts are short and dry and deliberately late. He hasn't asked to see her in two days.

Cas is angry at Samantha. He knows it's stupid and unreasonable to be mad at something that happened years ago, but he can't help it. He's jealous.

He's even angry at himself for being angry. *Here I am, lusting for Elizabeth, and I'm actually mad about something Sam did years ago?*

He knows he has to confront her and get past it if he wants to continue seeing her. The good thing about not dealing with any women in the past few days is he's been getting plenty of work done.

Cas sits at his desk, focused on the screen in front of him, typing away on the keyboard. The phone lights up with a phone call.

"Hello."

"Hey, Cas, what's up, stranger?"

He's happy to hear Samantha's voice.

"Hey, Sam. What's up, babe?" he says sweetly.

"Babe? Who's *babe*? I don't know any babes. I'm babe-less in these streets. I don't get no calls or nothing."

"I thought you were grading papers."

"So? You couldn't call?"

"True. I could've."

"Hey, what's up with you? You definitely seem distant; everything OK?"

"It's funny you say that because there's something I'm kind of apprehensive to ask you about."

"Really? Interesting. Well, ask away."

"Well, I really don't know how to ask something like this."

Samantha cuts him off, "I don't have herpes. So, if you have it, you gave it to me."

Cas pauses for a moment. "What? Hell no. I wasn't going to ask you about *herpes*."

She laughs. "Yeah, I was just joking."

"That was a good one."

"Thanks."

"I guess what I wanted to ask you is." Cas breathes in deeply. "Did you let Manolo hit it?"

Samantha coughs. "Sorry, what? Did I let him *hit it*?"

"Yeah, I mean, you know, did you sleep with him? Did you fuck him? Did you two have sex?"

There's a brief pause before Samantha responds.

"First of all, calm down, that's just gross. And secondly, why are you even asking me that?"

"I just think I should know. Manolo and I aren't best friends or anything, but we've known each other a long time, and we *are* good friends. So, I just feel like I should know. Don't get me wrong, this wouldn't change anything between us."

"If it wouldn't change anything, then why ask?"

"So, you did?" Cas presses on.

"Unfortunately."

"Really? Wow."

"What do you mean *really wow*?" Samantha sucks her teeth. "It was years ago, and you shouldn't be the one to talk."

"I didn't mean it like that. I'm not judging you, I was just hoping it wasn't true. That's all."

"Listen, that was years ago. It was a huge, *huge* mistake on my part."

"Why did you say *huge* twice?" Cas asks defensively, "What was so huge about it?" He's thinking about Manolo's *Grande Maduro* comment, feeling sick.

"It was huge mistake because I was young and dumb and drunk as shit. He's not even my type. And just everything about it was stupid."

Cas cuts her off, "How long ago was it?"

"I don't know. I was like 18 at the time."

Cas tries to do the math. "How old are you now?"

Samantha chuckles. "Really? Now is when you ask me my age?"

"Yup."

"24."

"So, if you were 18 at the time, that would make it six years ago."

"Well, there you go, math whiz. It was longer ago than I actually thought."

"It still sucks."

"Yeah, I know it does, but there is nothing I can do about it."

"Do you still like him?"

"What! Ewww... hell no. It was a stupid, one-time thing. Absolutely nothing more."

"You sure?" he presses again.

"Cas, I like you. You're good looking and funny, and something about you makes me want to explore this more. But I can't erase the past. So, if you can't look past it, you might as well say it now."

"No. I'm not saying that. It's not that big a deal. Of course, I wish it didn't happen, but it is what it is. It was a long time ago, and I can definitely look past it."

Samantha smile comes through the phone. "Good. Because if you had told me you can't, I would have kicked your ass."

He laughs. "Oh really?"

"Hell yeah." Samantha's voice is sexy and seductive. "You don't know it yet, but you're mine."

"What is this 'mine' you speak of?" Cas messes with her, "I am no one's; I am one with the earth."

"Yeah, OK. You gonna be one with my foot up your ass."

"Damn, why you so violent? Sheesh."

"I wanna see you," she says.

"When?" he asks.

"Tonight. I'll take you out to dinner, my treat."

Cas quickly moves the phone away from his ear to check for new messages; he doesn't have any.

He puts the phone back to his ear. "Sounds good to me. Let's do it, babe."

***

Three hours later, Cas arrives at the front of a small side walk restaurant in Harlem. He's meeting Samantha there. He goes in to get a drink from the bar while he waits for her.

He motions for the barkeep as he approaches a stool to sit on.

"Can I get a Long Island?"

"You got it." The bartender works the bottles and brings him the cola-colored drink. "12 dollars"

Cas slips him a $20. "Thanks."

As he waits for Samantha, he takes out his phone and begins scrolling through articles, absentmindedly sipping the Long Island continuously. He finishes the drink in a few minutes and is sucking up small bits of ice and water through the straw as he tries to get every last bit of the drink.

"Hey, chief." Cas puts the empty glass on the counter. "Let me get another one please."

"No problem. Hey, just so you know, we have a special on our Bulldog Fish Bowl. It would be a Long Island fish bowl, and in the middle of the bowl, there's another bowl of a frozen Long Island bulldog with a Corona in it and a shooter of Bacardi."

"How much is that?"

"On special, $30."

"Sounds good. Get me that."

A few minutes later, the bartender comes back with a huge drink, just as he described it. It's a literal fish bowl, instead of water in it, there's liquor – Long Island Iced Tea. The middle of the bowl is carved out to hold another bowl. In that bowl is a frozen Long Island Iced Tea slushy, with a small Corona beer bottle sticking in, neck down, and two small plastic shooter tubes filled with rum sticking out the side of the cola-colored ice.

"Shit." Cas is surprised by the monster-sized drink. "That's a lot going on."

The bartender laughs. "Yup. All you need is one of these, and you good for the night. Shit, you might be good for the week!"

Cas chuckles. "I hear you." He grabs the shooter and lifts it. "Cheers." He downs the shot of rum.

He waits around at the bar for another ten minutes, steadily sipping on his drink, but he's barely making a dent in it.

Samantha walks in through the front entrance. She looks stunning and professional.

Cas gets up eagerly. "Hey, babe, what's up?"

Her eyes light up when she sees him. She walks over, and they embrace.

"Sorry, I'm late. I had to finish something for my class, and I didn't have a chance to go home and change. I know I look like a mess."

"Are you crazy?" Cas cuts her off, speaking louder than he realizes, "You look fucking great. You look amazing!"

Samantha is caught off guard by his energy. "Thanks. You been drinking a bit, babe?"

"Yeah!" He says, still speaking loudly, "I got this drink for us." Cas brings her over to his seat at the bar.

She looks at the beverage in disbelief. "What the hell is that?"

He smiles broadly. "It's a Tiger Fish Bowl! One of these, and you're good for a week is what the bartender says. Here, have some." He removes the Corona bottle from the slushy and slides the rest of the drink towards Samantha.

"Kind of heavy for a Wednesday, no?" She slides the drink back over to him.

"I don't know. Why don't you want to drink? I got it for both of us. I thought you would definitely want some."

"No, I don't want any. If I was drinking anything, it would be a glass a wine. But definitely not that. I actually wasn't planning on drinking at all tonight."

"Really?" Cas takes a long swig from the beer bottle. "You not drink? Is that even possible?"

"What?" Samantha looks at him, completely confused.

"I just know you like to drink. You know? You like to have a good time, you like to drink. Me too."

"What are you talking about? I think you're the one who likes to drink. And a little too much, obviously."

"Oh, I drink too much?" Cas laughs and slaps his hand on the counter. "OK, Ms. Party Girl."

"I'm actually starting to get offended. What the fuck are you talking about? Is this about Manny?"

"No." He shakes his head and takes another swig from his beer. "I'm not worried about that. I don't care about that. So, you went out one night, got drunk, and slept with the guy." Cas pauses and rubs his chin as if he's thinking. "Hmmmm? Sounds familiar. Is that like your MO? Because that sounds exactly like what happened with us."

Samantha stares at him in silence, dumbfounded and hurt.

"I can't believe you." Her voice is low and dry with emotion.

Cas instantly feels bad. "I'm sorry, that was totally uncalled for. I..."

"Fuck you!" She cuts him off, "You wanna judge me for something I did years ago? I was a teenager, you fucking jerk! I've been nothing but good to you."

"I know. I'm just..."

"I wasn't finished. I have been nothing but good to you. And you think you can talk to me like that? Do you have a perfect past? Of course, you don't. You fuck married women. I'm so fucking angry with you right now. I'm such an idiot. Here I am, thinking you're different. You're just the same as your friends. It's OK for you to stick your dick in any bitch's pussy – who knows how many women you've had – but that's fine, because you're a man, you're a stud. I have one meaningless night with one meaningless guy and I'm some sort of party girl whore?"

Samantha pushes back the bar stool and quickly gets up. "Sad part is, I really thought we had something."

She turns around to leave, her heels clacking loudly as she walks away.

Cas pauses for a moment, watching her walk.

Suddenly, a huge wave of guilt and panic comes crashing over him.

"Sam, wait!" He yells as she hurries out the door and walks into the night. "Samantha!"

Cas rushes through the door and goes outside; he looks to the left and finds that she's already halfway down the street.

"Wait!"

He knows she can hear him because she starts walking faster. Samantha practically jogs to the corner and hails a cab; one quickly stops for her.

Cas makes a run for it. He knows that if she gets in and drives away, that might be the last he sees of her.

He reaches the corner just as she opens the car door.

"Wait! Don't go." He closes the door before she can get in.

"Leave me alone. I want to go home."

"Not yet, please."

The cab driver looks at them in confusion. "Are you guys getting in or what?"

Cas answers him before Samantha has a chance, "Nah, you can go ahead chief, we're good."

"Miss, are you OK?"

Samantha looks at the driver. "I'm fine."

The cabby shrugs and drives away.

"Sam, look, I'm sorry. I can be an idiot sometimes..."

"More like a fucking asshole."

"OK, I'm an asshole. But that's only because," he pauses.

"Because what?" Samantha looks annoyed.

"Because I like you a lot. If I didn't, I wouldn't have cared about the Manolo thing."

"So, because you like me, you get to act like an asshole? You see Cas, I don't have time for stupidity like that. I have to go, and don't block my cab because I'm gonna hit you."

"Samantha?"

She walks past him, steps off the curb, and waves for a cab.

"Samantha?" Cas pleads.

She ignores him.

A cab pulls up in front of her. As she opens the door, he jumps in her way.

"Get out of my way, Cas!" Samantha looks at him, her eyes intense with anger.

He can't help but be attracted to her passion.

"Don't leave," he says, gently grabbing her waist and pulling her in close.

She forcefully slaps his hands away and yells in his face. "Don't fucking touch me!"

He's not attracted to her passion anymore; he's scared.

"Damn, it's like that?" he asks with hurt apparent in his voice.

"It's like that," she answers immediately, her tone serious as she gets into the cab and closes the door. The car pulls away quickly.

"Damn." Cas's drops his head in defeat.

He stands there, contemplating his next move when someone taps him on the back.

"Hi. I'm sorry. It kind of looks like you're going through something, but do you want me to throw away your Bulldog Fish Bowl?"

331

Cas looks up the street and sees the car fading in the distance.

"No, don't throw it away," he sighs. "I'm coming in now."

***

An hour later, Cas has finished most of his Fish Bowl and has sent out 15 text messages to Samantha.

'I'm such a dick. Please call me, I'm beyond sorry.'

'Please call me... I'm sorry.'

'If you never want to speak to me again, I understand... but please call me.'

A few minutes pass and his phone finally lights up. He eagerly checks it.

It's a text from Jake, *'Yo! Come to my After-work Event on the West side. Bring Sam if you want. It's lit!!!'*

Cas disregards it and sends Samantha another text that's equally as apologetic as the previous ones.

After another 15 minutes, there's still no response from her.

He goes to his text to double-check. The last message is from Jake. *'Yo! Come to my After-work Event on the West side. Bring Sam if you want. It's lit!!!'*

Cas looks at his drink – he's completely finished the slushy part, and he has about a quarter inch of liquor left, covering the bottom of the fish bowl. He takes out all the straws and shooter tubes, removes the center bowl where the slushy was, grabs the entire main fish bowl, with a hand on each side, and brings it up to his mouth.

He tilts his head back and chugs down all the back wash from the bottom of the bowl. It drips down the sides of his mouth.

"Ahhhhhhh," he says as he finishes the drink, "That was good."

He takes out his phone, books an Uber, and sends Jake a text.

'I broke up with Sam. I'm a single man! On my way bro.'

Wiping off the excess alcohol dripping down his chin, he gets up and heads for the exit.

"Time   to   party."

CHAPTER 19

Brothers

Cas arrives at the trendy lounge on Lenox Ave in Harlem. He gets out of the Uber and walks into the place with as much composure as he can muster, considering how he drank a whole small aquarium worth of booze.

As soon as he walks into the place, he spots Jake and Chen. They see him and wave him over.

He approaches them, drunk and enthusiastic.

"Yoooooooo! Chicken Wing! Jake! What's up man!"

Jake can tell immediately he's drunk. "Hey, Novocain, I told you before. No one calls Chen *Chicken*..."

Chen cuts Jake off and leans in close to his ear, "Don't worry about it. He's drunk."

"Oh shit, oh shit, oh shit." Cas looks happy and remorseful at the same time. "My bad, Chen. I forgot, man, not cool."

Chen laughs. "No worries, brother."

Cas looks at them and suddenly gets emotional, tears welling up in his eyes. "You know, I don't have any real brothers, and I just want to say that you guys are my brothers. I love you guys. You are my brothers."

Jake and Chen look at each other, embarrassed by his drunken blabbering.

"Love you too, man." Jake pats him on the arm. "Hey." He looks at Chen. "Did Manny say he was going to the bathroom?"

Cas's emotional love fest is abruptly over. "Manolo's here?" he asks in a tone that is completely devoid of friendship.

"Yeah, he went to the bathroom." Chen nods towards the back. "There he is now."

Manny is walking back from the restroom, happy to see his friends.

"Juan Carlos, what's up, man? When did you get here?"

"I been here already."

"Really? I didn't see you."

"Maybe I just got here. Either way, I been here."

Manolo is confused and can sense some hostility, but he tries to ignore it.

"Alright. You been here, cool," he replies with a smile. "So, what's new, man? How are things with Samantha?"

Cas tilts his head to the side and looks at him intently. "Oh, you think you're funny?"

Manolo looks confused. "What are you talking about?"

Chen is confused by the animosity as well. "Yeah, what's up with you, Nova?"

"What's up with me is this mother fucker's making little sly remarks."

"Me?" Manolo is surprised. "All I asked is, 'How's Samantha?'"

Their conversation is interrupted by a waitress, oblivious of the ensuing argument.

"Shots?" She nods toward the tray she's holding with a dozen tequila shots.

Cas aggressively grabs one, his eyes leering over his friends before resting on Manolo. He brings the shot glass to his mouth and quickly downs the tequila; his face contorts from the taste, but his eyes never move.

"Arrrgghhhh," Cas grunts in satisfaction, finally taking his eyes off Manny and staring at the empty shot glass in his hand.

Manolo turns to Jake and Chen. "How drunk is this fool?"

All of them look at Cas.

He looks up and only stares at Manolo.

Manny stares back. "What the fuck is your deal?"

Cas clenches his teeth, and in one quick motion, raises the empty shot glass and throws it hard at Manolo's face. It hits him with force but doesn't break, the thick base of the shot glass bouncing off the right side of his forehead with a THUD!

Manolo's head snaps back from the hit. "Fuck!" He raises his hand to where he was struck, quickly touching the spot several times and looking at his finger to see if he's bleeding. There's no blood.

Manolo is furious and looks up at Cas to see if there's any sign of remorse.

Cas is standing there, feeling proud of his aim.

"That's it!" Manny rushes at him and slams Cas's back to the side of the bar, causing the bottles to rattle and clank against each other. A couple of them fall and shatter.

The people in the club are startled. The DJ stops the music.

Jake and Chen quickly grab them to break up the fight.

Cas shakes himself loose and stands with his hands balled up into tight fists, breathing heavily.

"Come on!" he growls, staring intensely at Manolo.

The group of people who were standing closest to them gasp and move away quickly.

Manny looks around and realizes people are staring at them; he's embarrassed. He relaxes his face and tries to smile.

"Listen, all I asked is 'How are you?' I don't know why you flipping out. Maybe you had too much to drink."

"Fuck you!" Cas responds loudly.

Jake tries to subdue him. "You alright, dude?" He moves in close and talks in a low voice, "Take it easy, baby, you're scaring people."

Drunk and angry, Cas yells and points at Manolo, "Tell this asshole to take it easy! This fucker here, he's a real smart ass!" He cries out with drool hanging off his curled lower lip.

The music is still off, and the people in the lounge can hear everything.

"Why didn't you tell me about Samantha?"

"Oh shit, drama!" Someone gasps in the background. The crowd moves back far enough to avoid getting hit but not far enough to miss the fight.

"Samantha?" Manolo looks at him with a half-smile. "That's what this is about? You're acting like an asshole because of that?"

"Oh damn!" adds another random patron's commentary.

"Dude, that was years ago. Like four, five years ago."

"Six!" Cas sharply interjects.

"There you go, six." Manolo continues, "Six years ago, man. That's a long fucking time. It has nothing to do with the here and now, *papa*."

"Why didn't you tell me about it!"

"Uhhh." Manolo's face is scrunched into a look of confusion. "For this very, exact reason. To avoid any awkward shit."

"You should have told me!"

"What difference does it make! It was years ago, she's mad cool, I know you're mad cool. I was trying to look out for you."

"Trying to look out for me but not telling me you banged her?"

"Wow!" a female voice comments in the background, "See how guys are?"

"However you want to process this is up to you. But when I tell you I honestly didn't mean any harm by not telling you, that's the truth." Manolo puts his hand out for a shake. "Look, I don't even know how or why you found out about that; I'm assuming it's from this asshole right here."

"Hey!" Jake is offended.

"Man, we go way back, Cas. I wouldn't try to play you on purpose." He motions his hand forward. "I'm willing to get past it if you are."

Cas looks down at his hand for a second. He slaps it away, hard.

"Really?" Manolo moves his hand. "Well, you know what? Fuck it. We can fight if you want. It's funny how you want to be all aggressive now but when we had the rumble at the baby shower, you didn't throw a fucking punch."

Cas looks overly bewildered. "The fuck are you taking about?"

"At my sister's baby shower; everybody fought except for you. You're the only guy who didn't throw a single punch."

"Hey," Jake cuts in, "I told you he was going to fight one of the guys but the guy didn't want to fight."

"Man, fuck that. Those guys crashed the party and hit my grandfather, and you asking if they want to fight? That's bullshit. That's why you got knocked out by a girl, like a little bitch."

"Oh yeah? Why don't you knock me out like a little bitch!" Cas lurches at him, but Chen quickly gets in between them.

"Hey, chill out! Chill the fuck out!" Chen yells at him. "Nova, you know you my dog, but you're totally out of line right now."

"No, let him go," Manolo insists, "If he really wants to do this, let's do it."

Before Cas can lurch again, Jake comes from behind, bear hugs him around the waist, and lifts him up. He quickly carries him to the back of the bar, through the "Employees Only" door, into the kitchen, where he puts him down.

"Yo, chill the fuck out, man! You're ruining my event. You're really fucking up my shit right now."

"Fucking up your shit?"

"Yeah, man. You're causing a scene, freaking people out; you have to calm down. People are going to start leaving."

"Fucking up your shit?" Cas repeats himself. "How about you? You're always fucking up my shit. You ruined everything! Everything!"

Jake looks at him perplexed. "What the hell are you talking about?"

339

"Samantha! Why you had to corrupt it?"

"How did I corrupt it? I didn't tell you to break up with her! I don't even know what happen, you just text me that you broke up."

"Because you told me that shit about Manny. That's what fucked it up."

"Oh, here we go again with this shit. I already explained exactly why I told you. I'm not doing this again, I'm not." Jake shakes his head. "Look, I'm sorry you broke up. But the fact of the matter is, you two were never in a real, exclusive relationship anyway. You haven't even dated long enough to make it official. So, I don't get why you're getting so bent out of shape?" Jake points at the door. "There are beautiful women right behind this door, right now, plenty of them, more to come too. And you're worried about Samantha? You dated for a fucking month, Cas. Fuck that bitch."

Tears of anger and pain trickle down Cas's cheek. "That's the problem. To you, they're all just 'that bitch.' Just another random woman, like they're fucking robots, not real people. Every woman is unique, Jake. Every woman is individually unique, and you can't replace one with another. People are not interchangeable."

"You say that, but yet, you tried to replace Tiffany with Samantha, and Samantha with Elizabeth. Interchangeable, no? It's the same thing."

"No, I didn't."

"Yes, you did."

Cas's drunkenness has him agitated and emotional. "You don't understand! We're all just people, and everyone's feelings and emotions are valid. But you don't care about that, you just look at it like one big game. Like women are pawns on the fuck fest game board of life."

"I think you're way overthinking this. There's nothing wrong with having fun. At least, I don't see anything wrong it."

"Of course, you don't. Because you're not a good person. You're an asshole, Jake. You're a self-centered asshole."

Jake looks genuinely insulted. "Fuck you, Cas."

Cas shrugs. "Really?"

"Yeah, fuck you. I'm self-centered? Who's always there for you when you're going through a depression? Me. Always me. I'm always trying to keep you up, I'm always trying to look out for you. You say we're brothers, but I show it. I always got your back, and you know that. So, for you, out of all people, to call me self-centered? That's crazy."

Cas drops his head. "I'm not saying you're not there for me."

"So, what the fuck you saying, then? You said I'm not a good person. You think you're better than me? Why? Because you *say* you care about people's feelings? Because you *say* you care, that somehow makes you better than me?"

"I don't *say* I care. I *do* care."

"Yeah, you care, you care so much that you do shit anyway. You run around, you fuck women, you manipulate, you lie, you cheat, and yet, you think you're better than me? You gotta be kidding." Jake laughs. "You're so much worse of a person than me. You actually see this as wrong, but you do it anyway. That's fucked up."

"How does that make me worse than you?"

341

"Because I don't see anything wrong with this. I see this as living. I see this as part of the fuck fest game of life, as you called it. But you, Mr. Everyone-has-feelings, you do care, and you do it anyway. Don't play all high and mighty with me, man, because I know you, the real you. You're a self-centered bastard, just like me. Except worse, because you like to judge and blame others for your fuck ups. You're a self-righteous prick, Cas, you have always been."

Cas just stares at him, absorbing what he's just said, coming to the realization that Jake is right.

After a moment, his adrenaline level drops. He sighs deeply. "You're right. I am no better. And I'm just angry because I fucked it up with Samantha. She's so dope. She's beautiful and funny, and she's a freaking teacher." Another tear trickles down his cheek. "She could have been anything she wanted to be, and she choose to help change the future of our nation. And I..." Cas looks at him, defeated, shaking his head. "I fucked it up. I'm so stupid, so self-centered."

Jake feels bad for his friend, he puts his arm around his shoulder. "Hey, man, if it's meant to be, it'll be. Just try to relax. Breathe."

Just then, Manolo and Chen come through the door. Cas quickly wipes his eyes and composes himself.

"What the hell is going on back here," Chen yells.

"Yo, lower your voice, man. Damn." Jake laughs.

"Hey, Manolo." Cas sticks his hand out. "My bad. I was totally out of line. I acted like a complete fool. I'm sorry."

Manolo reaches forward for Cas's hand and shakes it. "I'm sorry too, man. I had no idea you and Sam broke up today. Chen just told me. I could see how you might have thought I was being a douche."

"It was all me, man. I was just bugging out, totally my fault. I'm good now."

"Cool, because I was getting worried. You were looking like you wanted to kill me. It was getting a little dicey in there."

Cas laughs. "Yeah, my bad, I was a little over the top. I was just fronting, though, talking shit. You know how it is."

Manny smiles. "Yeah, I know."

"Aye," Jake cuts in, "Now that we're all on the same side again, let's get out of this fucking kitchen and see what's poppin' out there."

"Let's go."

They step out of the back room and into the lounge. Music is playing lightly in the background; the crowd has picked up.

The DJ points out at Jake. "We got my man, Jake the Snake, in the building. You already know. That's the man that put this event together. Yo, Jake, you good bro?"

Jake takes a few steps towards the booth and lifts his hand up; the DJ hands him a mic.

"I just want to thank everybody for spending your evening with us. Make sure you hit up all your friends, all your Snap, Face, Insta peeps, and let them know it's lit! And we always aim to please; so, for that little inconvenience earlier, we're giving everybody a free round. Hey DJ! Turn that music up!"

The DJ blares a bass heavy beat; the crowd erupts in cheers. "Yeeeaah!"

"Wait, DJ, turn it down for a sec." Jake motions for him to lower the music.

The DJ quickly kills the sound.

"Check it out." Jake smiles. "I was just joking, no free round."

The crowd sighs in disapproval. "Boooooo!"

"But! But!" Jake lifts his hand to get their attention. "We got half-price drinks! Half-price drinks. You have to buy one, and the second one is half price. Alright, buy one, second one half price. Yo, DJ, turn that shit up!"

The DJ blasts the music as the crowd bobs to the beat.

Jake hands him back the mic and goes to his friends.

"Fuck that, I'm trying to make some money." They all laugh.

Chen leads the guys to the bar. The counter has eight shots lined up and four slices of lemon. "Tequila this time. Let's go."

"Yes!" Manolo says.

The all grab one shot glass and a slice of lemon. They raise their shots for toasting.

"I'm sorry for acting like an asshole tonight, guys. You guys are my oldest and, in all honesty, my only true friends." Cas lifts his glass high. "Brothers."

"Brothers," they all say in unison.

They each drink the shot in their hand, take a bite of the lemon to chase it, then throw back the other shot, and bite the lemon again.

"Yo, Nova?" Jake says in between biting on his lemon slice to kill the taste of back-to-back shots, "You know what's the good thing about breaking up with Sam?"

Cas puts his head down on the counter, using his forearm as a pillow. His other hand is holding the lemon slice to his nose, inhaling deeply, with his eyes closed, and thinking that maybe the smell of the citrus will sober him up.

Jake continues, "The good thing about it is that you can really see what's up with Elizabeth now. Zero guilt. You know, since you care about that type of a thing."

"Who's Elizabeth?" Chen cuts in.

"Elizabeth is the beautiful, fucking MILF. She's gorgeous dude, and she's into this putz."

Cas quickly raises his head and looks at Jake. "Dude, chill out."

"Wait?" Manolo cuts in, "Which Elizabeth? My sister's friend?"

"Yeah," Jake answers quickly, "That super-hot MILF, your sister's friend. She fucks with Nova."

Cas stands up. "Dude! What the fuck?"

"What?" Jake gets defensive. "What the fuck? It's Manny and Chen."

"You just be telling my business to everybody. Everybody be knowing my shit because of you."

Chen and Manolo stay quiet.

"Alright, my bad." Jake sucks his teeth. "But yeah, her."

"Damn, Cas, you took her down?" Manolo smiles widely. "I've known plenty of dudes who tried to holler at her, but she never gives anybody a chance. Shit, I'm impressed. She's freaking beautiful, dude."

"Yeah, thanks, but, I'm trying to not talk about it. I don't want anybody to really know."

"Oh, for sure, I get it. You know she's married?"

"Yeah. Hence, why I want to keep this super-duper low key."

"You know who her husband is?"

"No clue." Cas shrugs.

Manolo shakes his head slowly in concern. "I heard he's a gangster."

"What?" Cas laughs.

"Like Italian Mafia style. A mob guy."

"Word?" Chen asks, "A mob guy? You serious?"

"That's what I heard from my sisters. I mean, I never met the guy; so, I can't say it's for sure, but that's what I heard."

"Well." Jake slaps Cas on the back of his shoulder. "If Nova goes missing, we know what happened. He's sleeping with the fishes." They all break up in laughter.

CHAPTER 20

You Only YOLO Once

Cas got home at 2 AM and vomited several times throughout the night, the last being at 3:30 AM.

He cracks open his eyes; his first thoughts are of Samantha.

Reaching for the phone on the night stand, he looks at the time, it's 9:45 AM. He checks his text messages; there's nothing new. He decides to send a text to Sam.

'Good morning.'

He's not very confident that she'll write back, but he feels compelled to message her anyway. After the text is sent, he lays the phone down on the pillow next to him, closes his eyes, and goes back to sleep.

When Cas opens his eyes again, it's 11:30 AM. He checks his phone; still nothing.

"Damn," he mumbles to himself and sits up in bed. He waits a moment before he tries to stand, giving himself a chance to see how his body feels after last night's bender. Surprisingly, he doesn't feel too hungover. He thinks that maybe the buckets of alcohol-filled puke that flowed out of his mouth like an open faucet emptied most of the toxins in his body after he got home.

He gets out of bed and heads to the bathroom for a shit, shower, and shave.

***

Two hours later, Cas is sitting at his desk; he still hasn't received a response from Samantha. He slouches in his chair, staring at his computer screen, clicking on sports scores.

Although he is not terribly hungover, he is very tired. *Maybe I'll take a nap.*

Suddenly, he hears the lock on the front door turn; someone's coming in.

"What's up, man?" Jake tosses his keys on a shelf near the door.

Cas gets up to greet him. "What's up, Jacob?"

"Yo, you were smacked last night. You got so trashed. I'm surprised you're even up."

"Really? I actually don't feel that bad. I'm crazy tired, but other than that, I feel alright."

Jake looks at him impressed. "Did you throw up?"

"Oh yeah." He grins. "A lot."

Jake laughs at his friend. "That's why you're good."

"I don't remember a whole lot." Cas shakes his head. "But I know I broke up with Sam, and that sucks."

Jake heads to his room. "Yeah, what's up with that? Are you going to try to make it work or what?"

"I don't know." Cas stands in the room's doorway. "I want to, but she won't respond at all."

"Really?" Jake asks as he gathers up his workout clothes and places them in his gym bag.

"Yup. Nothing."

"That blows."

Cas shrugs. "Anyway, what's up with you?"

"I got a session in a few."

"How was your night though?"

Jake looks up from the gym bag. "It was dope. I stayed the night at Cynthia's."

"Good times?"

"Great." He smiles. "The sex is so crazy."

Cas's phone beeps with a new message. He looks at it and immediately feels more awake. He looks up, smiling at Jake. "Guess who just texted me?"

"Samantha?"

"Elizabeth."

"Oh, hell yeah!" Jake says, tossing a pair of sneakers in the bag and zippering it up. "This is your chance."

"I was kind of hoping it was Samantha."

Jake pauses and looks at him. "I'm not fucking with you, Cas. Do whatever you want to do. I'm not giving you no advice or nothing. Do what you feel. What does the text say, though?"

Cas shows it to him. *'Hi handsome... How you been?'*

"Oh, it's on." Jake gives a wide grin of encouragement. Grabbing his bag, he makes his way out of the room. "If that had been sent to me? It would be so on."

"You think I should write back?"

"Yeah, why not? And don't be a bitch; ask for a pic."

"What about her husband being in the mob?

"I forgot about that. You think that's true?"

"I don't know. I know I don't want to fuck with a mob wife."

"Yeah, but you already did; so, it wouldn't hurt to get a pic for keepsake." Jake drops the bag in the living room and goes to the kitchen.

Cas thinks for a brief moment, looks down at his phone, and punches a few keys.

"Done. I texted her."

"For real?" Jake comes back from the kitchen with a bottled water.

"Yeah." Cas smiles, trying to suppress his guilt. "If she's offended, it's your fault."

"Why would she be offended? Stop putting her on a pedestal. You banged her in the bathroom of a bar, for crying out loud. She might be a mob wife, and you want to treat her like Princess Kate?"

Cas can't suppress a laugh. "That's true. But still."

"What did you text her?"

Cas hands him his phone. *'Hey, beautiful, send me a pic.'*

Jake hands it back to him. "I like it. To the point."

As soon as he gives it back, the cell phone vibrates again; it's a message from Elizabeth.

"Is it a pic?" Jake picks up his bag and starts heading for the door.

"I don't know." He exhales deeply. "Let me see."

Cas opens the text; it's a picture. Elizabeth is standing in front of a mirror with her back turned. She's wearing black mesh lingerie shorts, pulled up high, exposing the lower half of her big round ass and thick thighs.

He instantly gets aroused and stares, mesmerized, with his mouth half open. The picture has Cas drooling.

"Wow. Crazy."

Jake smiles widely, drops his bag, and comes back to the living room. "Let me see, let me see."

Cas pulls the phone close to his chest, covering the screen. "I can't."

Jake laughs. "Yeah right. Let me see."

Cas shakes his head. "Nah, sorry, man, I can't."

"Wait." Jake pauses, "You serious right now?"

He doesn't say anything.

"You know, you," Jake starts, "I can't believe you. You are the worst. How are you not going to show me the picture when I'm the one who gave you the courage to ask for it in the first place?"

"I know. I feel you," says Cas, "But messing with you, you'll have everybody knowing about it. I can't risk it, dude."

"I'm not asking for you to send me the pic so I can beat off to it. I'm just asking to see the damn shit on your phone."

"Alright, I'll show you but you can't tell anybody. Not Manolo, not Chen. I mean *no one*."

"I hear you, brother. Now, let me see the goods," Jake answers rubbing his hands together.

Cas passes him the phone.

"Damn!" Jake says, using his index finger and thumb to zoom in on the pic, "She is bangin'. Wow, she is *mad* sexy."

"Yes, she is. She's pretty bad." Cas gets up and walks to the kitchen.

As Jake watches Cas pass through the doorway and out of sight, he quickly presses a few buttons on the phone and forwards the picture to himself through a text. The message goes through instantly, and he deletes the sent message on Cas's phone so he doesn't know Jake has it.

As Cas walks back into the room with a bottled water, Jake hands him back the phone.

"Not for nothing, you might want to fall back a little until you've found out for sure what's up with that whole mob thing. We don't need some mafia hit men running up in here." Jake grabs his bag and opens the door. "I'm out. Lock up."

Cas gets tense but tries to hide it. "Eh, I don't think it's true. That mob thing. Look how quick she sent the pic. She doesn't seem to be worried about anything."

"Good point."

The give each other a fist bump, and Jake walks out. "Later, Nova."

As Cas locks the door behind him, the phone vibrates with a message.

It's from Elizabeth. *'What do you think of the pic?'*

Cas raises her eyebrows as he scrolls through the previous messages to look at it again.

"Wow." His mood soars as he stares at the pic.

'I think it's beautiful. The only thing more beautiful is you in person.'

Less than a minute passes and his phone vibrates with another message.

'What are you doing now? Maybe you can see the real thing in person ;)'

An adrenaline surge through Cas's body removes any last bit of fatigue he was feeling. *Oh, hell yeah.*

'I'm free right now if you are.'

'Great! Where do you want to meet?'

Cas hesitates for a second. *You only Yolo once.*

'My house?' he writes back.

He waits for an immediate response, but he doesn't get anything. After a few moments, the excited smile on his face begins to fade.

A few more minutes pass, and his phone still remains silent.

After 20 minutes, he gets up and begins to pace. He's starting to get nervous.

What am I doing? She's a married woman. You can't do this, man.

What if her husband finds out?

What if he already found out and that's why she hasn't written back?

What about Samantha?

The phone vibrates with a message. It's from Elizabeth.

'Send me the address.'

"Ha ha!" Cas jumps up in the air and yells out loud in the empty apartment. "Yessss! This is going to be so fucking epic! Thank you, God!"

Cas texts her his address, grinning ear to ear.

A brief moment passes before the phone vibrates again. He looks at it, the big smile is quickly wiped off his face.

'Thinking of you.' It's from Samantha.

He slouches back in his seat, thinking of what to write back.

'Hey, stranger, there you are,' he texts her.

'What are you doing?' Samantha responds.

'I'm good, just working on this article. Trying to meet a deadline.'

'I'll let you work. Call me later.'

'Will do.'

Cas feels a guilt pulling at his heart, but his lust for Elizabeth is overwhelming.

His phone lights up with a new message.

It's from Elizabeth. *'Are you sure you want me to come over?'*

Cas quickly responds, *'Definitely. Why not?'*

Elizabeth writes back, *'Think about it... me and you in a room, nobody around us. Who knows what could happen... Are you ready for that?'*

A rush of nervous excitement comes over him, resting uneasy in his stomach.

'Oh, I'm ready, baby.'

'You sure about that? Because you didn't seem ready the last time, lol'

'Wow, low blow! Lol... that was a pretty crazy experience.'

He waits for her to reply.

A few minutes pass – nothing.

***

It's been almost an hour since his last text, and he's still waiting.

Cas opens his phone to send Elizabeth another text. *'Hello?'*

After a few more minutes, his phone finally vibrates with a message; he quickly grabs it.

'So are you free tonight?'

It's from Samantha.

He sighs as anxiety and guilt come crawling over him.

'Sure,' he starts to write, but before he can finish, another text comes in.

'Be there in 5 mins.' This one is from Elizabeth.

Cas jumps up from the sofa. "Oh shit!"

He rushes into the bathroom to take a quick shower. Turning the water on, he remembers Samantha's text.

'Hey, I'm going with Jake to visit one of our old friends.' He sends the message and jumps in the shower.

He frantically glides the bar of soap over his body, trying to lather up and rinse off as quick as possible.

As he washes his face, he hears his door buzzer ring.

"Shit!" he says from the soap stinging his eyes. He smacks his face in the streaming water to quickly rinse off the suds.

Getting out of the shower, he wraps a towel around himself and heads for the intercom, leaving wet foot prints behind him as walks across his apartment.

"Who is it?" he says and presses the 'Listen' button.

Before he can release the button, there's a knock at his front door.

His heart races. "Who is it?"

A very feminine voice answers, "Me."

He opens the door. Elizabeth looks up from her phone and sees him standing in a towel, dripping wet.

"Oh, you showered for me? I feel special." She smirks as she walks into the apartment.

***

30 minutes later, Cas and Elizabeth are lying in bed.

Elizabeth covers her body with the bed sheets, Cas lies with his boxers on. There's an awkward silence.

"Um." He clears his throat. "That's never really happened to me before."

"Yes, that's a first for me. But just relax, no rush. Take your time. Maybe you're nervous."

"Yeah, I think I am." Cas is embarrassed by his woefully soft dick, a wet noddle. "I think I'm a little nervous."

Elizabeth leans over towards him and caress his chest, she gives him a soft kiss on the shoulder. "Don't be nervous. Everything is fine."

His cock finally nudges with a little life and starts to harden. "Thanks for understanding. You're so beautiful and sexy." Cas leans in for a kiss.

The intercom buzzes loudly. They both jump.

"Who's that?" They say at the same time.

"I'm not expecting anybody. It's probably the wrong bell."

The intercom buzzes loudly again.

Cas is reluctant to get up and check. He moves slowly, hoping they won't ring anymore. After a few moments, the intercom is silent.

"Wrong bell." He smiles at her.

His phone lights up with a text message.

'*I know you're prob in the shower, I'll be back in 20 minutes, I'm going to go to the store to get a bottle of wine.*'

The message is from Samantha.

"Uhhhhhhh," Cas leans back in bed. "Uhhhhhhh."

Elizabeth looks at him. "Are you OK?"

"Nahhhhhh, not really." He starts to slowly get up. "I think you need to go."

"Really?" Elizabeth looks at him shocked. "Who was that? Is someone coming here?"

"Ummm, well..."

She cuts him off, "You know what, doesn't even matter. It's cool." Elizabeth gets out of bed in her bra and panty and reaches for her clothes on top of his wardrobe.

Cas is quickly getting dressed as well.

"I'm sorry about this," he says as he puts on his pants.

"No problem. It was a dumb idea."

Cas is hurt. "No, it wasn't."

"For me, it was." Elizabeth zippers up her skirt, slips on her shoes, and walks out of the bedroom.

"I'll get you an Uber."

"No, it's fine. I have a car coming."

"You have a *car* coming?"

"Yup." She replies, walking past the desk, grabbing her purse, and opening the front door. "I have a car coming."

"Sounds fancy. It actually makes me want to ask. Just by chance, is your husband in the Mafia?"

"Don't ask about my husband." Elizabeth looks at him sharply. "What, are you crazy?"

She shakes her head and walks down the steps. "This was something else to say the least."

"Can I call you later?" Cas's desperate voice follows her down the stairs.

"Please don't. But don't worry, I'll call you," she answers back as she continues down the staircase. "Bye, Juan Carlos. Take care."

"Bye," he says, standing in the doorway, almost talking to himself.

As Elizabeth walks out of the apartment building, there is a black car waiting. The driver gets out and opens the door for her. The sedan pulls off.

On the far corner of the street, down the block, Samantha stands with her phone out, watching the car leave. She walks away from Cas's building, heading towards the Uptown subway station. As she gets into the train, she writes one last message. *'Just got the wine. Be there soon.'*

She sends out the text and gets on the train going to Washington Heights.

CHAPTER 21

The End

It's been a week since that day Samantha stood him up.

Cas called and texted her several times when she didn't show. Finally, at almost midnight, she texted, *'Sorry, something came up. I'll call you later.'*

The *later* never came. Since then, Cas has reached out countless times, but she hasn't answered any of his calls or texts. At this point, it's clear that Samantha is avoiding him.

Cas also can't get in touch with Elizabeth. They spoke once since their abbreviated encounter and were supposed to set up a reschedule date, but she hasn't responded to him in three days. He won't text without her texting him first, being that she's married and all.

As he wakes up today, his confidence is waning. He gets his phone and sends Samantha a text.

'Good morning.'

He sends her that every day – just as a reminder to her that he's alive, still thinking of her, that's if she still even cares, which he's doubting more and more with each passing day that she's ignores him.

***

A few hours later, Cas is sitting at his desk, eating a sticky bun, watching sports highlights. Jake comes out of his bedroom. Cas hadn't realized he was home.

"Morning bro," Jake grumbles while using the bathroom.

"Sup," Cas grunts back.

"I thought you were coming out last night?"

"Changed my mind."

Jake comes out of the bathroom. He peeks his head around the doorway, his tired eyes barely open.

"Did you hear from what's-her-face?"

"Which one?"

Jake shrugs. "Either one."

"Nope."

"You OK?"

"Yeah, I'm good. I'm not worried about it. Just chilling."

Jake nods and closes his eyes. "Good. Hey, I'm going down to the Caribbean next week for four days."

"What?" Cas looks at him, confused.

"Yeah, I'm going to Bahamas next week. Leave Thursday, come back Monday."

"With who? Who's going?"

"Just me and Cynthia." Jake yawns. "She found this great deal on Groupon. It's like 600 bucks for a four-star resort, air fare included. I'm already booked. We booked it last night."

"Sounds pretty good."

"You wanna come?"

"On a vacation with you and your girlfriend? Absolutely, not."

Jake sucks his teeth. "She's not my girlfriend. And who cares, just come party."

"I'll pass. That's total third wheel status."

"Well, let me know if you change your mind." He yawns again. "I'm going back to bed. Holler if you need me." Jake shuffles back into his room and closes the door.

A short while later, as Cas is staring aimlessly at his computer, the phone lights up with a text.

'Hey'

It's Samantha.

He sits up at his desk. *'Hey,'* he writes back.

'Are you busy?'

Cas quickly stands up. *'No, not at all. Why?'*

A few moments pass before his phone vibrates.

'I need to see you. Meet me at the Cafe Uptown. Can you be there in an hour?'

'I'll be there.' He rushes to the bathroom to take a shower.

***

An hour later, Cas is getting out of an Uber in front of a side-walk cafe on Columbus Ave. Samantha is already there. As soon as he sees her, he gets excited, a few butterflies flutter in his stomach.

"Hey!" He comes in for a hug and kiss on the cheek.

Samantha gently pushes him away.

"Hey," she replies with a timid smile. "No need for all the kissing and hugging. A handshake is just fine."

Cas's excitement soon simmers down to embarrassment, then anxiety hits him.

"Oh, OK. Um, do you want to go in and get a seat?"

"No, I'm not staying long." She reaches behind and picks up a backpack. "Here. You left it in my house." She hands it to him. "All the stuff you left is in there."

He slowly takes the bag from her. "But I don't understand? What happened?"

Samantha shrugs. "I can't see you anymore."

"What do you mean? Of course, you can see me."

"No, I can't." She looks at him plainly.

"Why can't you? I want to see you."

"Let me rephrase that, I don't *want* to see you anymore."

"Damn, you don't want to see me anymore? That's fucked up, Samantha."

"Yeah, well." She looks him square in the eye. "You're a pretty fucked up person."

Cas shakes his head. "What did I do? Do you know how much I care about you?"

"No, I don't know. And it's not very much, obviously."

"Then, give me a chance to show you."

Samantha laughs. "There's nothing more you can show me, Cas. You've shown me everything I need to know. You're completely full of shit."

"How? Why would you say that?"

Samantha shakes her head. "You know, you suck so bad. I thought we had something good. I was *so* into you."

"I'm into you too. What's the problem?"

She just stands there silently, looking down, shaking her head.

"Look, whatever it is, we can work through it." Cas smiles and grabs her by the waist to pull her in closer.

She quickly looks up at him and smacks his hands off her. "Don't touch me. Don't ever touch me."

Cas drops his hands; his eyes betray feelings of dejection. "Why it got to be that way?"

"Because you made it that way. We could have been something great, but you blew it."

"We can still be something great."

"Great?" Samantha shakes her head. "You had the audacity to come at me about something that happened years ago, when you didn't even know me. You made me feel so shitty about myself, and meanwhile, you're fucking a married woman?" She laughs out loud. "And I know the bitch. And you know I know the bitch, and you were with her anyway."

"In all fairness," Cas reaches for rationale, "I started talking to her before I was talking to you."

"Cas, don't play dumb with me." Samantha is starting to get angry. "Yes, you messed with her before me, but you fucked her again *after* being with me."

"What are you talking about?" Cas feels sick to his stomach; he starts sweating. "I don't even know what you're talking about?"

"You don't know what I'm talking about? That day I was going to come to your house and never showed up – you remember that day?"

He stutters, "Uh, yeah, I, uh…"

Samantha snaps and yells in Cas's face. "I saw her, Cas! I saw her leaving your apartment, you fucking asshole!"

Samantha pauses, panting with adrenaline. She closes her eyes and breathes slowly to compose herself.

She opens her eyes and talks in a low, measured voice, putting up her index finger to his face. "One day. One day? We break up for one day, and you fucked another woman? You couldn't wait for me more than one day?"

She knows! Casanova is horrified. The weight of the world comes crashing down on his shoulders; he drops his head. "I don't know what to say. I don't know what I was thinking. I'm ashamed. That wasn't me."

"No, it was you," Samantha aggressively nods her head in disgust. "That's the problem, it was definitely you. The sweet, nice guy you showed me? That wasn't you; that was a fraud, a phony. The asshole who guilts me about a partner I had years ago and then goes and fucks a married woman that I know? That's the real you."

"It's not. It's really not. For what it's worth, I didn't do anything with her."

"It's not worth shit," she sucks her teeth.

"I know it's not. I feel terrible about it. If there was any way to change it, I would do it in a heartbeat. Even the fact that I brought up Manolo, I would change that too. But obviously, I can't do that.

"What I can do is tell you I really, really care about you. I don't want to lose you, Sam. If you give me a chance, I know I can be everything you need in a man."

He gently grabs her hands, worried she might slap him, but she allows him to hold her.

"I'm not asking for forgiveness. I'm not asking for you to just forget everything and trust me like you did before. I know that has to be earned.

"What I am asking you for is a chance. A chance to prove myself. A chance to show you the real me, and what you mean to me. That's all I'm asking for. Give me a chance. Please."

Cas stares deep into her eyes, trying to connect with her soul. He sees a glimmer of hope.

"Samantha, please. Please, give me a chance. I ..." Cas's eyes begin to water. "I love you."

Samantha looks at him, as a tear slowly rolls down her cheek. "I can't."

Cas is crushed. "Why? Why can't you?"

"Because," she says as she slips away her hands from his, "I don't want you anymore. I honestly and truly don't want you.

"Any hint of sadness, like these tears," she says, wiping her cheek, "These tears are not because I *want* you, the sadness is because I *don't* want you. I'm hurt that the excitement I felt for you not so long ago is completely *gone*." Another tear rolls down her cheek, "And that's whats really sad." Samantha breathes in deeply. "I have to go."

"Sam, wait." Cas's at a loss for words. "Just wait."

She tearfully looks into his eyes. "Bye, Cas."

She brings her right hand to her mouth, gently kisses her fingers, then moves her hand to his mouth, gently touching his lips. "Take care."

Cas grabs her hand, holds it tightly, and looks at her, his eyes longing for her to stay. "Wait! It doesn't have to be this way."

Samantha forcefully pulls her hand away from him. "Don't touch me," she says, the last tear escaping her eye. "Don't ever touch me."

She turns around and walks away.

Cas follows her. "Wait."

She walks a few feet ahead of him, looking down at her phone.

She looks up and sees him. "Don't follow me."

Cas pleads, "I'm not following you, I just want to talk."

Samantha looks back down at her phone. "We already talked. There's nothing else to talk about."

"Samantha, please."

"Sorry, I can't. I don't want to, and someone is picking me up here."

"Somebody is picking you up?" Cas laughs, "Are you serious?"

"Yes. Any minute now."

"So, you already got someone else, that fast?" He shakes his head, "Let me find out you were seeing this somebody while you were seeing me?"

"No, I wasn't seeing anybody else but you. But that's done now; so, don't worry about me. Why don't you worry about the dirty pictures with your married bitch? That's what you should be worried about."

The statement hits Cas like a punch to the stomach; he's shocked that she knows about that. "Dirty pictures? What are you talking about?"

Samantha shakes her head. "What a joke."

Just then a black sports car pulls up.

"Sam!" Cas pleads desperately.

She looks him with dead eyes.

"Fuck you, Cas. You were a waste of time."

Samantha turns around and gets into the car. It pulls off, making a right at the end of the block and disappearing into the sea of the city.

Cas stands in front of the restaurant, dumbfounded, the fumes from the tailpipe still lingering in the air.

"Wow," he says to himself in disbelief. "What the fuck just happen?"

CHAPTER 22

The End?

Jake gets to the front door of his apartment and uses his key to undo the locks.

"Daddy's home," he says with a smile as he carries his suitcase to his room. He drops it off on the bed and heads to the bathroom. "Nova? You here?"

Jake comes out of the bathroom and knocks on Cas's door.

"You in there?"

He hears a faint moan coming from the room.

He knocks again. "You OK, man?"

A second later, the bedroom door opens.

Cas stands their bare chest, in his boxers, looking unshaven and disheveled. "Hey," he says dryly, "Welcome back."

The smell that emanates from the room makes Jake turn away.

"Oh shit, your room smells horrible."

"Does it? I definitely have to do laundry." Cas goes back into the room and lies on his bed.

Jake comes in and looks around. The shades are drawn, and the room is very dim. There are piles of clothes everywhere. Empty pizza boxes, fast food wrappers, and empty beer bottles are scattered about the whole space. He shakes his head at the mess.

"Dude, I've been gone a week; what the fuck happen?"

"Nothing," Cas grumbles and closes his eyes to go back to sleep.

"Oh no, get up." Jake goes to the window and lifts the blinds. Sunlight comes pouring in. The brightness causes Cas to squint.

"Get up, man." Jake goes to the other window and opens the blinds on that one as well. More light comes in. "It's a beautiful day outside. Get up."

"Why? For what?" Cas pulls the covers over his eyes.

"Come on, it's already 11. I just got home and want to hang for a bit. Come with me to get some food."

"I don't wanna," he grumbles from under the bed covers.

Jake yanks the bed sheet off him. "Get up! Come on, man, don't start this shit again. You were just getting out of a funk. We don't need you to start another one."

Cas covers his face with his pillow. "Start what? I'm just trying to sleep."

"Sleep later. You probably haven't been out of the apartment since I left. You have to get some fresh air, bro. Doctor's orders, remember?"

Cas stays still for moment.

He sighs deeply and slowly removes the pillow from his face. "Alright. I'll get up."

"Good, get ready. Let's get some food."

"Can you pass me those jeans?" Cas points at a pair of crumpled up pants on the floor.

Jake picks them up and tosses them to him.

Cas sits on the bed and begins to put the pants on.

Jake looks at him. "You not going to shower first?"

"I wasn't planning to." He shrugs.

Jake shakes his head. "Nova, take a damn shower. I'm not going out with you smelling like that."

"It's not that bad." Cas lifts his armpit and takes a whiff; his eyebrows quickly raise. "Alright, I'll take a shower."

***

About 20 minutes later, Jake is sitting in the living room, looking down at his phone. He's scrolling through his vacation pictures.

A text comes in; it's from Cynthia. *'Did you tell him?'*

Jake smiles at the text and writes back, *'Not yet. In a little while.'*

Cas comes into the living room, showered and fully dressed. "Ready."

Jake looks up at him. "No shave?" he asks as he stands up.

Cas lightly massages the thick stubble on his chin. "I'm a let it grow out for a little while," he says with a shrug. "Why not."

"A little lumber jack *chic*. I can dig it," Jake replies with a wink and smile. "Where you want to eat?"

"I don't care, you tell me."

"You want to go to the dinner on 3rd Ave?"

"That's the one Megan works at," Cas answers in a monotone.

"So?"

"I don't want to go there. We kind of ended on bad terms."

Jake laughs. "You went on one freaking date. How bad of terms could it be?"

Cas stares at him blankly. "Whatever. I don't care," he replies, deadpan.

"What's wrong with you?"

"Me? Nothing. I'm fine, just chilling."

"Oh, Nova," Jake walks up and pats his friend on the shoulder. "What am I going to do with you?"

Cas snaps back, "Leave me here while you go on fancy vacations. That's what you'll do."

Jake's mouth widens in shock. "Dude! I invited you. You didn't want to come."

"That was a bootleg invite. You invited me like two days before you were leaving. You didn't really want me to go."

"Bootleg invite?" Jake sucks his teeth. "It was a damn *Groupon*! We booked it on the spot. I told you that."

Cas doesn't say anything.

"Man, please," Jake is getting worked up and is about to say something else, but pauses. He looks at his best friend since the 7th grade and can't help feeling that pinch of empathy that sometimes crops up around Cas. After another moment he exhales, and nods at him. "I really wish you would've come, man. I missed you out there." Jake puts his hand out for a fist bump.

Cas puts his hand out too. "Thanks man. I should have went."

Jake turns around and heads for the front door. "We don't have to go to the diner on 3rd. We can go somewhere else if you want. Let's just get out of here."

They walk out of the apartment and lock the door.

"So, how was the trip?" Cas asks, following Jake towards the staircase.

"Awesome. You would have had a great time."

"Eh, maybe next time."

"Maybe."

Their voices fade and their steps grow faint as they walk down the stairs, through the lobby, and out into the bright New York City sunlight.

Thank you for reading!

Please visit www.**JLMejias.com** for more information on upcoming books or to leave feedback for the author.

www.ingramcontent.com/pod-product-compliance
Lightning Source LLC
Chambersburg PA
CBHW051321250626
47155CB00007B/2398